As superior storytelling often do McCusker unlocks doors to the heart so that truth can make its home there. Unrelenting action, powerful themes, and endearing characters—that's what you'll find in Passages. Readers will leap right into the fantastic world of Marus and discover biblical accounts brought to life in riveting new ways.

—WAYNE THOMAS BATSON

Bestselling author of The Door Within Trilogy: *Isle of Swords, Isle of Fire,* and *Curse of the Spider King*

Passages isn't just a good read, it's an exhilarating ride . . . and into a parallel realm ripe with adventure, suspense, biblical allegory, and pure imagination. This is storytelling at its best.

—THE MILLER BROTHERS

Award-winning authors of *Hunter Brown and the Secret of the Shadow*

Biblical truths wrapped up in a wonderful mixture of adventure and page-turning suspense.

—BILL MYERS

Author of the My Life As . . . series

What fun it is to realize that one character in Passages represents a real person in the Bible. New insight opens up as the reader walks with a child from [our world] in the world of Marus.

—DONITA K. PAUL

Author of the Dragon Keeper Chronicles

I love this series of books because you can find a similar Bible story. This is a great book for people who love adventure.

—ISAAC H., AGE 13

Colorado Springs, Colorado

The Passages books are so great! . . . I really like how they [are about] kids who've been exported to another world. . . . If you enjoy books about other world but can't seem to find any that are clean and spiritually uplifting, Passages is the series for you.

—CHRISTIAN A., AGE 14

Martin, Tennessee

Passages is now one of my favorite series. When I was reading them, I felt like I was there with the characters.

—GRACE O., AGE 14

Goodfield, Illinois

Arin's Judgment retells a familiar story with a new twist, and in my opinion, this book has an excellent one! I highly recommend it to any book lover or to anyone who is interested in finding out more about Passages!

—LUKE P., AGE 17

Franklin, Tennessee

VOLUME 1

PASSAGES:
THE MARUS MANUSCRIPTS

VOLUME 1

PASSAGES™

THE MARUS MANUSCRIPTS

DARIEN'S RISE

ARIN'S JUDGMENT

ANNISON'S RISK

PAUL M^CCUSKER

Tyndale House Publishers, Inc., Carol Stream, Illinois

PASSAGES: THE MARUS MANUSCRIPTS, VOLUME 1
© 2012 Focus on the Family.

ISBN: 978-1-58997-750-1

The books in this collection were previously published as
DARIEN'S RISE
© 1999, 2010, 2012 Focus on the Family. Internal Illustrations © 2010 Focus on the Family.
ANNISON'S RISK
© 1999, 2010, 2012 Focus on the Family. Internal Illustrations © 2010 Focus on the Family.
ARIN'S JUDGMENT
© 1999, 2010, 2012 Focus on the Family. Internal Illustrations © 2010 Focus on the Family.

A Focus on the Family book published by
Tyndale House Publishers, Carol Stream, Illinois 60188

Editors: Larry Weeden and Mick Silva
Cover design, cover illustration, and interior illustrations by Mike Harrigan.

Cataloging-in-Publication data for this book is available by contacting the Library of Congress
at http://www.loc.gov/help/contact-general.html.

Printed in the United States of America ·
2 3 4 5 6 7 8 9 /15 14 13

For manufacturing information regarding this product, please call 1=800-323-9400.

CONTENTS

PASSAGES™
MARUS MANUSCRIPT 1

THE CHRONICLES OF THE CHOSEN
DARIEN'S RISE

Manuscript date: October 3, 1958

Kyle and Anna pressed on through the thick, green forest.

"Come on!" Kyle ordered his younger sister impatiently.

Anna had been snagged by the wild underbrush. "I'm going as fast as I can," she insisted. "Why don't they have paths in these woods?"

"Because they're old woods, and nobody comes here anymore," Kyle answered. "You remember what Uncle Bill said. Now hurry up!"

"Uncle Bill might have been pulling our leg," Anna said. She broke free from the underbrush. Old twigs snapped like firecrackers under her feet. "Slow down, Kyle!" she called as she raced to catch up.

Kyle slowed a little, but not enough for Anna to notice. He was a stubborn 12-year-old who would never openly concede to doing something nice for his 10-year-old sister.

She puffed irritably behind him. "I knew this would happen," she said. "I should have stayed with Grandma."

"And get bored stiff," Kyle reminded her.

Anna didn't respond. Kyle was right. Since they'd come to stay with their grandparents at the beginning of the summer, they'd been bored. As a couple of "city kids," they found it hard to cope with the slower pace and less-sophisticated pleasures of a small town. Their grandparents did their best to keep the two kids active, but there was only so much that could hold their interest. Kyle and

Anna finally admitted to themselves that they'd made a big mistake when they let their parents talk them into going away for a month.

A glimmer of hope arose, however, when their uncle Bill came to visit just last evening and told them about an old, mysterious house in the middle of the woods. He said it had been empty for years. Some said it was haunted, others that it was magical, while still others claimed it once belonged to an eighteenth-century pirate who'd buried his treasure in the garden. "Whatever it is," Uncle Bill said, "it might be a fun way to pass the time."

Both Grandma and Grandpa pooh-poohed the story. Neither of them could remember an old house in the woods. But Uncle Bill insisted it was there, not far from Darien's Creek in what they called the Black Forest.

Kyle was immediately intrigued and wanted Uncle Bill to draw a map. Uncle Bill scribbled directions as well as he could remember them—he hadn't been there since he was a child, he admitted. Kyle said he would go the next day if it was all right with his grandparents.

"Sure, you can go," his grandfather said. "But you won't find anything."

Anna didn't agree to go with Kyle until the next morning. She didn't really want to, but she thought it would be better than holding Grandma's yarn while she knitted. Now—in the middle of the hot and humid Black Forest—she thought of that yarn and a tall glass of lemonade and wished she'd stayed behind in spite of the boredom.

Kyle tripped on a rock and fell, getting covered in dark mulch. Dead leaves stuck to his close-cropped, blond hair. Two circles of wet dirt formed on the knees of his jeans. "I'll bet nobody's walked through here in years," he said happily.

Anna didn't understand her brother. How could he be happy? It upset her to discover that her white sneakers were now a spotted brown. Her pants were streaked and smudged with dirt and decaying bark. She had torn the sleeve on her shirt. This expedition was turning into a disaster as far as she was concerned.

And what would they do if they didn't find a house? Worse, she thought, what if they did find it and it was all the things Uncle Bill had said? Maybe that pirate still haunted the house, scaring away strangers who hoped to dig up his treasure.

"That would be cool!" Kyle said when Anna told him her worries.

No, she didn't understand her brother at all.

Half an hour later, she was beyond trying to understand him and openly complained that it was time to go home. "The house doesn't exist," she said. "Uncle Bill was just teasing us."

Kyle wouldn't hear of it. "It's around here somewhere. It has to be."

Another half hour went by, and Anna began to worry out loud that they were lost.

"We're not lost!" Kyle snapped. "I never should have let you come along. All you do is gripe, gripe, gripe!"

"I want to go home," she said and abruptly sat down right where she was. "I'm tired and thirsty."

Kyle towered over her with his hands on his hips. "Then go home," he told her. "I don't care."

"I'll get lost," she said.

"That's not my problem."

"It will be if Mom and Dad find out you let me wander around alone in some strange woods."

He groaned.

"You know I'm right."

"You really get on my nerves," he said with a frown.

"That makes us even."

"Yeah, sure." Kyle glanced ahead longingly. He wanted to go on. But he had to admit—not out loud, though—that he was getting tired too. He sighed deeply, then said casually, "Okay, let's go back. But first you'd better knock that bug out of your hair."

Anna had long, thick, brown hair and lived in horror that a bug would hide in it somewhere. One night before bed, she had brushed a small spider out of it. She had screamed loudly enough to wake up the neighbors. The police had come. She'd had nightmares for a week.

If there had been any sleeping neighbors in these woods—or police—the situation would have repeated itself. She screamed out one long note, leaped to her feet, and danced wildly while flicking her hair with both hands. "Get it out! Get it out!" she shrieked.

Of course the bug flew away the instant Anna moved, but that didn't stop her from screaming, dancing, and flicking for a full seven minutes.

As Kyle tried to calm her down, he caught a glimpse of the house through the trees.

"This is incredible!" Kyle exclaimed. "I told you we'd find it!"

The house stood awkwardly in an area so thick with trees that the sunlight couldn't break through. It looked completely out of place.

"What's it doing here?" Anna whispered. "It's like it got lost from all the other houses and died here. Why would anyone want to build a house in the middle of nowhere?"

"I don't know," Kyle said breathlessly as he circled around to the front. It was everything Uncle Bill had said: big, empty, and mysterious. Part of it reminded him of an English castle, with walls made of large blocks of uncut stone and a tower sticking up from the corner. It had round, arched windows leading up to a conelike roof. Then it was as if the builder had gotten bored with that idea and decided to do something else. The rest of the house looked Gothic, with decorative gables, ornamental shingles, and shuttered windows jutting out of long walls. The porch was framed by intricate molding on the rails between the slim posts. It surrounded three sides of the house as if it were a belt meant to hold it all together.

Kyle's imagination went wild with images of pirates, secret meetings, and treasure. "Maybe Darien's Creek used to be a big river that led to the sea," he said. "I'll bet the pirates brought their ships in and hid here."

"Pirates?" Anna asked with a loud gulp. She hadn't forgotten the image of the ghost of a captain protecting his booty.

They slowly approached the steps leading up to the long front porch. Closer now, they could see how dark and dirty the place was. Windows were broken out. A tree had fallen and smashed through a wall on the far side. Portions of the roof had collapsed, the wood having given up its strength and decomposed a long time ago. Kyle reached the front door. It was made of heavy wood, worn and scarred, with panels of glazed glass, most of which were shattered.

"This is great!" Kyle said.

Anna lingered behind. She didn't believe in haunted houses, but this looked too much like the kind she'd seen in the movies.

"I don't like it," she groaned. "Let's go home." She knew Kyle wouldn't listen to her. He never listened to her. Nobody did, as far as she was concerned. She was just a little girl without a voice.

He tried the door handle. It turned, and the door opened with a loud creaking sound. Kyle winced at the smells of rotten wood, mold, and animal droppings.

Anna stayed by the steps. "Kyle!" she called.

"Stay out here if you want to," he said. He was turned away from her, so she couldn't see his wry smile. "I'm sure the bugs will leave your hair alone."

Anna hurried to Kyle's side and held on to his arm.

The house looked as bad on the inside as it did on the outside. Cobwebs clung to the corners of the cracked ceiling and chipped plaster walls. Black smudges outlined the places where framed pictures had once hung. Leaves swirled and spread across the floor like brown fairies. Nests of branches and bush filled some of the corners and the fireplaces.

"Cool," Kyle whispered.

The lower floor was made up of what was once a spacious living room, a library (with collapsed bookshelves), a dining room that led into what must have been the kitchen, and a small pantry. After their tour, Anna insisted that they go home.

"Not yet," Kyle said. "Not until I see the whole house." He started walking up the stairs. They protested with creaks and groans.

Anna looked around nervously and knew they'd made a mistake. They shouldn't have come here. Why didn't Uncle Bill learn to keep his mouth closed? Why couldn't she make Kyle listen to her?

"Hey! Is anybody here?" Kyle suddenly called out when they reached the top of the stairs.

Anna jumped. "Are you trying to give me a heart attack?" she protested.

"Do you hear that?" he asked her softly, cocking his ear.

"Hear what?"

He hesitated as he listened again. "Voices. I hear someone talking."

"You're trying to scare me," Anna said nervously.

"No, I'm serious," Kyle said, then crept along the second floor. "Back here."

"I don't hear anything."

They passed a couple of open doors that led into what were probably bedrooms. Their condition was the same as that of the rooms on the first floor.

"I don't like this," Anna whispered again. The floor beneath her felt wobbly. They were walking on loose boards. Kyle ignored her and pressed on down the corridor. He stopped at a closed door.

"In here," Kyle said softly. Putting his ear against the rotten wood, he listened, then whispered, "Someone's in here."

Anna watched her brother carefully. Was he teasing her, or had he been out in the woods too long?

"Can't you hear them?"

"No," she replied sullenly.

Kyle shot her an annoyed look, then knelt down and peeked in the keyhole. His eyes grew wider than she'd ever seen them. He gasped. "There are people in there!"

"Cut it out, Kyle," she demanded. "You're not funny." All her instincts told her to run away as fast as she could. But she didn't dare. She knew he'd never stop teasing her for falling for his joke.

He continued in a low whisper, "It's so weird! They're dressed in old-fashioned clothes. Like . . . like . . . uniforms and . . ." He couldn't find the words to describe it and gave up. "The room is full of furniture and paintings and . . ." His voice trailed off. "This doesn't make any sense. How can there be a room like this in an abandoned house?"

Anna tugged at his arm. "Let's get out of here!" she begged.

"But you have to see this," he insisted.

"I don't care! Let's go before we get in trouble!"

"Look first. I want to prove I'm not crazy." He stepped back so she could see into the keyhole.

Anna figured the only way to get Kyle out of the house was to do what he said. She bent down to look. At first she didn't see anything. She squinted and looked again. The room was there, but it was as empty and run-down as the rest of the house. "I don't see anything," she said.

"Look harder!" Kyle whispered.

She did. The room was still empty and run-down. "Kyle—" she began to say.

Suddenly they heard a loud crack. The floorboards beneath Kyle's feet buckled, then gave way. Kyle shouted as he fell backward. His hands clawed at the air. Anna reached for him, but it was too late. He crashed through the floor.

Anna crawled on her hands and knees to the edge of the gaping hole of old wood and splinters. "Kyle!" she screamed.

She couldn't see below. The hole was black except for a swirling cloud that Anna thought was dust from the ceiling plaster. The cloud spun around and around but didn't clear. If Kyle was down there, Anna couldn't figure out where he was.

"Kyle! Are you all right?" she called out. He didn't answer. Certain he was hurt, Anna got to her feet to run to the stairs. The floorboards in front of her also cracked loudly. *The whole floor is going to cave in,* she thought. She stepped back, pressed herself against the wall, then slid along to the closed bedroom door. "Kyle!" she cried.

She felt for the doorknob and prayed it wasn't locked, suddenly desperate for someplace safe. It turned easily. She pushed the door open and carefully inched backward into the room, turned on her heel to walk in, and was suddenly engulfed in a bright, white light.

Nobody ever listens to me was the last thing she thought before the light drew her in.

Kyle instantly realized three things. First, he knew that he'd fallen through the floor but hadn't landed on the ground below. He was in a sitting position, leaning against something hard. Second, he couldn't see anything because he was wrapped up in a large cloth. Third, he heard the distinct sound of a sword fight going on somewhere nearby. He was by no means an expert on sword fighting—all he knew he'd seen at the movies—but the sound of men's grunts and the *ching* of the sabers hitting each other was unmistakable.

He struggled to free himself from the cloth entangling him. He pushed hard with his arms in both directions and felt the fabric loosen. Another push, then one more, and he was uncovered. His mouth fell open at what he saw. Two men were sword fighting in the center of an ornate study. One was silver-haired with a thick mustache. He wore an impressive navy-blue uniform with epaulets and gold stitching around the sleeves. The other was much younger, with curly dark hair and a slender, clean-shaven face. He was dressed in a loose white shirt and old-fashioned breeches that tucked into his black boots.

Kyle stood up. With a glance, he realized he had been sitting behind a thick velvet curtain, his back to a wall containing an open window. It was night outside. *What in the world is going on here?* he wondered as he watched the two men fight. One thing was certain: The men were not practicing. With each thrust and parry, one tried to wound the other.

"No one needs to get hurt," the younger man said. "I want only your medals."

The older man wheezed as he dodged the younger man's sword and said, "And I want only your head!"

Several voices shouted from the hallway, "Commander! Commander!" Someone pounded on the closed door to the study. The handle turned rapidly but didn't open. The pounding grew more fierce. *They're going to break the door down,* Kyle feared.

With quick thrusts, the younger man drove the older man across the room until he was trapped against the large white marble fireplace. The fire in it popped and crackled, the flames threatening to lick the heels of the older man's boots. The younger man suddenly grabbed the older man's sword-fighting arm and banged it against the mantel with such force that the sword fell from his hand.

Pressing the point of his sword against the older man's throat, the younger man said breathlessly, "And now, your medal, please?"

The older man growled, "You dishonor yourself, sir."

"It wouldn't be the first time," the younger man answered with a laugh.

Seeing that he had no choice, the older man grabbed the medal on his chest and tore it from his jacket. "I hope you are satisfied," he said as he thrust the medal into the younger man's hand.

"Completely," the young man said. "Now, if you'll forgive me . . ." He grabbed a vase from the mantel and hit the older man across the head with it. The older man fell to the floor. "I'm so sorry," the younger man said sincerely. With a light step, he spun toward the window and saw Kyle for the first time. He held up his saber. "Hello, lad," he said. "I didn't see you there. Please thank your master for his hospitality."

"He's not my master," Kyle said. For some reason, he wasn't afraid of the swordsman. "I don't even know what I'm doing here."

The pounding at the door grew more rhythmic. The men were obviously throwing their full weight against it in unison. The wood began to crack around the frame.

"You had better figure it out soon," the young man said. "I don't think our friends on the other side of the door will take kindly to strangers."

Kyle felt a sick feeling in his stomach and looked at the door, just in time to see the older man silently struggle to his feet. He had a fire poker in his hand, and suddenly he lunged at the younger man's back. "Watch out!" Kyle shouted.

The young man swung around, raising his guard just in time to stab the older man in the side. The older man dropped the poker and fell to his knees, clutching his wound.

"Blast!" the younger man said with irritation. "I told you I didn't want anyone to get hurt."

The older man cursed at him.

At the window, the young man sheathed his sword and leaned toward Kyle. "You saved my life, and I thank you," he said. "Now, if you have no specific plans, I suggest you come with me."

"To where?" Kyle asked.

"Anywhere but here," the young man said with a smile and stepped through the window onto the ledge. Kyle followed instinctively.

"Whoa!" Kyle said when he saw that they were on the second floor.

Soldiers were gathering on the patio below, holding torches in their hands. One pointed up at them and shouted, "There!"

"Keep moving and don't look down," the young man said to Kyle. The ledge was only about half a foot wide, and they had to balance themselves carefully against the wall as they crept along the side of the mansion.

One of the soldiers fired a pistol at them. Chunks of granite sprayed the side of Kyle's face. "Ouch!" he cried.

The young man reached behind his back and produced a small handgun. He fired a couple of shots down toward the soldiers, apparently not to hit them but only to make them scatter. They did so with a lot of shouts and rude exclamations.

"Quickly now!" the young man commanded.

They shuffled to the corner of the building, where they leaped to an adjoining roof. Catlike, they raced along the roof, around another section of the house, and then jumped to the top of a small building. Kyle noticed that this building seemed to be part of a large wall separating the mansion and its gardens from a forest. Somewhere the soldiers were shouting things like, "I think he went this way!" and "No, over here!" But their voices grew distant as the young man led Kyle along a dark stretch of the wall. The young man then knelt down and swung himself from the top of the wall to a horse waiting below. Kyle hesitated.

"Come on, lad," the young man said. "You can be sure you're not welcome here."

Kyle crawled over the side of the wall. With helping hands from the young man, he landed behind him on the horse.

"Put your arms around my waist and keep your head down!" the young man shouted over his shoulder. He then nudged the horse to get moving. They raced into the dark forest.

How the young man or the horse knew where they were going in the black woods, Kyle couldn't guess. He knew only to hold on tight and pray they wouldn't be scooped from the horse by a wayward branch or tripped up by a fallen tree. To his amazement, they weren't. After a couple of miles, they reached an incline. At the top, they were suddenly surrounded by a dozen men, also on horseback.

"Did you get them, General?" one of the men asked as he saluted.

"I did," the young man said with a hearty laugh. "Is the train ready?"

"This way," another man said—and they were all off again.

As they rode through another forest, Kyle wondered, *Where is this place? Have I stumbled onto some strange fantasy land?* They splashed through a small brook and emerged into an open field. Something in the sky caught Kyle's attention: a brightness more luminous than any full moon he had ever seen. He looked a second time, not believing what he was seeing.

The sky held *two* moons. One was large and white, the other nearly half the size and slightly orange.

I'm not at home anymore, he thought.

Like Kyle, Anna found herself blinded. But she wasn't wrapped up in a curtain; she seemed to be in some sort of closet. *What happened?* she wondered. One minute she was staring into a bright white light, and the next she was sitting in thick darkness. Had she stepped into this strange place when she backed into the room? That didn't make sense. She had seen through the keyhole a big, empty *room,* not a closet. Had she fallen along with Kyle and was now unconscious and dreaming?

She pushed coats and other clothes aside and saw a sliver of light at the bottom of what was certainly a door. She reached for the handle and opened the door just a crack. She heard men's voices. She stopped, afraid of who the men might be. Maybe they were the men Kyle had seen through the keyhole.

Whoever they were, they didn't sound happy. They were in a full-blown shouting match. Anna tried to position herself to see what was going on. She caught a glimpse of one man pacing back and forth on a colorfully patterned carpet in front of several tall windows covered with white curtains. He was a large, older man with wild, brown hair and a heavy beard and mustache, all streaked with gray. His arms were clasped behind his back, except when he occasionally gestured frantically with his right hand. He had a set frown on his brow.

"I can't believe what I'm hearing!" the man shouted in a low, lionlike voice. "My own son plays the fool with me!"

Another man, this one much younger, stepped into view. He had all the looks of the older man, except he had nicely groomed, wavy hair and a thin mustache. Anna knew instantly that the young man was the son of the elder. Both were dressed in old-fashioned uniforms, the kind Anna had seen in her history textbooks. The coats had epaulets on the shoulders and an insignia of an eagle on their chests. She thought for a moment and remembered from historical movies she'd seen that men wore uniforms like that in England and Germany back in the late 1800s. She couldn't imagine why anyone would wear such clothes in 1958.

"Father, listen to reason," the son pleaded.

"Am I not the king?" the older man asked, gesturing wildly. "*King* Lawrence! Doesn't that mean anything to anyone? And aren't you my successor? Will you not be *King* George one day?"

The prince didn't answer. He leaned against a large wooden desk and folded his arms. His expression was one of weariness, as if he knew that there was no talking to his father when he got like this.

The king continued, "So what am I to think when the people of my nation talk about one of my generals as if *he* should be king instead of me? Eh? Answer me that!"

"You know how people are," Prince George appealed. "They're

fickle. General Darien is everyone's hero now. People talk like that about their heroes."

"They once spoke about *me* that way—and I was made their king as a result!" The king slammed his fist against the desktop. "Don't you see it, boy? All Darien has to do is simply *hint* that he would like to be their king, and we're done for! We'll have a revolution!"

Prince George shook his head and said, "But Darien wouldn't do that. Darien has no interest in being king. His allegiance is to you, Father. He knows you are the man selected by the Unseen One to be king of this country. He honors that. He honors you. Why else would he win so many victories against the Palatians in your name?"

"Your friendship with him has made you blind. He will betray me—and you—and our entire succession."

"Why worry about our family? With his impending marriage to Princess Michelle, we'll all rule as a family anyway." Prince George drifted toward a large bookcase and looked as if he were going to choose a book from the shelf.

The king laughed without humor. "He'll marry Michelle *if* he fulfills his vow."

Prince George turned to him. "That was a ridiculous vow, and I'm sorry you let him go through with it. Imagine letting your best general risk his life to retrieve a few medals—"

"One hundred medals is not 'a few.' It will be quite impressive if he can get them without dying in the process."

"But to dare him like you did! What could he do but accept your dare?"

The king spread his arms. "Darien is a peasant at heart. To marry the daughter of royalty would have seemed above his station. He had to do something to prove himself to us. Asking him to retrieve 100 Palatian medals seemed reasonable."

"Are you sure you weren't hoping he'd get killed along the way?"

The king looked deliberately at his son and said, "Whatever happens will be Darien's doing, not mine."

"But to go through all that for *Michelle*," Prince George said, exasperated. "She's beneath him!"

"Be careful what you say about your own sister. She'll keep Darien in his place."

"Mary was the one for Darien, and you know it."

"I needed Mary to wed the prince of Albany. It was good politics and good for our nation's security. With Albany as an ally, we'll be much safer in the Northern Territories."

"It was unconscionable to promise Mary to Darien, then give her to Albany," Prince George persisted.

The king shrugged. "You'll learn one day that the king must make many hard decisions for the sake of his people."

"It's interesting to me that you make these 'hard decisions,' and they all seem designed to hurt Darien."

The king smiled wryly. "Is Darien not man enough to handle it?"

"Darien is a great man!" Prince George exclaimed sharply. "And he will be loyal to you no matter what you do to him."

"We'll see about that," the king replied.

Prince George faced his father and said softly, "You continually wrong a man who has done you no harm. There are others in your army who need closer watching."

"Like whom?"

Just then the phone on the desk rang, the bell loud and shrill. Prince George picked up the receiver. "Yes?" He paused, listened, then frowned. "Send him in."

A few seconds later, a uniformed man with short-cropped hair, handlebar mustache, and a scar on his cheek entered. "Sire," he said with a quick bow.

"General Liddell," the king said. "What news do you bring?"

"I've received word from the Palatian border that General Darien has successfully returned from his mission and is on his way home to the capital by train. He'll arrive here tomorrow."

The king's face turned red. "What?" he roared.

"That *is* good news!" Prince George said with an eye to his father. "Did he capture the 100 medals?"

"I don't know," General Liddell said as he moved toward the closet. Anna shrank back, afraid he would see her through the crack.

"I'm sure he did!" Prince George clapped his hands happily. "If you'll excuse me, Father, I'd like to make arrangements for a feast to celebrate Darien's return."

The king waved a dismissive hand at him. Prince George strode out, laughing as he went.

The king slammed his fist on the desk again furiously. "What will it take to get rid of this man?" he asked.

"What would you like me to do, my king?" General Liddell asked.

The two men gazed at each other for a moment. "There are things we can discuss," the king said.

General Liddell smiled. "I'm sure there are. You need only say the word."

King Lawrence gestured to his general. "Let's walk in the garden for a while."

The two men left.

Anna waited a moment and tried to sort out everything that had happened. It was more than she could cope with. Where was she? Who were these people? How did she get from an abandoned house in the middle of the woods to this fancy room?

It was a dream, she decided. And the best way back to the real world was to get out of this closet—and out of this house. She gently pushed the door open, peeked around to be sure she was alone, and tiptoed across the room. The décor was more awesome than she could see from the closet. There were busts on marble pedestals in every corner, large sofas and chairs with upholstery of intricate tapestry, glass-covered bookcases, and an enormous fireplace. An ornate clock chimed in the corner. She gaped at the room, wishing she had time to look it over more thoroughly. She opened the door slowly and stuck her head into the hall. Suddenly, large hands grabbed her roughly.

"Just as I suspected," General Liddell growled from behind her. "A spy."

The king, who stood nearby, clucked his tongue. "However did you see her in the closet, General?" he said. "You're amazing."

"I'm not a spy!" Anna protested.

"Notice how oddly she's dressed," the king said, "as if she wishes to be disguised as a boy!"

Anna glanced down self-consciously at her blouse with the torn sleeve and her smudged pants. "I'm not disguised as a boy," she insisted. "These are *my* clothes." She added with a heartfelt plea, "You have to help me! I'm *lost*."

"Lost in the king's palace?" the general asked suspiciously. "How is that possible?"

In a torrent of words, Anna told the general and the king about the old house and the bright white light. They laughed at her.

"Normally we put spies to death," General Liddell said.

Anna began to cry. "I didn't do anything wrong. I don't know how I got here!"

The king looked over Anna carefully, then told General Liddell, "Give her to Titus. He'll know what to do with her."

General Liddell pulled Anna through the palace, up and down several flights of stairs, and down a long, dark hallway until they were in a quiet, nearly deserted section. He opened a large, wooden door that led into a little-used courtyard. Across the dirty pavement, past a dry, cracked fountain, sat a broken-down shack. "Titus!" the general shouted.

Titus was as round as he was tall. His torn trousers and stained shirt could barely contain his enormous form. His jowls flapped when he spoke, and his bald head glimmered with sweat no matter what the temperature around him. When he smiled, which he only ever did cruelly, one noticed that half his teeth were missing. Anna's first impression was that he was the kind of man you would expect to sell little kids into slavery. Her impression was right. That's exactly what he did.

Titus bowed as low as his bulky frame would let him. "My general," he said.

"We found this trespasser in the king's study. Sell her as a slave," General Liddell ordered as he pushed Anna to the ground.

"Very good, sir. The dealers meet in the morning."

"Don't explain," General Liddell said. "Just see to it." He turned and left the same way he had come.

"Hello, little girl," Titus leered, then poked a finger at her pants. "Or are you a girl? You dress like a boy."

"It's a mistake!" Anna cried out.

Titus dragged Anna from the courtyard and down into a damp cellar that could be best described as a dungeon. The door even had bars on the window. He took her to a corner littered with moldy straw.

"You won't make me stay in here!" Anna cried. "Please don't make me stay in here!"

Titus laughed. Using rope, he tied her to an iron ring attached to the wall. "Night night," he said and marched out, slamming the large door behind him. He peeked through the barred window. "I wouldn't sleep much if I were you. The rats like to nibble."

Anna screamed.

Kyle was on a steam train, the kind with an enormous chimney on top of the front engine. It puffed, whooshed, and whistled its way through the dark countryside. Kyle had followed the general—Darien was his name—onto the train, where the general told his entire regiment how Kyle had warned him about the fire poker and saved his life. The men gave Kyle extra-special consideration after that, offering him a hot meal and a comfortable berth in which to sleep. But sleep was the last thing Kyle wanted. He had dozens of questions about where he was and how he got there and who these people were. General Darien smiled at the boy and said they would talk after a good night's rest. Kyle was sure he'd never rest—until his head hit the pillow. He slept until dawn.

Kyle was awake before anyone else. He climbed down from the berth and discovered his clothes, washed and dried, hanging on a hook nearby. He put them on, then walked softly down the passageway. It stretched the length of the train car, with sleeping berths stacked up on both sides. He could hear some of the soldiers snoring behind the curtains that gave the small compartments their privacy.

A sentry stood guard at the end of the car. He eyed Kyle carefully, remembered who the boy was, and said that he could get breakfast in the dining car, two cars ahead. Kyle thanked him and stepped through the door into the chilly morning air. He lingered there only a minute—just long enough to be impressed with the beautiful green countryside they rolled past. The train jolted, and Kyle decided he should get into the next car. Unlike the previous car, with berths stacked up along the passageway, this one had room-sized compartments with doors. Apart from the rattle and hum of the train itself, everything was quiet.

Kyle went through to the next car, where tables were set up for dining, just as the sentry had said. A man in a white jacket smiled at Kyle and gestured to a window seat at one of the tables. Kyle sat down. Before he could say anything at all, the man had placed a glass of orange juice and a glass of milk in front of him.

"Compliments of the general," the man said. "He told me to give you the full treatment."

Kyle liked being treated like a hero.

Light poured in through the window. Kyle craned his neck to see if this world had more than one sun. He found himself squinting at just one, which was rising on the horizon. But the fields and trees that lay in front of it seemed somehow brighter, more vibrant, and greener than anything he'd seen in his world. He leaned back in the chair and wondered if it was a trick of the light or perhaps only his imagination.

The train whistle sounded as they passed through a station. Kyle looked out the window in time to see dozens of people on the platform. Some waved and shouted enthusiastically. Others held signs saying things like "Hooray General Darien!" and "General Darien, our hero."

"Wow," Kyle said to himself.

"They love him, you know," a man said to Kyle. Startled, Kyle looked over to the end of the table. The man standing there was dressed in a double-breasted gray uniform with medals on his chest. He had a wrinkled brow that made him look stern, though his face was young. He had wavy red hair and wore a goatee. The man pulled out a chair and sat down across the table from Kyle. "May I?" he asked after he'd already sat down. "I'm Colonel Oliver."

"I'm Kyle."

"Oh, I know who you are," Colonel Oliver said softly. "You're the boy who saved our general's life. And for that, we're eternally grateful. But I'd like to know who you really are and what you're up to."

The words came so fast and the tone stayed so pleasant that, for a moment, Kyle didn't catch on to what the colonel was saying. "Up to?" he asked.

"Don't toy with me, young man. How did you wind up in that room when the general was there?"

Kyle shook his head. "I don't know."

"You can do better than that."

"No, I'm serious—I don't know," Kyle said defensively. "One minute I was in an empty house, falling through the floorboards, and the next minute I was in that room. I don't know how it happened. See, I was visiting my grandparents, and my sister and I—"

Colonel Oliver held up a hand and said, "Spare me the details."

"I just wanted to explain that—"

"I knew you wouldn't answer directly." Colonel Oliver leaned forward on the table. "Be sure, boy, that I'll be keeping my eye on you. If you're really working for the Palatians, I'll find out about it. Even if you're not, I'm going to find out who and what you are."

A jovial voice called out from the doorway, "What he is? I'll tell you what he is, my dear colonel. He's my guardian angel!"

Colonel Oliver leaped to his feet and saluted.

General Darien stepped into the car and strode briskly to the table. He patted Kyle on the back. "Don't mind Colonel Oliver," he said kindly. "He's paid to be suspicious. It's what often keeps us all alive." Then, turning to the colonel, he said, "Thank you, Ollie."

Colonel Oliver understood the cue that he was expected to leave. He saluted again and, with one last glaring look at Kyle, walked over to a table at the opposite end of the car.

"Mind if I sit down?" General Darien asked.

"Yes . . . I mean, no. I mean, please sit down," Kyle said.

The general did and signaled to the waiter for a cup of coffee. "I only have a minute," he said. "Did you sleep well? Are you rested?"

"Yes, sir. Thank you."

"Good," the general said and fiddled with the buttons on his uniform. Like Colonel Oliver's, it was gray and heavily decorated with medals. "Sorry, but I can't stand to wear this thing. Uniforms give me a rash. Give me regular shirts and trousers any day." He smiled, and it almost seemed to Kyle that his teeth and eyes sparkled when he did. Kyle decided the general couldn't be much older than 25. He was like the older brother Kyle always wished he'd had—or would one day be.

The coffee arrived. General Darien dropped a splash of cream into it, then gazed at Kyle for a moment. "You don't look like a Palatian," he said. "And I wouldn't guess that you're from Marus, either."

"Marus? Where is Marus?" Kyle asked.

The general looked surprised. "You've never heard of Marus?"

"No, sir. Where is it?"

"You're riding through it, lad." The general chuckled. "Perhaps I should be quiet and allow you to tell me from where you've come. I'm curious—not suspicious, mind you, but curious."

Kyle drank his milk and ate a bowl of oatmeal and some toast with jam, all in the time it took to tell General Darien his story. The general asked one or two questions but didn't say anything otherwise. When Kyle finished, the general leaned back in his chair. "That's a remarkable story," he said.

"It's true!" Kyle said. He had no doubt that his story sounded crazy. It sounded crazy even to him.

The general rubbed his chin and told Kyle, "I've never heard of any of the places you say you're from. Explaining how you got here is probably impossible. I'd suggest it's all a dream, but you're real enough and so am I, so that knocks *that* out of our consideration." He thought for a moment. "When we have the chance, I'll take you to the Old Judge. He's wise about such things. Maybe he can explain it."

"I hope so," Kyle said. "I'm worried about my sister. She might get lost if she tries to find her way back to my grandparents. Oh— my grandparents! They'll be worried, too."

"Don't worry about it, Kyle. We're all in the hands of the Unseen One." Kyle wanted to ask who the Unseen One was, but the general stood up. "Meanwhile, you're my personal guest. It's the least I can do for the service you did for me. Now, if you'll excuse me, I have to meet with my officers. A boring business meeting." He winked and smiled as he left.

Later in the morning, Kyle came upon a group of boys in another car who were polishing boots, cleaning pistols, and shining swords. They were cadets whose sole purpose at this stage of their life was to make sure the officers were catered to. Kyle was pleased to meet up with boys his own age. The adults were polite enough, but none of them besides the general had gone out of his way to speak to him.

The boys were extremely curious about Kyle and weren't shy about asking him more questions than he had answers for. Once again, he told his story about how he wound up in the Palatian general's mansion. They were silent as they listened and went about their work. Kyle couldn't tell if they believed him or not.

One of the boys finally said, "That's quite a story. I *hope* it's true. Otherwise you're one of the best liars I ever met."

Kyle protested that he wasn't a liar, but he knew it wouldn't make any difference. Why should anyone believe him?

"Since you've been asking me a lot of questions, do you mind if I ask you a few?" he said.

The boys said they didn't mind.

"For starters, where are we going?"

A fair-haired boy replied, "We're going to our capital. It's called Sarum. General Darien is taking back his 'prizes' "—at this the rest of the boys giggled—"from the Palatians. They're our enemies, by the way. And then the king will let General Darien marry his daughter."

"I don't understand," Kyle said. "General Darien went into enemy territory to bring back prizes so he could marry the king's daughter? If he's a general, why didn't the king just say yes?"

The fair-haired boy smiled indulgently and answered, "You honestly don't know *anything* about Marus, do you?"

"I really don't."

"Well," the boy began, "General Darien wasn't always a general. In fact, he wasn't even raised to be a soldier. A couple of years ago, he was just a farm boy out in one of the crop-growing counties. But after he killed Commander Soren—"

"Commander Soren?"

"He was Palatia's greatest leader," another boy interjected.

The fair-haired one continued. "Commander Soren and the Palatian army invaded—"

"As *usual*," the second boy said with mock boredom.

The fair-haired one shot him an impatient look. "Anyway, they had our army cornered near Glendale. That's a town in the southwest part of the country, near the mines. We rode past it in the middle of the night."

"He doesn't want a geography lesson," one of the other boys said, then spat on a boot to polish it.

The fair-haired boy went on. "The story goes that Darien and his brothers had decided to enlist in the army to battle the Pala-

tians. They arrived at Glendale just when it looked as if King Lawrence was about to surrender to Soren.

"When Darien heard this, he was furious. He couldn't believe
that the people of Marus would ever surrender to the Palatians,
under any condition. He made such a fuss about it that an officer
grabbed him and dragged him in front of the king to get permission to put him to death for treason. Darien laughed at the idea. He
said it was better to be put to death for treason than to become a
slave to the Palatians.

"The king was amazed at Darien's arrogance. Darien said that
the king, of all people, should know that the Unseen One would
protect them and give them victory. The king called him a fanatic
and said that if he was so confident about the Unseen One, maybe
he should go out and do something about the Palatians himself.
Darien took the dare and said that he would.

"The whole army watched with their mouths hanging open as
Darien headed straight across the battlefield. He didn't have on a
uniform, he didn't take a pistol or a rifle—he didn't have any protection at all." The fair-haired boy stopped for a moment. By now,
every boy in the car had put down his work and was listening.

"Commander Soren was told by his soldiers that a boy from
Marus was walking across the field. Soren was angry. He expected
King Lawrence to come himself to surrender. 'He sent me a boy?'
Soren yelled. 'Give me my rifle. I'll send that boy back with a
message—as a corpse.' Soren took his rifle and headed across the
field toward Darien.

"They got closer and closer to each other. Soren started to curse
at Darien. Darien didn't flinch. Then, still walking, Soren lifted up
his rifle and took aim at Darien. Darien didn't lose a step. He kept
on going. Soren laughed and started to squeeze the trigger. Darien
yelled, 'To the glory of the Unseen One!' and that made Soren angry.

"'I won't shoot this pup,' Soren said and threw down his rifle.

He pulled his sword from its sheath. 'I'll send him back to King Lawrence in pieces!' Meanwhile, Darien kept walking toward Soren, who raised his sword. When he was just a few feet from Soren, Darien pulled out a pocketknife—the one he whittles with. It's a little thing; maybe he'll show it to you sometime. Anyway, with a flick of his wrist, Darien threw that little knife at Soren. It hit him right in the heart. My father was there, and he saw the whole thing. It hit Soren in the heart, and he died right where he stood.

"Did Darien stop and turn back? No. Darien kept right on walking, went up to the commander's dead body, grabbed his rifle, and started firing like a madman at the Palatians. Everyone was so shocked that they didn't have time to think. The Palatians started to run, and King Lawrence, seeing the opportunity, yelled for his men to attack. They did, and they beat the Palatians back to the border."

"That's amazing," Kyle said, wide-eyed.

The fair-haired boy nodded. "Since then, he's become one of our greatest generals. Ever. The whole country loves him."

"And it all started with just a pocketknife?"

"A pocketknife and the power of the Unseen One," another boy said.

Kyle cocked an eyebrow. "So who is this Unseen One that everybody keeps talking about?"

"Not everybody talks about the Unseen One," the fair-haired boy answered. "We do because we believe. But once you get off this train, you won't find very many people who believe anymore."

"But what is the Unseen One?" Kyle asked.

The fair-haired boy opened his mouth to speak, but a bell suddenly rang. "The officers want us," he said, and, quick as rabbits, the boys jumped up and raced out of the train car.

Her wrists tied with a thick rope, Anna was led by Titus like a dog on a leash. From the palace, they weaved their way through litter-strewn alleys and passages until they emerged in a large market area. At the edge, Titus untied Anna but instantly grabbed her arm in his big hand. "You'll behave or suffer the consequences," he said.

She winced at the dazzling sunlight and felt as if her eyes were being assaulted by brighter colors than she'd ever seen before. Titus led her past booths and stalls filled with fruit, vegetables, meat, newspapers, household items, and even live animals. Men in smocks and women in aprons busied themselves with their work, while some chatted idly about the weather and the state of the economy. All had a look and clothes that reminded Anna of pictures she'd seen in her history books of the Civil War. The market smelled of animals and earth, with an occasional hint of freshly baked bread.

Anna hadn't eaten or slept all night. Though no rats had come to nibble on her, she hadn't wanted to take the chance that they might. She had spent the entire night awake and hoping she'd snap out of this awful dream.

She pleaded with Titus whenever she had the chance. She told him again and again that he was making a big mistake and even threatened him with what her parents would do if they found out he was treating her so badly. He told her repeatedly to shut up or he'd belt her. But he did let go of her arm.

Halfway across the market, Anna tripped and fell into a puddle of mud. That made Titus angry, and he began to kick at her to get up. She easily dodged the thrusts of his short, stumpy legs. That made him even angrier.

"Get up!" He kicked out harder and harder. She quickly evaded him. He thrust out his leg in the hardest kick of all, lost his balance, and fell into the mud with a large *splat.* If the situation weren't so serious, Anna might have giggled over how silly the two of them must have looked. A crowd had gathered and did what Anna dared not: They laughed.

"You're going to get yours!" Titus spat, his face beet red.

Before she could get out of reach, he roughly grabbed her arm. He climbed to his feet, not caring whether he twisted her arm this way or that to do it, and yanked her up. "I'm not sure what your value will be once I thrash you for this," he growled, "but I don't care anymore!"

"Help me!" Anna called out to the crowd on the gamble that they might respond. "He's going to make me a slave!"

The crowd immediately went about their business as if nothing had happened—or was about to happen—to the poor girl. Anna felt the sting of despair as Titus jerked her out of the mud.

"What goes on, Titus?" inquired a low, gravelly voice.

Titus swung around to see who spoke. "What?" he said.

An old man stepped around from behind a vegetable booth. He had a slender, pale face with wild, white hair and a thin beard and mustache. He wore a long, black overcoat that seemed to droop from his skeletal body. Underneath, Anna noticed that he wore a collarless shirt, waistcoat, and old-fashioned breeches, stockings, and shoes—like the people who had lived during the American Revolution. It was an odd contrast to the way everyone else was dressed.

"I want to know what you are doing," the old man said.

Anna heard Titus's sharp intake of breath. He recognized the old man. "You're here!" Titus said. "I thought you were . . ."

"Dead?"

"No, no, of course not. The entire nation would know about that. I just thought that you were . . . were ill."

"Too ill to come visit our lovely capital?"

"I thought you and the king . . . had an understanding."

"The king and I have an understanding. But it's probably not the same understanding. However, there is one thing I do understand: Slavery was outlawed in Marus years ago. Before you were born. How do I know? Because I was the one who outlawed it. Now let the girl go."

Titus tried to sound tough. "I obey the king and his officers. You have no authority over me."

"Don't I?" the old man asked as he took a step forward. Titus stepped back, his grip loosening on Anna's arm.

"No," Titus said, less sure of himself.

"Let me tell you a little something about authority," the old man said with a smile. "It is given, not taken. My authority comes from the Unseen One. From where do the king and his officers get their authority?"

"From . . . from . . ." Titus stammered, but he never found an answer.

The old man held up a finger. "A man your size shouldn't wrestle around in the mud with small children. It's not healthy. Your heart might not be up to it. Perhaps you should have a rest."

Titus suddenly gasped, then collapsed back into the mud. His eyes rolled up in their sockets, then closed, and his massive form relaxed.

Anna quickly moved away from him. "What happened?" she asked. "Is he all right?"

"He's having a little nap," the old man responded. "He'll wake up sooner or later." The old man stooped to look Anna full in the face. "Tell me your story, young lady. You're not from around here, are you?"

"No, sir."

"You're not even from this country, am I correct?"

"Yes, sir. You're correct."

The old man gazed at her thoughtfully. "You're not safe here. I suggest you come with me."

"But . . . why? Who are you?"

The man smiled again. "I am the Old Judge."

The name meant nothing to Anna, but he had saved her, and that was reason enough to go with him. As she and the Old Judge walked past staring eyes in the marketplace, a train whistle blew in the distance.

"That will be the king," the Old Judge said.

"The king is leaving?" Anna asked.

"No, he's just arriving."

Anna was confused. She had seen the king in the palace the day before. Had he left and was now coming back?

"I'm talking about the *real* king," the Old Judge said, sensing Anna's confusion. "The chosen."

Watching from the train window, Kyle was amazed by the large number of people who had crowded onto the station platform to greet General Darien and his men. They cheered loudly as the train hissed and screeched its way to a stop. A delegation of men dressed in brightly colored military uniforms and hats emerged from the crowd. They looked serious and formal as they waited for General Darien to step from the train.

A train-car door swung open, and Colonel Oliver climbed onto the platform. He was followed by several other officers from General Darien's regiment. The crowd grew silent as they watched. Then General Darien appeared in the doorway. The crowd went wild with cheers, flag-waving, and applause. General Darien blushed, then smiled and waved. The delegation stepped forward the second Darien's feet touched the platform. A young man in uniform with wavy dark hair and a thin mustache broke ranks and unceremoniously embraced Darien.

"Darien!" he cried out happily.

"Hello, George," Darien said with a laugh as they thumped each other on the back with all the affection of close brothers. A military band struck up a tune Kyle had never heard before.

"Sorry about all the fuss, but word got around that you'd made it back safely, and, well . . ." The one called George gestured at the crowds, the soldiers, and the band. "I'm afraid we'll have to return to the palace with a lot of pomp and circumstance."

General Darien nodded. "Then let's get on with it. What about my men?"

"We have cars for them to follow in," George said. "There'll be a brief reception in the Great Hall, and then we'll let you all get some much-needed rest."

Kyle joined the rest of Darien's men in large, old-fashioned touring cars. The tops were pushed back so that everyone could wave at the throngs who lined the streets leading to the palace.

Kyle had never seen such a display of affection for a public figure. Nor had he ever seen a city as grand as Sarum. Wide avenues of beautiful green trees and manicured lawns stretched out to majestic buildings of brick, stone, and marble. Some had broad stairs leading up to magnificent porticos and colonnades and the biggest windows Kyle had ever laid eyes on. The avenues spilled

onto circles and squares containing monuments and statues acknowledging people and places Kyle had never heard of. Once again
he was struck by how vibrant the colors were.

As the parade of cars pulled to the front entrance of the king's
palace, Kyle looked to the left and the right. Both wings of the royal
residence disappeared into a forest and rounded off in a way that
looked as if they went on forever. The main building was adorned
with a golden rotunda with a statue of an angel on top.

The king's servants met the entourage and led them through an
arched door into an ornate foyer filled with paintings, statues, and
a wide marble staircase. Kyle imagined that a tank could drive up
those stairs without any trouble. They detoured down a grand hallway lined with more paintings, alcoves with statues, gold-leaf borders, and lamps hanging from carved pilasters.

Finally, they swung off through a double doorway into the Great
Hall. It was great indeed, with high walls of carved wood, cornices,
ornately framed portraits and mirrors, and tall, triangular windows
that seemed to point to an elaborately painted ceiling filled with
frescoes of muscular men engaged in battles of all descriptions. The
room looked as if it could accommodate hundreds of people without
anyone feeling cramped.

Kyle sat with the rest of the troops in chairs facing a stage with
wingback chairs and a lavishly designed podium. Kyle suspected
by the way the other members of the audience were dressed that
the room was filled with dignitaries and officers from other parts of
the country. The king—there was no mistaking him with that
crown on his head—took the podium and welcomed the soldiers
home from their daring adventures. The audience applauded.

The king continued, "It is with great pride that we honor you
today. Your escapades have been the talk of all the nations. Our
enemies now know that nothing is beyond the abilities of General
Darien and his fighting forces!"

At this, General Darien's men shouted and clapped.

The king waved his arms for the men to quiet down. Then he continued, "General Darien, I believe you have a presentation to make?"

General Darien strode across the stage to another round of applause. When he had reached the podium, he began, "Sire, fellow officers of the royal army, ladies and gentlemen, I am proud to stand here before you today." He smiled wryly. "I'm proud to stand *anywhere,* in fact. We had some close calls in our encounters with the Palatian officers." Everyone laughed.

Darien went on, "As you know, I'm little more than a farm boy who has been blessed beyond his dreams. When the king said he would allow me to marry one of his daughters, I felt humbled and unworthy. It seemed that the only way to accept his graciousness was to do something to prove myself. Most of you know that I agreed to bring back the medals of 100 Palatian officers." He gestured to Colonel Oliver. The colonel and another soldier carried a box forward and placed it on the stage. "Your highness, I'm pleased to report that I have brought you the medals of 200 Palatian officers!"

Pandemonium broke out as the crowd leaped to its feet. The people began to chant, "Darien! Darien! Darien!" over and over. Kyle watched with fascination. He thought for a moment that General Darien could have told these people to do anything—anything at all—and they would have done it. But their admiration wasn't shared on the stage. Kyle couldn't help but notice that the king looked sour-faced, as did many of the officers with him. Was it possible that the king wasn't happy with Darien's success?

When the noise died down, Darien concluded by saying, "Sire, these are only tokens. But I believe they symbolize the power and determination of your people to serve you at home and abroad, in the luxury of peace or in fields of war. May your name bring joy to our allies and strike fear in the hearts of our enemies!" The crowd applauded enthusiastically again as Darien stepped away from the podium.

The king's face worked from a frown into a forced smile. He said, "Thank you, General Darien. Two hundred medals? I'm sorry, but our laws don't allow for you to marry two of my daughters!" The people laughed as he went on, "You do us a great honor, General. And it gives me added pleasure to announce my permission for you to marry my daughter Michelle, in the Sarum Cathedral, *next Saturday*."

Wild applause followed once more. A beautiful young woman with long chestnut hair and large eyes that darted around nervously appeared in the wings of the stage and was led to General Darien. The king clasped their hands together. Kyle assumed it was Michelle. The king raised his arms, and the people got to their feet again with shouts, chants, stomping feet, and clapping hands. The roar of the ocean could not have been heard in that hall, Kyle thought.

But Kyle couldn't take his eyes off the king. For all the bravado and praise, Kyle thought that he looked like a very unhappy man.

The Old Judge helped Anna into his horse-drawn wagon. He gave her some fruit to eat and then told her to rest while they drove to his cottage in the small village of Hailsham, several miles from the capital. Resting was easy; it was a glorious summer's day. Anna stretched out to greet the warmth of the sun, which somehow seemed bigger here, and let it soak into her body. She still hadn't gotten over the dampness of the dungeon. She dozed for a while and only woke up when the wagon wheel bumped a large rock on the unpaved road.

Anna yawned and looked around. Shafts of light shone on the green hills and groves of trees and highlighted the village of Hailsham, which, as she now saw, sat in the center of a valley. It was composed mostly of a small cluster of shops and offices and a few cottages sprinkled around the outskirts. Nearby, the railroad track cut like a scar into one of the hillsides. Somehow it didn't take away from the beauty, though. The whole scene looked to Anna like the kind of village you'd find on a picture postcard of New England.

The Old Judge's cottage sat between a field and a forest. It was a simple building, mostly white except for dark beams of timber that ran from the thatched roof to the ground. The leaded windows were shuttered and had window boxes filled with flowers of all kinds. Roses, carnations, pansies—Anna couldn't name them all. When Anna and the Old Judge had climbed out of the wagon, he lifted the latch on the heavy brown door and invited her in.

The main room had dark paneling, a fireplace, and two comfortable-looking chairs sitting on a colorful carpet. Off to one side were a large hutch and several bookcases filled with books of all kinds. A grandfather clock watched them indifferently, its arm swinging from left to right and back again.

A second room served as the kitchen, with a stove, sink, and open cupboards containing a modest array of dishes and food containers. Anna noted three doors leading to what she guessed were the bedrooms. The main room was naturally cool since the trees from the forest blocked the sun when it was at its highest point. She sighed contentedly. It might have been the most charming place she'd ever seen in her young life.

"After I take care of the horses and wagon, I'll make us some tea, and then we'll have a little chat," the Old Judge said. He went to put the wagon in his small barn and unhitch the horses to run in the field.

Anna sat down in one of the chairs and glanced at the clock. It was 3:02. Without meaning to, she fell asleep again. When she awoke, a small fire was crackling in the fireplace, and the Old Judge was reading a book in the chair across from her. "I'm sorry," Anna said sleepily. "Did I sleep long?"

The Old Judge closed his book and peered at her over his reading glasses. "Not long," he said.

She glanced at the grandfather clock. It said it was 5:17. "Oh," she said, sorry to have slept for more than two hours.

The Old Judge pointed to a cup and saucer and plate on the end table next to her. "I made you a fresh cup of tea," he explained, "and there are some pastries for you to munch on."

She thanked him and devoured the pastries. She had forgotten how hungry she was. When she finished eating, she still felt hungry and wondered when dinner would be.

"Would you like more?" the Old Judge asked. "Are you still hungry?"

Her parents had taught her that asking for more was rude, whether one was hungry or not. "I'm okay, thank you," she said.

"I don't think you're being honest with me," the old man said. "You're still hungry or *those* wouldn't be there." He tilted his head toward the end table.

Anna looked over and barely stifled her surprise. The empty plate now had several more pastries on it. She looked around to see if the Old Judge had a servant waiting on them. The cottage was empty, however, except for the two of them. She rubbed her eyes and thought, *I must be very, very tired. Or am I still dreaming?*

The Old Judge watched her with a fixed smile as she ate two more pastries. "Is that better?" he asked.

"Yes, sir," she replied. Her hunger was taken care of, for the moment. She reached over to the end table for her cup of tea and was startled yet again. The plate of pastries was empty. *But I only had two, and there must've been seven or eight on the plate,* she nearly said out loud. She bit her tongue, however, and didn't say a word. She thought she *must* be dreaming.

"Let's talk about your situation," the old man said.

"My situation?" she asked.

"Tell me why you're here."

"I don't know why I'm here," she answered. "I don't even know how I got here."

"You've been chosen for something. You don't know what it is?"

"No, sir. All I know is that one minute I was in an abandoned house in the middle of the woods, and the next minute I was in the king's closet."

The Old Judge took off his glasses. "That's very interesting."

Surprised, Anna asked, "You believe me?"

"Why wouldn't I?"

"Nobody else has."

"We're surrounded by men of little imagination and no faith," the Old Judge said wearily.

"I'm not sure that *I'd* believe me," Anna confessed.

"Do you believe you?"

"Yes."

"Then I believe you too."

Anna was genuinely puzzled. "But . . . *why* do you believe me?"

"Because the ancient ways of the Unseen One are full of mystery. Just because your homeland can't be found on any of our maps doesn't mean it isn't real. Obviously *you're* real, so there must be something to your story. And I know that the Unseen One is real, so there you are."

"There I am? *Where* am I?" Anna asked.

"In the middle of a wonderful mystery!" the Old Judge exclaimed. "Now, drink your tea."

"I think it's gotten cold," Anna said.

"Is it?" he asked as he put his glasses back on.

Anna reached over for the teacup. It was filled to the brim and steaming hot.

"That's strange," she said.

"What is?" the Old Judge asked. His voice was farther away than it had been. He now stood in the doorway to the kitchen, a tray in his hand containing two cups of tea. She shook her head. He'd been sitting in the chair a moment ago. How did he move so fast?

"I must be dreaming," she said. She looked at the grandfather clock. It now said it was 3:06.

The Old Judge smiled at her. For the first time, she noticed that his eyes were different colors. One was blue, the other green. "Were you dreaming, or are you dreaming now?" he asked.

∞

The celebration banquet in the Great Hall ended, and Darien released his men to go home to their families. Kyle waited, unsure of what to do or where to go. He worried that Darien had forgotten him now that they were back in the capital. But Darien hadn't. He insisted that Kyle return home with him until they could figure out what to do next.

Darien lived in a manor that the king had given him after he'd defeated the Monrovians in a long, grueling battle. Built in a Gothic style with pointed arches, ornate stonework, and elaborate gables, the manor was on the outskirts of the city, nestled in a cozy corner of the royal forest. It wasn't as large as it was complicated, with halls and rooms twisting and turning in different directions.

"It has more rooms than I ever expect to use in my lifetime," Darien explained to Kyle. "I don't bother with the east wing of the house. The west wing suits me perfectly." That wing had a kitchen, dining room, library, and four bedrooms. They established that Kyle would sleep in the room that overlooked the garden. It didn't matter much to Kyle where he slept. He was more worried about his sister and his family. By now he'd been gone for more than a day. Everyone at home would be alarmed. Maybe even the police were searching for him.

In the library, Darien sat down at a grand piano and began to play a tune that, to Kyle, sounded classical. A maid interrupted to take instructions from Darien for their dinner. He simply said to fix him his "favorite." Kyle wandered over to a tall suit of armor with a colorful shield and a long sword clasped to its side. He could see his reflection in the shiny chest plate.

"We'll rest tonight," Darien said as he played. "Tomorrow I'll take you to see the Old Judge."

Just then, someone tapped on the glass of the double doors that led into the garden. It startled Kyle, but Darien acted as if he'd expected the noise. He got up from the piano, parted the curtains, and opened one of the doors. Prince George stepped in. The two men shook hands and clapped each other on the back and said the kinds of things men say when they haven't seen each other in a long time.

Then Prince George saw Kyle and smiled. "So this is the boy who saved your life," he said.

"He is indeed," Darien replied. "Kyle, this is our beloved Prince George, the son of the king and my greatest friend."

"Hi, Your Honor—er, Highness—er, *sire*." Kyle blushed as Prince George laughed.

"Our servant Damaris is fixing dinner. Are you hungry?" Darien asked George.

George shook his head. "I can't stay long. My father is expecting me for some state function tonight. But I wanted to talk to you about something urgent." He darted an uneasy glance at Kyle as if to ask, "Can he be trusted?"

Darien nodded. "Say what you must. We are all trusted friends here. Aren't we, Kyle?"

Kyle replied, "Yes, sir. I'm in big trouble otherwise."

The two men laughed, then sat down on a thick red sofa next to the dormant fireplace. Prince George's face grew earnest.

"I'm here to warn you," he said. "The king is in a dangerous frame of mind. I'm not sure what has seized his disposition, but it's something dark and threatening."

"Are you in any sort of danger?" Darien asked.

Prince George sighed. "I'm not, but you may be."

"Me?" Darien's face lit up with surprise. "I've done nothing against the king. I've served him well, I thought."

"You've served him *too* well. Your successes make him think he's a failure. Your popularity makes him feel unappreciated. Your acceptance makes him feel rejected."

"But he's the *king*," Darien said.

Prince George nodded. "He's the king, yes, but he feels that his position is threatened. He imagines that you may be maneuvering your way to become the next king."

"He is my king as long as he lives!" Darien exclaimed. "I would do nothing to take his throne away from him . . . or you."

Prince George stood up and paced thoughtfully. "There's no point in fooling ourselves," he said after a moment. "I will never be king. You are the chosen one. You will reign one day. The Old Judge said so."

Darien implored, "He said I was chosen, but never for what or even for *when*. Stop this nonsense, George. I'm a loyal subject of the king, your father. I would not lift a finger against him."

"I know that, Darien. But my father doesn't."

"He used to. He has treated me like a son. Would I spit on that? Would I shove a dagger in the back of a man who treated me so well?"

Prince George moved closer to his friend. "My father isn't himself these days. You know he hasn't been the same since his last argument with the Old Judge. He's fearful and suspicious. I don't know what they said to each other, but it's changed my father. That's why I'm here to warn you."

The two men gazed at each other silently for a moment.

"Thank you, George," Darien said softly.

"Surround yourself with only those you trust wholeheartedly. My father has eyes and ears everywhere." George crossed the room to the double doors and opened one. The smells of the flowers in the garden wafted in. Halfway through the door, he turned back and said, "And, Darien . . ."

Darien faced his friend.

"When you do become king, remember me." Then he was gone.

Darien was in a thoughtful mood for the rest of the evening. He didn't eat much of his dinner, which annoyed Damaris because she'd fixed his favorite meal of lamb, potatoes, carrots, and a bread-like pastry that Kyle didn't recognize. Kyle thought the food was delicious and wolfed it down as politely as he could.

Just as Damaris was clearing away their plates, a messenger arrived from General Liddell. He was a young man dressed in a smart, gray uniform. After a quick salute, he said, "A renegade group from Adria has crossed the border and attacked a town in the Territory of Peace. General Liddell wants you to join him and his brigade in driving the Adrians back into their own land."

"Tell the general that my men are in no condition to fight so soon after their return," said Darien.

"General Liddell anticipated your concern," the messenger said. "The general doesn't want your men. Just you."

Darien considered this for a moment, then nodded. "All right. Tell the general I'll come."

The messenger saluted again and, with a click of his heels, turned and left.

"What's your pleasure, Kyle?" Darien asked when they were alone again.

"My pleasure?"

"You can stay here until I return, or you can go with me as my personal assistant."

Kyle was surprised. "You want *me* to go into a battle with you?"

"I doubt it'll be much of a battle. A small skirmish mostly." Darien leaned back in his chair. "It'll mean a delay in our speaking with the Old Judge about getting you home."

Kyle considered it for a moment. He could rush back to his worrying sister and grandparents or get to see a real battle. If only he could send a message somehow! But he couldn't. So what should he do? "I'll go with you," he said finally.

Darien smiled. "I thought you might."

The battle—if that's what it could be called—took place in the town of Krawley, some two miles inside the Territory of Peace. In theory, the Territory of Peace was a neutral zone between Marus and Adria, established 100 years before in the Treaty of the Kings. "But the Adrians are barbarians at heart," Darien explained to Kyle on the train the next morning. "Seven years ago, they slaughtered their king and his entire family. Now they're a loose collection of rebel factions who are trying to take over the entire country. Every once in a while, they decide to venture into our realm just to stir things up. It's annoying mostly."

"It seems like you're surrounded by people who like to attack your country," Kyle observed. "The Palatians, the Adrians . . . Is everybody out to get you?"

Darien chuckled and nodded. "I think they are. Ours is a beautiful and blessed country. Our rival nations believe that if they can conquer us, they'll share in what we have. But they don't understand that it's the *people* who make a nation great, not the land. If you conquer us, you'll conquer the very thing that makes Marus worth having. It's like caging a bird for its song. Once caged, the bird will stop singing."

When Kyle and Darien went to meet with General Liddell in his private car, Kyle noticed that the general was a stern-looking man with distinctive features: primarily a handlebar mustache and a scar on his cheek. He ignored Kyle—even though Darien introduced them—and got down to business with Darien about how to attack the Adrians. Kyle sat quietly in the corner while General Liddell, Darien, and several other officers made their plans.

In Lester, a town a few miles from Krawley, the train stopped and unloaded Liddell's soldiers, artillery, horses, and provisions. The local garrison met them and, together, they numbered almost 1,000. "Can you ride a horse?" Darien asked Kyle.

Kyle had to confess that he couldn't.

"Then you'll ride with me," Darien said. On horseback, they joined the cavalry and rode toward Krawley.

The battle for Krawley was nothing like what Kyle had imagined. He thought there would be a lot of shooting and hand-to-hand combat. There wasn't. For one thing, they found that the Adrians had retreated from the town itself and were now hiding in the nearby hills. For another thing, Marutian cannons on large wheels were rolled in to drive the Adrians out. They fired shells at the hills mercilessly for an entire morning. The constant *boom, boom, boom* gave Kyle a headache.

When the Adrians stopped firing back, the Marutian army marched into the hills to see if the Adrians had deserted or were prepared to surrender. Kyle again rode with General Darien on his horse. Once in the hills, they found evidence that the Adrians had indeed been there. A few bodies littered the camps and rocky inclines where the shells had hit with the most force. Kyle got physically sick at the sight. They were men. And they were dead. It was awful. He retched behind one of the gun carriages.

Darien patted him lightly on the back and handed him a canteen full of water. "It doesn't get better," he whispered.

"Spread out and search for prisoners," General Liddell ordered. As second only to the king, General Liddell could command Darien like no other officer. "You check those rocks to the north," he told Darien.

"They've retreated, I'm sure," Darien said.

"Check anyway," General Liddell insisted.

With a handful of men, Darien and Kyle went up into the northern part of the hills.

"They'd be fools to stay after that shelling," Darien told Kyle as they sat down on a large rock a few minutes later. They shared water from a stream.

"General Liddell was pretty sure he wanted you to look around, though," Kyle said.

"So he was."

Kyle glanced at the soldiers canvassing the area. From a distance, they looked like wild animals grazing in the grassy knolls. A flicker of light from farther above them caught Kyle's eye. He squinted as an odd feeling settled in the pit of his stomach. A man was leaning against a rock with a rifle pointed in their direction. *How strange,* Kyle thought, the feeling in his stomach making him nauseated.

Then he realized what the man was doing. Kyle leaped up and threw himself at General Darien. They both tumbled off the rock to the ground as splinters of gravel sprayed upward from a bullet that had just missed them. A fraction of a second later, they heard the sharp report of the gunfire echo around them. A great commotion broke out among the soldiers. Some knew instantly what had happened and fired in the direction of the man. Others rushed to make sure General Darien hadn't been hit.

What they found was the bizarre sight of their general with his back on the ground and Kyle lying on top of him.

"Are you all right?" Kyle asked as he rolled off of Darien.

"You have more strength than I would've given you credit for," Darien replied pleasantly. He called out to his second-in-command, "Bryson! Bryson!"

Colonel Bryson came around the rock, his face panicked. "Are you all right, sir? Have you been hit?"

"No," Darien said. "Thanks to my guardian angel. Was it an Adrian assassin?"

"We don't know yet, sir." Colonel Bryson disappeared from view again. More shots were fired, then someone yelled, "Over here!"

Darien leaned against the rock. "What am I going to do with you?" he asked Kyle. "This is the second time you've saved my life. I'm in your debt and deeply grateful to you." He shook Kyle's hand vigorously. "If I were a king, I'd knight you . . . Thank you."

"You're welcome," Kyle said, turning a deep crimson.

They stood up, careful to stay behind the cover of the rock, and dusted themselves off. "I'm hesitant now to ever let you go back home. No doubt I'll be killed the instant you go."

Colonel Bryson returned just then and said, "We got him, sir."

"Is he alive?"

"I'm afraid not." Colonel Bryson shuffled awkwardly for a moment.

"Well?"

"He's one of ours."

"What do you mean?"

"He's not an Adrian. He's one of our soldiers, though I don't know with whom he serves."

"One of our own men tried to kill me?" Darien asked, perplexed.

"It would appear so, sir."

Darien tapped his chin thoughtfully. "Now why would he want to do a thing like that?"

A few minutes later, when they had explained the incident to General Liddell, he promised to conduct a full-blown investigation into the murder attempt. A look in his eye, however, made Kyle think the case would never be solved.

∞

Three days passed. While Kyle chased the Adrians and then returned to Sarum with Darien, Anna stayed with the Old Judge at his cottage. She mended her clothes with a thread and needle the Old Judge had given her, walked through the lush green forest and over the small hills, and, at night, stared with an insatiable curiosity at the two moons.

Part of their routine—one that Anna suspected the Old Judge had been doing for years—was to begin the day with prayer to the Unseen One and reading from the Sacred Scroll. Since Anna didn't know much about either, the Old Judge used the time to teach her.

"The Unseen One is the Creator and Sustainer of all things," he explained. "He is everywhere at all times; all-seeing, all-knowing, all-powerful."

"Like our God," Anna said, relating the description to what she knew from her world.

"Not *like* God," the Old Judge corrected. "The Unseen One *is* God. The God of love and justice."

Anna pointed to the large roll of paper spread out in front of them. "Is that your Bible?"

He pondered her question. "The word *bible* means 'book.' In which case, the Sacred Scroll might be considered that. It contains an account of the relationship between the Unseen One and the created. It spans history back to the beginning of time. It tells the story of the faithful and the faithless, of despots and statesmen, of common folk and warriors, of heroes and cowards. I'm writing sections of it now myself, recounting my own work as a chosen voice for the Unseen One."

"Chosen? You keep using that word. What does it mean?"

"It means several things. We are chosen because of the Unseen

One's love for us. That love reaches out to us, and we, in turn, respond to it by faith—by our belief in the Unseen One."

Anna nodded. That much she could understand.

The Old Judge continued, "Yet we, the faithful, are also chosen in specific ways, to do specific tasks for the Unseen One. I was chosen before I was born."

"Before you were born?" Anna said, surprised. "Then how did you know you were chosen?"

"My parents had dedicated me to the Unseen One at my birth. I was a child when they gave me over to the priests to be trained."

"Your parents gave you away?"

"They knew I was chosen—or called—by the Unseen One. It was their duty to give me to those who would help me hear that call more clearly. We had many priests in those days. Very few are left."

Anna was still thinking about the Old Judge's being separated from his parents. "Didn't you miss them?" she asked.

"I still saw them. We visited often. But I would not have refused the Unseen One's call even if I could."

Anna knitted her brow. "But . . . how did your parents . . . or *you* know you were called?"

"That's part of the mystery, I suppose," he said. "My mother knew from the moment I was conceived. I inherited that knowledge from her. Others are called later in life."

"How do *they* know?"

The Old Judge patted his beard thoughtfully. "It is a matter of faith, child, and it works differently from person to person. My parents had faith in the Unseen One, and their faith extended to me—that is, until I had faith of my own to believe."

Anna still didn't understand. "So which part comes first? Your faith or being chosen?"

"That's like asking whether the sun first rises or the sun first sets." The Old Judge smiled. "All things begin with the Unseen One. We could not have faith unless the Unseen One first gave us the capacity for faith. We believe because He makes it possible to believe. Once we believe, then it's safe to assume we are chosen. Chosen for *what* is part of the mystery. But know this: Where there is faith, there is calling."

Anna shook her head. It was too much to take in. "But *how* do you know what the calling is?"

"Sometimes the knowledge comes in visible and tangible ways. For most, though, it comes through prayer and the study of the Sacred Scroll. In time, the voice is unmistakable. The calling is there. Sometimes the knowledge comes through an old prophet like myself. I identify the one who has been called, even before they know it themselves. As I did to make Lawrence the king. And as I did to make General Darien the king."

"Lawrence and Darien—both kings?" Anna asked. "You called both? But won't that cause a lot of trouble?"

"It certainly will," the Old Judge said sadly. "But the trouble is not from the Unseen One. The problems come when a man is disobedient to the call—allows himself to be seduced by man-made powers and forces—and turns his back on the Unseen One. He is leading this nation to faithlessness. So a new king had to be chosen. General Darien is that king."

"I don't think King Lawrence will like that very much."

"It's the way of man to avoid the consequences of his faithlessness. King Lawrence will cling to an imaginary crown for as long as he can and lead the people of Marus even further away from the Unseen One. However, in his heart, Lawrence knows his rule is over. He rejected the Unseen One, and now the Unseen One has rejected him. Does he accept it? No. It drives him to madness even now."

At night, Anna had troubling dreams. They weren't nightmares but dreams that left her feeling disturbed when she awoke in the morning. Twice, the Old Judge came to her in the dreams. "You've been chosen," he said. "But your heart is not ready. In your heart, you must have faith in the Unseen One. Then you will be His voice."

Anna argued, "But nobody ever listens to me. I couldn't even keep my brother from going into that old house."

The Old Judge smiled and said, "A greater power than your brother was at work. You two were brought here to be a voice and a protector."

"A voice and a protector?"

Then he faded away. She woke up.

Other times, in the middle of the day, she would be doing something normal like working in the garden or reading one of the Old Judge's books, and suddenly it was as if she were no longer where she was but had been transported to another place to witness scenes of other people. The scenes made no sense to her. In one instance, she saw King Lawrence throwing a temper tantrum in his study.

"Still alive?" he screamed.

"The assassination attempt in the hills near Krawley failed. The fool missed," reported someone Anna couldn't see.

The king swept his arm across his desk, sending the paper, pens, ink blotter, telephone, and decorations exploding away. Then, suddenly, Anna saw him alone. He wept like a child.

"Please," he prayed with tear-filled eyes, "let me have the kingdom back."

When the prayer didn't bring him satisfaction, he marched around the room angrily, pouting like a spoiled brat. Anna found it a pathetic thing to watch.

Then, just as suddenly, she was back at the cottage, in the same position, doing the same thing she'd been doing before the weird "daydream."

She didn't tell the Old Judge about her dreams. She was afraid he would think she was crazy or hallucinating. Anyway, she knew, adults rarely believed her when she told them unusual things. When she was younger, she had an active imagination, often thinking up other lands and people and stories about them. But when she told her parents or teachers about her imaginings, they just smiled and nodded dismissively. "What an imagination!" they'd say, then tell her to get back to her math homework or science project. As she got older, she stopped imagining so much. It wasn't practical or helpful with her grades at school. "Stick with the *real* world," the adults told her. So she did. But now that the real world had disappeared, she wondered if her imagination had taken over again. For all she knew, this whole experience was just a dream and, in reality, she was lying with a high fever in a bed somewhere.

"When can I go home?" she asked the Old Judge on their third day together.

He shrugged and said, "I wish I could tell you."

"Does that mean you know and can't tell me or that you don't know?"

He gazed at her. His odd-colored eyes captured her. "These things must be taken by faith—one day at a time," he replied. He waited as if he expected her to tell him something. She was tempted to tell him about the dreams but resisted. He sighed. "One day at a time," he said again.

The night before the wedding of Darien and Michelle, King Lawrence threw a small banquet at his palace. The king was there with his entire family, including Prince George; his two brothers,

Andrew and William; their sister Mary; and her new husband, Frederick, the prince of Albany. (The king's wife, their mother, had died a couple of years before.) Darien and Michelle were there, of course. Darien's family, who lived on the opposite side of the country, couldn't attend the banquet but were to arrive later that night for the festivities the following day. General Liddell was also there and stayed at the king's elbow the entire evening. There were dozens of servants and attendants as well, including Kyle, who stood off to the side and looked uncomfortable in the formal uniform he'd been made to wear.

The skirmish with the Adrians seemed to dominate most of the discussion that night. General Liddell spoke proudly of his men's skill in battle. Kyle noticed that he didn't refer to Darien by name. In fact, to Kyle's surprise, no one mentioned the attempt to kill Darien at all. At first he thought it was because most people would've considered it rude or bad luck to bring up such a subject on the eve of a wedding. But as Kyle watched the various guests—the king and General Liddell in particular—he had a strong feeling that there were more sinister reasons to keep the subject under wraps. A thought came to him suddenly and for no apparent reason: *The king himself arranged the murder attempt.* Kyle tried to make the thought go away, but it wouldn't.

Darien and Michelle were attentive to each other. He kissed her hand while she blushed shyly, then gently teased her and treated her playfully as one might treat a friend.

But something was missing. Kyle remembered how his mother and father sometimes looked at each other with a deep affection. Kyle didn't see it in Darien's eyes. Michelle, on the other hand, was nervous and self-conscious. Kyle thought of a girl at school who had developed a crush on him. She had talked to him with ease up until then, but she suddenly became speechless around him. Her feelings got hurt quickly, and she sometimes punched him in the arm for no apparent reason. Michelle reminded Kyle of that girl. It was as if she had a schoolgirl crush on Darien. Was that love? Kyle didn't know for sure.

On the way to the banquet, Darien had briefly explained to Kyle that people often didn't marry for love. They married because their parents had arranged it. Or, in the case of kings and governments, marriages were politically expedient to secure relationships and allies. Kyle had told Darien that he thought those kinds of marriages were sad. "Not always," Darien had said. "Some marriages start out of necessity, then grow into love. Sometimes they begin with basic respect, and that's enough."

Watching Darien and Michelle as the evening went on, Kyle knew they did not love each other. Maybe they shared enough respect to make them happy. Time would tell, he figured.

After dinner had been served, the crowd urged Darien to play a few pieces on the grand piano that stood in the corner of the room. He reluctantly agreed and performed songs that made Kyle want to cry and leap for joy at the same time. They stirred something in his heart in a way that he never thought music could do. The guests were so moved that, when Darien finished the last song, no one stirred or applauded.

King Lawrence downed a gobletful of wine, then clapped his hands. He announced in rather slurred speech that he had some surprises for the happy couple. Two servants brought out beautifully wrapped presents for his daughter. She opened them to discover a necklace, earrings, and a ring that had belonged to her mother. Michelle wept and hugged her father in gratitude. For Darien, King Lawrence had an antique crossbow.

"It works!" he said to Darien as he loaded a small arrow onto the horizontal bow. He put the stock against his shoulder and pulled the string back until the arrow was nestled and cocked in its slot. To everyone's dismay, he pointed the crossbow around the room as if he might fire at whatever—or whomever—struck his fancy.

"Sire," General Liddell said and rested a hand on the king's arm.

The king laughed and put the crossbow onto the banquet table. "Oh, don't be so peevish, General," he said.

Crowds had been gathering outside the palace the entire evening, and now they broke into a familiar chant for Darien. "Darien! Darien! Darien!" they called.

Prince George broke the tension by saying jovially, "I believe the crowd would appreciate an appearance by the bride and bridegroom on the balcony." He stood up and waved for a servant to open the double doors. The roar of the crowd intensified. "Darien! Darien! Darien!"

"Go on, Darien," someone encouraged. "Show the world your bride!"

Darien stood up, took his bride's hand, and led her to the balcony. The rest of the banquet guests joined them.

The sight of Darien and Michelle threw people into a frenzy of cheering and shouts. In return, Darien smiled, waved, then kissed the hand of the bride-to-be. The people shouted more loudly in appreciation.

After several minutes of this, Darien indicated that they should go back in to the banquet. "Let's not bore them," he said pleasantly as they turned back toward the banquet hall.

"Bore them?" Prince William said boisterously. "You could never bore them, Darien. They love you. You can do no wrong as far as they're concerned!"

What happened next happened so quickly that Kyle barely had time to act. He glanced over in time to see the king, who was slumped in his chair, reach toward the crossbow. It didn't look like a purposeful act. He casually placed his hand on the stock of the weapon and rubbed the wood lightly. Kyle felt an odd feeling in the pit of his stomach, a sense that something wasn't right. *Does he mean to shoot Darien?* Kyle wondered. But the king's manner was so careless that Kyle couldn't be sure. Yet that feeling, so like the one he had had on the Krawley hillside, said that Darien was in danger. How could he warn Darien without causing a scene?

Kyle looked over at the glass-paned double doors where Darien, Michelle, and the other guests were returning from the balcony. Michelle entered, with Darien following. The king fiddled with the crossbow. His fingers stretched toward the trigger. Kyle reached into his pocket and pulled out a round brass button shaped like a marble, an extra to the same buttons along his waistcoat and cloak. With a quick flick of his wrist—barely noticeable to anyone around him—he threw the button across the floor toward Darien.

Michelle and the guests continued walking into the hall. Darien, who was crossing in front of the grand piano, had turned to say something to one of the guests when his eye caught sight of the button sliding toward his feet. He bent down to pick it up. Suddenly there was a loud *click* and a hissing sound, followed by the arrow from the crossbow slamming into the upright lid of the piano. The force splintered the wood and sent a discordant note shivering through the instrument. It had missed Darien only by inches and would have hit him if he hadn't stooped down. Kyle breathed a deep sigh of relief.

Some of the guests screamed and moved back. Darien turned in the direction from which the arrow had come. All eyes followed. The king looked up sullenly from his place at the table, his hand still on the crossbow. He said in a wine-filled voice, "My dear boy, I'm so sorry! I was reaching for the confounded thing, and it simply went off. A light touch on the trigger. I do apologize. Good thing I wasn't aiming, eh?"

Darien glared at the king without speaking.

"Father!" Michelle cried out.

Prince George strode to the table and snatched up the crossbow indignantly. "You could have killed him!" he growled. He turned quickly. "General Liddell!" he barked.

"Yes, sir." General Liddell broke from the crowd and stepped forward.

"My father has had too much to drink. See him to his room, if you please."

"Yes, sir." General Liddell rounded the table and helped the king to his feet.

"It was an accident!" the king protested drunkenly as General Liddell led him away. "Do you honestly think I'd try to kill my greatest general—the greatest in the entire land? The greatest in history?"

After the king had gone, Darien turned to Michelle, kissed her hand once again, and said, "I will see you tomorrow, my princess." He signaled Kyle, and together they walked toward the door.

"So soon? So early?" Prince Andrew called out. "Now that Father's gone, this party can really heat up. Do stay, Darien."

"I'm sorry, but I must think of tomorrow," he said from the door. He gave them a half-salute and walked out, closing the door behind him.

"That was a close call," Kyle said as they walked down the hall.

"Too close, as far as I'm concerned," Darien replied. He handed the button back to Kyle. "This is yours, I assume?"

Kyle nodded.

"Someday you're going to have to explain to me how you always know when my life is in danger."

"I don't know," Kyle said simply as he pocketed the button again. "So Prince George was right. The king wants to kill you."

"It would appear so."

"Unless it really was an accident."

Darien gave Kyle a look of disbelief. "If it was an accident, it would have been an awfully *convenient* accident."

Anna had just finished washing for bed. She grabbed a towel, dried her face, and looked in the mirror. She gasped. Instead of seeing her reflection, it was as if she were looking through a window into a large bedroom with an enormous bed surrounded by thick curtains. At the foot of the bed, King Lawrence sat with his legs stretched out. General Liddell pulled at the king's boots. They were in an animated conversation, though Anna couldn't hear it. The king was angry about something, as usual. Suddenly Prince George stormed into the room. He shouted at his father. His father shouted back. Prince George paced, shook his finger at the king as if rebuking him for something, then left.

More calmly, King Lawrence and General Liddell spoke to each other. They had the look of two conspirators hatching a dangerous plot. The king was emphatic about what he wanted done. General Liddell finally saluted and marched out of the room.

The king staggered to the side of the bed and threw himself facedown onto the thick cushions. The room was still for a moment. Then a shadow moved in the window. The curtains parted, and a woman Anna had never seen before stepped out. She glanced nervously at the king on his bed, then crossed the room and leaned against a wall next to a bookcase. Watching the king closely, she reached over to the chair rail that lined the wall and pressed something along the top. A secret door in the wall opened, and she slipped out of the room. The secret door closed, and the wall looked as solid as it had before.

Anna trembled for a moment, and then the room disappeared, replaced by her face in the mirror. She looked pale. Her knees felt weak, and her arms ached from clutching the washstand tightly. Composing herself, she splashed water on her face again, dried off, and then stepped into the hallway to go to her room.

The Old Judge stood there, waiting for her. "Are you well?" he asked.

Anna swallowed hard. "Yes, sir, I am," she said.

"You look shaken," he said.

She avoided his gaze as she walked past him. "I'm all right," she affirmed.

But she knew his eyes were on her as she slipped into her room. In bed, she pulled her pillow close. *What are these scenes I keep seeing?* she wondered. *Why am I seeing them?* She eventually closed her eyes for a night of restless sleep.

At home once again, Darien sat down at his piano and played songs that were alternately mournful and passionate. Kyle sat nearby and watched him. Darien's playing wasn't an idle amusement. He was thinking as he played, trying to decide what to do next.

Kyle shifted in his seat nervously. "What are you going to do?" he eventually asked.

"A very good question, lad," Darien said. He stopped playing, closed the lid on the piano, and rested his elbows there.

"If you think the king tried to kill you, you'd be crazy to stick around," Kyle said. "Shouldn't you escape while you can?"

Darien shook his head. "What about the wedding tomorrow?" he asked. "I can't simply disappear in the night without an explanation. What would I say? 'Oh, sorry, but I couldn't marry the princess because the king tried to kill me with a crossbow.' It would be an accusation—my word against the king's."

"What if you just don't show up?"

"Another scandal. How could I insult the princess and her royal family like that? The entire nation would be up in arms."

Just then, they heard a light tapping at the French doors leading to the garden.

Kyle's face brightened. "I'll bet it's Prince George," he said. "He'll know what to do."

Darien crossed over to the doors but didn't open them. Instead, he stood next to the wall and carefully lifted the curtain for a peek. His face registered surprise, and he quickly opened the doors. Princess Michelle, dressed in a black cloak with a hood, rushed in. Kyle, also surprised, stood up.

"What brings you here, my princess?" Darien asked.

"We haven't much time," the princess said. "They're on their way."

"Who is?" Darien asked.

"General Liddell's guards. They've been instructed to arrest you."

"On what charge?"

"Treason."

"That's insane!"

"Insane or not, it's what my father wants."

Darien fumed. "No one will believe it," he insisted. "How could they prove such a thing?"

"You underestimate my father. He has it all worked out. They're going to claim that the man who tried to assassinate you outside Krawley had learned that you were hatching a plot to overthrow the king. You had him killed to keep him quiet."

"I didn't have him killed! The soldiers there will attest to that."

"What soldiers? *General Liddell's* soldiers?" the princess asked, shocked at Darien's naïveté. "They're duty bound to whatever the general and the king tell them. You must leave—*now*."

Darien eyed her warily. "You're the king's daughter. Why should I believe you?"

The princess opened her mouth to speak, but tears fell from her eyes instead. "I know my father wanted me to marry you so I'd keep an eye on you for him. And I know you're marrying me only because the king wants you to. No one stopped to ask *my* feelings, though. And the truth is, I love you. I have from the first time I met you."

A sympathetic smile crossed Darien's face, and he took the princess's hands in his and kissed them both. "I'm humbled and undeserving of your love, my princess," he said.

A hard pounding at the front door interrupted their tender moment. Darien, Princess Michelle, and Kyle raced into the hallway just as Edward, the head servant, made his way to the door.

"Wait!" Darien told him. "You have to stall them, Edward. Tell them I'm in bed. Give me time."

Edward's dull expression didn't change as he bowed slightly and answered, "Yes, sir."

The three of them turned and raced up the steps to the second floor and Darien's room.

"What do we do now?" Kyle asked after Darien closed and locked the door.

Darien quickly pulled the covers down to the foot of the bed and then went to the corner of the room, where he grabbed a suit of armor that stood there indifferently. *Do they have suits of armor in every room?* Kyle wondered.

"Help me," Darien said to Kyle. Together they pushed the armor onto the bed. Darien yanked the covers over it. He then dimmed the light in the room so that it genuinely looked as if someone were asleep in the bed. "There," he said. "Sleeping like a baby."

Deep voices shouted in another part of the house. Darien went to the window and threw it open. Satisfied that no one was waiting below, he turned to Kyle and asked, "Are you coming?"

"Where else would I go?" Kyle said.

Darien then turned to Princess Michelle. "It's going to look bad for you," he said sympathetically. "Liddell's men will wonder why you're here. Tell them I threatened to kill you if you didn't help me. Attempted murder won't surprise them if they think I'm a traitor."

Michelle nodded silently.

Darien kissed her. "I suppose our wedding day will have to wait," he said with an ironic smile.

She smiled sadly as a tear slipped down her cheek. "I suppose it will," she agreed.

Heavy footsteps invaded the hall just outside the room. Someone jiggled the handle, then began to break down the door.

"Farewell," Darien said to Michelle. Then he hoisted Kyle out of the window, where he grabbed on to a branch of a nearby tree. Darien started to follow, then stopped. "I've forgotten my pistol and my sword!" he exclaimed. "Where are they?"

"You don't have time!" Michelle said firmly.

Darien frowned, then leaped to the tree. He and Kyle climbed down to the ground and ran off into the night.

In her dreams, Anna saw a woman standing in a bedroom. It wasn't the king's bedroom this time—this room was smaller and more modest—but it was the same woman she had seen before. The room wasn't lit very well, so Anna had a hard time making out the shadows. The woman moved to the bed and sat down. Someone slept under the covers. Whoever it was didn't stir. Anna had the impression that the woman was a nurse taking care of someone ill.

The bedroom door was suddenly thrown open. Several men stood silhouetted in the doorway. They were dressed as soldiers, with guns in hand and swords at their sides. The woman stood up and crossed quickly to the men before they could enter the room fully.

The men stopped, surprised to see the woman there. She gestured in appeal to them and then back to the bed as if to say that they shouldn't disturb the sleeper. One of the men waved his arms anxiously at the woman and also pointed to the bed. The woman responded. Finally the man waved her aside and approached the bed with his sword drawn. He threw back the covers. A suit of armor glimmered in the dim light.

Dreams have no sense of time or place. Just as Anna saw the suit of armor, the scene quickly changed to a dark wood. A man Anna didn't know moved hastily through the trees. He was followed by a boy.

"Kyle!" Anna gasped.

Kyle and the man emerged from the woods and stood for a moment on the crest of a hill. They looked out over a valley that Anna recognized. In the distance, she saw the town of Hailsham. Kyle and the man headed for the town.

Seconds later—or was it minutes or an hour?—Anna was awakened by a knocking sound. She sluggishly crawled from her bed and ventured out to the main room of the Old Judge's cottage. The Old Judge, still fully dressed as if he'd never gone to bed, held a lamp high and opened the door.

"Hello, Darien," he said warmly as the man in Anna's dream stepped in. They clasped hands and shook vigorously. Then the Old Judge said, "And you must be—"

"Kyle!" Anna cried out as she rushed to the door.

Kyle turned to his sister, a stunned expression on his face. She gave him a long, hard hug.

Morning came just as Kyle and Anna finished swapping stories of their time in Marus. They were both amazed at their respective adventures and wondered anew about their reason for being in Marus at all. Anna didn't tell Kyle about her bizarre dreams. Nor did Kyle mention how he'd saved Darien's life three times. They talked instead about the effect their disappearance would have on their family.

"Do you think Grandma and Grandpa are worried?" Anna asked.

"Probably," Kyle said. "Maybe the police are looking for us."

But there was nothing they could do about it. Both were resigned to that fact. What neither of them dared mention, though, was the possibility that they might never get back to their own world. That was a worry they didn't dare put into words.

Meanwhile, in another part of the cottage, Darien told the Old Judge everything that had happened with King Lawrence, including the attempt to kill him with the crossbow and the narrow escape from his bedroom thanks to Princess Michelle's warning.

The Old Judge listened and nodded thoughtfully. "This was inevitable," he said.

"Was it?" Darien asked.

"You were chosen by the Unseen One. Lawrence knows it but won't accept it. What man would?"

"But the king has nothing to fear from me," Darien said firmly.

"Oh, but his madness tells him he does," the Old Judge said. "He knows you've been chosen to replace him."

"I don't know that. No one ever told me I was chosen to be king."

"Perhaps you won't admit it openly, but you've known in your heart that it is true," the Old Judge said, casting a steely gaze at the young man. "Don't you remember when I secretly went to your father's house? Do you think it was for a cup of tea and a pleasant chat? I was sent there by the Unseen One to find you."

"I remember," Darien said quietly. "You laid your hands on my head and claimed I was chosen for an important purpose."

"To be king."

"And now King Lawrence wants to see that it doesn't happen. Nor will I force it to happen. I will not lift a hand against him. You know I won't." Darien folded his arms resolutely.

The Old Judge smiled like a shrewd negotiator. "We're in the hands of the Unseen One."

"I wish someone would tell me who the Unseen One is," Kyle said as he and Anna walked into the room.

"Your sister will explain it as you walk to the village," the Old Judge stated.

"We're going to the village?" Anna asked.

The Old Judge waved her on. "Yes. Bring me back a newspaper. I'd like to see what the king is saying about the cancellation of the wedding."

The children complied, and on the way to the village, Anna told Kyle what she could about the Unseen One.

"The Unseen One must be God," Kyle said, coming to the same conclusion that Anna had.

"Yeah, but here the Unseen One seems so . . . well, it's like He really does things here."

Kyle thought about it for a moment and then said, "Grandma and Grandpa say God does things in our world, too—but you have to believe in Him in your heart to see what He's up to."

Anna remembered the dream she had where the Old Judge said almost the same thing to her. "You must have faith," he'd said. *Do I have that kind of faith?* she asked herself.

"I get the feeling there aren't a lot of people left who believe in the Unseen One," Kyle said.

"I get the same feeling," Anna agreed. "The Old Judge says that King Lawrence and the rest of the country have come up with some kind of do-it-yourself religion. He says it's man-made and that everyone thinks that things just happen because they happen— sort of like fate with a capital F. But the Old Judge thinks the king believes in it because he can't stand being rejected by the Unseen One. If he pretends the Unseen One doesn't exist, he'll get to be king longer."

They reached the village, and Anna slipped into a corner shop that sold groceries, tobacco, and newspapers. When she returned to the street, she was ashen-faced. She handed the newspaper to Kyle.

"Plot to Overthrow King Thwarted!" the headline in the *Sarum Herald* shouted in large, black type. The article went on to say that a plot to overthrow the king had been exposed just in the nick of time. For security reasons, the wedding had been canceled. Though it didn't say so directly, the newspaper hinted that General Darien may have been part of the plot. The royal family was leaving the capital city for a safer place until the extent of the plot could be determined.

"The king didn't waste any time, did he?" Kyle said.

Inside the paper were stock black-and-white photos of the royal family. In the center of one page was a photo of Darien and Michelle on stage in the Great Hall on the day the king announced the wedding. Anna put her hand to her mouth with alarm.

"What's the matter?" Kyle asked.

"Is that really the princess?" she said.

"Yeah."

Anna shook her head and spoke so softly that Kyle had a hard time hearing her as she observed, "Weird things are happening here."

Kyle looked curiously at his sister. "Like what?" he asked.

She led Kyle down Hailsham's main street toward the road that would lead them back to the cottage. When they reached an open field, she said, "I keep having dreams, seeing things."

Kyle sounded annoyed at having to wait so long for that statement. "Everybody sees things in their dreams," he said.

"But these are real things," Anna explained. "I saw the king in his bedroom having an argument with that General Liddell guy. I saw the princess, too. She was in the bedroom spying on them. She escaped through a secret door. And then I saw her in another bedroom."

Kyle said impatiently, "She was in Darien's room. She helped us escape. I told you the story. I think you're getting mixed up."

"No. I saw what happened *after* you escaped from his bedroom."

"That's impossible."

Anna shook her head. "Soldiers came in, and the princess stopped them. There was someone in the bed—or that's what I thought. But the soldiers pulled the covers back, and it wasn't a person. Someone had put a suit of armor in the bed."

Kyle's face went pale. No one had mentioned the suit of armor back at the cottage. There was no way Anna could've known about it. "You dreamed that?" he asked.

"Sort of," Anna said, relieved that Kyle seemed to believe her now. "But it's more like a daydream than a dream. It's like . . ." But the words to describe it escaped her. She couldn't say any more.

"Maybe it's because we're in this country," Kyle offered.

"Maybe it's the Unseen One. The Old Judge said that I've been brought here for a reason. If I was, then you were, too. You came here before I did, remember? We were chosen for a reason."

"What kind of reason?"

Anna shrugged. "The Old Judge said something about us being a voice and a protector. Maybe he meant that *I'm* the voice and you're the protector."

Kyle thought about that for a moment. *Protector.* It made sense—and his face reflected the realization.

"What are you thinking?" Anna asked.

Kyle told his sister about the three times he had saved Darien's life. He concluded, "I get this sick feeling in the pit of my stomach. And then the next thing I know, somebody tries to hurt Darien and I save him."

Anna shuddered. "This is very strange."

"Anna . . ." Kyle hesitated as if he wasn't sure he should say more. But he did. "Do you believe in the Unseen One?"

Anna considered her answer carefully, then said, "There's no other way to explain all the things I've seen with the Old Judge, or in my dreams, or our being here. So, yes, I believe in the Unseen One."

They walked on silently for a while. The cottage appeared just ahead.

Eventually, Kyle asked, "Do you think the Unseen One is on our side? I mean, if we're here for a reason, will the Unseen One take care of us and get us home again?"

"I hope so," Anna said, then added, "I think so."

Kyle sighed deeply. "I hope you're right."

Back at the cottage, Darien read the newspaper, then threw it across the room. "This is unbelievable!" he snarled.

"Unbelievable? *Predictable* is the better word," the Old Judge said.

"At least they didn't say you were a traitor," Kyle said to be helpful.

Darien frowned. "They didn't say it outright, but they implied it. People will be watching."

"The king will pay me a visit," the Old Judge said. "Of that you can be sure."

"Why?"

"Why not? He'll know that you've come to see me." The Old Judge scratched at his beard. "Frankly, I'm surprised he hasn't tried to sneak up on us already."

Darien shook his head. "He'd send someone to arrest me. He wouldn't come all this way himself."

"All this way? He's just over the hill."

Darien looked at the Old Judge quizzically. "What are you talking about?"

"Think about it, son. If they left Sarum for security reasons, where would they go? The king's country estate—and that's all of two miles from here. It is peaceful and secure. Being so close, the king will not resist coming to me."

"Let him come," Darien said. "I won't be here."

"And where will you be?"

"At the king's country estate," Darien said simply.

"What?" Kyle asked. "Are you nuts? I mean, are you nuts, *sir*?"

"If the royal family is there, that would include George. I want to see him."

"To what end?" the Old Judge asked.

"He's my friend," Darien replied. "I want him to know that these allegations are all lies."

"If he's your friend, he knows it already," said the Old Judge.

"And I want to see if he can speak to the king," Darien continued. "Maybe there's a way to appease him, to make him see that I am not his enemy."

The Old Judge scrutinized Darien's face. "You say that so sincerely," he said. "Do you believe it? Do you believe King Lawrence will ever allow you to return to his court?"

"I want to believe it's possible, even if it's impossible."

The Old Judge placed a hand on Darien's shoulder and said gently, "The wheels are in motion, my son. Nothing can be the way it was."

Darien didn't reply but went to the door and pulled it open. Kyle followed.

"Don't go, Kyle," Anna said as he and Darien walked out. "You'll get caught—or hurt."

Kyle looked back over his shoulder and smiled bravely. "Me get caught?" he said lightly. "I'm in the hands of the Unseen One."

"That doesn't mean the Unseen One won't let you get caught," she said.

But the door closed and they were gone.

The Old Judge was right. Shortly after Darien and Kyle left, a handful of soldiers came to the cottage and demanded to see Darien. The Old Judge said truthfully that he wasn't there. When the soldiers declared that they would search the house, the Old Judge blocked their way, fixed a dark eye on them, and said, "You must find it terribly funny to think that Darien would hide in an old cottage like this."

To Anna's amazement, the soldiers began to laugh. "Yeah, it is funny," the captain said as his laughter turned into side-splitting hysterics. The soldiers guffawed uncontrollably, to the extent that they sank to their knees and rolled on their sides. Some of them doubled over with stomach cramps from laughing so hard, and others couldn't breathe. After a few minutes, the captain begged the Old Judge for mercy.

The Old Judge said, "You desire mercy? Then leave this place and you'll have it."

Between chortles and gasps, the captain commanded his men to withdraw. They helped each other up from the ground and stumbled away, their laughter still echoing through the valley as they went.

Anna looked at the Old Judge with an unspoken question.

"Weak-minded men," the Old Judge said offhandedly. "We'll see how the next batch hold up."

"The next batch?"

Sure enough, two hours later, another company of soldiers arrived. They were a harder-looking bunch than the previous men, with expressions that said they probably hadn't laughed in years. The officer in charge seemed to know the Old Judge. "None of your tricks," he barked. "We want Darien."

"He's not here," the Old Judge said.

"We'll see about that," the officer growled. He directed his men to search the house.

Again the Old Judge stepped forward to block their way to the door. "But it's so sad that a man as respected as Darien should be hunted like an animal," he said. "Don't you find it terribly sad?"

"I don't find it sad at all," the officer said. But his eyes filled with tears anyway.

His men began to sob.

"Stop it!" the officer shouted through his own tears. "Don't you see what's happening? He's tricking us!"

The Old Judge gazed at them innocently. "A trick?" he said. "Since when are laughter and tears part of a trick? They are gifts from the Unseen One."

"Keep your gifts to yourself!" the officer said as he wept. "We have to search this house."

"Am I stopping you?" the Old Judge asked.

By now, the soldiers had fallen to their knees, their faces hidden in their hands, the tears pouring from between their fingers. The officer, strong though he was, eventually succumbed and also dropped to the ground. The weeping and wailing of the men brought tears to Anna's eyes, too.

"I'm afraid I'm all out of tissues," the Old Judge said.

Through heaving sobs, the officer told his men to retreat. "This is humiliating!" was the last thing he cried before they were out of sight.

Within the hour, there came a stern knock at the door. "That would be General Liddell, with King Lawrence not too far behind," the Old Judge said to Anna. He went to welcome them.

General Liddell stood erect in the doorway, his face red and the scar a sliver of white on his cheek. "The king wants to speak to you," he said formally. He tapped the handle of the pistol he had tucked in his belt. "I wouldn't do anything clever."

"Clever?" the Old Judge said with a smile. "I'm too old to do anything clever."

Anna followed at a discreet distance as the Old Judge stepped into his front garden and crossed to a large tree where the king waited silently. General Liddell glanced at Anna and gestured for her to stay back. His face registered a moment's recognition, but then he ignored her.

The king bowed slightly to the Old Judge. "Hello, you old fox," he said.

"Greetings, my son," the Old Judge replied as he nodded.

"My royal army doctors are up to their eyeballs in soldiers," the king said. "One regiment seems to be suffering from severe cramps from laughing too hard. The other can barely see from the soreness in their eyes. Do you know anything about it?"

The Old Judge spread his arms. "What could I know?" he asked.

"Just as I thought," the king said. "Where is Darien?"

"Hither and yon," the Old Judge answered.

"He's under suspicion of treason. You would be committing a crime by harboring a fugitive."

"Committing a crime against whom?"

"Against your king."

"*My* king? And who, pray tell, is *my* king? You know to whom I pledge allegiance, and it is no king that I see here."

Lawrence's face turned bright red, and he quickly pulled his sword from its sheath. He pointed it at the Old Judge's neck. "I'm not some fool that you can make laugh or cry, old one!" the king spat. "It would be within my right and my strength to strike you down here and now."

"Within your strength, perhaps," the Old Judge said coolly. "But not within your right. You waived that right when you turned your back on the Unseen One."

"The Unseen One turned His back on *me,*" the king snarled.

The Old Judge frowned. "Is that so? Shall I recall your rebellion in front of this small audience? Do you want your general and this young girl to hear how you willfully disobeyed the One who made you king? I have held my tongue until now, Lawrence, but I will not hesitate to tell the world how you betrayed the ancient ways. And in betraying them, you have betrayed your own people. Where the blessings of the Unseen One could have been a harvest in your life, His curses will now fall upon you in ways you cannot comprehend!"

The king quivered for a moment as if he might thrust his sword through the Old Judge. The Old Judge simply blinked. An apple fell from the tree and hit the king on the top of his head.

The king looked up, perplexed. "This is no apple tree," he said. Another apple fell and hit him. Then another. And another. Soon it was raining apples on him. He ran away from the tree. The apple shower followed him. He began to laugh at the absurdity of the situation. Quickly, though, his laughter became uncontrollable. Then tears poured from his eyes. The king was laughing and crying at the same time. He gasped, desperate for breath.

General Liddell pointed his pistol at the Old Judge. "Stop it," he ordered, "or I'll kill you."

"Kill me and it will never stop until the king himself is dead," the Old Judge responded with a steely gaze.

General Liddell returned the pistol to his belt and asked, "Then what do you want me to do?"

"Take the king away, and he'll soon be back to his sour self," the Old Judge instructed. "And never—*never*—return to my cottage. The day that you do will be your last."

General Liddell, obviously shaken, helped the king, still helpless from his laughter and tears, get onto his horse. Once Lawrence had mounted, he brokenly said to the Old Judge, "Your conjurings won't stop me, old man. I will find Darien."

"Perhaps Darien will find *you*," the Old Judge said.

King Lawrence and General Liddell galloped away.

When the dust of the road had faded into the air, the Old Judge turned to Anna. "I have a mission for you," he said.

Balmovia, the king's country mansion, was a sprawling estate with acres and acres of royal forest, marshes, and groves inhabited by royal deer, rabbits, badgers, and other woodland animals. The forest rolled like a thick green carpet to the mansion itself, which stood on top of a hill. The house had more than 100 rooms, a grand banquet hall, a huge library, and endless corridors. It sat on a well-manicured lawn with gardens, adjoining tennis courts, a swimming pool, a maze of intricately carved shrubs, and an archery range. Because the woods were thickest on the side approaching the archery range, that's where Darien and Kyle ventured first.

"Considering the king's life is supposed to be in danger, they don't seem to have many guards around," Darien observed.

Kyle also noticed the absence of soldiers, police, or security guards watching the area. It seemed that Darien and he could have strolled in as if nothing had ever happened at the banquet the night before.

Through the trees, they could see that someone was practicing on the archery range. They heard the sound of the arrows sailing through the air and the dull thuds of the sharp points hitting a solid target.

"Maybe you should hide here while I go ahead," Kyle suggested. "If they see me, it won't matter. They're not looking for me. But everyone around the house will be watching for you."

Darien deferred to Kyle's idea. "I'll be here," he said.

Kyle crept to the edge of the forest, staying close to the ground. He hid behind a large tree and peered around it, which gave him a clear view of the field. His heart started to race. Prince George was alone, shooting at the target. Kyle looked up toward the house to see whether anyone there might spot him if he came out to signal George. The angle from the house would make the view difficult if not impossible.

Kyle waited until the prince exhausted his quiver of arrows, then stepped out into the open. At first George looked annoyed at the intruder. "What do you want?" he demanded.

"To speak to Your Highness on behalf of a friend," Kyle said.

George squinted at Kyle, and then his face brightened with recognition. "Kyle! Good heavens, boy, what are you doing here? Is—?" He stopped himself and looked around to be sure no one could see or hear him. "Is Darien all right?"

"Follow me and you'll see," Kyle replied.

George obeyed, following Kyle to where Darien had hidden.

Darien bowed to George and said, "My prince."

George grabbed Darien and embraced him heartily. "What are you doing here?" he asked. "Why have you taken this risk? I had hoped you'd be miles from here by now."

"I had to see you. To be sure."

"I'm so sorry about what's happened," George said. "I'm afraid my father has lost his mind."

"So you don't believe the allegations in the *Sarum Herald*," Darien said, relieved.

George looked indignant. "Of course not!" he said. "I'm not privy to my father's scheming, but I knew he'd gone over the edge when he took a shot at you with that crossbow. I can't imagine what he was thinking."

"You're certain it wasn't an accident? He'd been drinking . . ."

George frowned at his friend. "Didn't I warn you that something like this might happen? He's beside himself with jealousy. I believe something snapped when he heard the crowds calling your name beneath the balcony. All that nonsense in the newspaper was probably concocted by General Liddell."

Darien sat down on a log. He sighed heavily. "Then the king wants me dead."

"Dead or arrested," George said. "Though I doubt there's much difference between the two."

The two men were silent for a moment.

"Look, Darien, you have to get out of here—and out of the country," George continued. "You're not safe here at all. My father won't make a public spectacle of his desire to get rid of you, but he'll work quietly. He'll send his men after you. He already has, in fact. They went to the Old Judge's cottage to find you."

"Where can I go?" Darien asked sadly. "This is my homeland."

"I don't know," George replied with equal sorrow. He gave his mustache a quick brush with the side of his finger. "How about Prince Edwin? The people of Gotthard have always been friendly to you. Remember the fuss they made when you vacationed there last year? You were a celebrity. Prince Edwin himself couldn't do enough for you."

The idea seemed to appeal to Darien. "If he can give me refuge until your father's mind changes, maybe that will be enough."

"It's certainly worth a try," George said. "But I'd stay away from the trains or main roads. My father has spies everywhere."

A twig snapped loudly nearby. Darien, George, and Kyle all jumped and turned quickly to see if someone was sneaking up on them. It was a deer.

"You must go," George said, turning back to Darien. "It was foolish to come here."

"I couldn't have left the area without knowing for certain that we were still friends, no matter what happens with your father."

George clasped Darien's hand in his. "Our friendship is secure, my brother," he said with feeling. "May the Unseen One be our witness."

"So be it," Darien said, smiling.

"Now go," the prince urged.

Back at the Old Judge's cottage, everyone sat down for dinner. While they ate, Anna told Darien and Kyle about what had happened to the king's soldiers and then to the king himself. Kyle was astounded.

Darien cast a troubled glance at the Old Judge. "Is it appropriate to torment the king of our country that way?" he asked.

The Old Judge snorted impatiently. "You deal with the king in your way and I'll deal with him in mine," he replied. "Remember, son, that I have known him much longer than you have."

Darien didn't reply to that but said, "It's time to leave. I want to go first to see that my family is all right. After that, I'll travel to Gotthard. Prince George believes that Edwin and his people will receive me."

"So they might," the Old Judge said. "There is a remnant of believers in the Unseen One there."

"You agree?" Darien asked, surprised.

"Why wouldn't I?" the Old Judge asked.

"I thought you would probably have another plan worked out—something better from the Unseen One."

"Something easy, perhaps?"

"Yes."

"A quick snap of the fingers and everything will be taken care of?"

Darien nodded. "It would be easy enough for the Unseen One."

"Easy, yes," the Old Judge said with a smile. "But the Unseen One rarely makes things easy for us."

"Why not?" Kyle asked.

"Because the Unseen One knows our hearts. When we are given things easily, we dismiss them easily. When the Unseen One makes us work and sweat and struggle a little for what we have, we respect and treasure it." He turned to Darien. "You will respect your crown when you have struggled to win it." His face then went dark. "But even your respect will not be enough to keep it on your head."

Darien groaned. "I'm not even king yet and you're predicting trouble?"

"I predict nothing," the Old Judge said. "Know this, however: For all your attributes, Darien, there are weaknesses. Beware your weaknesses. There are those who wait to see them and exploit them."

Darien waved the warning away. "Enough of this talk," he said. "I have a long journey ahead of me."

The Old Judge clasped his hands under his chin. "All of you do," he said.

"All of us?" Darien asked.

Anna suddenly realized what the Old Judge was saying. "Me, too?" she said.

"Darien, I would like you to make your journey past the town of Dorr," the Old Judge instructed. "There's a convent there. Go to Sister Leona. She can help you. It's important, though, that you don't explain to her *why* you're traveling."

"Then why would I want to go there?" asked Darien.

"Because I want Anna to stay with her."

"What?" Anna cried out. "Why?"

The Old Judge reached over, laid a hand on her arm, and

explained, "Because your gift is still new and hasn't been properly developed."

"Gift?" Anna's face went alternately red, then white, then red again.

"Do you really think I don't know about the dreams and visions you've been having?"

Anna's mouth fell open. "You know about that?"

"My dear child, why do you think you are here?" The Old Judge asked the question as if the answer should have been obvious to everyone. He didn't elaborate further but said, "Now you must go to Sister Leona, for she will help you with your gift."

Anna looked puzzled. "How?" she asked.

"You'll find out when the time is right."

Darien stood up, along with Kyle. "We must leave if we hope to make it to Dorr before daybreak," Darien said.

Anna hesitated. She knew she had to leave the Old Judge. And only now did she realize how deeply she cared for him. "But sir . . ." she began. She searched for words that wouldn't come. "I don't want to say good-bye."

"Nor do I," he said warmly. "You have been a breath of fresh air to me, a beautiful light. But it's necessary that you go."

"Will we come back?" she asked. "Will I see you again?"

"We are in the hands of the Unseen One. I make no promises, but I hope that one day we will." His eyes suddenly filled with tears. "I do not envy you your journey, child. It will not be without its share of suffering. But often it is in suffering that we see the ancient ways of the Unseen One most clearly."

Anna struggled to keep back her tears as they walked to the front door. She hugged the Old Judge quickly. "Thank you," she said.

"You're welcome," he replied warmly.

Darien shook the Old Judge's hand with silent gratitude. Kyle did the same.

The shadows of dusk surrounded them as they crossed from the house to the edge of the forest. Darien and Kyle looked back to wave at the Old Judge, who stood in the doorway, framed with golden light. Anna kept her eyes forward.

The three travelers had an uneventful journey and arrived at the village of Dorr shortly before morning. It had been a long walk, and Kyle and Anna were exhausted. The only thing either of them wanted was a bed.

The convent the Old Judge had mentioned sat on the village outskirts. It was a modest stone compound with high walls and a huge door on the front. Darien banged the simple iron knocker several times. Five minutes passed before a young, sleepy-eyed girl wearing a hood opened the door. When Darien introduced himself, the girl stumbled and stammered that they should wait right there while she went to get Sister Leona. She disappeared into a dark corridor.

Sister Leona, the head of the convent, came to the door in her dressing gown. Her white hair was tousled and stuck out at odd angles under her hood. Her eyes were puffy from sleep. "Come in, come in!" she said and led them in. They took a path through a beautiful courtyard with flowers and a fountain and eventually arrived at a small building on the other side of the enclosure. It housed a primitive kitchen and long, wooden table. Sister Leona and another girl quickly warmed up a meat stew, even though Darien assured her it wasn't necessary.

After the food had been served and a blessing said, Sister Leona turned to Anna. Her eyes were piercing in their intensity. "So the Old Judge wants me to teach you?" she said. "You must be very special for him to send you to me."

Anna blushed and said, "I don't know what he thinks I'll learn."

"You'll learn what you're willing to learn," Sister Leona answered. Anna then noticed that, like the Old Judge, Sister Leona's eyes were two different colors—one blue, the other green. "Is there something wrong?" she asked.

Anna averted her gaze. "No, ma'am."

"General Darien, why are you traveling so late at night—and without your attendants and soldiers?" asked Sister Leona. "Are you on your way to a battle?"

"No, Sister," Darien replied and ate some bread. Kyle and Anna exchanged uneasy glances.

"Had we known you were going to visit our humble convent, we would have made proper arrangements for you," Sister Leona said. "Normally an official at the king's palace informs us when—"

Darien interrupted her: "The king's officials aren't involved in this enterprise. This is a secret mission."

"Then the allegations that you are part of a plot against the king are false?"

"I can assure you that they are false. I am not part of a plot against the king." Darien toyed with his bread. "As it happens, we were passing this way, so the Old Judge asked us to bring Anna to you. That's all. It would be helpful if you didn't ask any more questions."

"I see," Sister Leona said politely. "Is there anything I can give you for your mission? More food?"

"Beds for a couple of hours' sleep would be most appreciated."

"Anything else?"

"A pistol and a sword," Darien said as a joke. "I'm traveling without my weapons."

Sister Leona didn't laugh. She merely tapped her chin with her index finger. "I may be able to help you with one of those items," she said seriously.

A few minutes later, they were in Sister Leona's private study. On the wall above the fireplace hung a large golden sword. Darien reached up, unclasped it, and carefully brought it down. "Amazing!" he said softly. "I had no idea it was here."

"Is there something special about it?" Kyle asked.

"It's the sword that belonged to Commander Soren of the Palatians," Sister Leona explained.

Kyle looked at the sword with awe and said, "You mean the one the commander used to try to kill General Darien?"

"The very one."

Darien held the sword up. The light from the gas lamps caught the edges of the sword, sending thin beams of yellow in all directions. "How did you come by it?" he asked.

"It was a gift to our order from the king," Sister Leona said. She searched a nearby closet and pulled out the sword's belt and sheath. "But it is yours by right, General. If you need it for your secret mission, then you must take it."

"I'll borrow it," Darien said.

They slept only a couple of hours before Darien was ready to move on to his family's farm. He woke Kyle up first, then together they went to Anna's room to say good-bye. She sat up in her bed and rubbed her eyes sleepily. When she realized they were leaving her, she was immediately distressed. "I'm afraid," she whispered to her brother.

"So am I," he admitted. "But it's probably a good idea for you to stay here."

"What if something happens to you?"

"I'm the protector," he said as bravely as he could. "Nothing can happen to me."

Neither of them believed it, but they didn't say so.

"How will I know where you are?" she asked. "How will I find you?"

"*We'll* find you," Darien assured her. "Or we'll send for you."

Kyle smiled. "Yeah, we'll send somebody with a secret code. He'll say: *Uncle Bill wants to see you.*"

"That's silly," Anna said.

Kyle nodded. "Yep," he agreed.

Darien put a hand on Kyle's shoulder. "The sun is up," he said. "We have to go." Then he left the room. Kyle lingered, looked at his sister with a worried expression, then spun on his heel and left.

Anna buried her face in her pillow and prayed to the Unseen One, "Please don't let anything happen to them."

Darien and Kyle walked around the village of Dorr, staying close to the outlying fields so they wouldn't be spotted. The only living creatures they ran into were a flock of sheep and their shepherd. Darien said hello to the shepherd as if they were on a morning stroll rather than a couple of fugitives on the run. The shepherd smiled back and said "Good morning" pleasantly.

Kyle felt that sick feeling in the pit of his stomach again and immediately prepared himself for something bad to happen. Maybe the shepherd was going to attack Darien with his crook. The shepherd just looked curiously at him, however, then walked on. *That's strange,* Kyle thought. *Is my "protector antenna" going wrong?*

Anna, asleep in her bed, saw the encounter with the shepherd in a dream. But she also saw what Darien and Kyle didn't: The shepherd waited until they were out of sight and then ran to the village. In her dream, she felt peaceful and unalarmed. When she awoke, however, her heart beat furiously in her chest. Panicked, she looked around her room. The thick curtains on the single window were drawn. The small wooden washstand, the bedside table, and the rectangular brown carpet on the floor all seemed to be cast in a single shadow. Suddenly the door was thrown open and a man rushed in, his sword drawn. Before Anna could scream, he ran her through in a single thrust.

And then she was truly awake. It had been another dream. Her room was filled with the half light of a sunny day that pushed through the drawn curtains. The door was closed.

She tried to figure out what the two dreams meant but didn't know how. Chilled and feverish, her eyes burning in their sockets, she tried to stand up. Her legs gave way, and she collapsed onto the floor.

That's where Sister Leona found her later in the morning.

"Father!" Darien cried as he and his father embraced.

The stooped and bearded old man held his son. "Darien!" he exclaimed.

His mother joined the embrace as the three clung to one another.

It was late afternoon, and the four of them met in a small cabin on the outer limits of Darien's family property. Just in case King Lawrence had people watching, Kyle had run ahead to the back door of the house to secretly tell Darien's parents where their son was. "Tell him to meet us at the old house after dark," his father had instructed.

"Is it safe?" Kyle had asked.

"No one but our family has any idea it's there," Darien's father had replied. "I am Torbin, by the way. This is my wife, Evelyn. You must be my son's guardian angel."

Kyle had nodded as a reply and said, "We'll see you there after dark."

He had run back to deliver the message to Darien. They had then made their way to the old house, so called because it was where Darien's ancestors had lived when they first settled the land. It was a one-room cabin that reminded Kyle of an oversized playhouse. Inside were a few items of furniture—a cot, sofa, and kitchen table—and not much else. The cot had captured Kyle's eye first. He was tired and felt as if he'd been in a relay race most of the day. All he wanted to do was stretch out and rest while Darien conversed with his parents around the small kitchen table. So he did.

"The king's men were here yesterday," Darien's father said, his tanned face wrinkled and folded like a plowed field. "They're probably watching now, too. But we were too smart for them. I had two servants dress like us and ride to town while we slipped out the back door."

"Is everyone all right?" Darien asked. "Did the king's men do anything to you?"

"Oh, they were abusive and pushed us around a little, but nothing serious," Torbin said.

"They broke my mother's china," Evelyn complained. "The bullies!"

"They could've broken more than that," Torbin said.

"How about the rest of the family?" Darien asked.

His father rubbed his beard absentmindedly. "They are well. They're wondering what brought this on. Why would the king suddenly turn on you?"

"He thinks I want his job," Darien said wryly.

"Ah," Darien's mother said. "Then he knows about our visit from the Old Judge."

Darien shrugged. "Maybe he does."

"Or maybe he's worried because of your success as a general," Torbin suggested.

"This is terrible! Just terrible!" said Evelyn. "You never should have left the farm. If you'd stayed here with your family, none of this would've happened!"

Darien reached over and stroked his mother's face. "My place was not on this farm," he told her. "I was called to other things."

"Yes," Evelyn said with a frown. "And one day I will have words with the Unseen One about that!"

Darien ignored her comment and said, "Meanwhile, we have to be sure you're safe. I think the prince of Gotthard will give you sanctuary until we can sort out this mess."

"Gotthard! You want us to leave our farm?" Torbin asked.

"I don't see that we have a choice. The king may decide to punish you as a means to get to me. So you must pack your things while I try to make contact with the prince on your behalf."

"On our behalf? You're not coming with us?" Evelyn asked, her voice laced with worry.

Darien shook his head. "The prince can give you refuge without much trouble. To help me directly would threaten his relationship with King Lawrence. What with their various treaties and agreements, he dare not take the chance. I will find other places to hide."

"Other places to hide . . ." Torbin groaned and hit the table angrily. Kyle opened an eye to look at them. "The greatest general in our land, and you have to hide. May the Unseen One see our plight and deliver us from this madness!"

Darien agreed, "And so He may. But until He does, we have to take every precaution."

Kyle reluctantly gave up the cot to follow Darien and his parents outside. While Kyle waited on the porch, Darien hugged and kissed his mother and father good night. Then they began the long walk home across the field. It was a beautiful summer's night. The chirping crickets and flashing fireflies went about their business as if the world hadn't been turned upside down for this family. Darien and Kyle watched Torbin and Evelyn until they disappeared over the dark horizon.

"Now, how am I going to get in touch with Prince Edwin?" Darien muttered as he turned to go back inside the cabin. Suddenly, without warning, a loud shout seemed to come from all around them. Darien quickly reached for his sword, forgetting that he'd left it inside. It was too late anyway. They were surrounded.

"A man of your experience should be more on his guard," a voice said. From the darkness of the woods, Colonel Oliver approached carrying a torch. Like phantoms bearing candles, almost 100 of Darien's most faithful soldiers came forward.

"What are you doing here, Colonel?" Darien asked after briskly shaking his hand. He was amazed. "How in the world did you find this place?"

"The Old Judge sent the girl to me a few nights ago," Colonel Oliver said.

"Anna?" Darien asked.

"Yes. She told us where and when to meet you. I got the word around to those I knew would want to come."

"But *what* are you doing here?" asked Darien.

"We're with you, sir," Colonel Oliver said resolutely. "Wherever you go, we go. None of us desire to serve under any other commander, even if he *is* supposed to be a scoundrel and a traitor."

Darien looked around at the faces of the men, knowing well what they were sacrificing for him. "I cannot ask you to do this," he said in a choked voice.

Colonel Oliver nodded. "Nor do we expect you to ask," he said matter-of-factly. "Which is why we've come of our own free will. Now, are we going to stand here all night or are you going to tell us what you need us to do?"

They spent most of the night discussing their options. Having so many men to help made all the difference in Darien's attitude. He became a general again.

Kyle sat on the edge of the cot, knowing he wouldn't be able to sleep now. Instead he wondered about Anna—the bold errand girl for the Old Judge. Somehow she seemed so different from the whiny little sister he had wanted to desert before this adventure began. He hoped she was being well treated at the convent.

Sister Leona took care of Anna personally. She fed her soup and spoke gently to her while dabbing her forehead with a cool, damp cloth. Anna felt as if she was constantly drifting between her dreams and reality—to the point where she wasn't sure which was which.

"The Ancient Fathers and Mothers had dreams," Sister Leona said. Though they had only begun to talk, Anna had the feeling that they had been chatting for hours and this was a conversation in the middle of it all. "The Unseen One used dreams to speak to the chosen ones. Only a handful are left who have the dreams or know how to interpret them. These are the days of abandonment, when the leaders and their people turn away from the ancient ways and the Unseen One."

"I don't like my dreams," Anna said through a voice like sandpaper.

"No. Few of us do." Sister Leona wrung the cloth out, then reapplied it to Anna's face. "To be a voice for the Unseen One can be a great burden. Sometimes it involves suffering—even sharing the suffering of others. But our faith in the Unseen One carries us through. Do you have that kind of faith, Anna?"

"I want to."

"Then feed that faith with prayer and study, silence and soli-tude. Will you do that?"

Anna closed her eyes. "I'll do my best."

When she opened her eyes again, the room was empty.

She slept until evening. Sister Leona knocked gently on the door, then walked in. She wore a cloak, as if she were about to leave.

"How are you feeling, Anna?" she asked.

Anna took a deep breath. The burning in her eyes had stopped. She felt weak but much better and said so.

"Good," said Sister Leona, taking Anna's hand and sitting beside her on the bed.

"Have we been talking?" Anna asked.

"A little," Sister Leona said.

"Then it was a dream. I dreamed we talked a lot."

Sister Leona smiled and patted her hand. "I hope it was a pleasant dream," she said. Then she stood up and explained, "I have to leave for a while. I've been summoned."

"Summoned?"

"The king has come to Dorr and asked to see me."

"King Lawrence?"

"There is no other king that I know of."

Anna sat up quickly. Her head spun. "Sister . . . I had a dream about soldiers and swords and . . ." She couldn't bring herself to say the word *death*. "And danger," she said.

"We'll talk about it when I return," Sister Leona said. "In a little while."

"Will you also teach me?" Anna asked. "The Old Judge said you would teach me how to use my gift—and you'd give me something."

"You have all you need," said the sister with a knowing smile. She handed a small mirror to Anna and left.

Anna wasn't sure what she was supposed to do with the mirror. Was she supposed to say "Mirror, mirror on the wall"? She looked at her reflection. Her face was pale and gaunt. Her eyes sat atop dark circles. *Her eyes!* Her entire life she'd had brown eyes. Now they were two separate colors; one was blue and the other green. She put a hand to her mouth as if to stop her sudden intake of breath. She stared at them, unsure what to think.

After a moment, Anna lay back in her bed. The wheels of her mind spun wildly, and her heart raced. *What does this mean?* she wondered. She heard voices whispering in the hallway, and then a young girl walked in. She was pretty, with long, braided hair and freckles on her nose. She said her name was Dawn and that Sister Leona wanted her to sit with Anna for a while.

"I don't need anyone to sit with me," Anna said. "I'm all right."

Dawn reached over and touched Anna's forehead tenderly. "Are you sure?" she asked.

"Yes, I am," she replied, and then she fell asleep again.

Her dreams were fitful. In them she saw Sister Leona walk down a dingy hallway and into a room with candles and lamps set up in odd places, as if the room normally wouldn't have so much light. The walls were covered with cheap paintings and documents that looked like legal papers and diplomas. A rolltop desk, also covered with papers, sat in the corner. In the center of the room, King Lawrence leaned back in a large thronelike chair that didn't belong in the office at all. On one side of him stood a short, bald-headed man who kept wringing his hands. On the other side, General Liddell stood as straight as any ruler. Sister Leona knelt out of respect for the king, then waited.

"Get up, get up," the king commanded wearily.

Anna was surprised because this was the first time she'd had a dream about the king where she could hear him clearly.

"What can I do for you, sire?" Sister Leona asked when she stood up.

The king rested his elbow on the arm of the chair and his hand against the side of his face. "Tell me about General Darien," he said.

Sister Leona looked puzzled. "General Darien?"

"Don't play innocent with me," he said. "General Darien came to see you last night. Or should I say earlier this morning? What did he want? Why was he here?"

Sister Leona glanced around nervously. "Your Highness should know better than I would."

"Indeed? Tell me what I should know."

"General Darien is on a secret mission. That's as much as he said. I assumed it was a mission for you."

"Were you not aware that he is suspected of being a traitor?" the king asked.

"The newspapers hinted at the idea, but I haven't seen any official papers or warrants for his arrest. I'd be a fool to believe everything I read in the newspaper. Besides, General Darien denied it."

"He would deny it, wouldn't he?" the king scoffed.

"He would if he were a liar," Sister Leona said. "But I have no reason to think he'd lie."

The king jerked forward in his chair. His eyes were aflame, his face twisted into a scowl. "Yet you would believe your king to be a liar!"

"Why would you say such a thing to me?" said Sister Leona indignantly. "I'm a loyal subject."

"Are you?" the king bellowed. "Then explain to me what you, my loyal subject, did for General Darien!"

"Did for him? I don't know what you mean."

The king waved his hand. "Oram!"

A tall, hairy man dressed in a vest of sheepskin stepped from a corner behind Sister Leona. "Yes, Your Highness?" he said.

"She doesn't understand me. Please enlighten her."

"Eh?"

"Say what you know!" the king commanded impatiently.

"Oh," he said, shuffling his feet like a small child. "Well, like I told you, sire, I was walking this morning with my flock, and I saw General Darien and a boy walking from the sister's convent. We said hello in a friendly manner. I knew it was Darien but acted like I didn't because I read in the paper how he might be plotting against you. And then I saw that he was wearing a long gold sword. So I thought, *Hold on, that's the sword that was in the sister's study,* 'cause I seen it there myself when I had business in the place once or twice. I was then wondering if maybe the general didn't rob the sister of the sword. So I ran to Phipps here, our magistrate—"

With this acknowledgment, the bald-headed man nodded.

"—and he told me he'd contact you if I went to the convent to see if it'd been robbed. Well, I happen to know one of the girls there—she's one of the few girls who'll give me the time of day, the rest being holy snobs and all—and I asked her right away what was up with General Darien. Did he come in the night to rob them? And she said that the sword wasn't stolen but *given* to General Darien by Sister Leona, along with some food."

The king gestured to Sister Leona as if to say, "Well?"

Sister Leona said firmly, "Are you accusing me of something?"

"Apart from giving food and a weapon to my sworn enemy, then no, I don't suppose I am!" the king shouted ironically. His face had turned bright red.

Sister Leona didn't flinch, and her voice remained calm. "General Darien has been an honorable and dutiful servant to you. I had no reason to think he was otherwise. What I did for him, I did because I believed him to be on a mission for you. If there were more to know or reasons to distrust him, they are beyond me."

"*Beyond* you? I thought you prophets for the Unseen One knew everything!"

"We don't."

"That is truly unfortunate." The king sneered. "Now get out of my sight."

Sister Leona said in a stern voice, "Your Highness—"

"Go!" he screamed at her.

She bowed slightly and walked out.

The king leaped out of his chair and prowled around the room. "These people—these believers in the Unseen One—will all side with Darien against me. I know it!" he said. "We have to send a message to them. They have to understand that I will not tolerate their treason!"

"What kind of message, sire?" General Liddell asked.

"I want those sisters killed. Every last one of them."

General Liddell stared at the king in disbelief. "Killed! No, sire, that would be extreme," he cautioned.

"Did I hear you say no to me?" the king asked menacingly. "Is that what I heard?"

General Liddell changed his tone. "Sire, as your loyal general, I can only say that such a move would be disastrous. If anyone saw members of the Royal Guard committing such an act, the entire nation would turn against them—and you. It could spark an uprising that none of us could contain."

The king clasped his hands behind his back and growled, "Then get somebody else to do it! I want it done, and I want it done by tonight!" The king left no time for answers or questions as he stomped out of the room. Phipps the magistrate followed anxiously.

General Liddell folded his arms, his face a frozen mask. He then looked at the shepherd. "Oram?" he said.

"Yes, sir?"

"The convent owns a lot of the land around here, doesn't it?"

"Too much, if you ask me."

"You'd like that land for your sheep, wouldn't you?" Liddell's voice was oily with opportunity. "Imagine all the grazing they could do."

"Yes, sir. I've imagined it. Even talked to the lady—that one in charge—but she wouldn't agree."

"You've heard what the king wants done. Can you do it quickly, in exchange for the land?"

Oram's expression didn't change. "Me and the boys can do it right away. Never cared for those women and all that nonsense about the Unseen Thingy watching over us anyway. Dangerous superstition, I figure."

"Dangerous—yes," the general said.

Anna woke up. Dawn sat next to the bed, reading a book. Her lips moved ever so slightly. She was praying.

"Dawn," Anna said with a parched throat.

Dawn put a finger to her lips. "Wait. I'll get you something to drink," she offered.

"No," Anna said. Her voice rose as the panic within her grew. "Something awful is going to happen."

The door opened slightly, and Sister Leona peered in. "Ah, you're awake," she said.

"Sister Leona! I just had a dream," Anna said quickly. "You were with the king."

Sister Leona began to take off her cloak. "You knew I was going to see him," she said.

"He accused you of helping General Darien," Anna said.

A shadow crossed Sister Leona's face. Her voice took on a tone of urgency. "What else did you see in the dream?"

"They're coming."

"Who is?"

"The shepherd. He's coming to—"

In another part of the building, there was a loud crash. Someone screamed.

"Wait here," Sister Leona said. "Both of you. And lock this door behind me." She rushed out of the room, closing the door behind her.

Dawn moved nervously to the door and locked it. More screams echoed through the halls, increasing in number and intensity. "Mercy!" Dawn whispered.

Anna crawled out of the bed. Her clothes were neatly folded on the bottom shelf of the bedside table. She grabbed them and dressed as quickly as she could.

Men's voices intermingled with the screams. They came closer down the hall. Sister Leona shouted at someone, but her voice was suddenly silenced. Dawn began to cry as she backed away from the door. Anna threw the curtains aside. The window frame was small, but it looked as if she and Dawn could squeeze through.

"We have to get out of here," Anna said.

"What's happening?" Dawn cried. "What are they doing?"

"They're going to kill us!" shouted Anna. The latch on the window stubbornly refused to move. It probably hadn't been opened in years. The shouts and screams came closer and closer.

"Have mercy!" Dawn said again, her hand to her mouth. Someone was at the door. The handle moved up and down quickly. A man shouted.

Anna tugged at the window latch with all her might. It gave a little and then completely. She threw open the window just as someone began to beat against the door. The old wooden frame splintered, and the door handle broke loose.

"Hurry, Dawn!" Anna screamed.

Trancelike, Dawn drifted toward the door. Her hand reached out. "No," she said softly.

The frame gave way to the blows of whoever was on the other side. A large man burst in, surveyed the room in a glance, and caught Dawn by the hair. He drew his sword back.

Instinctively, Anna grabbed the lamp on the bedside table and threw it at him. It crashed against his side, the fuel catching his sheepskin vest on fire. He yelled angrily and ran his sword into Dawn. She fell at his feet. The man staggered toward Anna, then swung out and caught her on the side of the head with his fist. She fell back against the wall. The man threw himself onto the bed, squirming and writhing to put out the flames. He had little success as the flames spread to other areas of his clothing, then onto the bed itself.

Anna scrambled for the window.

The man's agonizing cries followed her as she fell from the window to a makeshift roof one story below. It gave way under her weight and she crashed through, landing on her side on a hay-covered dirt floor. A sharp pain shot through her hip and down her legs. Struggling to her feet, she half ran and half limped away from the convent and into the night.

Word came to Darien, then Kyle, about the massacre at the Dorr convent through one of Darien's soldiers. The blame was placed on unknown marauders and vandals who killed the women, then set fire to the building. There were no witnesses to claim otherwise. General Liddell, who visited the scene of the destruction, promised a full investigation into the tragedy. "Justice will be served," he proclaimed on the steps of the burned-out shell.

"Anna! What about Anna?" Kyle asked urgently.

"There were no survivors," Darien replied, his hand held firmly on Kyle's shoulder.

Kyle's voice trembled. "No. I don't believe it!" he insisted. "We didn't come here for Anna to die! I have to see for myself!"

Darien signaled Colonel Oliver. "It's only a couple of hours on horseback. Will you take him?" he asked.

Colonel Oliver nodded and went to saddle the horses. Kyle closed his eyes to fight back his tears. *What kind of world is this?* he asked himself. *The Unseen One wouldn't allow Anna to die!*

Dorr was crowded with soldiers from the royal army. Though the king and General Liddell had left, government officials and detectives remained to ask questions and make a good showing of sympathy to those who'd died. Grieving relatives arrived to identify their dead daughters who had joined the convent in high hopes of serving the Unseen One with their lives. In a way, Kyle thought, they had.

The stone walls of the convent stood tall, as if nothing had happened. But the wooden beams that held up the roof, the frames around the windows, and the large oak doors were all gone or turned into fallen black sticks of no distinction. Kyle's heart sank as he looked at the charred ruins. The local police wouldn't let them any closer than the gate. Phipps, the local magistrate, was keeping a tight seal on the area.

Colonel Oliver used his influence with a friend in the army to get a list of those who'd been found in the convent. He scanned it, then handed it over to Kyle. Breathlessly, Kyle ran his finger along the names of those who'd been claimed and the descriptions of those who hadn't. None of them fit Anna.

"She's not here," Kyle said, afraid to hope.

"Are you sure?" Colonel Oliver asked.

Kyle tapped the list. "It says that all these girls were teenagers or older. Anna isn't here!"

"I got the impression that she's a very resourceful girl," Colonel Oliver said. "Maybe she escaped."

Kyle scanned the crowds nearby, the town, and the rolling green fields around them. Dark clouds were moving in. "Then where did she go?" he asked.

It began to rain.

The rain tapped like impatient fingers on the top of the old tin roof. Anna opened her eyes and immediately recoiled from the squalor of the place. A makeshift sink was filled with dishes and rotten food; a nearby rat sniffed at it with disdain. The walls and floor were made of loose-fitting boards that easily let weather, dust, and mud through. She thought she heard the buzzing of flies nearby. Looking down, she realized she was on a bed of straw.

She groaned as she reached for her aching head. It was bruised and tender to touch. Swinging her legs over the side of the bed, she winced. Her hip and legs also hurt. The pain worked through the fuzziness of her head, and she remembered what had happened at the convent. She stifled a cry, resolved to be strong, and instantly prayed to the Unseen One for the families of those who had died, for she knew without a doubt that everyone had—particularly Sister Leona and Dawn.

Only afterward did she realize how strange, yet natural, it was for her to pray at all.

"Hello there, little one," a croaking old voice said.

Anna looked up. A shriveled old woman in a patched-up peasant dress and shawl walked in. She was hunched over as she carried a bucket and still hunched after she put it down next to the lopsided, wooden table. Her dirty gray hair dripped with rain but looked as if it might drip even in the sunshine.

"I wouldn't get up too fast if I was ye," the old woman said.

"Who are you?" Anna asked. "Where am I?"

"Ye're in the house of Anastasia—*my* house," the old woman said happily. "I lives near Wollet-in-Stone. Stumbling around in the dark, ye were. Thought ye were a beggar, I did. Nearly turned ye away, excepting I had a torch and saw yer eyes. Then I knew better. Better indeed. Ye walked miles."

"What do *you* care about my eyes?"

The old woman named Anastasia poked a bony finger toward Anna's face. "Two colors, ye have. One of the marks of the Unseen One. 'She's special,' I said to myself and put ye to bed. Bad luck otherwise. I found foreign coins in yer pockets. They will serve as payment for my help." She held out a quarter, a dime, and two nickels that Anna had been carrying.

Anna rubbed her eyes to be sure she wasn't in another dream.

"Ye said much in yer sleep," Anastasia went on. "Came from Sister Leona's holy house, I reckoned. Sister Leona never liked me, but I'm sad that she was made dead. A tragedy, it was. I heared that the king himself wept over the news."

Wept for joy, Anna thought and bit her tongue to keep from saying it. "Why didn't Sister Leona like you?" Anna asked instead. Her tongue felt numb, her speech slurred.

"Because I'm not like her, I'm not. I make a business that she don't approve of."

"What kind of business?"

The old woman laughed in a horselike manner. "Questions. So many questions ye have. The spirits of the departed is my trade. I speak to them and they visit me, they do."

Anna then noticed an old, faded carnival poster hanging on the wall. "Anastasia the Mysterious," it said in large, curly letters. Beneath it was a crudely rendered painting of a much younger Anastasia with her hair flowing and shimmering around a round face with magnetic eyes. Her hands were raised up as if she were conjuring something, her nails a bright blue. Anna shivered involuntarily. The rat at the sink eyed her for a moment as if it understood her feelings.

"It's the rain, isn't it? Ye're cold," Anastasia said. She walked to a rusted potbellied stove in the corner and stoked the tiny embers. They spat defiantly at her. "Warm ye up, this will."

Anna tested her legs to stand, and, though it hurt, she was pleased that she could. "Thank you for your kindness, but I have to find my brother," she said politely.

"Go? In this rain? Ye mustn't," Anastasia protested.

"But he'll be worried about me," Anna said, imagining how Kyle would react to the news about the convent. "He doesn't know where I am."

Anastasia sat down at the lopsided table and shuffled some cards. "Do ye know where he is?" she asked. "We can contact him without yer walks in the rain."

Frowning, Anna asked, "How?" *Card tricks? A séance? Maybe a crystal ball?* she wondered.

"Call."

"Call?" Anna asked, puzzled.

The old woman pointed to a box on the wall. It had thin, exposed wires running from the top and out through a hole in the wall. "Yes. It's called a telephone, it is. Have ye not heard of it?"

Placing Anna's call took some doing. First, an operator had to be called. That operator transferred Anna to another who handled inquiries about phone numbers. When Anna didn't know Darien's parents' names or in what town they lived, that operator then connected her to the Ministry of Information in Sarum. The clerk there was less than helpful when he realized Anna wanted information about General Darien's family. The palace had put a seal on any information related to General Darien. Anna tried to reason with the clerk. "It can't be *that* big of a secret," she said. Finally the clerk allowed that the general's family lived several miles from a town called Leapford. That was as much as he would say before he hung up on her.

"I could have told ye that," Anastasia said with a smirk on her face.

"Why didn't you?" Anna said.

"Ye didn't ask."

Anna went back to the operator who handled inquiries about phone numbers and asked about Darien's family's phone number in Leapford. The operator said she would have to connect her to the

Leapford operator. Once that was done, the Leapford operator, who had been friends with Torbin and Evelyn for years, warily transferred Anna to what she called the "public line" for the house. A servant answered and promised to deliver Anna's message to either Torbin or Evelyn, though he claimed not to know anything about Darien or his whereabouts.

Anna hung up, exhausted from all the effort. *It would've been easier if I'd walked,* she thought.

Three things happened as a result of Anna's trip through the telephone maze. First, the servant told Torbin about the call from Anna. Torbin ventured out to the old house, where Darien and his men were making final preparations to leave for Gotthard. Darien dispatched Kyle and Colonel Oliver to go get Anna from the old woman's shack near Wollet-in-Stone.

Second, Kyle got a crash course in horseback riding, having his own mount for the first time.

And third, the Leapford operator told her boss about the call. The boss, who was under strict orders to report any activity connected to Darien's family, phoned the palace to tell them about the girl's call. This news, combined with another report from the Ministry of Information, told General Liddell that Darien must be somewhere near his parents. Liddell passed the news on to King Lawrence.

Kyle hugged his sister without restraint or embarrassment there in front of the Wollet-in-Stone post office. It was the only building in the village. The rain had diminished to a light sprinkle.

"Ouch," Anna groaned, her entire body now one big pain.

"I knew you weren't dead," he said in her ear. "The Unseen One wouldn't let you die."

Anna smiled at her brother's affection and his conviction about the Unseen One. Somehow the two of them had gone from doubting His existence to faith that He was with them on this adventure.

"What happened to your eyes?" he asked.

"I'll tell you some other time."

Colonel Oliver, atop his horse, beckoned the two of them to hurry up. "General Darien is waiting for us," he reminded them.

Kyle rubbed his aching legs. "Okay. You ride with me," he told Anna.

"Not a chance," Anna said and climbed onto Colonel Oliver's horse.

Back at the old house, the three of them arrived to the chaos of Darien's family and army finalizing the preparations for their journey to Gotthard. Darien embraced Anna when he saw her, then took her and Kyle aside. He wanted to know what had happened at the convent.

"King Lawrence sent the men in to kill us," Anna said as the memory of her dreams and the attack returned to her. Her bottom lip quivered as she told him everything.

"I blame myself," Darien said angrily. "Those poor women and girls lost their lives because I visited them."

"But you only visited them because the Old Judge told you to," Kyle offered.

"The Old Judge told me to take Anna there—not stay for food or take Soren's sword. If I'd done exactly as he said, it wouldn't have happened."

Kyle and Anna watched Darien as he brooded. The business at hand demanded that he not brood for long.

"If I am ever made king," he finally said, "I will set these things to right. There will be justice in this land."

The rain moved on to other parts, but the journey to the Gotthard border still took most of the day. To Kyle's and Anna's relief, nothing bad happened. Kyle never felt that sick feeling in his stomach. Anna didn't have any troublesome dreams. The only real difficulty was Kyle's inexperience riding his own horse—a cantankerous old beast named Bethesda—and the added bruises it gave him.

Once at the border, Darien sadly said good-bye to his parents and handed them over to Prince Edwin's officials for safekeeping. Darien was assured, by letter from the prince, that they would be made comfortable and kept secure under royal protection in a secret location.

"I am proud of you, my son," Darien's father said. "Be strong."

"Be *safe*," Darien's mother added. She wept loudly as they rode away.

Darien and his officers decided to head south from Gotthard toward the section of Marus that adjoined Palatia, to a walled-in town called Kellen. It was large enough to accommodate the 100-strong regiment that traveled with Darien, but remote enough to hide them for a while. It also stood at the entrance to an area called the Valley of the Rocks, a rough wilderness where they could escape if King Lawrence found them and decided to attack.

"Do you think he would be so obvious?" Colonel Oliver asked as they strategized. "You haven't been declared a criminal as such. Why would he take such direct action?"

"He sanctioned the massacre at the convent. He's capable of anything," replied Darien.

As they drew closer to the town that evening, the woods opened up to a long stretch of flat fields. Darien noticed that the road seemed unusually deserted. "This is the only paved road to this part of the country," he said. "One would think that it'd be busier."

Farther on, they saw that some of the telephone and telegraph poles had been knocked down, the lines cut.

"This looks awfully suspicious," Colonel Oliver noted. "I'll scout ahead." He nudged the horse with his heels, and it picked up speed. They watched him for a few minutes until the road took him over a small hill.

Darien held up his hand for the soldiers behind him and slowed their pace. If there was trouble ahead, he didn't want to rush into it.

Half an hour later, Colonel Oliver returned. He looked frazzled. As he brought his horse to a stop in front of Darien, he reported, "Palatians. They have taken Kellen."

"No! Kellen is a good two miles inside Marus land!" Darien said.

"They're a brazen bunch," agreed Colonel Oliver. "Let's attack immediately!"

"Not so fast," Darien insisted. "Not until we have a plan." He quickly looked around, then pointed to a hill in the distance. "Let's camp there until we decide what to do."

The debate among Darien and his officers on the hilltop went on for an hour. Some of them said there was little they could do to help the people of Kellen since they had only sidearms, a few rifles, and their swords. Others said it was the king's responsibility to save Kellen, not theirs. He'd learn of the Palatian attack soon enough and would have to respond, they reasoned. Colonel Oliver felt strongly that they should attack the Palatians and drive them from Kellen—it was their duty as Marutians—but he confessed that he didn't know how.

Darien listened to the debate, sitting with his hands folded under his chin. Apart from a question or two, he didn't contribute to their arguing. From the top of the hill, he looked out across the flat green fields and to the Valley of the Rocks far beyond. "Majestic," he said.

The debate ceased as his officers turned to him. "What did you say?" they asked.

"Majestic," he repeated. "Look at the beauty of this land. It speaks of the glory of the Unseen One."

"Haven't you been listening to us, General?" an officer with a wolflike face asked irritably.

Darien stood up and walked over to Kyle and Anna, who'd been watching the debate with undisguised boredom. They would have entertained themselves with something else or rested from the journey, but Darien had asked them to stay nearby. They were about to understand why.

"What do you think, Kyle?" Darien asked.

Kyle was shocked to be put on the spot like that. He blushed, then stammered, "What do I think?"

"You're my guardian angel," Darien said with a smile. "Would I be in danger if I attacked the Palatians?"

Kyle struggled with his answer. He wanted to impress Darien and his officers with his cleverness and insight. But the truth was nothing in his gut instinct helped him one way or the other. However it was that he knew when Darien was in danger, he couldn't manufacture the feeling or predict when it would come. Finally, he shrugged and answered, "I don't know, General."

A few of the officers chuckled. Darien ignored them. "Anna?" he asked.

"Yes, sir?"

"You have been taught by the Old Judge and Sister Leona. You, better than most of us, know the ancient ways."

"I don't know that much," Anna said, also embarrassed about being made the center of attention.

Darien leaned close to her and said gently, "Yes, you do. You see what we cannot see, then speak what we can't hear."

She searched Darien's face and watched as it suddenly transformed from the confident face she saw now into a dirt-smudged, sweaty, and weary face in her dream. "Darien—" she began to say, but he turned away from her. He was in front of a roomful of people where he raised a chalice and said, "May the Unseen One receive glory from our victory!"

Standing in the corner of the room was a group of scowling soldiers—Anna didn't recognize their uniforms but guessed they must be Palatians. Next to them, standing like a proud guard, was the mayor of Kellen, a grin stretched across his chubby face. How she knew who he was, Anna couldn't say. But she recognized him as surely as if she'd seen him a dozen times.

"To the Unseen One!" everyone shouted as they drank from their cups.

Darien turned back to Anna. His face was no longer smudged or tired. He looked as he had before. "Anna?" he said.

Anna blinked a couple of times. The room, the people, and the Palatian soldiers were gone. She was back on the hilltop. "What?" she asked.

"Will you tell us what the Unseen One wants us to do?"

"You'll win," she responded. "You'll save Kellen and win."

Darien smiled and told her, "Thank you."

Anna sat back and rubbed her burning eyes.

Addressing his officers, Darien said, "All right, we'll attack the Palatians."

"No!" the officer with the wolflike face said. "It'll be a slaughter! We can't go against them with the weapons or men we have."

"The Unseen One goes with us."

"Because this *girl* said so?"

Darien looked at his officer with a determined expression. "She is a voice," he said. "We will have victory because of the Unseen One."

Colonel Oliver stood up. "You heard the general! Now let's get everyone ready!" he ordered.

After Darien and his officers walked away, Kyle asked Anna, "How did you do that?"

Anna slowly shook her head, a helpless look on her face. "I don't know how it happens. How do you know when Darien is in danger? It just happens, right? It's the Unseen One who does it."

"But you're sure we'll win?"

"We'll win."

Kellen was a walled town, fortresslike in appearance, with a large gate that served as its only formal entrance. But it also had smaller entry points along the seemingly endless circular wall for bringing in livestock and getting rid of rubbish. General Darien disguised a dozen of his men as traders and shepherds, then sent them in one and two at a time to position themselves at those entrances. The Palatians would be looking for a large army headed by the king of Marus, Darien knew. They wouldn't be on the lookout for stealth fighters.

The Palatian officers had taken over the mayor's offices and residence. The remaining Palatians—almost 1,000 in all—camped in the open spaces around the town. The citizens of Kellen were beaten into submission by the Palatians, then told to go about their business as usual and be ready to serve the Palatians as needed.

On Darien's signal, after the sun had gone down, the rest of the men casually entered the city and began to quietly capture or kill the soldiers who'd been put on guard duty.

While his disguised men carefully dispatched pockets of Palatian soldiers, Darien and Kyle walked past the guards at the front gate. (They had been captured and replaced by Colonel Oliver and other Marutian soldiers.) They made their way to the center of the city. Kyle was dressed in his normal clothes, while Darien was dressed in his general's uniform.

"I sure hope this works," Kyle whispered once they were positioned in the middle of the main marketplace. Torches blazed on all sides, casting an eerie yellow glow on the two of them. As a first impression, Kyle thought Kellen looked like a cross between a Western town (like Dodge City) and a village from Robin Hood's days.

Darien winked at Kyle, then shouted, "I am Darien! Come and take me!"

He had to shout it a few times before the Palatians could be stirred to respond. As they surrounded him, Darien crouched down and began to jump around like a monkey, making screeching and hooting noises.

A Palatian officer broke through the circle of soldiers. He had dark, slicked-back hair and a pointed beard. "What's going on here?" he demanded.

Kyle rushed forward to him. "Please, sir, I found this man wandering in the forest," he said. "He kept screaming that he was General Darien. I brought him here for the reward you Palatians said you'd give for handing him over."

On hearing his name, Darien screeched even louder: "Darien! Darien!" He made faces at the soldiers, tugged at their shirts, and even tried to climb on the shoulders of a guard.

"I don't have time for madmen," the officer said, clearly not believing what he was seeing.

"Mad?" Darien cried. "Me mad? Mad me? I am Darien! Take me to your leader!"

"My leaders are busy," the officer growled. "Now go away."

Darien wouldn't be so easily brushed aside. He howled like a dog, then screeched and danced like a monkey. "Take me to your leader!" he yelled over and over.

Kyle grabbed the officer's sleeve and asked, "If this man is really Darien, what'll your bosses say if you let him go?"

That stopped the officer.

"Take us to your general," Kyle said. "Let's talk business."

The officer signaled for two of his men to help lead Darien to the mayor's office.

General Gaiman, head of that particular Palatian regiment, wasn't pleased to see his officer, Darien, or Kyle. He frowned wearily, the deep lines on his dark forehead bunching up over his nose. "He looks like Darien, but he's obviously mad as a hatter," he concluded.

Darien was racing around the room, knocking things off the desk and walls.

"Get rid of him," General Gaiman said.

"How?" the pointy-bearded officer asked.

"Throw him back outside the gate or lock him up—I don't care. I'm more concerned about Lawrence's army, which will likely show up any time now."

The officer sighed, then gestured for two guards to take Darien back out.

"What about my reward?" Kyle complained.

"Your reward is that I'll let you go free rather than kill you," the general said. "Now get out."

At the doorway, Kyle and Darien exchanged a quick look and then sprang into action. Darien pushed the two guards into the hall and closed the door on them. Kyle pulled out a small pistol he had tucked under his shirt and fired it at the front window. The sound of the shot and the breaking glass were the signal for Darien's men to attack throughout the town.

In one fast motion, Darien deftly swung around, grabbed a large marble bust from a nearby pedestal, and brought it crashing against the officer's head. General Gaiman dashed to the desk, where a pistol sat in a holster hanging from the chair. But Kyle, who was closer, reached it before him and snatched it up.

"Give me that!" the general snapped.

Kyle threw the pistol to Darien, who caught it with one hand and then pointed the muzzle at the general. He smiled. "Now sit down so we can go over your terms of surrender," he ordered.

Within two hours, Kellen was once again a Marutian town. While many Palatians were wounded, killed, or had fled from the town, not a single member of Darien's army was hurt.

In a banquet room at Kellen's largest (and only) hotel, Darien raised a toast to the Unseen One and the victory He'd given them. The Palatian officers scowled, the mayor of Kellen grinned a chubby grin—and Anna smiled because the scene was exactly as she remembered it.

The stranger arrived at Kellen first thing the next morning. He came on horseback and wore a long cloak and a wrap that hid his face and protected it from the sun. Darien's guards at the front gate let him through but used the phone in the guardhouse to alert Darien that the stranger was coming. Darien was having breakfast with some of his officers, along with Anna and Kyle, at the Kellen Hotel's restaurant.

When told that the stranger had reached the front of the hotel, Darien threw his napkin onto his plate and got up. He walked from the restaurant, through the plush lobby, and out onto the front sidewalk just as the stranger dismounted. Kyle felt nothing in his stomach to alert him to any danger. Anna was silent.

"Darien!" the stranger said warmly and pulled the wrap from his face.

"George!" said Darien happily. The two men shook hands, embraced, then went back into the hotel. Darien offered the prince some breakfast.

"I'm afraid I don't have much time," George said. He looked older than Kyle remembered. Could he have aged so much in just a few days?

Darien sipped some coffee. "Then tell me what you're doing here," he said.

"The king knows you're here," George answered. "He's been tracking you ever since you left your parents. In fact, word is getting around the entire country about the battle with the Palatians."

"How could they know so fast?" Darien asked, surprised.

"The way they know everything faster than we expect," George replied. "My father and General Liddell contacted the newspapers."

"To what purpose?"

"They reported that you came here to negotiate with the Palatians, but a loyal royal regiment attacked and drove the Palatians away. The *Sarum Herald* is saying that my father and General Liddell will come to secure the town and capture you for your treason."

Darien couldn't believe what he was hearing. He fumed, "How could they spread such lies and still call themselves honorable men?"

"They dispensed with calling themselves honorable men a long time ago. My father is truly insane. I see that now." George hesitated, then added, "I've come to affirm my allegiance to you and your future kingship—and to warn you that you'll be grossly outnumbered when my father's troops arrive."

"Does the king know you're here?" Darien asked.

"No. He left Sarum without asking where I was or where I would be going. I'm not sure he trusts me anymore. He does things without consulting me."

"Like attack Sister Leona and the women at the convent?"

George went pale. "That wasn't my father's doing," he insisted. "He may be insane, but he's no barbarian."

Darien glanced over at Anna, who was nibbling on a crescent roll. "I know otherwise," he said grimly. "The attack was his idea."

George looked as though he might be sick—or argue—or both. But he didn't.

"Stay with us, George," Darien urged. "Don't go back to him."

"I . . . must," George said, grieved. "While he lives he's still my father and my king, and I have to support him."

"In everything?"

George shook his head. "Not everything. But my remaining with him will be useful to you. I can send you information about his plans, to the best of my ability."

Darien thought it over, then reluctantly agreed. "All right," he said, "but please be careful, George. And know this: If and when I am king, you will rule with me. That I promise."

"Ruin," Anna suddenly said. She had a distant look on her face.

"What?" Darien asked.

"I see ruin. A terrible battle. The king and his family will not survive against you."

"Against *me*? I will not fight the king—or his family."

"I see many wounds and blood and . . ." Anna suddenly gasped. She dropped her roll without seeming to notice. In a different tone she said, "Darien, the people of Kellen will hand you over to the king."

"Will they?"

The mayor, who sat eating at a nearby table, blustered, "Hand our champion over to the king? Never! What kind of thing is that to say?"

Anna said plainly, "The king will surround the city and demand that they deliver you. They will. You must leave Kellen now."

"Thank you, Anna," Darien said.

Anna's eyes cleared, and she turned red to see everyone staring at her. "What's wrong?" she asked.

"We're leaving," Darien announced and stood up.

Prince George left and, within an hour, Darien's men were mobilized to leave Kellen. The mayor was insistent to the last minute that Darien could stay. Darien said he appreciated his offer but felt it would be better for all if they left.

As they rode out of town, Anna looked back at the mayor, who stood waving at the front gate like a bowling ball overdressed in a coat and vest, a gold watch chain linked from his vest button to a small pocket on the side. In her mind's eye, Anna saw that the watch had belonged to someone close to the king. Just as the watch was in the mayor's pocket, so was the mayor in the king's pocket. He'd been reporting to the king's spies everything that had happened.

That meant the king and his army were closer than any of them realized. Anna saw them on the horizon as clearly as if they'd really been there.

"We have to hurry up," she told Darien.

Darien didn't question or argue with her statement. He simply ordered everyone to pick up their pace.

The Valley of the Rocks was well named. It was mostly desert, with only spots of vegetation near what was left of a dying river. The rest of it was dirt and tumbleweeds. The rocks, which rose canyonlike on two sides, were a beautiful reddish pink—Kyle and Anna had no idea what they were called—and jutted up in formations that could easily be seen as faces or figurines. They surrounded Darien's army on all sides.

"We'll have to find good hiding places or we'll be surrounded by more than just rocks," Darien said. He gave instructions for the 100 of them to split up into four groups of 25 and then camp at strategic places around the valley.

"But if we split up," Colonel Oliver observed, "the king will have a better chance of defeating us."

"But if we stay together, he'll have a better chance of finding us," Darien countered. "It's easier to hide small groups of 25 than a whole army of 100."

"But General—"

Darien held up his hand. "I know it's a gamble. And unless Anna has words of wisdom for us, I think it's the best thing for us to do."

Anna didn't have any words of wisdom. She closed her eyes, but no dreams or visions came.

Darien and his group of 25, including Kyle and Anna, slowly wove their way through the rocks on the north side of the valley. It was a tortuous climb for both people and horses. They went up and up until they found a large cleft in one of the rocks that would shelter them all. It curved into a deep cave where they had plenty of room. It also afforded them a vantage point to the valley in all directions. Darien was troubled only by the existence of a ridge above them, one that might give the king's army a chance to trap him. But he had to take a chance. His people were exhausted, and they were running out of places to hide.

While they set up camp, Kyle got a sick feeling in the pit of his stomach. He looked around quickly to see what was causing it. The soldiers were busy arranging their provisions or unpacking their knapsacks. Darien sat quietly in the corner. He was either thinking or praying—or both. Still, the sick feeling grew worse.

Kyle walked over to Darien. "I'm sorry to bother you," he started to say. But just then, a shot rang out. The entire squad drew their pistols and swords instantaneously. Darien leaped to his feet and went to the edge of the cave.

"Surrender now and we may be merciful!" someone shouted from afar, the voice bouncing and echoing around the rock walls. Darien recognized the voice. It was General Liddell.

"I'll check their position," a young soldier said. Before Darien could stop him, he had crept out of the cave and raced to a rock farther out in the open. He looked around, then signaled to Darien that the king's army was situated in four places on the long ridge above them. Darien cursed himself for not paying closer attention to his instincts. They were trapped.

"Yes, trapped!" General Liddell called out as if he knew what the signals meant. "We've been watching you for hours. Did you think we were so foolish as to not anticipate that you'd come to the Valley of the Rocks to hide? We've been hiding here since you defeated the Palatians at Kellen last night. The king is here. He wants desperately to see you."

"It's true, my son!" the king shouted. "Come! Embrace me!"

Darien's face was expressionless. He said nothing.

General Liddell then said, "To demonstrate how effectively you are trapped . . ."

Another shot rang out, and the young scout suddenly clutched his chest and fell behind the rock he mistakenly thought was protecting him.

"No!" Darien cried out, and he would've run to the young man if he hadn't been grabbed by some of his other soldiers.

"What are we going to do?" one of them asked.

"I'm going to surrender myself to them," Darien replied quickly.

Another soldier immediately protested, "No! You can't! They'll kill you!"

"Better for me to take that chance than for everyone here to die in this trap."

"Well?" General Liddell shouted.

Another soldier stepped forward. "Maybe Colonel Oliver and the others will see what's happening and rescue us."

"If *they* haven't already been captured," Darien reminded him. "Though, if George was right, we're so outnumbered that they couldn't do us much good anyway."

"But you're our future king!" the first soldier said. "If you die, the rest of us will die anyway for having joined you."

"Better to die fighting!" a third soldier added.

"If I'm to be your future king, I'm in the hands of the Unseen One anyway," Darien said. "He will do with me whatever He wills, whether I stay here or go."

With the mention of the Unseen One, Darien looked over at Anna. She sat on a rock nearby and trembled. Her eyes filled with tears. The Unseen One hadn't given her any sort of dream or vision about what they should do. She shook her head and slumped sadly.

The discussion continued for a few more minutes, the soldiers arguing that surely the Unseen One wouldn't have brought them this far only to have Darien "throw his life away" now. Finally, Darien beckoned everyone to kneel. "A moment of silent prayer," he said.

Five minutes later, he stood up. "I will go," he said and pushed through his soldiers, ignoring their protests. He went to the mouth of the cave. Taking a deep breath, he stepped out into the open. Darien didn't know what he expected. But he certainly didn't expect *nothing* to happen. Scanning the ridges above, he was surprised to see that they were empty. He suspected that General Liddell's soldiers were simply out of view.

"Hello?" he called out. He thought someone—General Liddell or the king himself—would appear. He got no response, not even sniper fire.

He ventured farther out, past the body of the dead scout. "All right, General, you win," he shouted. "Tell the king I will surrender myself—provided you let my men go!"

General Liddell didn't respond. No one did. Again, nothing happened.

The feeling in the pit of Kyle's stomach went away. "General?" he called out.

Darien waved him back. "Hello?" he shouted to the valley. "Are you playing games with me?" No one answered. Darien moved farther out and climbed up on a rock. He waved. "Hello? Is anybody out there?" Shielding his eyes from the sun, he scanned the valley and the rock walls. He looked back at the cave and shrugged.

Kyle, Anna, and the soldiers wandered out into the open.

Darien stepped down from the rock. "I don't understand this at all," he said.

Small pebbles fell at their feet. They all looked up in time to see Colonel Oliver scurrying down across the rocks toward them. "It's unbelievable!" he said breathlessly as he got closer. "Unbelievable!"

"Slow down, Colonel," Darien ordered.

The colonel panted but smiled as he reported, "We were surrounded. On all sides. No chance of escape. They had us, General."

"I know all that," Darien said. "But why haven't they captured us? Where are they?"

"They left."

"Left! They had us where they wanted us, and they simply up and left?"

"Yes! We watched them leave! They were poised to attack us, and then they suddenly retreated. I've never seen an army move so fast."

"But why?"

Colonel Oliver eyed them for dramatic effect. His red complexion was alight. "We picked up on our shortwave wireless the very thing that *they* picked up. A distress call. The Palatians have attacked Furnchance, just to the south. A massive Palatian army. Retaliation for your victory in Kellen, probably. There was no time to lose. They couldn't capture you *and* fight the Palatians, so the king and General Liddell left! It was that simple." Colonel Oliver was laughing now.

Darien watched him, the news still slowly sinking in.

Colonel Oliver clapped him on the back. "You, my dear general, were saved from your worst enemies *by* your worst enemies!"

With that, they all began to laugh. They laughed long and hard—not the laugh of those who were amused but of those who felt a great sense of relief.

14

The battle of Furnchance was no small skirmish. It marked the beginning of a war between Marus and Palatia. The Palatians, a civilization founded on principles of conquest and domination, unleashed everything they had in the southern part of Marus. King Lawrence, General Liddell, and their best advisers were busy for weeks keeping the Palatians on their own side of the border. No one had time to think about Darien or where he and his men had gone.

They had, in fact, hidden in the hills of the Territory of Peace, in the far north of Marus where Darien had helped to thwart an attack from the Adrians and was nearly assassinated by one of General Liddell's men. (There was no doubt about it now.)

A network of communication developed throughout the country as Darien's secret got around. Anyone who had ever been abused or victimized by King Lawrence joined Darien's side. Some stayed in their own towns and contributed money or food to Darien's men. Others actually traveled to the Territory of Peace, where they pledged themselves to help Darien in any way they could. Kyle and Anna took on simple duties and responsibilities to help around the camp, all the while wondering and worrying about their family and friends back in their own world. When could they go back? In time, they began to second-guess themselves. Did they really *want* to go back?

"Of course we do!" Anna said one afternoon as they were picking vegetables from a makeshift garden. "We have to go back!"

"Don't you like it here?" Kyle asked.

"Yes! But that's not the point. Mom and Dad will be worried about us. And who knows what this has done to poor Grandma and Grandpa? We've been gone for weeks!"

Kyle wiped a spot of dirt from his sister's chin. "But I like being a helper to the future king of Marus," he said honestly. "It'll be so boring to go back to our world and school and normal things and be . . . just *me* again."

"But we're chosen by the Unseen One," Anna replied. "Aren't we chosen there as well as here?"

"I hope so, but it won't be the same," Kyle observed sadly.

Anna knew he was right. Somehow—though she didn't understand how—she realized that whatever power she had as a voice and whatever it was that made Kyle a protector, those gifts would be gone if the two of them left Marus. She wondered then, as later, if God would give them different kinds of gifts or choose them for different tasks in *their* world. What had her grandparents said about it? That all believers were called to serve Him. But Kyle was right. It wouldn't be the same.

She sighed. "But we still have to go back," she insisted. "I'm going to ask Darien about it at dinner tonight. I'm going to ask him to let us go back to the Old Judge and see how we can get home."

True to her word, Anna sat down next to Darien near the fire where dinner was prepared. Kyle sat on his other side. They both noticed that Darien looked worried and preoccupied.

"Have you seen anything lately?" Darien asked Anna before she could speak.

Anna had to admit that she hadn't. Occasionally she had dreams of the king in battle against the Palatians, but they were fuzzy, unspecific dreams, like old newsreels of somebody else's war somewhere. It had been awhile since she'd had the kinds of visions and dreams that had helped them.

"The Unseen One has been so quiet," Darien said. A twinge of sadness in his voice alarmed Anna and Kyle. "It's as if He is allowing His voice to . . . to . . ." He stopped. A tear slid down his cheek.

"What's wrong, Darien?" asked Anna anxiously.

"The Old Judge is dead."

"No . . ." Kyle said.

"What?" Anna was stunned.

"He died in his sleep this morning. The Unseen One has taken him away."

Kyle stared into the fire. He didn't know what to feel.

Anna began to cry. "But he *can't* die!" she insisted. "He can't *ever* die!"

Darien pulled her close with one arm, then wrapped another around Kyle. "Yes," he agreed, "he should have lived forever."

They all wept together.

Against the advice of his officers, Darien decided to disguise himself and take a train to Hailsham for the Old Judge's funeral. He explained to them that it was the least he could do after all the Old Judge had done for him. Colonel Oliver insisted on going along. So did Kyle and Anna. They were also determined to pay their last respects to the old prophet. Darien's other officers harrumphed and argued with them up to the very last minute.

By now, Darien was hard to recognize. He hadn't shaved since the narrow escape at the Valley of the Rocks and had a full beard and mustache. His curly hair also had streaks of gray in it. With his country-folk clothes and hat, he could have been anyone. Few would've guessed that he was the great General Darien.

The small party booked a first-class compartment on a train from Krawley and traveled without incident south toward Hailsham. They knew they were scheduled to stop in the main terminal in

Sarum, but they didn't worry since the king was reported to be with General Liddell at Kellen. Kellen had become an important headquarters for the king and his leaders since the war with Palatia had begun. Besides, no one thought much about Darien anymore. The war was on everyone's minds, first and foremost.

As the train pulled into the Sarum station, Darien looked wistfully at the capital city. "I wonder if I will ever be able to return here," he said softly. Considering he was a die-hard country boy, he was surprised to find that he'd fallen in love with the city.

"You're going to be king here!" Colonel Oliver insisted with feeling.

"I wonder . . ." Darien said.

Anna opened her mouth to assure him that he would be king. There were few things on earth of which she could be absolutely certain, but Darien's kingship was one of them. Something prompted her to keep silent, however. Somehow she knew that Darien would have to see—and believe—for himself.

The train to Hailsham sat at the station longer than they had expected. Five minutes, ten minutes, then half an hour went by. The train didn't move. Even the people on the platform seemed to thin out until it was virtually empty. Colonel Oliver got nervous and went into the hall to ask a steward what the holdup was. When the colonel returned a few minutes later, he was white as a ghost.

Kyle felt that sick feeling again in his stomach.

"It's the king," Colonel Oliver said. "He's getting on the train!"

"What train?" Darien asked. "He has his own train, and it's in Kellen, where *he's* supposed to be."

Colonel Oliver gestured wildly as he explained, "He's not in Kellen, he's *here*. And his train is having mechanical problems, so he's getting on *this* train. He's going to Hailsham for the Old Judge's funeral!"

Darien put a hand over his mouth to keep from laughing.

"You think this is funny, General?" Colonel Oliver asked indignantly. "They're putting him in the carriage ahead of us. He has a compartment *right in front of us*. I think we should get off now, while we can."

"And I think we should go up and say hello."

"This isn't amusing."

"Sit down, Colonel. If we make a run for it now, they'll suspect us. Let's just stick to our plan, all right? The king isn't a politician. He won't venture back here to shake our hands or ask how our families are. He'll stay in his carriage, and we'll stay in ours."

Colonel Oliver looked at him skeptically. "And when we get to Hailsham?"

Darien sat back casually. "We'll get off the train with the hundreds of other people who are on it and lose ourselves in the crowd. Don't panic."

"Panic? Who's panicked?" the colonel said as he wiped beads of sweat from his freckled forehead.

With a jolt, the train suddenly began to move from the station. Within a few minutes it was going full speed.

"Half an hour is all it should take," said Darien. "They won't make any more stops with the king on board." He had a mischievous look on his face. A smile crept onto his lips. "Maybe I *should* go say hello to the king."

"What?" Colonel Oliver cried, exasperated.

"It's dangerous," Kyle warned, his stomach still churning.

"Just a quick little visit. Why not?" Darien said.

Anna shook her head silently, like a mother with a precocious child.

"You're going to kill him then?" Colonel Oliver asked.

"Kill him! He's the king," Darien said earnestly. "Chosen by the Unseen One. I won't raise my hand against him."

Colonel Oliver pointed a finger at him. "Well, if you're going to all the trouble of dropping in on him, I suspect you'll have to kill him as well. He's not going to give you a nice, big howdy-do and let you go."

"No, I suppose not," Darien admitted thoughtfully, then brightened again. "A quick peek won't hurt, though. I won't have to speak to him. You said his compartment is just ahead?"

"Yes, but—"

Before Colonel Oliver could say anything else, Darien was on his feet and opening the outside door to their compartment. Wind rushed in, nearly yanking the door from his hand. The inside door, the one that led into the carriage hall, rattled in its frame.

"How are you going to get there?" Colonel Oliver asked, his face the picture of worry.

"Plenty of rods and rails to hold on to," Darien said as he stepped halfway outside. The wind pounded against him, pressing his hair back and turning his shirt into a billowing sheet. "Each door has its own step. I'll simply pull myself from one to another until I find his compartment."

"And if someone reports you *before* you get to his compartment?"

"Then I'll jump off the train and meet you later in Hailsham."

"Oh, that's a comfort."

"It's something fun to do!" he said like a little boy. "I haven't had any fun since I got those Palatian medals. Bye!" He slipped out the door. They watched him as he clung to the side of the train like a spider, inching his way forward, swinging from one step to the next. The train went into a black tunnel, and when it emerged into the light again, Darien was gone.

"How's your stomach?" Colonel Oliver asked Kyle after a few minutes.

"I feel sick," Kyle said.

"So he's still in danger?"

"I guess so. But I can't be his guardian angel if he's going to do stuff like this."

Colonel Oliver nodded. "Agreed," he said. "He sometimes makes it difficult for all of us." The colonel paused, but it was clear he still had something on his mind. Finally he looked at Kyle and said, "When I first met you, I spoke harshly to you. I didn't trust you and suspected you were out to hurt General Darien. I was wrong, of course, and I want to apologize to you for thinking the worst." He reached out his hand, and Kyle shook it. "No hard feelings?"

"No hard feelings," Kyle said.

"Thank you."

Fifteen minutes later, Colonel Oliver was aggressively pacing their compartment, stopping only to peer out the window to see if Darien was coming back. Kyle squirmed in his seat, chewing fingernails that were already chewed to the nub, and Anna prayed that the Unseen One would be merciful even though Darien didn't deserve it.

Five minutes later, all three of them were pacing circles with Colonel Oliver. The steward announced that they would be arriving in Hailsham station in a minute.

"Do you think he jumped off the train?" Kyle asked.

"I have no idea," Colonel Oliver said, "but I could kill him myself for doing something like this."

The train began to slow as it approached Hailsham. Anna stood at the window and thought sadly about the Old Judge. She had hoped to see him again. Now she never would. Colonel Oliver and Kyle joined her at the window. Darien was still nowhere to be seen.

Just as the train came to a stop at the platform, the inside door of the compartment opened behind them. Darien stepped in from the hallway with a wry smile on his face. He was dressed in a steward's uniform and cap.

"I could make a living doing this," he said as he tossed the cap onto the sofa and began to unbutton the steward's vest. "The pay's rotten, but the tips are pretty good."

"Well, what happened?" they all demanded.

Darien put on a disappointed expression. "Sadly, the king was sleeping," he answered. "He didn't even wake up when I slipped into his compartment. I nearly tucked him in and kissed him on the forehead, he looked so sweet and innocent."

Colonel Oliver groaned.

Darien's expression changed to one of disapproval. "It's a terrible comment about the king's security when a man like me can get in to him like that. I should write to someone about it."

"I'm sure General Liddell would love to hear from you," Anna giggled.

"And so he shall! Imagine leaving the king to ride on a train with only a few guards around him. Just because he's battling the Palatians doesn't give him the excuse to—"

"So how did you get back?" Colonel Oliver interrupted.

"Easy. A steward knocked on the door and came in. The king told him to go away and rolled over. I quietly gave the steward a wad of money for his coat and hat and 10 minutes of silence. He accepted the offer. I came out and walked back here without any questions or problems." He glanced at his watch. "Though the 10 minutes are almost up, and that steward is going to have to explain why he's been sitting in the king's toilet while on duty."

"Let's get out of here," Colonel Oliver said and headed for the door.

"Good idea." Darien didn't move but fished in his pocket and pulled out a large gold medallion on a red ribbon. "Do you think the king will miss this? I took it as a memento of my visit."

Colonel Oliver went bug-eyed. "The king's medallion?" he said. "You stole the *king's medallion*?"

"It looked so pretty sitting there. How could I resist?"

"The king's medallion?" Kyle asked. "Is it important?"

"Oh, not at all," Colonel Oliver said sarcastically. "It's only the medallion the king is given at his coronation."

"He shouldn't have taken it off and left it lying around."

"I don't want to hear about it," Colonel Oliver said.

"I'll give it back to him one day."

Colonel Oliver waved him away. "Don't say another word."

When the crowd was at its peak on the platform, the four of them got off the train and seemed to disappear among the people. As they walked past the window of the king's carriage, they saw two stern-looking guards interrogating a steward.

15

Anna had never been to a funeral before, at least not that she could recall. She'd gone to her grandfather's funeral as a baby, but she had no memory of it. This was the first time someone had died that Anna knew and, in her own way, loved.

The service for the Old Judge was held in an old church in Hailsham. The stone building was beautiful with its tower, pillars lining the inside, stained-glass windows, and smooth wooden pews. It reminded Anna of a miniature cathedral. She sat with Kyle, Darien, and Colonel Oliver in the back, among a crowd of local people. Dignitaries like the king and his guards sat in the front pew. The coffin was also in the front, by the altar, as a simple tribute to the man inside.

"But he isn't inside," the priest said in his eulogy. "This shallow encasement, this empty vessel, is not the man we loved and who loved us. He is somewhere else. The Old Judge is with the Unseen One, in the paradise created for all those who believe in Him."

Anna squeezed her eyes closed, not to ward off any tears but in the strong desire to "see" the Old Judge. She wanted a vision of him now, in that paradise. "Just let me see a little bit of it," Anna prayed. But nothing came except black and orange circles as her eyes readjusted to the light.

The service was over in 20 minutes. A line of mourners formed to pray beside the coffin or to touch it, but the top was closed and there was no final look at the man who'd been the Unseen One's voice for so many years.

"I want to see his cottage one more time," Anna pleaded. "Please."

Darien saw no reason not to go, so the four of them sneaked out the back door of the church and stayed off the beaten path to get there. If they had gone on the main road, they would have seen the large touring car waiting there, not far from the cottage. As it was, they walked up along the rear side, past the vegetable garden, and slipped in the small door that led into the kitchen. They crept in— and then stopped suddenly. The king stood alone in the middle of the living room.

Darien felt quickly for the pistol tucked into his trousers. Colonel Oliver put his hand on the hilt of his dagger. Anna and Kyle hung back a few steps, just in case something happened. Strangely, though, Kyle did not feel anything resembling a sense of danger.

The king didn't react to their arrival. He merely looked at them with red-rimmed eyes sunk into a deeply lined face. He looked so much older than the last time they'd seen him. He coughed wearily and said, "I thought I saw you in the back of the church."

"You did, Your Highness," Darien replied. "We didn't want to miss our last good-byes to the Old Judge."

The king waved his hand toward the room and continued, "I can't believe he's gone. It doesn't seem possible."

"I know what you mean, sire."

"It's *all* gone, isn't it? The days pass so quickly, and then . . ." He didn't finish the thought but looked at them, anguished.

They waited.

He sighed deeply. "And then come the days when you no longer know your friends from your enemies."

Darien stepped forward and said softly, "You have no enemies here, my king."

"Don't I?"

"No, sire." Darien was only a foot or two away from the king.

"Listen no longer to those who whisper evil in your ear. Ignore the voices who say that I mean to do you harm. They are liars. You have been like a father to me. Would I turn my hand against you?"

"Others have."

"But I have not." Darien pulled the king's medallion from his pocket and held it up. The gold seemed to glow artificially in the shadow of the cottage.

The king instinctively put a hand to his chest, as if feeling to be sure the medallion wasn't there. "My medallion!" he exclaimed.

"It was within my power to take your life, just as I took this medallion," Darien said. "But I didn't. You are the chosen one, and I would be in defiance of the Unseen One to raise my hand against you." He handed the medallion to the king. The king took it with shaking hands. Darien continued, "I have done you no wrong, my king. Nor will I. May the Unseen One vindicate me in your eyes."

The king lowered his head. Then his shoulders began to shake as he started to weep, his whole body joining in. He grabbed Darien and cried out, "Darien, my son! What is this madness that afflicts me? How could I ever believe that you would hurt me?"

Darien held the king close. They both wept for several minutes.

The guards who'd been waiting by the touring car came to the door and knocked. "Sire? Are you all right?" they asked. "We must return to Sarum now. General Liddell will be calling."

"Yes, yes," the king said impatiently. He gazed into Darien's face, touched the side of it softly, and told him, "The Old Judge was right. There is no doubt that you will be king. I pray only that you'll find it in your heart to have more mercy on me and my family than I did on you and yours. Good-bye, my son."

With that, the king turned away and left. He yelled at the guards as they walked to the car, as if they'd done something terribly wrong. "Just take me back to the station!" he concluded.

Darien slumped into a chair—the Old Judge's favorite—next to the cold fireplace. A chill swept through the room, and Anna thought then that the cottage would never be warm again.

The four of them spent the night at an inn halfway between Hailsham and Sarum, and then they caught the first train back to Krawley the next morning. Anna and Kyle spent most of the trip in silence, watching the rolling fields and thick forests wash past like gentle waves of green. Apart from the sadness of losing the Old Judge, the question that dominated their thinking was this: *How are we going to get home?* If the Old Judge was the only one who knew, they were now stuck.

Darien and Colonel Oliver spent the trip discussing plans for their future. "You don't believe King Lawrence will simply sit back and allow you to become the new king, do you?" Colonel Oliver asked.

"No," Darien said with a sigh. "His grief and remorse at the cottage were genuine enough, but once he returns to the splendor of his palace and the great power and the servants waiting on him hand and foot, he'll change his mind. He *likes* being the king and wants to keep it that way."

"So where do we go from here?"

Darien rubbed his hand over his beard. "I think we should keep on as we have."

Colonel Oliver wasn't satisfied. "But we've grown so much," he pointed out. "We have over 500 people in our group now. And the men are getting restless. It's driving them crazy sitting in the Territory of Peace while every fighting man is at war with the Palatians."

"What do they want to do?"

"Fight the Palatians, of course."

"I wish we could," Darien said ruefully. "But for us to openly join the war would invite the king to murder us on the battlefield and then blame the Palatians. No, it's too risky."

"There must be *something* we can do!" Colonel Oliver growled, frustrated.

Darien leaned toward the colonel. "There is," he affirmed. "We must pray. Then maybe an answer will present itself."

When they stepped onto the platform at the station in Krawley, Colonel Henri, one of Darien's officers, greeted them. "Welcome back," he said, then led them aside, close to the stationmaster's office. "A baron from Adria has come to meet with you. He and his servants waited for you all day yesterday. He said they wouldn't leave until they had a chance to talk to you."

"Where are they now?" Darien asked.

"The Lion's Head Pub in the center of town," Colonel Henri answered.

"Are they safe?" Colonel Oliver asked. "I wouldn't put it past our king to hire Adrians to kill us."

Colonel Henri nodded. "We searched them thoroughly. They're unarmed except for weapons they keep on their horses for when they travel. They won't be near their horses when they meet you."

"Then I suppose I should talk to them," said Darien.

"What about the kids?" Colonel Henri asked. "Do you want me to take them back to our camp?"

Darien didn't need to think about it. "Of course not," he replied. "I wouldn't dare meet the baron without my prophet and my guardian angel."

They walked straight to the Lion's Head Pub and went inside. Like most pubs, it was decorated in dark paneling, dark furniture, and dark paintings. Even the light through the windows seemed dark. The baron, who couldn't have been missed in any circumstance, was a big, ostentatious man dressed in a large cloak laced with orange fur. He had a thick, heavy brow that kept his eyes in constant shadow and round, wobbly jowls that shook when he laughed. His mannerisms, even before he spoke, included flamboyant gestures with his hands and an affected accent that no nation would want as its own. Most noticeable was his size. He stood up to receive them, and Anna guessed he was at least six-foot-five. His two guards, who were also tall, looked like dwarves next to their boss.

"I wonder why he even *needs* guards," Kyle said softly to Anna as they crossed the room.

"Thank you for meeting with me. I am Baron Orkzy," the man said in a thunderous voice.

"I knew who you were instantly," Darien said. "Your reputation is known by everyone."

"You're too kind."

Kyle noticed that Darien didn't say exactly what sort of reputation the baron had.

Darien introduced everyone. The baron shook hands, his bear-like paw swallowing each of theirs, then invited them to sit down at the table with him.

"We need to discuss a matter of business," the baron said once they were comfortable. "As you know, I'm a man with many friends and many enemies. My wealth intimidates some, and my work in— shall we say, *negotiations*—with certain parties annoys others."

"In other words, there are people who hate you because you'll do anything for money," Darien said flatly.

The baron laughed, and his jowls shook. "Yes! Yes! Precisely! Straight to the point. Score one for you, General."

"What can I do for you?" Darien asked.

"I want to hire you."

"I beg your pardon?"

The baron rested his elbows on the table. It tilted beneath the weight. He feigned a great weariness and said, "The war between your country and the Palatians is a nasty affair. Frankly, I don't feel safe anymore. Because of my past dealings with the Palatians, I'm afraid your people—or your allies—may attack me. Because of my past dealings with the Marutians, I'm afraid the Palatians and *their* allies will attack."

"Why come to me? Adrians are known for their love of war. It seems like there are plenty of tribes around to protect you."

"And that is where you've hit the nail directly on the head. My country has been torn apart by petty differences for years. Few of the leaders will stop bickering long enough to see the bigger picture. They're barbarians, mostly. I don't trust a single one of them." He placed his hand against his forehead melodramatically. "Alas, I am a man without a country. Much like you, I dare say."

"I understand," replied Darien dryly.

"I want to hire you and your *entourage* to be my bodyguards. I want you to help me to protect my interests. You'll be my own personal army, as such. In exchange, you'll be well looked after. Your people will even have better accommodations than you have here. Imagine living in houses rather than tents on a hillside. Gas, electricity, plumbing, proper sewage . . ." The baron lifted an eyebrow coaxingly.

Darien's tone and expression betrayed no answer one way or the other. He said simply, "I'll have to give it some thought, Baron."

"Yes, yes. Consult with your officers."

"Can we meet again tomorrow morning?"

"I'd be delighted," the baron said with a flourish of his hand. He pulled a handkerchief from his sleeve and dabbed the side of his nose. He waved the handkerchief at them as they stood up and left. "Until tomorrow!"

As they walked out of the pub, Darien said to Colonel Oliver, "Check the grapevine and find out what he's really up to."

"Yes, sir," the colonel replied.

"Don't you trust him?" Kyle asked.

"Baron Orkzy is a mercenary who'll greet you with one hand and stab you in the back with the other," Darien said.

"Then why are you going to meet with him again?" asked Anna.

"Because it's possible that we can suit our own purposes while trying to suit his."

That evening at the camp, Anna and Kyle were summoned to Darien's tent. Just as they arrived, Colonel Oliver brought in a man who looked surprisingly like a rat. He had a pointed nose, small teeth, and whiskers that spread out from his face like fur. He even held his hands in front of him like a rat when it's on its hind legs, looking for food. And he was called, appropriately enough, the Rat.

"Sit down," Darien said.

"I'd rather stand, if you don't mind," the Rat replied. "I get fidgety sitting down."

"The Rat has some useful information for us," Colonel Oliver explained.

Darien smiled graciously. "We've paid well for it, I assume?"

The Rat's head jerked up and down quickly. "Oh yes," he said. "The general always pays well. I hope to honor you with my information in return."

"Then tell us what you know."

"I have it from reliable sources that the baron's offer to you is a good one," the Rat began, his nose twitching. "He can and will provide you with an entire town in which to live. It's called Lizah, just inside the Adrian border. What he wants from you in return is to see that he is kept safe and that some of his 'product' gets safely to market."

"What product?" Darien asked suspiciously.

The Rat smiled, his lips turning into a giant *U*. "Ah, this is where it gets most interesting. The baron is a partner in a firm that has created the parts for a new long-range cannon. It shoots farther than anything in existence—up to 300 yards farther. But the Adrians don't have the internal stability or the factories to build the cannons themselves. That's why the parts must be delivered."

"Delivered where?" asked Darien.

"Monrovia."

Darien and Colonel Oliver glanced at each other. "Monrovia?" the colonel asked.

"Yes. They assemble the baron's cannon parts with their own."

Colonel Oliver pressed on. "Why is Monrovia interested in this cannon? They're not at war with anyone."

"They're not at war now, but they might be one day." The Rat's eyes flickered.

"You know something else," Darien said. "Out with it."

"I have it from another good source that the Monrovians are going to sell the assembled cannons to the Palatians."

"I see."

Colonel Oliver stood up and began to pace. "With that kind of firepower, the Palatians could defeat our armies in a matter of weeks," he observed.

The Rat sniffed. "In exchange for the cannons, the Palatians will give the Monrovians part of your territories."

"Carve us up like a Christmas goose," the colonel said. "Is that what they have in mind?"

"Likely."

Darien mused, "Does the baron know about this?"

"I can't say for sure. Though there is little that the baron doesn't know."

"Is it possible that he wants me to be his bodyguard to get me out of the way?" asked Darien. "He knows I'll do anything to help our army if the war turns against them. Maybe he wants to neutralize me."

"Wouldn't you, if you were in his position?" Colonel Oliver asked.

"Unless he has something else up his sleeve."

Darien gratefully dismissed the Rat and called in his officers. While he waited for them, he asked Kyle and Anna what they thought.

"I get confused by all the double-dealing," Kyle complained. "It's like you can't trust anybody around here."

"You can't," Darien confirmed. "Marus is surrounded by countries that want our land. Allegiances change almost as quickly as the weather."

"Then what are you going to do?" Anna asked.

"Perhaps we can play both sides for a while," Darien said.

"How?"

A thin smile crept across Darien's face. "We'll give safe delivery of the cannon parts to Monrovia so the baron will get his money. That's what he'll be paying us to do."

Kyle didn't understand. "What good is that?" he asked. "Then the Monrovians will build the cannons and send them to the Palatians."

"How do you suppose they'll get the cannons to the Palatians?" Darien said, pointing to a map hanging on the side of the tent. "They either have to take them south through Gotthard—which Prince Edwin will never allow since he is *our* ally. Or, more likely, they'll transport them by train to the west of Gotthard. That's wide-open wilderness. Anything can happen to those poor trains on the way."

"You'll sabotage the train tracks?" Anna asked.

Darien nodded.

"They'll figure it out eventually," Kyle observed.

"Maybe they will," Darien agreed. "But in the meantime, we'll find the plans to that cannon and get them to our own experts. That'll even things out a little."

The officers entered Darien's tent and wondered why Darien, Anna, and Kyle were smiling.

16

For nearly three months, the plan worked just as Darien had hoped. While he and his army gave safe conduct to the baron's supplies from Adria to Monrovia, a team of his guerrilla fighters blasted the railway lines west of Gotthard. The Monrovians switched their transportation from trains to trucks and horse-drawn wagons, but the result was the same. No matter how they tried to smuggle the cannons through, Darien's fighters thwarted them. In that time, only six cannons got through to the Palatian front lines, not enough to make a big difference in the war.

One night, in a daring raid, Darien broke into the plant where the Monrovians built the cannons. The blueprints for the cannon were kept in a safe in the president's office. The Rat, who was also skilled as a safecracker, got the safe open. Darien used a new con-traption called a *photographic camera* to take pictures of the plans. Then Darien and the Rat crept away, and no one knew they had been there.

Darien had the blueprints delivered anonymously to General Liddell's weaponry office. Darien was quite proud of himself.

In those three months, Kyle and Anna lived with Darien's army in the town of Lizah. It was a mining town settled in an area of Adria where the lush green beauty of the Marus terrain and the Territory of Peace gave way to brown sand, cacti, and dry air. The Marutians found it barren and boring. Darien insisted that Kyle and Anna receive lessons from a tutor; he saw no reason for them to stop learning just because they weren't in their own world. It annoyed Kyle more than Anna, since he disliked doing homework more than she did.

"If I have to go to school and do homework, I may as well be back home!" Kyle pouted. He often felt as though he'd lost his sense of purpose. He didn't get that sick feeling in his stomach anymore, so he had become just another kid in the camp. He didn't like it, and he began to question whether there had ever been an Unseen One to give him the power in the first place.

Anna, on the other hand, studied hard. It wasn't unusual for Kyle to find her reading the Sacred Scroll that Darien had given her or walking and thinking in the wilderness alone.

"Don't you get bored silly?" he once asked her.

She looked at him with the same indulgent expression their mother often gave him when he'd asked a ridiculous question. "No, I think it's nice out here," she said.

"Okay, so it's nice. But when are we going home?" he asked.

Anna shrugged. She had no idea.

"Don't you care? Aren't you worried about Mom and Dad, Grandma and Grandpa?"

Anna had to think about it before she could answer. "I'm not worried," she replied after a moment. "Somehow the Unseen One will work it all out when we go back."

"*If* we go back," Kyle said. "I don't think the Unseen One is interested—*if* He's even out there."

Anna gazed at her brother for a moment. "You're upset because you don't feel special anymore," she observed.

"What are you talking about?"

"You know what I mean," Anna replied. "Being chosen doesn't mean excitement day in and day out. It doesn't mean we're always being used in obvious ways by the Unseen One. Sometimes it means waiting and being patient and staying faithful."

Kyle folded his arms. "Don't preach at me," he said grumpily.

"You're not sure you believe anymore."

"Leave me alone."

"Can't you believe without that feeling?"

"Oh, that's easy for you to say!" he snapped. "You get those dreams and visions all the time. If the Unseen One gave *me* dreams and visions, I'd believe, too."

Anna shook her head. "I haven't had those dreams in a long time," she said. "But I don't need to have them to believe."

"Well, maybe I do."

"Then you're believing in the wrong thing," she snapped.

"I don't want to talk about it anymore." He turned and walked away from her. She was right in what she said, he knew. The truth was, he felt deserted and rejected by the Unseen One. It was time to take matters into his own hands.

That night, Kyle ventured out from Lizah to see if it would help him think the way Anna thought. The desert evening was cool, so he started a small campfire. He brooded next to it, bugged that he still didn't know what to do to get home. He heard a rustling behind him. Before he could see who it was, the Rat was standing next to him, warming his hands over the fire as if he'd been there all along.

"You scared me," Kyle said in an accusing tone.

"My apologies," the Rat said. "What ails you?"

"Nothing."

"I see you sitting here alone, and I think to myself that you are not happy. Then I think that I am the Rat and able to find things that might make you happy."

"You can't find anything that will make me happy," Kyle said testily.

"Don't be so certain, young protector."

Kyle looked up at him. His eyes looked like embers in the firelight. "I don't have any money. Well, none that you can use."

"On the contrary. You have money from your world."

Kyle frowned. "What do you know about my world?"

"I'm the Rat. I'm supposed to know everything I can. You want to go back to your world. That much I know."

"Yeah, but the Old Judge is dead, and there's nobody else who can help us," Kyle said. He jabbed at the fire with a stick. It spat back at him.

"The Old Judge was not the last of his kind."

"Anna doesn't know how either."

"Anna is not the last of that kind," the Rat said. "There is another. A woman. She can help you."

Kyle brightened up. "Really?"

"I would not say so unless I was sure." The Rat rubbed his hands together and waited.

"Where is she?" Kyle asked. "How can I talk to her?"

The Rat spread his arms. "She's a long way from here. Back in Marus. You'll have to journey a day and a half to get to her."

"I don't care. I'm ready to go."

"Then give me some of your otherworldly money and the Rat will take care of everything."

Kyle dug around in his pocket. He found a couple of dollar bills and 63 cents in change, and he thought he'd better hang on to a dollar.

The Rat smiled as Kyle placed the rest of the money in his palm. "You're too generous," the Rat said. "Meet me here in an hour."

Kyle was beside himself with joy and ran to tell Anna the news.

Anna wasn't in her room. Darien had asked her—and Kyle—to come to the briefing room in his headquarters at what was once a schoolhouse. When no one could find Kyle, Anna went alone. The

briefing room (actually, one of the old classrooms) was crowded
with officers and the elected leaders of the community. To the left
of the podium, Baron Orkzy sat, regal and erect. He could have
been the principal for this school. Darien called everyone to silence.

"I have important news. The war with the Palatians is dead-
locked," Darien announced. "The Palatians are fed up."

"They're ready to surrender then?" someone asked with a
chuckle.

Darien didn't smile. "No. They're ready to conquer. The baron
and I met this evening. He tells me the Palatians are calling in all
debts from the nations who're friendly to them. As of midnight
tonight, the Monrovians are going to join the war on the side of
Palatia."

The room erupted in shouts and protests.

Darien waved his arms to get them quiet again. "It's worse than
that," he continued. "Many of the leaders of the Adrian tribes are
ready to side with Monrovia and Palatia as well."

"Even the baron?" another voice called out.

Darien gestured to the baron. "Please tell them what you told
me."

The baron stood up, a giant in the room. "I despise this sort of
thing, I have to confess," he began. "I prefer neutrality. It makes for
better business. But the Adrian leaders are putting a lot of pressure
on me to swear allegiance to Palatia."

"And what about us?" a woman shouted.

"To put it bluntly, they don't trust you," the baron said. "They
seem to suspect that you've had something to do with all those
nasty explosions on the Monrovian railway lines. Imagine that.
They believe that you actively thwarted the delivery of the cannons
to the Palatians."

The room was silent. A few knowing smiles were exchanged.

The baron pulled a handkerchief from his sleeve and dabbed the side of his nose. "Naturally, it's none of *my* business since the parts I'd promised to them were delivered. I'd rather *not* know whether you were involved as saboteurs. Now, however, they're forcing me to be involved. They want me to make a decision. And by forcing *me* to make a decision, they're forcing *you* to make a decision."

"What kind of decision?"

"Whether you're going to stay here and behave yourselves, or whether you're going to side with your countrymen." The baron leaned against the podium dramatically. "One will ensure that you live in peace, the other will put you at risk as enemies of our allies."

A wave of murmuring rolled through the gathering.

"I've been told to offer you a deal, though," said the baron.

"What kind of deal?" Colonel Oliver asked from the side of the room.

"Everyone knows of the conflict between King Lawrence and General Darien. It is also well known that General Darien will likely win out as your next ruler."

Colonel Henri stood up. "What's your point, Baron?" he asked.

The baron looked at the colonel with disdain. "Side with the Palatians and you will be given a significantly large portion of Marus's northern counties. General Darien will be installed as your king. This the Palatians promise to you if they are victorious."

The room erupted again in a commotion of catcalls and dissension.

"You have until tomorrow to decide," the baron said over the noise, and with a grand flourish, he left the room.

Darien returned to the podium and tried to get control of the crowd. Then the arguments among them began. Anna didn't stay. She felt an odd but strong desire to take a walk.

∞

The dream took her by surprise. She hadn't had one in such a long time and had resigned herself to the idea that she might never have one again. But there it was, more vivid and real than any she'd ever had before.

She saw King Lawrence. He was thin and wild-eyed, pacing with his hands clasped behind his back in what looked like a tent. General Liddell stood nearby, a dark and sour expression on his face.

"Well, sire?" Liddell asked.

"I don't know! I don't know! How can I know?" the king cried out.

"A decision—orders to attack—*anything* will be helpful at this time." The anger in General Liddell's voice was unmistakable. "In just a few hours, we'll have not one but *three* enemies to contend with. What do you want us to do?"

The king paced more quickly. "If the Old Judge were here, he'd know. He would tell me what to do. Why did he desert me?"

"Because he's *dead,* sire. That's what happens to people. They die. *We'll* die if you don't make a decision soon."

"That's where you're wrong, General. He's not dead. He's around here somewhere. We just have to pick up the phone and give him a call." The king put his thumb and pinkie against his face as if he were talking into a phone.

General Liddell worked his jaw, clenching and unclenching his teeth. "Of course," he said with open sarcasm. "Why didn't I think of it before?"

"I want our armies to stay right where they are for the time being," the king suddenly commanded. "Don't move. Not an inch, not a muscle. I have to find someone to consult with."

"Like who?" General Liddell looked as if he might slap the king if he mentioned the Old Judge again.

"There's a woman. I don't remember her name. She has the power. We'll visit her, and she'll tell us what to do."

"A woman?"

"Yes, yes. Don't be so thick. She lives near . . . Dorr. That's it. I can find her if we go there." The king stopped pacing and leaned over a table with a map on it. He pointed. "That little town right there."

General Liddell didn't bother to look. "You're going to leave your troops *now*? Sire, with all due respect, if they see you leave, they'll panic."

"They won't see me leave. We'll disguise ourselves. That's what we'll do. We'll disguise ourselves, go to the woman, then come back. Just tell the men that we're in conference and can't be disturbed."

"Sire, please—"

"No! Stop arguing with me!" the king screamed. "We have to go! We have no hope of winning if we don't go!"

Anna woke up, alone in the desert. Something made a chirping noise nearby. An owl hooted.

Was this a dream to report to Darien? She wondered. Nothing in it would help them with their decision to stay in Adria or join the king's troops. Then again, maybe she simply couldn't see it. She made her way back to Darien's headquarters. It was deserted except for Colonel Oliver, who was locking the door. He informed her that General Darien had gone off somewhere to think and pray. Whatever she had to tell him would have to wait until morning.

She thanked him and walked to the room she shared with Kyle at the Lizah Hotel. It was dark.

"Kyle?" she called out as she lit a lamp. "Are you here?"

She looked around, her hand brushing against a piece of paper on the table in front of her. It was a note from Kyle.

"I've gone to see someone who will help us get home," the note said in his distinctive cursive. "I'll be back in a couple of days. Then we'll go home!" He had underlined *go home* in heavy strokes.

Anna sat down in a chair and buried her face in her hands.

17

The sun hadn't fully risen yet when someone knocked on the door. Anna, who hadn't slept all night and was still fully dressed, padded across the room.

"Who is it?" she asked.

"Darien," the familiar voice said.

She opened the door, and before he could say anything she thrust Kyle's note into his hands. He read it, then frowned. "He needs a good kick in his backside," he growled. "It's the wrong day to do something like this."

"You made a decision?"

"I think so," Darien replied. "Unless you have a message for me. Have you had any dreams lately?"

Anna told him about the dream of King Lawrence.

"What am I supposed to make of that?" he asked.

"I don't know," Anna said, distressed.

Darien went to the window and looked out on the street. Colonel Oliver was beginning to assemble the officers and community leaders below. "Your dream may be the confirmation of my decision. The king is obviously losing his grip. He's not capable of fighting the combined allied armies. He needs our help."

"No," Anna said. "That may not be the message at all. Maybe it means to stay away. Maybe you should wait until—"

"Until what, Anna?" he shouted at her. "Until the Palatians have conquered our country?"

She winced as if he'd struck her in the face, her eyes tearing up.

He checked himself and continued more quietly. "What you mean is that you want me to wait until Kyle comes back. I can't do that. Whatever we do, we have to do quickly. Right now."

"I understand," Anna whispered.

"I've decided that we won't stay here. All the civilians will go back to where we camped in the Territory of Peace. You'll be as safe there as anywhere."

"What about your army?"

"We're going south to join the royal army," Darien said. "We have to help them fight against the Palatians. It'll be a massacre otherwise."

"What if King Lawrence has you arrested—or you're killed?" Anna asked.

"Then we've all been terribly misled and the Unseen One didn't really choose me to be king."

The Rat and Kyle took a night train from Lizah to Krawley. From there they caught a train that took them south to Sarum. They arrived the next morning, just in time for a connecting train to Dorr. Kyle slept most of the way, though he awoke with a sick feeling in the pit of his stomach.

"I hope I didn't make a big mistake," he said.

"Do you think it would be a mistake to find your way home?" the Rat asked.

Kyle didn't answer.

The Rat glanced at a map on the wall of the Dorr station. "Only a few miles' walk," he said, "then you'll have your answer."

An hour later, they passed the post office for Wollet-in-Stone. "I know this place," Kyle said. "This is where we picked up Anna after she escaped from the convent!"

Five minutes later, they were standing outside a wooden shack with a tin roof. A red palm was painted on the doorway. "That's the sign of a seer," the Rat said. He knocked on the frame since the door was hanging wide open. "Hello?" he called.

Someone shuffled and banged inside, as if the person had been startled and tipped something over. An old woman, older than any Kyle had ever seen, appeared in the doorway, wiping her hands on the skirt of her peasant dress. A tattered shawl hung like cobwebs from her shoulders. "Yes? Anastasia, I am," she said. "What can I do's for ye?"

"The boy needs to talk to you," the Rat explained. "About matters of another world."

"Come in and sit ye down! Sit ye down!" she said, clearly delighted.

Kyle followed her in and immediately regretted it. The place was a dump. The woman scooted a skeletal cat from one of the chairs and positioned it next to the table in the center of the shack. Kyle reluctantly sat down, then noticed that the Rat hadn't joined them. He stood in the doorway.

"Come in," Kyle said.

"This is your affair, not mine," the Rat said. "I'll meet you at the station when you're done."

Before Kyle could say anything, the Rat was gone.

"Matters of another world?" Anastasia asked.

Kyle surveyed the room. Besides the obvious dirt and trash, he noticed an old, faded carnival poster hanging on the wall. "Anastasia the Mysterious" the headline read in large, curly letters. The woman in the painting bore little resemblance to the old, shriveled person in front of him, however. That woman was dark and beautiful, with wild hair and eyes that probably caught the hearts of many men.

Anastasia cleared her throat. Her hand was held out for payment.

"Oh, sorry," Kyle said. He dug into his pocket, found his last dollar, and gave it to her. "I hope that's enough."

She held up the greenback and giggled. "Money from the other world. Oh yes. I'll add it to my collection, I will." She opened a small tin confectioner's box. Kyle thought he caught sight of an American nickel before she shoved the dollar in and closed the box up tight.

"I want to go home," Kyle said when Anastasia turned her attention to him once more.

"Home! Yes, yes. We all want to go home. Give me yer hand."

He held out his hand to her. She took it quickly, then just as quickly let it go. Her face looked as if she'd been jolted with electricity. "No. Ye are tricking me, ye are."

Kyle was confused. "What do you mean?" he asked.

The old woman had the tin box open again and was fumbling around for the dollar. "Ye are not true. Ye should not be here, no." She threw the dollar back at him. "Go! Hurry!"

"What's wrong?" Kyle asked as Anastasia came around the table and nearly pulled him from the chair. "You're supposed to help me."

"I cannot help ye. No. Why didn't ye tell me ye were a chosen protector? Are ye trying to kill me?" She pushed him to the door, stopping only when the sound of approaching horses could be heard above her gravelly commotion.

"Tell you—" Kyle was bewildered.

"It's too late!" the woman cried. "It's too late!"

The horses were reined to a stop next to the shack. Two men dressed in what looked like monks' hoods climbed off and strode toward the door. The woman stumbled backward and slumped into her chair. Kyle looked at Anastasia, then back at the two men. They yanked their hoods off. King Lawrence and General Liddell walked in.

"Oh no . . ." Kyle said.

"Oh yes," General Liddell replied, then backhanded him. Kyle was halfway to the ground when Liddell grabbed him and yanked him back to his feet. Dazed, Kyle tried to speak, but he couldn't. He felt a sliver of warm blood trickle from his mouth.

"Do you know this boy?" King Lawrence asked.

"Don't you remember him?" Liddell replied. "He was with Darien."

The king's eyes came alive. "Is he the boy they keep talking about? The one who keeps saving Darien's life?"

"Saved him from my marksman in the Territory of Peace," General Liddell growled.

"I remember now. We met at the palace. Or at the Old Judge's cottage. Or somewhere. How nice to meet you again," King Lawrence said with a smile. "Your timing couldn't be better."

"He'll make a wonderful hostage," Liddell said.

The king glared at his general. "Hostage! You're mistaken, my friend. He will be my aid and my assistant!"

"Sire—"

The king continued, "He'll be *my* protector. My own lucky charm! If he saved Darien, he can save me! This is wonderful!" The king's face was aglow, like a child who's just found all the answers to an important test ahead of time. Then he suddenly looked confused. "But what's he doing here?"

"Nothing, my lord," Anastasia said. "We were just chatting, that's all. Talking, we were. Passing time away, la-di-da."

The king pushed Kyle toward a chair. "Sit down, my protector," he ordered. "Your visit here may be—*must be*—providential. You may give this old charlatan a little help. A boost for her failing powers!" He laughed, pulled up another chair, and sat down.

He's insane, Kyle thought. *The king has gone completely over the edge.*

Anastasia said fearfully, "Powers, my lord? I'm just an old woman trying to make her way through life. What powers?"

"Oh, be quiet," General Liddell said. "We know what you are, though I don't believe in it myself. The king wants your advice."

The king cocked an eye at her. "You don't think I know what the red palm means? You think I don't know about you? I'm the king of this country, and I *know.*" He brought his fist down against the rickety old table. It nearly collapsed. "Now tell me what I must do! Tell me and *be right,* blast you!"

Anastasia fumbled around for a moment, picking up a deck of cards, then putting them down again. She then reached for a small gold pendant, thought better of it, and put it back. "I'll need a moment, I will."

"*Now,* hag," General Liddell said from his place by the door.

Anastasia had a new idea. "Dark," she said. "It must be dark. Close the door, you must. Pull the drapes."

"You pull the drapes," Liddell said as he closed the door. "I wouldn't touch them with a 10-foot barge pole."

"Pull the drapes, General!" the king shouted.

Liddell obeyed grudgingly. The shack was now in a hazy darkness. Light still peeked through the spaces and holes in the wall's wooden planks.

"What now?" the king asked.

"Close your eyes," she said nervously.

She's stalling, Kyle thought. He wiped the side of his mouth, which now felt numb. The bleeding had stopped. Through his half-closed eyes, he looked around to see if there was any way to escape.

Liddell was still standing next to the door. The only door. There was no other way out.

"What do ye want to know?" Anastasia asked.

"Will I be victorious against the Palatians?" King Lawrence asked.

The old woman stammered, "The Palatians. Oh yes. Them. Victorious. Well . . . I think . . ."

"I don't care what you think!" the king growled. "I want you to ask *him*."

"Who?"

"The Old Judge!"

"No . . . please. I can't call the Old Judge. Calling him would be like . . . like . . ."

"Asking for the Unseen One?" the king said. "Yes, I know. Now call him! He'll tell me what I need to know. Say his name."

"No!" Anastasia cried.

King Lawrence reached across the table and grabbed her by the throat. "Say his name!"

"No one has said his name in years!" she shrieked.

"Say it!" he screamed at her. "Say it! Say the name!"

Anastasia gasped as the king tightened his grip around her throat. She had to say the name or die, that much was certain. So she said it in a hoarse whisper. "Samuel."

"Louder!"

"Samuel!" she screeched.

The king let her go and looked around. "Now what?"

She whimpered and fell from the chair to her knees. "No!"

"What do you see?"

"It's rising from the earth," she said. "An old man in a cloak."

The king spun around. "Where? I don't see it."

Kyle had no idea if what he saw next was something that

appeared to his eyes or to some other senses, but it was definitely the Old Judge. But he didn't appear like a ghost or a spirit, nor did he appear as a living person. He was a presence that seemed to fill the room, standing at all points simultaneously, no matter which way one turned.

"Why are you troubling me?" the Old Judge asked, annoyed.

The king's voice trembled, not from fear but from relief. "Ah!" he said. "The Palatians are going to attack, and I don't know what to do. You were my last friend—my only friend—and I need your help. Tell me what the Unseen One wants me to do."

"Why do you ask me now?" the Old Judge asked. "I have told you all there is to know. You have turned your back on the Unseen One, and so He has taken the kingdom from your hands and given it to another. You have not obeyed. You have not believed. You did not remain faithful. Now it is too late. You have led the people of Marus to disaster. Death waits for you!"

The king threw himself to the ground. "No, Samuel! No! Save me! You must save me! Samuel!"

The Old Judge held up his hand. "Speak my name no more," he commanded. Then it was as if he turned to Kyle, though he didn't actually move, and he said, "You are in bad company, boy. You should have had faith. You should have been patient."

"I know, but—"

The door suddenly blew open, the curtains were ripped from their flimsy rods, and light poured in. They all covered their eyes and, when they could see again, the shack was as it had been when they arrived. The Old Judge was gone, leaving only a trace in the memory that he had ever been there at all.

General Liddell was obviously shaken. He helped King Lawrence to his feet. "Sire, we must go," he said.

"Yes, we must," the king agreed.

Kyle considered making a dash for the door, but the two men blocked the way. General Liddell guided the king out, and Kyle hoped they had forgotten him. Suddenly the king reached back, catching Kyle by the shoulder. "You're coming with us," King Lawrence snarled. "Your power as protector might be greater than his power as a prophet."

"No!" Kyle cried, struggling against him.

The king leered at him, madness gathering like foam at the corners of his mouth. "You'll be my lucky charm!" he shouted.

General Darien and his soldiers had left to fight the Palatians. Anna, along with the rest of the civilians, packed a few provisions for the journey back to the Territory of Peace. She had just put her hands on a few of Kyle's belongings when the vision came. It hit her like a lightning bolt, and she fell to the floor. She saw Anastasia's shack, and in it were Anastasia, King Lawrence, General Liddell, Kyle, and the Old Judge. She heard every word of condemnation the Old Judge passed on to the king. She felt the burning fury of the Old Judge's anger. Yet behind it, she also felt sadness and disappointment.

Then it was gone.

Her mind raced to interpret what she'd seen. Surely it wasn't real. How could the Old Judge, who was dead, be in the shack with the king and General Liddell? And what was Kyle doing there? The dream was all mixed up, as if someone had thrown images together in the wrong place. *It wasn't a dream,* she decided. *I'm just worried about Kyle.*

From outside, she heard a shot and a scream. Then the sound of horses' hooves came in like thunder. *Another dream?* she wondered as she looked out the window.

It wasn't a dream. The Adrians were attacking.

Gathered together in the Lizah Hotel, Anna and the rest of the civilians—some 200 people in all—found themselves guarded by Adrian soldiers. Apart from being pushed and shoved, no one was hurt. One of the community leaders, an old man named Morlock, demanded to know why they were being held. The guards refused to answer; instead they gestured with their guns.

Early afternoon, a commotion arose by the hotel front door. A moment later, Baron Orkzy walked in. His normal composure was replaced by breathless worry. His hair was tousled, his clothes askew. He'd obviously been manhandled, though Anna couldn't imagine anyone being large enough to do such a job.

The baron asked everyone to gather around. Then he addressed them, punctuating his comments with flutters of his handkerchief. "Ladies and gentlemen, I've been asked to explain your situation," he said. "As it stands now, you're being held hostage."

"Tell us something we don't know," Morlock snapped.

"Please don't interrupt," the baron replied wearily. "You're being held hostage as a bargaining tool. General Darien will be intercepted and given a message from my Adrian rulers. Essentially, the message will inform him that if he does not return to Lizah immediately, you will all be killed."

Several women cried out. Someone began to sob.

"Now, now, none of that," the baron said. "My Adrian leaders aren't really interested in hurting you."

"What *are* they interested in?" Morlock asked.

"They're interested in keeping General Darien and his soldiers from helping King Lawrence. By using you as collateral, they have a good chance of succeeding."

Morlock refused to yield. "What makes you so sure General Darien will come back? He may choose his duty to the king over our lives."

The baron sniffed. "That would be most regrettable since, if he doesn't return, you *will* die."

Morlock quickly stepped forward, a knife in his hand. "What will stop us from taking *you* hostage?"

The baron looked at Morlock's face, down at the knife, then back at his face. "You old fool," he said angrily, "I'm already a hostage! Don't you understand? This whole business wasn't *my* idea. I'm only the messenger. Now I have to wait here with you for Darien's return. So put that little blade away like a nice little man, and stop being so overdramatic."

Morlock's face turned red against his white beard, but he put the knife away. "What do we do now?" he asked glumly.

"Wait for Darien's answer," the baron said. "And hope that this hotel has decent coffee."

A couple of hours passed. Anna sat alone in a red velvet chair to the side of the hotel lobby. She read portions of the Sacred Scroll, prayed, then read some more. She dreamed without sleeping, a variety of images clearly presented and understood.

A blast of cologne suddenly filled her nostrils, and she looked up. The baron stood over her.

"May I sit with you for a moment?" he asked.

"Yes, sir," she said.

He sat down next to her. Even then he was as tall as she. "You're one of those . . . oh, what do they call them? A *voice*. For the Unseen One. Do you know what Darien will do?"

Anna did. She had already seen the Adrian messenger stop

Darien and the troops. She decided not to say so, though. "General Darien is torn between his duty to the king and his love for the people here," she offered.

"I know that," the baron said. "But will he come?"

"I cannot answer that," Anna replied.

"Because you don't know or because you won't say?"

Anna gazed at him without answering.

The baron examined his fingernails for a moment. Then he asked, "What will become of the king?"

Anna's heart ached, as if somehow she shared in the pain and disappointment the Unseen One felt at that moment, like a father who had to punish a rebellious child. "The king will suffer the full consequences of his faithlessness."

The baron let the subject drop. Then, as if he'd just remembered something else, he said, "You have a brother. Where is he? Did he go with Darien?"

"No," Anna said, her eyes starting to burn. "He is with the king."

The baron lifted his eyebrows. "Oh, dear. What will happen to him?"

"He will go home."

The battle against the Palatians was a catastrophe from the start. King Lawrence ignored his generals' advice to spread his battalions out over strategic areas to the south, west, and north of Kellen. He thought they would be more effective as one solid army, concentrating on the Palatian troops to the west. This allowed the Palatians to circle from the south and southwest, while the Monrovians and Adrians circled in from the north and northwest. Prince Edwin of Gotthard hastily assembled his army and cut off part of the Monrovian and Adrian forces, but it wasn't enough.

King Lawrence found himself outflanked and outmaneuvered in the Valley of the Rocks. Where he had once trapped General Darien, he was now himself trapped. The Palatians bombarded the king and his soldiers with cannon fire, then moved in for hand-to-hand combat.

Kyle witnessed it all firsthand. The king would not let Kyle out of his sight after they left Anastasia's shack. "You're my lucky charm," he said over and over.

Kyle explained in despair that he wasn't anyone's lucky charm. "I'm just a kid," he insisted.

"You protected General Darien," the king said. "You'll protect me."

"I can't," Kyle pleaded. But his words had no effect. The king dressed Kyle as one of his attendants and insisted that the boy stay nearby wherever he went. That included the battle against the Palatians.

The Palatians broke through the front lines of the Marutian army and aggressively made their way along the edges of the Valley of the Rocks toward the Royal Guards—those who were committed to protecting the king. The Royal Guards fell quickly at the hands of the Palatians. The king's sons, including Prince George, rushed to counterattack. Kyle saw the Palatians strike them down.

King Lawrence watched from his hiding place, his sword drawn. "Tell me what to do!" he commanded Kyle.

"I don't know!" Kyle cried.

The king grabbed him. "Then we'll run."

Blindly, they stumbled through the passages and crevices of the rocks, the roar of cannons and gunfire in their ears. No matter how far they went, however, the Palatians' shouts seemed close behind. Somehow they wound up at the very cave that Darien had found months before. It seemed like such a long time ago, Kyle thought.

"Maybe they won't find us here," the king said breathlessly, panic in his eyes.

Kyle fell to the floor of the cave. It was muddy and cold. "Help me!" he prayed to the Unseen One. "I don't deserve it, but please help me."

The Palatians were coming. Kyle could hear their voices echoing in the rocks around the cave.

"Tell me," the king said to Kyle, "are we safe here?"

Kyle shook his head and began to cry. "I don't know!" he said.

The king slapped him. "Prophesy for me! You're supposed to be my protector! Tell me your dreams!"

Kyle put his face in his hands.

The Palatians weren't far from the mouth of the cave now. Kyle felt sick to his stomach, but it wasn't a warning. He knew they were doomed.

The king looked around, wild-eyed. "They can't capture me!" he shouted. "They'll humiliate me—torture me. I can't be captured!" He thrust his sword handle at Kyle. "As soon as they arrive, you have to kill me."

"No!" Kyle said, pushing the handle away. "I won't."

"You have to!" King Lawrence demanded.

Kyle refused.

Just then, a Palatian soldier appeared at the mouth of the cave. King Lawrence drew his pistol and shot him. Kyle scrambled behind a nearby rock for cover.

"You won't have me!" the king shouted to the Palatians. He followed Kyle and begged, "Please, take my life! Don't let me die in dishonor!"

Kyle looked helplessly at the king. "No. I can't!"

The king leaned against the cave wall, looking like a puppet that someone had casually thrown there. "This is the end," he said mournfully. "Oh, that it should come to this!" A tear slid down his face. "This is what it's like to die as a coward, without faith. May the Unseen One forgive me." He lifted the pistol and put it to the side of his head.

Kyle realized too late what was about to happen. He turned away as the king pulled the trigger. The sound of the blast exploded through the cave.

Kyle didn't remember much after that. He crawled away from the king on his hands and knees, the mud on the cave floor sticking to him like tar. His body convulsed from his sobs. With little strength left, he got to his feet. The Palatians were in the cave now. One raised the butt of his rifle and brought it crashing down on Kyle's back. The pain shot through his body and he thought, *This is what it's like to die as a coward. Without faith.* His mind was filled with images of pirates and adventure, of abandoned houses and a room with whispering voices, of guardian angels and being chosen by the Unseen One. *I was going to be a hero,* he thought. *But I didn't have patience. I didn't have faith.*

He closed his eyes as stars spun in his head. For a moment he thought he saw Anna peering at him through a hole in a ceiling.

Anna didn't tell Baron Orkzy what Darien had decided because she didn't want to spoil the element of surprise. She feared that the baron might blab to the Adrians that Darien was coming back to rescue them. As it turned out, the baron had bribed one of the guards and departed long before Darien's return.

Darien and his army didn't approach Lizah by the normal route. They circled around the south of the town, to the west, and caught the Adrian soldiers completely unawares. Darien's attack was swift and merciless. The Adrians who managed to escape told of the "mad Marutian general" for years to come. Others called it "Darien's Fury."

Darien never forgave the Adrians for the deception that took him away from the king in his hour of need.

Anna was still sitting in the red, velvet chair in the lobby of the Lizah Hotel when Darien and a handful of men burst in. The hostages cheered him. He ignored them and went straight to Anna. He knelt in front of her, his face dripping with sweat, his eyes a picture of worry.

"Well?" he asked.

"The king is dead," she said in a voice that seemed far, far away.

Darien lowered his head. When he looked up again, the sweat had been replaced with tears. They traced lines through the dust on his cheeks.

Colonel Oliver suddenly joined them. "General, we just heard on the shortwave," he said. "Our armies were defeated. Prince George was fatally wounded . . . and the king has been killed."

Somewhere in the room, a shout of joy went up.

Darien leaped to his feet and furiously cried out, "No! Be quiet, all of you! There'll be no joy. We'll have no celebration. The king—God's chosen—is dead. Let there be mourning and lamentation. Our king is dead."

The crowd was silenced, and the people slowly made their way out of the hotel.

"We must go to Sarum," Colonel Oliver said softly to Darien. "The nation needs your leadership now."

Darien looked at Anna. "Is it true?" he asked.

Anna nodded. "You are the king now."

"Will we be victorious over the Palatians?"

"You will, but at a great cost."

Darien gazed at her for a moment. "You're not going back to Sarum with me, are you?"

She shook her head slowly. "I'm going to find Kyle."

Darien didn't understand. He couldn't have. But he accepted it anyway. Kneeling again, he kissed her hand. "May the Unseen One allow us to meet again," he said softly.

She smiled at him. She hoped He would.

Darien and Colonel Oliver strode quickly from the hotel. Anna was alone. She felt a heaviness in her heart that seemed to weigh down her feet as well. She stood and walked sluggishly up the stairs to her room. She wasn't sure what she would find there, but she felt compelled to go.

Opening the door to her room, she saw that it was different. "Oh," she said. The furniture and carpets were gone, replaced by broken boards, peeling wallpaper, and dirt. A white light flashed, grew in intensity, and seemed to swallow her up.

Anna was on her hands and knees in the bedroom at the abandoned house back home. Somewhere, someone was groaning. She followed the sound to the door. Careful to avoid the section of the floor that had collapsed, she peeked through a large hole to the floor below. Kyle was lying there on his back. He was wearing his normal clothes. He moved his head slightly and groaned some more.

"Kyle!" she called out.

He didn't answer.

Anna navigated the upstairs hallway back to the stairs. She took them two at a time, then raced into the room where Kyle still lay, semiconscious from the fall.

"Don't move," she whispered in his ear. "I'll get help."

The little sister who had seemed to hate adventure and screamed at bugs ran with all her might back through the woods. How she found her way to her grandparents, she didn't know, but she did.

"What in the world . . . ?" her grandmother asked when Anna burst through the back door into the kitchen.

"In the woods—" Anna gasped, her breathlessness getting in the way of her words.

Her grandmother shook her head. "Calm down, child," she said. "Take a deep breath while I get you some lemonade."

"But Grandma—"

"I knew going to those woods was a bad idea," Grandma said as she started to pour a glass of lemonade. "I figured you were gone an awful long time. Two hours was long enough, but when it got to be three, well . . ." She *tsked* with her tongue.

"Three hours?" Anna said, shocked. "But we've been gone for months and months!"

"Don't exaggerate," Grandma scolded. "Now, where's your brother?"

"That's what I'm trying to tell you!" Anna cried out. "He's hurt!"

Grandma nearly dropped the pitcher of lemonade. Then, quickly regaining her composure, she shouted for Anna's grandfather to come quickly. Anna told them both about Kyle's fall. Grandma called an ambulance while Anna and Grandpa retraced Anna's steps to the abandoned house.

Kyle was kept in the hospital overnight. His back was bruised, and the doctors were worried that he might have fractured a rib in the fall. More than that, though, they wanted to be certain he didn't have a concussion. He seemed delirious when the ambulance brought him in. He kept talking about Darien, King Lawrence, and "a protector."

That evening, Anna sat alone with Kyle in his room. They didn't speak at first but seemed to scrutinize the room as if they'd never seen anything like it before. The silver metal on the bed frame above his head reflected the room in distorted shapes. The sheets on the bed were crisp and clean and smelled of detergent. A radio on the bedside table played a song by Doris Day. This was America. It was 1958.

He looked into her eyes. "They aren't different colors anymore," he finally said.

"I know."

"Was it a dream?" he asked.

Anna shrugged. "It seems like it now."

He looked away from her, and Anna thought he might cry. "I failed," he said miserably. "I stopped believing. I should've listened to you and waited."

Anna put her hand on his arm.

"I liked being a big shot," he said. "But I forgot who made me what I was."

A slight smile crossed Anna's face. Her brother seemed bigger, much older somehow.

He faced her again. "Are we still chosen?" he asked. "I mean, does it work that way here?"

Her gaze moved upward to a symbol above the bed—a cross. "Yeah," she said. "The Unseen One is here. We're chosen."

"But . . . for what?"

Anna shrugged. "That's what we're going to have to figure out. We were chosen for one thing in Marus. Maybe we're chosen for something else here."

They sat quietly together and thought about it until the nurse said it was time for lights out.

That night, Anna slept without dreams.

PASSAGES™
MARUS MANUSCRIPT 2

THE CHRONICLES OF THE DESTROYED
ARIN'S JUDGMENT

Manuscript date: September 18, 1945

PASSAGES™
ARIN'S JUDGMENT

Desert

ADRIA

KE
TER

The Wilderness

MECHLITE
TERRITORY

Field of the Great

MONROVIA

GOTTHARD

Great Canyon

Forests of Gotthard

MUIRK

PALATIA

Age of
Apostacy

BOOK 2
ARIN

Timeline = 2000 years

Glennall

IV

ALBANY

N
W E
S

Albany Road

The Downs

SARUM

LAHAMITE
TERRITORY

Liven's Mansion

Tyran's Castle

hailsham

Legend

~~~~~ River
----- Road

ONEN
RITORY

of the Rocks

Fendar   Period of   Darien Draven   Annison
          the Judges

VI   ////////   I   V   III

A punch to the stomach sent Wade Mullens doubled over to the ground. Black spots pulsated before his eyes, and he barely heard Steve Calloway mutter, "Kraut-loving freak!" before he walked away.

Bobby Adams rushed up to Wade. "Are you all right?" he asked. His voice seemed miles away.

"I . . . can't . . . breathe . . ." Wade croaked.

"Stay calm," Bobby said. "Relax."

Wade rolled around on the ground, gasping like a fish out of water. After a few minutes, the air came back to him and he sat up.

Bobby knelt next to him. "Oh, boy, you're going to have a shiner," he announced.

Wade gently touched his left eye where Steve had punched him right before the decisive blow to his stomach. He could feel the eye swelling up.

"Can you stand up?" Bobby asked.

Wade nodded. Clasping hands with Bobby, he was tugged to his feet. His legs were wobbly.

"Where are my books?" Wade asked.

"All over the place," Bobby replied. Silently the two boys retrieved Wade's books, which had been littered around the school yard by Steve and his gang.

Bobby, a stout boy of 11 with curly brown hair, grunted at the exertion of bending over for the books and bits of paper.

Wade dusted the dirt from his blond hair and checked his clothes. A black eye was bad enough, but if he'd torn his trousers or shirt, his mother would have a fit. Apart from smudges of grass and mud, however, they seemed to be all right.

Bobby shook his head. "You shouldn't have said it. How many times did I tell you not to say it?"

Wade shrugged. "I was just stating a fact."

"Fact or not, you can't go around talking about German airplanes as if you *like* them," Bobby said.

"All I said was that the Messerschmitt has a sleek design. What's so bad about that?"

"And you said that the German Me-262 has turbojet power and beats anything we've invented."

"It's true. It has a top speed of 540 miles per hour, and that's a lot faster than—"

"You don't have to tell me! I'm the one who first told you about the Me-262, remember? But Steve's dad was at Omaha Beach on D-Day! You can't talk to people like Steve about the Germans unless it's something you *hate* about them. Otherwise you sound like a traitor."

"I'm not a traitor. Steve's dad came home after the Germans surrendered. My dad is still—" Wade stopped, unable to continue. America had just dropped two atomic bombs on Japan a month before, and the Japanese had surrendered, but Wade and his mother still hadn't heard anything about his father. He'd been missing somewhere in the South Pacific for several weeks.

"You know that and I know that, but Steve doesn't know." Bobby handed him a sheet of paper he'd picked up from the ground. It was a picture Wade had drawn of the B-29 Superfortress, number 77. *Bockscar,* it was called. It had carried the second A-bomb to Japan.

In Wade's picture, the plane flew through clear skies. Somewhere below lay the great shipping center called Nagasaki, represented by a distant shoreline and dots depicting buildings. There were no people in Wade's picture because, like most Americans, he didn't want to think about the thousands who'd died from the two bombs. But, also like most Americans, he was glad that the force of those bombs, equivalent to 20,000 to 40,000 tons of TNT, had persuaded the Japanese to surrender. Now maybe they'd find his dad and let him come home.

Wade took a moment to assemble his textbooks so he could carry them home. Jammed between the books were comic books about space travel and war, a science-fiction novel, and one of the academic journals lent to him by Mr. Curfew, his neighbor. He'd brought that in for show-and-tell, and to tell the class about the various weapons of war. He had told them about the B-17G, the "Flying Fortress Bomber," which was able to carry more than 6,000 tons of bombs over 2,000 miles. He'd also described the Hawker Tempest Mark V, with its ability to go faster than 400 miles per hour; it was one of the few Allied planes that could catch and destroy the German "buzz bombs" (the V-1 jet-powered bombs). Then he'd mentioned the superiority of the Messerschmitt's design and the Me-262's speed. This last part had guaranteed his afternoon fight with Steve Calloway.

Wade had tried to explain to Steve that he didn't like the war or the Germans, but that didn't stop him from learning about the machines and weapons they'd used in the war. Steve wouldn't hear it, and the fists had begun to fly.

"Remember Pearl Harbor!" Steve had proclaimed when he hit Wade in the eye. "Remember the death march on Bataan!" he had then shouted before hitting Wade in the stomach.

Wade and Bobby made their way toward home.

"Do you want to stop by my house to clean up?" Bobby asked.

Wade nodded.

"Good, because there's something I want to show you."

Bobby's mother worked afternoons at the downtown Hudson's Drug Store, so the two boys could move around the house without adult supervision. Wade gave himself a quick wash in the bathroom while Bobby's seven-year-old sister kept asking why Wade's eye was so puffed up. *It looks bad, all right,* Wade thought as he inspected it in the mirror. It was already taking on the telltale tones of blue, black, and yellow.

Bobby gestured for Wade to follow him into his bedroom, then nearly closed the door on his younger sister, who whined and protested for a few minutes.

"Look what my cousin sent me," Bobby said quietly. He looked around the room and out the window, then double-checked to make sure his sister was gone before spreading some pages out on his desk. On them were rough drawings of what looked like a large bomb.

"What are these?" Wade asked.

"Top secret," Bobby said.

"Top secret?"

Bobby's voice fell to a whisper. "This is from my cousin Lee in *New Mexico.*"

"So?"

"So! New Mexico is where they've been working on the atomic bomb."

Wade looked from Bobby's face to the pages, then back to Bobby's face again. "You mean . . . ?"

"My cousin Lee's dad—my uncle Walter—is a scientist who's been working on the atomic bomb. Lee made these drawings from some papers and photos he'd seen in his dad's briefcase."

Wade's heart lurched. "Are you crazy?" he asked breathlessly.

"There are spies out there who would *kill* to get their hands on stuff like this."

"Yeah, I know," Bobby said. "Why do you think I'm being so careful?"

Wade pointed to the next page. "What's all this stuff?"

"I think it's how they make them. See?"

Wade glanced over the list: "Uranium 235 . . . Uranium 238 . . . plutonium . . . nuclear fission . . . isotopes . . . altimeter . . . air pressure detonator . . . detonating head . . . urea nitrate . . . lead shield . . ."

"Lee said he scribbled down everything he could," Bobby explained.

Wade's mouth was hanging open now. He read about how the various components interacted to cause an explosion. He also saw a page about the effects of radiation on human subjects after the bombs exploded. Many were burned, and some got sick and died. It also warned of radiation getting into water systems and sources of food. "We shouldn't be seeing this," he said finally.

"I know," Bobby said, smiling. "That's why I showed it to you."

"We have to get rid of it."

"I figured I'd throw it in the furnace as soon as we looked it over," Bobby agreed. "Uncle Walt would put Lee on restriction for the rest of his life if he knew Lee had mailed this to me."

Suddenly a voice at the door said, "Bobby?" It was his mother. The door handle turned. Acting quickly, Bobby grabbed and folded the sheets of paper and shoved them under Wade's untucked shirt. "What's going on in here?" Bobby's mother asked.

"Nothing," Bobby answered with a voice that said just the opposite.

His mother eyed him suspiciously, then looked at Wade. "Good heavens! What happened to you?" she said. "Is that a black eye?"

Wade stammered incoherently.

"He fell down on the way home from school," Bobby lied.

"Looks more like you were in a fight," his mother said. "I think you should go home right away."

"But—" Bobby started to protest.

"No 'buts' about it." She put a hand on Wade's shoulder and guided him out of the room. "You go home and get that eye looked at," she instructed him.

Bobby's mother stayed with Wade all the way down the stairs to the front door. He tried to think of a way to get the papers back to Bobby, but Bobby's mother was in the way the entire time. She handed him his jacket and books. Bobby shrugged helplessly at Wade as Wade walked through the door and it closed between them.

On the front porch, Wade zipped up his jacket and pressed his books to his chest. He could feel the papers under his shirt. He looked around nervously. What if there were spies watching him? What if the government found out that Lee had sent the drawings to Bobby and secret agents were coming to arrest them even now? Wade swallowed hard and walked quickly down the steps of the front porch and out onto the street. His walk soon became a run as he took off for home.

Every casual glance from people he passed took on sinister meaning. *They know about the papers,* he kept thinking. A large black sedan drove past, then suddenly pulled up next to him. *It's them! It's the agents!* Wade thought. The door opened, and Wade cried out—then blushed with embarrassment as an older woman got out of the car to put a letter in the curbside mailbox.

He ducked down some back alleys and zigzagged through his neighborhood, just to make sure he wasn't being followed. When he finally reached his own home, he burst through the front door and raced up the stairs to his room.

"Wade?" his mother called from the kitchen.

Wade dropped the books on his bed, pulled out the papers, and shoved them under his mattress. It was the only place he could think to hide them on the spur of the moment.

His mother called for him from the bottom of the stairs. Forgetting about his black eye, he went back to the top and smiled down at her. "Hi," he said innocently.

"What in the world are you doing?" she asked.

"Putting my books away."

"Why the rush? Didn't you hear me call you from the kitchen?" She wiped her hands on her apron.

"I'm sorry," he said.

"What's that on your face?"

"My face?"

"Come down here," she ordered. Wade went down the stairs to her. She gasped. "Your eye! You've got a black eye!"

"I—"

"Who was it this time, Richard King or Jim McClendon?"

"It doesn't matter," Wade said, shuffling uncomfortably as she ran her fingers gently around his eye.

"Oh, Wade!" she said. "Into the kitchen right now. We're putting an ice pack on it."

Wade groaned.

"And don't make a fuss."

As he walked down the hall toward the kitchen, he suddenly sneezed. It made his eye throb. Then, in the kitchen, he sneezed again.

"Are you coming down with a cold?" his mother asked.

Only then was Wade aware that his nose was running.

It *was* an illness. And in spite of Wade's protests, his mother insisted that he have a bath after putting an ice pack on his eye and then spend the rest of the evening in bed. As the night progressed, he began to feel worse. By bedtime, he had a full-fledged flu of some sort. His mother made him stay home from school the next day. And the day after. What made Wade feel worst of all, though, was knowing Steve and his gang would think Wade had missed school because of his black eye. When he returned to class, they would call him a sissy and a baby, and the teasing would be far more difficult to take than if they'd gotten into another fight.

In his illness, Wade dreamed of evil-looking men trying to sneak into his bedroom to steal the drawings of the atomic bomb. He dreamed of being arrested by government agents who accused him of being a spy. He saw his name in horrible accusatory headlines on the cover of every newspaper in the country. "Spy!" they said. "Hang him!" the editorials demanded. His mother would live in shame, and his father would never be allowed to come home from wherever he was.

A scraping sound echoed distantly in the heat duct near the door. The sound penetrated his deep sleep. He knew instantly what it was: His mother was in the basement, trying to throw some life into their old coal furnace. From the sounds of it, she wasn't having much success.

Wade swung his legs over the side of the bed and pushed his feet into his slippers. The cool air of the room made him realize his pajamas were slightly damp. His fever had broken, he knew. He stood up, expecting to feel light-headed. To his surprise, he felt normal—good, in fact. His eye didn't hurt as much, either. A glance in the mirror showed him that the swelling was nearly gone and the color wasn't as bad as it had been. He grabbed his robe from the back of the door and suddenly had an idea: Now would be the time to burn the papers about the atomic bomb. He slipped them out from under the mattress, tucked them inside his pajama top, then wrapped his robe snug around him.

"Mom," Wade said when he rounded the furnace in the basement.

Wade's mother looked at him. Her face was smudged with coal. Black streaks also covered her hands, the sleeves of her blouse, and her apron. His mother had never learned the knack of working the furnace, and she got tearfully upset with it. More than once, she'd said that she could endure nearly everything about the war except that furnace. "When your father gets home, we're going to tear it out and get a new one," she'd say. "Do you hear?"

Wade always nodded and agreed.

"What are you doing out of bed?" she asked now, her face flushed.

"I came down to help you."

Mrs. Mullens jabbed a shovel at the inside of the furnace. "I don't need your help," she said. "You should be in bed."

"I'm feeling much better," he replied. He reached up and put his hand on her arm to take the shovel. She frowned, then surrendered the shovel to him. Wade smiled.

"You're the expert, aren't you?" she said as she stroked his blond hair—hair just like hers. "Planes, bombs, and furnaces. Your father is going to be very proud to see how you've grown up."

Wade poked at the fire. "We need more coal."

"He'll be home soon, you know," she said.

Wade turned to her with an expression of understanding. "I know."

But the truth was, he *didn't* know. Neither of them did. The chaos of the war against the Japanese in the Pacific—the many soldiers who had fought on the tiny islands around the Philippines—caused a lot of confusion about who was where. No one was sure what had become of Henry Mullens as the war came to a close. He may simply have been one of many soldiers who'd been separated from his unit. Or he might have been captured, wounded, or killed.

"I would like some tea, please," he said to his mother as he went to the coal cellar in the back corner of the basement. "I'll fix the furnace and then come right up."

She pondered him, then turned to go upstairs. "I hate this furnace," she said as she walked away. "When your father comes home, we're going to—"

"Tear it out and get a new one," Wade called out.

"Brat!" she said with a smile in her voice. He heard her footsteps going up the basement stairs.

Wade wrenched open the door to the coal cellar. Black soot swirled up and around him. He flipped the switch for the single light that hung by a bare wire from the ceiling. It didn't turn on. "Bulb's out," he said.

Enough light shone in from the furnace room for him to get a bucket of coal, however, so he stepped inside to do just that. Retrieving the empty bucket from where it hung by a peg on the wall, he went to the edge of the pile of coal and started shoveling. Now that his mother was gone, he would throw the papers about the atomic bomb into the furnace with this coal.

He was glad he felt well again. He hated being sick; he missed his talks at lunch, during recess, and after school with Bobby Adams. For the two of them, fascination with the war had taken the place of their fascination with sports. They spoke of the various armed services the way other boys spoke about baseball teams.

He even missed being in his classes, annoying his teachers with his obsession about the war and his extensive knowledge of the weapons and machines that had brought the war to a conclusion. He wondered what they would think if they knew he had top secret drawings of the atomic bomb.

The doorbell rang upstairs, and Wade heard his mother's footsteps go across the floor. *I wonder who's here?* he thought, and then he suddenly realized, *It may be government agents! They've come to arrest me for having these papers!*

Wade spun around to rush back to the furnace. He could burn them quickly, and no one would ever know. But just then the cellar door blew closed.

"Oh, brother," he said in the sudden deep darkness. He made his way carefully to the door and pushed at it. Nothing happened. He pushed again, but it wouldn't budge. He fiddled with the latch, which lifted easily enough, but still the door wouldn't open. He pounded on it and called out, "Mom? Mom!"

He listened, but she didn't reply.

"Mom!" he called out as loudly as he could. Then he pounded some more with the back of the shovel. "Mom!"

He heard heavy footsteps outside the door and relaxed. He was sure that between the two of them, they could get the door unstuck.

The effort wasn't necessary, however. The door suddenly swung open without any problems.

"Thank you," Wade said.

"You're welcome," an old man he'd never seen before replied.

The old man carried a lantern and held it high for a closer look at Wade. His eyes narrowed beneath thick gray eyebrows. "Heaven help me!" he exclaimed. "What are you doing here?"

"What am *I* doing here? What are *you* doing here?" Wade asked indignantly.

The old man's eyes widened. Wade noticed that they were two different colors, one blue and the other green. "Why, I'm about to feed Bethel," he said.

"Feed Bethel? In my basement?" Wade challenged the stranger. His father had always said that the best way to put off an intruder was by being forceful. Never show fear, he'd said. Wade raised the shovel like a weapon. "Where's my mother?" he demanded to know.

"Your—? I have no idea. Come out of there before you're bitten."

"Bitten?"

"Bethel doesn't take kindly to strangers." The old man gestured to the corner behind Wade. A horse stood there, gazing at Wade with disdain.

Wade stepped back, mouth agape. The coal was gone. Straw and hay covered the floor. Where the bucket had been sitting a moment ago, now sat a trough. The cement wall that had enclosed the coal cellar was also changed; it was now made of wooden slats. "What happened?" Wade stammered.

"Come out now," the old man said patiently. "You've been caught. You may as well confess."

"Confess?"

"You're one of those vandals from town, aren't you? Come to do me mischief."

"No! This is my house!"

"This place may be a lot of different things, but it's certainly not your house." The old man beckoned to Wade. "Come out and explain yourself."

Wade, still staring at what used to be his coal cellar, slowly walked out. His basement was gone, too—no furnace, no workbench, no boxes of keepsakes or the furniture his father had intended to donate to charity. Instead, Wade now looked at what seemed to be a large barn—a *very* large barn, the biggest he'd ever seen. It must have been as long as a football field, maybe even as wide. Along the sides were compartments of stalls, pens, and cages. Pipes stretched the length of the ceiling, some of them feeding down into the various compartments. Lanterns dotted the walls, casting a bright, ethereal yellow over the expanse. Wade blinked, sure that he was dreaming. *I must be dreaming,* he thought. *Why else would I be hearing a lion roar, a pig snort, and a monkey chatter?*

The old man closed the door to Bethel's stall. "Stay put," he said to the horse. "I'll be back."

Wade turned to the old man. He was tall and thin, with a slender, clean-shaved face and a mop of white hair. He wore a long tunic that was belted in the middle. "Something's wrong," Wade said.

"Obviously." The old man reached out and tugged at Wade's sleeve. "What do you call this outfit? The latest city fashion?"

Wade looked down and realized he was still in his robe, pajamas, and slippers. "I'm dreaming," he said.

"Maybe so. Or maybe *I'm* the one who's dreaming. It wouldn't be the first time." He quickly caught hold of Wade's hair.

"Ouch!" Wade cried out. "What are you doing?"

"I wanted to see if it's real." Satisfied, the old man let go.

"It's real. What did you think, I was wearing a wig?"

The old man smiled. "I don't know where you'd ever find a wig that color. Now tell me what you're doing in Bethel's stall."

"I wasn't in Bethel's stall. I mean, I wasn't before. I was getting coal for our furnace, and the door closed behind me and I couldn't get out." Wade spoke as much to himself as to the old man, trying to retrace what had happened.

"I heard you pounding on the door," the old man said, as if confirming that part of Wade's story was true. "But there's no coal or furnace. Just Bethel."

"I must be hallucinating. My fever. That's it. I'm in a feverish delirium." Wade felt his forehead. "But I feel fine. I feel great. This is very strange."

"Listen to the way you talk. 'Delirium.' What kind of boy uses such a word?"

"My teachers say I'm precocious," Wade replied simply.

"Where are you from?"

"America."

"I've never heard of it."

Wade felt a cold rush go through his body. *Never heard of America?* He had to think. Either the man was crazy or he was. "Then . . . where do *you* think I am?" he asked.

The old man chuckled. "It's not where I *think* you are. It's where you *are*. You're standing in my shelter."

"Shelter."

"Yes, my shelter. How you got in here is a mystery to me, I have to say. We've only got two doors, one that's always locked, except when we're bringing the animals or supplies in. We have to keep a close eye on things, what with the vandals and troublemakers."

"I don't understand."

"Neither do I, but that's the way of things. Let's start with the basics. My name is Arin."

"I'm Wade Mullens."

"Glad to meet you, Wade Mullens, providing you aren't some kind of spy," Arin said, half-bowing to the boy. The word *spy* stopped Wade for a second. He wondered if this strange situation was because of the papers tucked under his pajama top.

"*I'm* not a spy," Wade insisted.

"And this had better not be some sort of trick," Arin warned.

"If it's a trick, it's being played on me."

The old man put a firm hand on Wade's shoulder and directed him onward. "Well, there's no point in standing here asking a lot of confusing questions. We'll get to the truth when you say what you've got to say. Let's go up to the house."

They crossed the floor to a large steel door that opened to a wide ramp leading upward. At the top, Arin turned a knob on the lantern, and the light faded. Only then did Wade realize that the lantern didn't generate light from a flame, as he had assumed, but from a thin tube. Arin hung the lantern on a hook, then opened another steel door. Wade had to shield his eyes from the bright sunlight outside.

"This way," Arin said, his hand still on Wade's shoulder.

When Wade could see clearly, what struck him first was that he was in a beautiful forest, thick with foliage and rich with growth. He could *feel* the life, if such a thing were possible. And the colors! The greens of the grass and leaves on the trees seemed much greener, the sky above much bluer, the shafts of dancing light through the trees much more golden than he'd ever seen before. It reminded him of the Technicolor films he and his mother some-times saw at the movies. It was all so much *realer* than real.

He also noticed the sweet perfume of the flowers lining the

path ahead. He had no idea what they were, only that they filled the air with fragrances that made him think of vast gardens and fresh-cut lawns. He took several deep breaths as if he couldn't get enough of the scents.

His eye caught Arin watching him. "I'm sorry," Wade said. "It's so . . . beautiful."

"Yes," Arin said. "This was the first garden. The one from the beginning."

"The beginning?"

"This is where the Unseen One started, when our world was first created."

"I don't know what the Unseen One is."

Arin *tsked* loudly. "And they wonder why our world is so evil! Little surprise that you're a vandal."

"I'm not a vandal!" Wade complained. "Please don't say that. I . . . I'm either dreaming or I'm lost. I don't know which."

They reached a tall stone wall and veered around on the path to the right. Directly ahead was a cottage, also made of stone. At the door, Arin paused to touch his forehead and heart lightly with his forefinger before going in. "Muiraq!" he called out.

Inside, the cottage was plain but comfortable in a homey way. The front door opened to a sitting room with a few wingback chairs, a sofa, a coffee table, and a hutch in front of a fireplace. Everything was constructed of dark wood with ornate, carved swirls and curves. Wade instantly suspected it had been handmade.

Up three steps was a dining area and a larger staircase leading to another floor. A woman emerged from a room off the dining area. She wiped her hands on an apron as she entered, giving Wade the impression she was working in the kitchen. Round-bodied and round-faced, she reminded Wade of Grandma Milly, his father's mother. The thought put him at ease.

"Yes, Arin?" she said. She saw Wade and put a hand to her mouth to stifle a gasp. Composing herself, she simply said, "Oh, hello."

"This is Wade Mullens. My wife, Muiraq."

"It's a pleasure to meet you." She half-curtsied.

"I found him in the shelter. In Bethel's stall, to be precise."

"Honestly? And she didn't bite him?"

"No. I'm surprised, too. But no more surprised than to find him there at all. He has an unusual explanation."

"Does he? Then he should sit down. Is he hungry? I was just preparing lunch."

"Are you hungry?" Arin asked Wade.

Wade wasn't sure, and in the second it took him to think of an answer, Muiraq had already disappeared into the other room. "Of course he is," she said from the kitchen. "What boy isn't?"

"You're going to feed me?" Wade asked as he followed Arin to the dining table.

"The Unseen One would have us treat even our enemies with kindness. And if you're not our enemy, we should be hospitable anyway."

Wade sat down. He wasn't sure he followed the logic of Arin's statement, but he accepted it anyway.

Muiraq returned with a plate of sandwiches, fruit, and cheese. "Help yourself," she said and sat down. Arin poured a sweet fruit juice into wooden cups from a large jug in the middle of the table.

Wade had already put a slice of apple in his mouth when Arin and Muiraq bowed their heads to pray. Embarrassed, Wade stayed still until the blessing was said, then resumed eating. He was hungrier than he had thought.

"Tell us your story," Arin prompted. "You said you're from a place called America and that your furnace needed coal." He bit into a sandwich.

Wade started again, telling them how he'd been in bed with a flu and—

"Flu?" Arin asked. "What's a flu?"

"An illness, when you have chills and a fever and runny nose and—" He paused. "You've never heard of the flu?"

"Not the kind you describe. Carry on with your story."

"Anyway, I felt better and went down in the basement to help my mother with the furnace."

"Furnace?"

Wade nodded. "A coal furnace."

"Coal?" Arin's face lit up with surprise. "You use a *coal* furnace?"

"Yes, sir. Don't tell me you've never heard of a coal furnace either?"

"Oh, we've heard of them. We just never met anyone who's used them," Arin said.

"Where is your father?" Muiraq asked.

Wade noticed that her eyes kept going from his face up to his hair and back again. "He hasn't come back from the war yet," he answered.

"War?"

"Not just my hometown, the whole country. The United States of America. It was at war with Germany and Japan and their allies."

"I've never heard of any of those countries," said Arin.

"It was a big war. Nearly everybody was fighting in it."

"Was? The war is over?" Arin speared a piece of cheese with his knife and tossed it onto Wade's plate.

"Thank you," Wade said and ate the cheese. It was sweet, unlike any cheese he'd known. He continued with his answer, "We beat Germany, and then we dropped a couple of atomic bombs on Japan, and they surrendered just a few days ago."

Arin and Muiraq exchanged glances.

Wade thought they didn't believe him. "It's true!" he insisted.

"We don't doubt you, lad," Muiraq said soothingly.

"You don't?"

"No," said Arin.

Muiraq turned to her husband. "Do you think—?" she said. "Look at him. Is it possible that he's the sign?"

Arin looked at his wife, choosing his words carefully. "Yes, Muiraq, I believe he is," he replied. "It all fits, doesn't it? The final sign."

"I'm a what? A sign?" Wade asked.

Suddenly, a man with curly hair and beard burst into the room. He said breathlessly, "Come quick, Father. They're—" He caught sight of Wade and stopped midsentence in astonishment. Recovering himself, he continued, "They're back."

Arin was immediately on his feet and raced out the door on his son's heels.

Muiraq sighed deeply. "Why won't they leave us alone?" she asked as she stood up and followed Arin. Unsure of what to do, Wade went along.

The tall stone wall that served as a fence around Arin's estate had a large gold gate in it. As Wade approached, he could hear what sounded like a battering ram hitting the gate again and again. Arin and the bearded man were there, along with two younger men and three younger women. They spread out around the gate as if they weren't certain whether it would withstand the blows. Rocks and garbage were hurled at them over the wall, causing them all to duck and dodge. Shouts of abuse were also thrown at them.

"What's wrong? Why are they doing this?" Wade asked Muiraq.

"A drunken mob with nothing better to do with their time, I think," she replied. "It's happening more and more these days."

"What should we do, Father?" the bearded one asked.

"I'll go out and talk to them," Arin responded.

"They'll tear you apart," one of the other young men said.

"They don't have the courage," Arin said. "They're brave as long as this wall stands between us. Face-to-face, they know with whom they're dealing. They won't harm me. It's not within their power."

Arin went to the gate. Within its frame was a smaller, man-sized door. He lifted the enormous bar that secured the door and handed it to the bearded man, who struggled against its weight. Only then did Wade have some idea of how strong Arin must be. Arin nodded to his wife, took a deep breath, then opened the door to the crowd. The people went silent at the sight of the old man.

Arin asked in a calm voice, "What do you want?"

No one replied.

"Simply out for an afternoon stroll and some vandalism, is that it?" Arin said with a wry smile.

"We want to know what you're up to behind those walls!" a man shouted.

"You know very well what I'm up to. I've made it clear to you for years now."

"We want to see," challenged a woman.

"Ah, but that you will not do," Arin said and held up his hand. "Repent, turn your hearts to the Unseen One, and you will see. Until then, you'll remain in your blindness and ignorance."

A husky-voiced man called out, "Just who are you to call us blind? Who made you our judge?"

Arin spread his arms as if reasoning with them. "I am not judging you. Only the Unseen One judges. And He has judged you. The wickedness of this generation has reached His nostrils like the stench of a decaying corpse. He has given you every chance to repent, to return to Him. But you refuse. So His judgment is coming. It's closer than you think."

"You've been saying that for years!" another man shouted.

"Yes!" Arin replied. "And to think that you've had all those years to repent, to show good faith in the Unseen One. But have you? No! But the day is coming—it is here!"

A man laughed scornfully. "He's going to wipe us all out, is that what you're saying?" he challenged. "The Unseen One's going to destroy us all!"

Arin turned to Muiraq. "Bring the boy," he instructed.

Muiraq put her hand on Wade's back. Wade resisted when he realized he was the boy Arin wanted.

"It's all right," she said softly. "You won't get hurt."

"Why does he want me?" Wade asked. "I don't have anything to do with this."

"Oh yes, you do. More than you know."

Wade allowed himself to be guided forward to the door. Anybody who looked like Grandma Milly wouldn't do anything to harm him, he reasoned.

"The final sign is here," Arin announced to the crowd. "See for yourselves." With that, Arin pulled Wade into view.

The crowd gasped and shrank back. Some of them cried out.

Wade wanted to run back inside the gate. He couldn't imagine what was so hideous about his features that people would react that way. He hoped it was the robe. He had never liked the color of it. It had been a gift from his aunt Priscilla.

"It's a trick!" someone said.

But no one stuck around to find out whether the statement was true. The people backed farther and farther from the door, then turned and scattered in various directions down the street. Many of them kept looking back with expressions of fear. One man lifted a rock and came forward as if he might throw it at them, but Arin's steely look made him think twice. He dropped the rock and ran away.

Arin and Wade stepped back inside. Arin's son secured the door again.

"I don't understand," Wade said. "Why did they act like that? Why were they scared of me?"

"Because of your hair," Arin said.

"My hair?"

"Your golden hair," Muiraq affirmed. "The final sign of the Unseen One's judgment was to be the arrival of a child with golden hair."

Back inside the cottage, Arin began to explain, "When I was a young man, the Unseen One spoke to me."

"Wait, please," Wade said. "I still don't understand who the Unseen One is."

"The Unseen One is the creator and sustainer of all things. He fashioned us from the earth, breathed life into us, and chose to love us in spite of our rebellion. He exists in your world, I'm sure. Your world would not exist without Him."

Wade thought about it. "Our 'Unseen One' is called 'God,' if that's what you mean."

"God may be another name for the Unseen One. But in our world, the name *God* is easily confused with the false gods many of the people worship. From the ancient days, we have called Him the Unseen One."

Wade had never thought much about God. His mother and father were good people who seemed to believe in God. They talked about God when good or bad things happened. But they never took Wade to church or asked him to read the large family Bible that decorated the end table.

Arin continued, "The Unseen One spoke to me—"

"How?" Wade interrupted again.

"How?" Arin seemed perplexed by the question. "The same way one person speaks to another. How else?"

"You heard Him?"

"Yes."

"A voice," Wade pressed. "You heard a voice?"

"A voice, yes. *The* voice."

"What did He sound like?"

Arin frowned impatiently. "I wouldn't know how to tell you, lad. I've never found the words to describe it. Nor could I do an imitation."

"I'm sorry," Wade said. "I won't interrupt you anymore."

Arin went on, "He told me that the sins of this generation were more than He could stand. The people have given up His truth for their own lies. He's been repeatedly rejected by His own creation, and He now wishes to begin again. He called me to speak His message of repentance to the people while I built a refuge."

"You mean the shelter I saw, the one underground."

Arin affirmed Wade with a nod. "It is our protection when His judgment comes."

"He *told you* to build the shelter?" Wade still had a difficult time believing that God, or the Unseen One, literally talked to Arin.

"He gave the specific design to me. Every inch, every detail is from Him. I have spent the past 60 years building it. When my sons were old enough, they helped as well."

"There were animals down there, too," Wade said.

"The Unseen One told me to gather the animals, to save them from the destruction."

"What kind of destruction?" Wade's mind continued to try to sort through these facts.

"I don't know. That's something He didn't care to let me in on."

Wade glanced around the room. Everyone in the family stared back at him, their eyes drifting at one time or another to his hair. He felt like a freak. He didn't like being the center of attention. "What about the signs—my 'golden hair'?" he asked.

"Ah, that," Arin replied. "The Unseen One told me that the wickedness of His creation would increase throughout my lifetime. Forces of evil would be invited into the hearts of all mankind, destroying their humanity and replacing it with depravity and decadence."

"That's always the first thing to go when people turn their backs on the Unseen One," Muiraq said sadly. "Their humanity."

"That's because the Unseen One is the source of our humanity," Arin agreed. "Once we have dispensed with Him, we have dispensed with our true selves. So what's left? Men who commit heinous and immoral acts become heroes, giants in the land. Lives become expendable to wicked ideals and causes. We celebrate inhumanity because we no longer understand what it is to be human. Corruption spreads to the very root of mankind's being. So the Unseen One said He would lay the ax to the root. He would obliterate what He's created and we—my family and I—would begin anew."

"That makes you pretty lucky, I guess," Wade said.

"Lucky? There is no luck. The Unseen One has chosen us. And as is often true of being chosen, sometimes it is a blessing, but other times it is a curse. I have spent most of my life being mocked and ridiculed. What you saw today was only one small incident. We've had worse. Much worse."

"Arin," Muiraq interjected. "The signs. He asked about the signs."

"Oh yes," Arin said, recovering himself. "The signs. One was the wickedness of mankind. Another was mankind's rejection of the Unseen One for other faiths and idols. A third was the emergence of corrupt leaders, of which we have many, with not a single faithful person among them. The final was the arrival of a golden-haired child in this land of dark-haired individuals. Until you arrived today, I had always believed it would be a baby. Perhaps one of my sons and his wife would give birth to this golden-haired child. But now you are here."

"But I'm not from the Unseen One. I'm from America," Wade said. "Don't you see? It's a bizarre coincidence."

"Wherever you are from, however you came here, I have no doubt that you're the one. You're the final sign. It is now only a small matter of time."

Wade's mind was reeling. It was all too much to take in. He looked around the room at their faces. Arin and Muiraq wore expressions of a gentle tolerance, as if they understood more about his doubt and confusion than even he knew.

He glanced at the two young men he'd seen at the gate, now sitting on the sofa. They were Pool and Riv, Arin and Muiraq's second and third sons. Pool was round-faced, like his mother. Riv was slender, with his father's narrow face and sparkling eyes. Next to them were their wives, Nacob and Hesham. Even though Wade was still too young to like girls much, he appreciated that Nacob and Hesham were pretty. One had straight black hair, dark skin, and penetrating blue eyes; the other had shorter, curly hair, a fairer complexion, and eyes like half moons, as if they were smiling all the time.

Next to the fireplace stood the bearded man who'd come in earlier to tell them about the attack. His name was Oshan. He was the oldest son. He stood quietly while his wife, Etham, sat nearby, knitting an item of clothing. Wade found he couldn't take his eyes off her. She had an angelic face, with wide eyes and a pleasant mouth that turned upward at the corners, as if she were remembering a joke she couldn't tell. Her curly dark hair fell like waves upon her shoulders. And there was something about her eyes. She reminded Wade of his mother.

Wade stood up and said firmly, "I tell you I'm not from the Unseen One." His voice caught in his throat. This didn't make sense. None of it did. "Excuse me," he said, then he raced outside to throw up.

When he had wretched as much as he could, Arin appeared with a cup of water for him. He rinsed his mouth, spat, then drank the water in earnest. "Thank you," he said when he could speak.

"You honestly don't know what's happening to you," Arin said sympathetically.

"No. I want to go home. I want my mother." He began to cry.

Arin pulled him close in an embrace that, if Wade had closed his eyes, might have been his father's. "If the Unseen One has brought you here, then perhaps He will take you home, too."

Wade thought that was a lot to ask a kid to believe, especially one who didn't believe in the Unseen One. For all he knew, these people were completely insane. Maybe he'd gone insane, too.

Somewhere in the distance, a low pounding filled the air, like someone banging rhythmically on a bass drum. "What's that?" Wade asked.

"Bombs and antiaerocraft cannons," Arin replied. "They're trying to destroy the aeroplanes from Belgarum that are bombing the city."

Wade was dumbfounded. "You're being attacked by airplanes?"

"We are at war on all sides," Arin replied. "There are no neighbors to our country anymore, only enemies."

"What kind of planes are they? Spitfires? Mustangs? Messerschmitts?"

"We speak the same language, but sometimes I don't understand a word you say," Arin said with a chuckle.

"I wonder what kind of planes they are," Wade said, trying to be more clear.

"I couldn't tell you. Weapons of destruction never interested me. I couldn't help but feel that they were yet another indicator that the end is coming."

"Are we safe here?"

Arin patted the boy on the back. "The Unseen One keeps His promises. We're safe."

Wade was taken inside and given clothes that Muiraq had made for Riv when he was Wade's age. The outfit consisted of long cotton trousers, a shirt of the same style as a T-shirt, and a thin robe with a belt covering both. The trousers had deep pockets on the sides, so as he put them on he carefully folded the papers of the atomic bomb plans and slid them into the left pocket. He then strapped on a pair of leather sandals. Wade was impressed with how comfortable the outfit was, and he said so when he thanked Muiraq.

She blushed a deep crimson. "It's my honor to provide them for you," she said. "Now, we'll be eating dinner shortly, so make yourself at home.

"May I look around?" he asked.

"Of course."

Wade's first inclination was to look at the many books on the shelves lining the rooms on the second floor. He was surprised to find that they were printed and bound with a greater quality than any books he'd owned. The reference books—encyclopedias, manuals, and educational texts—had full-color pages and photographs. This was something he'd rarely seen, and only in the most expensive books. The other books covered every topic imaginable: law, medicine, science, the arts, and, mostly, essays and instructions about the Unseen One. Wade skimmed through them all but felt as if they were written in another language. This world—whatever and wherever it was—had a different history from his own. He'd hoped to find an overlap somewhere, something to show that maybe he wasn't in a different world after all. But he couldn't find one, except maybe the being he knew as God and the one they called the Unseen One.

Turning his attention from the books, Wade was curious about the technology of the house. It seemed a lot like his own, until he realized that none of the rooms had power sockets. This wouldn't have been unusual if they didn't have electricity, but they did. Or they seemed to. The lights in the guest room had switches on them. As expected, they made the lights go on and off. But something was wrong.

"Don't you have lights where you come from?" Riv asked when he caught Wade toying with a light in the front room.

"Yes. Just like these," Wade said. "But your lamps aren't plugged into the wall." Wade gestured to the one he had been examining. "See? No wires."

"Should they have wires?"

"How else would the power get to the lightbulbs?" asked Wade.

"From the sun."

Wade was confused. "I don't follow you."

"The power comes from the sun," Riv said more slowly. He held up the lamp. On the side was a small, square, silver-colored panel. "This panel receives its power from that panel there." He pointed to a similar panel discreetly placed on the wall, next to the window.

"Where does that panel get its power?"

"From the larger panel above the house. It captures the rays of the sun and transmits those rays as power throughout the house— all over the compound, in fact."

"Then you don't have electricity?" Wade asked, amazed.

Riv laughed. "We haven't needed electricity for years. It's considered primitive now, like outdoor toilets."

"Power from the sun . . ." Wade mused.

"Unfortunately, because the sun has provided so much, people now worship it instead of the Unseen One," Riv said sadly. "They consider the sun and nature to be the source of life and creation. They no longer believe that the Unseen One provided the natural order to bless us."

Wade pondered it all through dinner. On one hand, this world gave him the impression of being simpler than his own. On the other hand, it seemed to be more technologically advanced. He couldn't think of how that was possible. "May I see the city tomorrow?" he suddenly asked. "I'm dying to have a look around."

"I'm afraid not," Arin said after swallowing a mouthful of potatoes.

"Why not?"

"Frankly, I'm afraid of what they'll do to you."

"Or what you'll do to them," Pool added with a chuckle. "You might cause a riot."

"Then I'm trapped here?"

"You're *safe* here," Arin said. "You're protected here from those who would do you harm or lead you to do harm to others."

Wade fell into a disappointed silence. What was the point of coming to another world and being stuck inside someone's compound?

A messenger from the city elders arrived after dinner. He was heavily bearded and as round as a bowling ball.

"The elders have heard about your guest," the bowling ball said.

"So?" Arin said.

"They want to meet him."

"Then they are welcome to come here."

"You know that's not possible," the bowling ball replied. "Not since . . . well . . ."

Arin smiled. "Not since I threw them out the last time they came."

"They'd rather the people did not see them come to you," the bowling ball said. "It would make them appear as if they were negotiating with you or giving you respect."

"Which they dare not do," Arin stated sarcastically.

"You understand, I'm sure."

"I understand completely. But they cannot see our guest unless they come here. The choice is theirs to make."

"Must you be so difficult about everything?" the bowling ball asked.

"Indeed I must," Arin replied. "Now, here are some cakes my wife made. They'll comfort your journey back."

The bowling ball's face lit up. "Thank you, Arin," he said sincerely. "And thank Muiraq for us."

"You're welcome, Flabian."

"Who are the elders?" Wade asked after Arin had returned from seeing the bowling ball to the gate. "And from what city?"

"The elders of Sarum," Arin answered as they stood outside the front door of the cottage. "It's our capital city, the city that surrounds us even now. Or maybe I should say that it's the central city of the confederacy."

"What do you mean by 'confederacy'?"

"The simplest way to explain it is to say that the country we're in—Marus, it's called—is a collection of little countries. It's a confederacy of factions or *tribes*. The elders represent those tribes and make the laws accordingly."

"You don't have a president or a king?"

"No. There was a time when the Unseen One was considered our king, but those days are long gone. Now there are elders. However, there is a man who wants to change all that. He wants to be our king, though he hasn't been honest enough to say so directly."

"This is a very strange world," Wade said softly.

Arin looked at the boy, then said wistfully, "One day, when the

Unseen One's judgment has come and gone and a new generation has risen up, then Marus will be united under a true ruler. But that will be a long time in the future."

"Look at that!" Wade suddenly cried out.

Arin spun around. Wade was staring up at the clear night sky.

"Do you see that?" Wade asked.

"What?" Arin said, looking but not seeing what could have caught Wade's attention.

"There are *two* moons up there! Do you see?" Wade was pointing wildly in excitement. One was large and white, the other nearly half the size and slightly more orange.

Arin laughed, then said, "We've always had two moons. How many moons do you have in your world?"

"Just one."

"How sad," Arin said, then headed back into the cottage.

"May I walk around?" Wade asked.

"Be my guest," Arin said. "But don't leave the compound. Remember what I said."

Wade didn't answer but continued to stare at the two moons. He walked slowly away from the cottage, hoping to see if the sky held any other surprises. He followed the path that took him back toward the shelter. The stars blurred together until he lost interest in them.

The main entrance to the shelter lay just ahead, he remembered. It occurred to him that if he returned to Bethel's stall, it might magically turn into the coal cellar once more and he'd be home again. *But the door will be locked*, he thought. *Arin wouldn't leave it open at night.*

He tried anyway. Sure enough, the door was locked.

Strolling around to the left of the top of the shelter, he noticed how much it looked like the roof of a large and long house sticking up from the ground. It reminded him of a military bunker—made of thick cement and with a gently sloping roof.

He wondered if he could see over the compound wall if he stood at the pinnacle of the shelter. Glancing around, he hoped to find something to climb on, something high enough to get him onto the roof. His eye caught sight of a ladder leaning horizontally against the shelter wall. He ran over to it and was pleased to see that it might be long enough for him to see over the compound wall, which was about 15 feet high.

I could climb the ladder to the top of the wall and look out at the city, he thought. Then another idea came to him: *Maybe I could find a way to climb down the other side, check out the neighborhood, then come back again. No one has to know.*

He looked around. Arin and his family were nowhere to be seen. Moving as fast as he could, he dragged the ladder over to the nearest section of wall and hoisted it up. It reached nearly to the top.

Wade's heart raced. Now he'd be able to see more of this new world he'd discovered! He climbed the ladder carefully, but even standing on the uppermost rung, he was still a few feet short of the top of the wall. The only way he'd be able to see over would be to jump up, grab on to the top, and pull himself up the rest of the way.

But then how would he get down again? He eyed the wall, the ladder, and then the wall again. He decided that when he was ready, he could hang from the ledge of the wall and drop back onto the ladder. *Easy,* he thought.

Taking a deep breath, Wade crouched on the top rung, then sprang up as hard as he could. His fingers crooked over the top of the wall. He kicked his legs wildly as he tried to climb up. One of his feet caught the ladder, not just once but two or three times, and knocked it aside. To Wade's horror, the ladder slid along the wall and fell to the ground.

"Oh, no!" he gasped. He waited for a second, then mustered all his strength to pull himself to the top. It was a painfully slow process since his arms weren't that strong. The rough cement of the wall dug into his fingers. He felt beads of sweat form on his forehead and upper lip. He pulled and pulled until, eventually, he worked one elbow over the ledge, then another, and then he swung his right leg up, followed by his left. Finally, he was lying completely atop the wall. He stayed there, panting, for a few minutes.

When he felt slightly recovered, he rolled onto his side. The wall was a couple of feet thick and gave him enough room to sit up. He was facing an alleyway with several tall brick buildings directly across from him. They looked like warehouses, with large leaded windows that were now dark and barren of any people or activity. *No view of the city from here*, he thought with disappointment. He looked in both directions and decided to make his way to the right. Maybe he could see more if he followed the wall to that end of the alley. Looking like a squirrel, he scurried along as fast as he could on hands and knees. When he reached the end of that wall—and the corner of the compound—he stopped. To his disappointment, he'd come to another alley. *Will I have to scurry all the way around to the front gate in order to see the city?* he wondered.

He decided he wouldn't try. The chances were good that Arin or one of his sons would spot him. Looking back into the compound, he searched for a tree branch he might jump onto. He couldn't see any that were close enough, however, and then he realized Arin was too smart to allow a tree to grow close enough to the wall for an intruder to break in that way.

Wade turned to look in the other direction and only then saw that he was face-to-face with some kind of pole that stuck up from the corner of the wall. At the top of the pole was a rectangular piece of metal tilted down toward the street. It was a sign of some sort. Wade twisted around to get a look at what it said.

The sign read: "Warning. This is a high-powered security wall." Then it had symbols that looked like lightning bolts, followed by the word *Danger.*

Wade felt his heart jump into his throat. This was a hazardous wall, probably like an electric fence! Yet another way that Arin kept intruders out.

Why isn't it turned on? Wade wondered. *Does Arin have it on some sort of timer? Is it about to come on at any moment and shock the living daylights out of me?*

He tried to decide what to do. He could hang from the side of the wall and let himself fall back into the compound, risking a twisted ankle or, worse, a broken bone. That didn't appeal to him. Maybe he should call to Arin for help, admit he was wrong, and hope they'd let him back in. That didn't appeal to him either. There had to be another way.

Just then, he heard a couple of voices from below. He froze where he was. The voices came from the street, not the compound. Two men walked up the alley, one carrying a flashlight that he occasionally shone along the wall. Wade moved carefully and gently around the sign pole. Suddenly the man with the flashlight flicked the beam up toward Wade. It was a casual gesture; he didn't know Wade was there. But it startled Wade, who jerked back and banged the large sign.

The men stopped and looked up, searching the area with the light. "Who's there?" one of them barked.

"It's someone," the other man said to his partner.

"I guess the power isn't turned on," the first man said.

The second man called out, "Identify yourself! We see you up there."

Wade leaned over the ledge. "It's me," he said. "I mean, it's Wade. Who are you?"

"We're . . ." the first man hesitated. "Guards, I guess you could say."

"How did you get up there?" the second man asked.

"A ladder."

"A ladder!" the first man growled. "What ladder? We've been around this compound at least twice tonight, and we haven't seen a ladder."

"There's a ladder on the inside, but it fell down."

"So you're saying you're stuck up there?" the first man asked.

"Yes."

The two men laughed.

"It's not funny," Wade said indignantly.

"Don't get snippy with us, boy," the second man said. "What possessed you to get on top of that wall? Don't you know that old Arin could be turning on the power any minute now?"

"I wanted to see the city," Wade explained.

"That's not a very smart way to see it," the first man observed.

"Do you belong in there or out here?" the second man asked.

"In here."

The flashlight beam hit him again, and the two men consulted between themselves in low tones. Wade thought he heard one of them mention his blond hair.

"We could help you," the second man said. "Just crawl down and dangle your legs over. Then let go and we'll catch you."

"Then what?" Wade asked.

"What do you mean?"

"What'll happen to me if I let you help me?"

"We'll take you around to the front gate and let you in."

"How? By telling Arin?"

"No, we'll let you in with our key." The first man held up some keys and jingled them.

"Why do you have a key?" Wade asked.

"You ask a lot of questions, don't you?" the second man complained. "We have a key because we're guards for Arin."

"Really?"

"Yes!" the first man said. "Why would we lie to you?"

"Why *wouldn't* you lie to me?" asked Wade.

"Stay up there and cook, then."

The two men made as if they might walk off.

"Wait!" Wade called out. "I'll trust you."

"All right, just climb over and hang down," the first man instructed.

"Okay." Wade did that very thing: He sat on the edge of the wall, rolled over onto his stomach, slowly slid down until he hung by his fingers, and finally let go. He felt the two men grab his legs, then carry him to the ground.

"That wasn't so bad, was it?" the first man asked once Wade was standing on firm ground between them.

"No, it wasn't," Wade said. "Thank you."

The second man chuckled and said, "You're welcome, you gullible boy."

"Gullible?"

The two men grabbed him with heavy hands. One clamped down on his nose and mouth before he could shout. He couldn't breathe. Then everything went black.

4

Liven, an elder of the confederacy and the only one who actually lived in Sarum, carefully moved the thick blackout curtain an inch to the side. The curtain was designed to keep the meeting room's light from shining outside so the enemy airplanes wouldn't be able to see the building in the dark. In the distance, flares went up and shells exploded like fireworks in the sky. They lit up the skyscrapers and lower rooftops. He wondered what kind of rubble they'd have to sort through in the morning.

"Close the curtain," Acad, another elder, said in a weary drone from the conference table. "It's bad enough that I have to argue with you men. I don't want to die with you."

Liven pulled the curtain tight and turned to the room. *What a sight!* he thought. A blanket of smoke from too many cigars and pipes covered the assembled leaders in a haze. The table, around which they'd gathered, was littered with papers, half-empty coffee cups, filled ashtrays, and food wrappers. *They're pigs,* Liven thought. He frowned. They had been arguing all day, and it looked as if they were going to argue well into the night—all while his beloved city went up in flames. "Can't we stop for a while?" he asked. "My brain hurts."

Dedmon, a heavily bearded man from the Mechlites, wagged a finger at Liven. "I promised my people I would not rest, nor return, without a final agreement," he said.

"I'm not bound by the promises you make," Liven said. He was grumpy now. He would just as readily have assassins kill these men as speak to them. But he needed them; they needed one another to keep from being overrun by their enemies.

"Have we made *any* progress?" Greave of the Kenans asked. He brushed his hand absentmindedly across his bushy gray eyebrows. They stuck out like wild branches from his thin face.

"We've agreed that we must combine our resources to ward off our attackers," sniffed Krupt. He was from the Shonens, a wealthy faction from the south, and spoke with a thick, stuffed-nose accent.

Acad groaned. "We had agreed on that much before we entered the room this morning!" he complained. "The question is, how much are we each willing to commit?"

"I'm overextended," Dedmon said. "I've poured all we have into battling those pesky barbarians from Gotthard. We're keeping them at bay, but I can't say how long we'll last."

Liven threw his hands up. "Your problem is *everyone's* problem, Dedmon!" he exclaimed. "We're besieged on all sides."

Dedmon picked his teeth casually. "I'm only saying that if we don't come to agreement here, I'll be forced to negotiate my own peace with the Gotthardites."

"You'll have no peace with the Gotthardites," Acad droned. "Only surrender."

"Which will leave the rest of us vulnerable!" Greave snapped.

Dedmon turned on Acad. "It's easy enough for you. You have nothing but sea to the east. What battles do you have?"

"Only the Palatians sending boats from the south, plus the Albanites with their big ships from the north," Acad whined. "They send their marauders in day after day. My coastal towns are panic-stricken."

"If you think the Palatians are vicious on the water, try engaging them on land," Krupt said, then yawned. "Gentlemen, I will die of boredom if something doesn't happen soon. This gathering was tiresome when it began and has not improved since."

Just then, a knock came at the door. Madalay, Liven's assistant, opened it and peered in. "Sorry to bother you, sir, but he's still waiting," he said.

"Yes, of course he is," Liven replied.

"Who is?" Greave asked. "This is supposed to be a closed meeting."

Liven rubbed his eyes. "It's Tyran."

"Tyran! What's he want now?" Dedmon growled.

"Only to address us for a moment," Liven said. He gestured to Madalay and instructed, "Bring him in."

"I don't trust him," Krupt said simply.

"You don't trust anyone," Greave countered.

Krupt waved a hand to everyone present. "Do you blame me when I have to deal with cutthroats and double-crossers like you?"

The men regarded Krupt and his comment silently. He was right. They were united now only because of their enemies. If they weren't being attacked from without, they would be attacking each other from within. It was the way of the world, Liven thought. In their own way, they were each playing King of the Hill. A handshake, a stab in the back, and, ultimately, the survival of the fittest: Those were the only rules they lived by these days.

The door opened again, and Tyran strode in.

If nothing else, Liven thought, Tyran knew how to make an entrance. When he walked into a room, he did so with a theatrical flourish and an unmistakable confidence that drew all eyes to him. And yet he was only medium in height and build; his hair was kept unfashionably short; and his skinny mustache—something no one in good society would wear—hung above his thin lips like a black slash on a pasty-white page. His eyes were magnetic, though—black and mesmerizing. His voice was commanding, a deep boom from an otherwise small cannon.

"Gentlemen," Tyran said, gesturing respectfully. "How go the negotiations?"

"None of your business," Dedmon said.

"Not well, then," Tyran said pleasantly.

"You have one minute," Liven informed his guest.

Tyran stood at the head of the table, leaning on the surface with his knuckles. "I will be succinct then," he said. "This confederacy, as you call it, is a joke. You meet for hours and days and accomplish nothing."

The elders reacted with indignation. "Throw him out!" Krupt demanded.

"Throw me out at your own peril," Tyran said, raising a hand to silence them. "I am here to tell you that the *people* are fed up with your politics and bureaucracy."

"People? What people?" Acad demanded to know. "*Whose* people?"

"People from all your districts, the people in the streets," Tyran said. "While you debate and argue uselessly, I have been talking to those you claim to represent. Their confidence and patience are gone. They trust *me* now. I am now the voice you must listen to. I am the one you must respect."

"Nonsense!" said Krupt.

Tyran leaned forward, staring each man down in turn. "I am here to warn you. The people are weary of your ineffectiveness. They are tired of war. They want someone to take charge, to take action. Divided as you are, you cannot accomplish anything."

"And what do you propose?" Liven asked as calmly as he could.

"A united nation. No more factions, no more individual tribes—the Mechlites, the Shonens, the Lahamites, the Kenans. We are the people of Marus, and we should be one!"

"You're living in a dream," Greave said.

"I am living in the *future*," Tyran said. "You may join me or die in the past."

Acad shifted uncomfortably in his chair. "Are you threatening us?" he asked.

"Not a threat but a warning." Tyran spun on his heel and marched out of the room.

"Nonsense," Krupt said again.

Deep crevices formed on Greave's forehead. He stroked his chin. "Is he capable?" he asked. "Does he have the support of the people like he says? My spies haven't reported anything to me about this."

"Your spies are probably working for him," Liven answered.

Greave looked as if he might disagree, but he thought better of it and kept his mouth closed.

Liven addressed the men: "I believe we should take Tyran very seriously. He wouldn't be so emphatic unless he had substantial power behind him."

"It's a bluff," Krupt snorted.

"I'll have some of my men kill him," Dedmon offered.

"And we'll have riots all over the land," warned Liven.

Dedmon was not deterred. "They'll make it look like an accident," he said confidently.

"We'll still have riots," Liven said. "Please, let's put aside our barbaric tendencies for just a moment and consider what we can do to save ourselves. Tyran may well know how the people are feeling, and if we don't take decisive action soon, we may find ourselves on the wrong end of the assassin's knife."

The rest of the elders began to argue Liven's statement. He wearily turned again to the blackout curtain and pushed it aside. To the north, the sky was nothing more than a blood-red stain.

Wade was half-dragged, half-carried to a waiting car. There the two men bound and gagged him with a heavy-duty tape. They then threw him into the trunk of the car and slammed the lid down. Enveloped in darkness, Wade woke up and listened as the car pulled away.

A moment later, Wade tried kicking at the trunk as hard as he could. It was solidly shut. He lay still for a minute and tried to think. But there was nothing to think about. He was a stranger in this world, and he had no idea who his kidnappers were or where they were going. So he waited, hoping that someone in Arin's house had heard the noises or the car and was now in pursuit.

From the few seconds he had seen them, Wade knew his captors were dangerous. They had the look of street thugs. What were they doing at the compound? Were they trying to break into the shelter, or had they come for another reason?

The car hummed beneath him. It wasn't the normal hum his parents' Ford made, he realized. This was softer. It lacked the noise of a proper engine. Wade sniffed the air. He didn't detect the telltale smells of gas or exhaust. Was it possible that this car was powered by the sun like so much else in this world?

Nearly 15 minutes later, the car came to a stop. Wade listened as the two men got out and walked to the rear of the car. He considered kicking at them when they lifted the trunk lid, but he realized he wouldn't accomplish much with his ankles and wrists bound the way they were. He'd probably only make them mad, and then they might hurt him.

The lid popped open, and the two men gazed in at Wade. "Hello, boy," the first man said. He had a face filled with deep lines and a drooping mustache. His brown hair was cut close and thinning on top.

"You behave yourself," the second man said with a thin smile on his pudgy face, "and you won't get hurt."

They reached in, pulled him out of the trunk, and leaned him against the car. "I'll hold him while you get him ready," the pudgy one said.

"Right," the mustached man responded. He leaned down and removed the tape over Wade's mouth and, with a quick flick of a knife, from around his ankles, leaving his wrists bound.

"Don't think about running," the pudgy one advised. "You won't get far."

Wade glanced around. They seemed to be in some kind of alley that stretched for blocks between high-rise buildings. A yellow light shone down on them from a nearby door. It reflected off the black sheen of the car. Wade craned his neck to get a better look. The car was like something out of a science-fiction comic book. Long and sleek, it had a delicately curved body, with a low top and narrow windows. "Wow," Wade said more loudly than he'd intended.

"You like the car?" the mustached man asked.

The pudgy man laughed and said, "Maybe we'll give you a proper ride in it sometime."

Just then, a bomb exploded in the distance. It sounded closer now than when Wade was in Arin's compound. He was still in Sarum, he knew. But why had they brought him here?

"Let's get him inside," the pudgy man said.

They led Wade into the building through a door marked Staff Only. The hall was dark, but a safety light ahead allowed Wade to notice the marble floor and the pillars that reached up on both sides to the arches overhead. The style reminded Wade of movies about ancient Rome. He expected Julius Caesar to appear around a corner.

Once more, the scene didn't make sense to him. It was as if this world contained a mixture of styles. Arin's cottage and compound looked as if they had been built in medieval England. His family's clothes, too, were a reflection of that period and style: tunics and robes and sandals. Wade's captors, in contrast, dressed as anyone in Wade's world might have dressed, with worn suitcoats, vests, baggy trousers, and regular-looking black shoes. But against this Roman architecture, they seemed out of place. *What kind of world is this?* Wade wondered as he had before and would again.

"I'm Movan," the mustached man said for no obvious reason.

The pudgy man said, "I'm Simpson."

"You ever need any odd jobs done, you think of us," Movan said.

"That's what we do," added Simpson.

Wade hesitated as a man walked into view ahead of them. He was dressed in a long tunic, just like an ancient Roman senator. *Julius Caesar!* Wade thought.

Movan prodded him on. "No need to be afraid," he said. "It's only Madalay. He's Liven's assistant. Do you know who Liven is?"

Wade shook his head no.

"Only the head of the elders," Movan replied, clearly impressed.

"He's not the head," Simpson corrected him. "Only the host. He's like a . . . a . . . mediator for them. Does that make sense to you, boy?"

Wade nodded.

Madalay was directly in front of them now. "You have him," he said.

"We sure do," Simpson said. "Just like we promised."

"He came to us, actually," Movan said.

"Shut up," Simpson snapped as he poked Movan in the ribs with his elbow. "Your messenger created a nice diversion while we sneaked in," he lied to Madalay.

"Good," Madalay said. "Liven is eager to meet him." Madalay took a step back to get a better look at Wade in the light. "His hair. It's astounding. Straight out of a storybook."

"Never seen anything like it," Simpson agreed.

"Liven hopes his appearance will have an impact on the elders. Follow me." Madalay started walking back the way he had come.

"We're going to the elders themselves?" Movan said. "How're my clothes? Not too dirty, I hope."

"Suitably shabby, as usual," Simpson said.

The hallway deposited them into a large reception area. Here the pillars reached way up to ornate balconies far above. At the top was an enormous stained-glass dome covered with pictures of angels and celestial beings dancing in a blue sky. Wade stumbled as he craned his neck to see it all, though it was darkened and the detail was hard to make out.

Simpson tugged at his sleeve. "This way," he ordered.

They walked past large wooden doors embellished with patterns of oak leaves and vines. Wade's mind went to a field trip he'd taken with his class to the Connellsville courthouse. It had looked something like this, but on a more modest scale. They soon reached a smaller but equally ornate door. A hand-painted sign said Chambers.

"Wait here," Madalay ordered, and he slipped into the room.

In the moment the door was open, Wade could hear men arguing inside. Madalay's appearance sparked complaints about another interruption. Finally, one man silenced them and instructed Madalay to bring in their guests.

Madalay opened the door wide.

Movan and Simpson stepped forward, blocking Wade from being seen. They smiled proudly to the men in the room.

"Well?" one man droned. "We know these two men. We've all employed their services at one time or another."

Movan and Simpson then moved aside. They obviously wanted Wade to make a dramatic entrance. The group of men—the elders—gasped as if the devil himself had walked into the room.

"He has golden hair!" a man exclaimed as he backed away to the far wall.

Wade felt his face turn red.

"Unbind him," the man in charge instructed Wade's captors.

"Are you sure?" the droning man asked.

Another man wrung his hands and inquired, "Does he have powers?"

"I heard he caused quite a commotion today," one said. "Hundreds of people ran in fear just from the sight of him."

The man in charge said impatiently, "They fled because they are superstitious fools." He spoke to Movan. "Did he offer any resistance? Did he strike you blind or give you boils?"

Movan grinned. "Yes, sir, all of the above," he said sarcastically. "But we recovered."

"Unbind him, then," the man in charge snapped.

Movan quickly undid the tape around Wade's wrists. He was free. But the two men stayed close in case he tried to make a run for it.

"Do you know who we are?" the man in charge asked.

"No, sir."

"We're the elders of Sarum," he said. "I am Liven. That's Greave of the Kenans, Dedmon of the Mechlites, Krupt of the Shonens, and Acad of the Lahamites."

Wade wasn't impressed. "Arin's going to be really mad about this," he replied with as much menace as he could muster.

Liven showed mock concern. "Do you think so?" he said. "Will he call down fire from the Unseen One to rescue you? Maybe the holocaust he has been predicting for the past 60 years will finally come true. Sit down, boy."

Wade sat on a chair next to the wall. All eyes were on him. He didn't like it.

"Where are you from?" Krupt asked.

"America."

"Where, exactly, is that?" inquired Dedmon.

"The planet Earth."

The men laughed.

"As you are a guest, I won't strike you for your impertinence," Liven said. "Next time, I'll forget you're a guest. Now kindly tell us how it is that you're with Arin."

Wade took a deep breath, which caused him to cough. *The smoke in the room*, he thought. When he recovered, he explained to them everything that had happened since he woke up in his bed that morning. *It feels like years ago*, he told himself.

The elders listened to him thoughtfully as he spoke. After he finished, they glanced at one another.

Greave shrugged as if to say, "Well, what do we think?"

"It's more nonsense," Krupt said.

"Everything is nonsense to you," Dedmon complained.

Acad droned, "He's a peasant boy who's been put up to this by Arin. He always said that a golden-haired child would come, and now he's pulled this trick to make us believe him."

"It's probably not the real color of his hair," Greave suggested. "We could arrest him for gross physical alteration."

"I'm telling you the truth," Wade said through clenched teeth.

"To make us believe you're from a different world or time or dimension, you'll have to be a bit more persuasive," Liven stated. "Tell us how your world is different from ours."

"I haven't seen much of your world," Wade responded. "Only Arin's compound."

"Didn't you see our city on the way here?"

"Your goons put me in the trunk of their car."

"I'm sorry," Liven said without meaning it. "Now, what differences have you noticed?"

Wade thought for a moment, then said, "Their car didn't smell."

"Smell like what?"

"Like exhaust, like gas fumes."

"Automobiles in your world do?" inquired Acad.

"Yes."

"My word, are you saying your world uses *petrol-burning* engines?" Krupt asked with an undisguised air of disdain.

"Internal combustion engines, yes, sir."

"Next you'll be telling us you still use electricity!" Greave said with a laugh.

Wade swallowed hard. "Yes, we do."

"You've not harnessed the energy of the provider of our very lives, the source of our very existence—the *sun*?" asked Dedmon.

It was Wade's turn to ask, "Do you use the sun for everything?"

"Of course we do!" Dedmon replied. "It drives our autos, our aeroplanes, our ships. It provides energy to our homes and buildings, gives us light by night, coolness for hot days, warmth for cold ones. It is . . . everything."

"Even your weapons?"

Liven said quickly, "We're still developing our weapons. War was fairly unknown to us until the last hundred years. We were too busy developing our arts, sciences, and medicines."

"What kind of weapons do you have in *your* world?" Krupt asked Wade.

Wade thought about it for a moment. "Rifles, machine guns, hand grenades, torpedoes, artillery cannons, bombs—"

Liven gestured wearily. "That's more than enough," he said.

"What kind of bombs?" Acad asked.

"The kind that explode."

Acad was not amused but said sarcastically, "What sorts of bombs do you use: *gas*-powered bombs? Electric bombs, perhaps?"

Wade was tired of being made fun of, so he said to impress them, "We have atomic bombs."

The elders looked puzzled. "What kind of bombs?" Liven asked.

"Atomic," Wade repeated.

"You're going to have to explain that to us," Liven said.

Wade feigned boredom, like a teacher with silly schoolchildren. "It's based on nuclear fission," he explained. "You see, the bomb is made of plutonium or uranium, and neutrons are shot into it, which causes a chain reaction, and then *boom*, the explosion. It could destroy your entire city in just a few seconds."

The men sat silently, assessing what Wade had said.

"Your world has obviously spent a lot of time developing its warfare," Liven observed.

"Or your imagination has!" Krupt snorted. "I don't believe a word of this drivel. This boy is making it all up. Uranium, plutonium, chain reactions . . . it's nonsense!"

Krupt's statement triggered a chain reaction of its own as the elders began to argue among themselves. They were divided over whether or not to believe Wade. This then spun into a debate about what to do with Wade now that they had him in custody.

"You have to take me back to Arin!" Wade insisted.

Liven shook his head. "Arin will wait," he said. "If you are who you say you are, a boy from another world, we dare not let you loose. If you aren't, we dare not allow Arin to wreak havoc among the people by using you as a means to frighten them. Morale is low enough right now. We can't have Arin's message of doom and gloom taking it any lower."

"But what if he's right?" Wade asked.

"Right!" Greave cried out. "He's a lunatic! He can't be right!"

Liven signaled to Movan and Simpson to take Wade out. "Take him to the security house," he ordered. "Keep him there until I tell you otherwise."

"Yes, sir," Simpson said.

"You're making a big mistake!" Wade shouted to the elders as he was taken away. Madalay closed the door behind him, cutting off their laughter.

Madalay said, "You have your instructions," and walked away.

"We have our instructions all right," Movan said with a smile filled with gray teeth.

When Madalay was out of earshot, Simpson added under his breath, "Too bad they aren't the instructions Liven gave us."

Wade was taken back to the car, but this time he was allowed to sit between Movan, who drove, and Simpson. The seat was plush and comfortable. The car's dashboard was lit up like a Christmas tree, with red and green lights next to symbols Wade didn't understand. Movan pushed a button, and the car drifted forward, as if on air.

"Is it fast?" Wade asked.

"Is it fast!" Movan said with a chuckle. "You just watch." He moved the steering column forward slightly, and the car took off. They flew down the city streets, past large skyscrapers and smaller office complexes, all with the same Romanesque architecture. But street lamps burned yellow nearby. *It's like Rome with electricity*, Wade thought.

They zoomed past other cars with body styles similar to the car they were in. Wade looked carefully to see if the cars were actually riding on tires. The ride was so smooth that he doubted it, but the tires were there, spinning quickly.

Simpson frowned. "Stop showing off," he said. "If you get us pulled over, we'll be in big trouble."

"How can we get in trouble if we're on official business?" Movan asked.

"If we were going to the security house, we *wouldn't* get in trouble," Simpson said slowly. "But we're not going there. Remember?" Simpson reached over and tapped Movan's temple. "We're going to Tyran's castle. Remember?"

"Oh, yeah," Movan said, slowing the car down.

"Tyran's castle?" Wade asked, perplexed.

Simpson glanced down at Wade. "We got a better offer for you," he said simply.

They drove south, reaching a spacious section of the city where the skyscrapers and offices gave way to homes scattered on large plots of land. At the top of a large hill sat a genuine castle with a moat, a gate, turrets, and towers peering at them majestically from all sides.

"It is a castle!" Wade gasped.

"Would we lie?" Movan said.

"Who is Tyran, and why does he want me?" asked Wade.

Simpson replied, "He's one of the richest and most powerful men in the city. As for why he wants you, that's for him to know and you to find out."

A winding lane took them up to the castle gate. Triggered by some unseen signal, a drawbridge lowered smoothly over the moat. They drove inside and parked in a large courtyard. A man with short dark hair and a thin mustache strode up to the car as they climbed out.

"Tyran," Simpson said and bowed slightly.

"I am glad you made it safely," the man said formally, then looked at Wade. "You are our alien visitor, I take it."

"My name is Wade Mullens."

"I know," Tyran said.

"So, what now?" Simpson asked.

"You are to make it look as if someone attacked you and kid-napped the boy," Tyran said. "It would be best if everyone thought Arin or his sons had done it."

"But, sir!" Movan said. "Our reputations will be ruined if peo-ple think Arin and his sissy sons stole the boy from us."

Tyran gazed at him with a steely expression. "Your vanity is no concern of mine," he said. "Do as I say."

Simpson sighed sadly. "You heard him, Movan," he said miserably. "We have to make it look like we were attacked."

"As you wish," Movan said, then punched Simpson in the jaw.

Simpson staggered back, then returned with a hard right to Movan's eye.

With grunts and groans, the two men pummeled each other. Tyran led Wade into the castle as they continued.

"The elders are a collection of idiots," Tyran said. "I heard how they treated you in that meeting. Abominable! They have a guest from another world in their midst, and do they treat you with respect? Do they listen to you? No. They disbelieve and ridicule you. A travesty!"

"How did you know that?" Wade asked.

"How do I know what?"

"How they treated me. You weren't there."

A shadow of a smile crossed Tyran's face. "I have listening devices in the room. I would not let those buffoons gather together without knowing what they were saying."

Wade shuddered as a cold chill shot through his body. *Why did he tell me that?* he thought. *How does he know I won't tell the elders about his listening devices? Unless he's planning to keep me here . . .*

"Are you hungry? Would you like something to eat?" Tyran asked.

They locked eyes for a moment, and Wade felt instantly drawn in by them. They were friendly eyes, the eyes of a compassionate preacher or a good-natured uncle. He saw nothing to be afraid of in those eyes. "No, thank you," Wade replied.

"Then allow me to tell you what is going on here," Tyran said as they strolled down a long hallway lined with suits of armor and brilliantly colored tapestries. "I am a man who has grown very tired of the various factions, tribes, fiefdoms—call them whatever you want—that have divided Marus for too many years. I think it is time that they are united under one vision, one leader."

"You want to be that leader, right?" Wade said, thinking of another leader who had said the same kind of thing and led his world into war.

Tyran nodded. "From my childhood, I knew this was what I was called to do. I was chosen to bring our nation together."

"Chosen by whom?"

"Fate. Destiny. The Almighty Sun. You choose a name."

"The Unseen One?"

"You may use that name if you like. I do not believe in Him myself. But it is a suitable name for whatever power makes things happen in this life." Tyran gestured to a large doorway. They walked in. The enormous room had lavish antique furniture, wall-sized bookshelves, and a harpsichord.

"Why did you bring me here?" Wade asked.

"Because, like Arin, I believe your coming is preordained. I believe you are from another world and have been sent to our world to bring about a new age."

"Arin thinks I'm the final sign of the end of the world."

"That is Arin's opinion," Tyran replied dismissively as they continued walking toward the far side of the room. "But I think you are the final sign of the *beginning* of the world. That sounds so much better than Arin's idea, does it not? Would you not rather help *start* something than end it?"

"Well . . . yes," Wade said.

"I thought so." He smiled at Wade. "I suspect that you and I are not so different. In you, I see myself as a boy. I will wager that you get picked on at school. The other children do not understand your intelligence. The teachers do not know what to make of you."

Wade was silent. It was all true. Bobby Adams had said that

Wade was too smart for his own good. His mother said the same thing.

Tyran placed a gentle hand on Wade's shoulder. "Those days are over. Everyone who works with me will appreciate you. They will understand the gift you are to us. You were brought here to help me unite the world in peace."

"How?" Wade asked, wanting to believe him but remaining skeptical. "I'm just a kid."

"You are not just a kid," Tyran challenged. "You are a visionary, like me. I heard what you said about your world and its weapons, your description of that bomb—the one that can destroy an entire city within seconds."

"The atomic bomb?"

"Yes. If you can tell us about that, there are other things you can tell us. The weapons from your world may help our world. They may help me to bring about peace."

"I only know a little about them," Wade said. "I don't know how to *build* them."

"Do not worry about that. I have a very smart man who will take care of the construction. All you have to do is tell him everything you know. Somehow we will find a bridge between our inferior weapons and your superior technology."

"What man?"

"Dr. Lyst."

They had arrived at a door on the far side of the large room, and Tyran now threw it open, revealing a huge laboratory filled with electronic gadgets, beakers on burners, test equipment, and blackboards with complex formulas written from one edge to the other. At the far end of a lab table, a man in a white coat stood bent over a microscope.

The man straightened up and quickly approached with a broad smile and outstretched hand. "Is this him?" he asked.

"This is Wade," Tyran replied.

The man shook Wade's hand vigorously. "A pleasure to meet you," he said. "I've never shaken hands with someone from another world!"

"It feels the same as anywhere else," Wade offered.

The man laughed. His slender face reminded Wade of an exclamation point. Something about his expression was bright and alive.

"I am Dr. Lyst," the man said. "You and I will be working together, I understand."

"Only if Wade wants to. He has not said he will," Tyran explained, then gazed at Wade. "If you want to go back to Arin, now is the time to say so. I will not stop you. But I think your purpose in this world will be better fulfilled with us."

Wade didn't know what to say or do, and he had already forgotten Tyran's last instructions to the kidnappers. "I'm a stranger here," he replied after a moment's hesitation. "I don't know where I belong."

"Then you may as well stay with us," Dr. Lyst said.

"I guess so."

Dr. Lyst suddenly flapped his hands at Tyran in a shooing motion. "Go away now," he said playfully. "He's mine."

Tyran laughed and said, "I look forward to seeing what you two come up with."

"Yes, yes, now go away." Dr. Lyst walked Tyran to the door and saw him out. He closed it firmly, then turned to Wade. "This is going to be fun," he said with a smile.

Dr. Lyst's face was ageless. Wade guessed he was in his forties but couldn't be sure. He had black hair, with gray at the temples that made it look as if his head had grown wings. He also had a smooth, babylike complexion; the only lines were the crow's-feet that had gathered at the corners of his green eyes. He was square-jawed and had high cheekbones, which gave his wide mouth room to smile in a big way. Wade found the face reassuring.

"Let's sit down and you can tell me everything," Dr. Lyst said, pulling a chair close. He had an expression of pure delight on his face, as if he'd just made a brand-new friend. "I read the transcript of your statement to the elders."

"Transcript?"

Dr. Lyst motioned with his thumb toward some papers on the table. "Word for word. Everything you told them. I'm fascinated. I could spend days—*weeks*—trying to figure out how you got here. Just think what it would be like if we could jump at will from place to place, dimension to dimension."

"You believe me?"

"Why wouldn't I? You're here, aren't you?"

"But I could be from this world. I could be lying to all of you."

"Not with that hair you aren't."

"You don't have blonds—er, people with golden hair—in this world?"

"Perhaps in some undiscovered part somewhere. And if you were from an undiscovered part, it would be the same as if you had come from another world. Why does it bother you that I believe what you said?"

Wade shrugged. "I keep thinking that I must be dreaming. I'm going to wake up in the coal cellar with a bad fever."

"Ah! Thank you for reminding me," Dr. Lyst said. "I want to do a quick physical on you, if you don't mind."

"A physical? Why?"

"To see if you're made of the same stuff as we are: flesh and blood."

"I am."

"I'll be the judge of that," Dr. Lyst said playfully. He reached into a nearby drawer and pulled out a small box. He opened it and retrieved what looked to Wade like a stethoscope and a blood pressure gauge. "This won't hurt a bit."

"What are you going to do?"

"Check all your vitals." Dr. Lyst touched a button on the side of the box, and the inside of the lid lit up in a colorful array of blues, reds, and greens. Then they faded to gray. Wade looked closer at the lid and realized it was a small transmission screen. He had seen the new television sets at a downtown appliance shop, but he didn't expect to see anything like that here. "Is something wrong?" Dr. Lyst asked.

"Is that a television?" Wade asked in a whisper of wonder.

"It's a monitor." Dr. Lyst picked up the stethoscope. But rather than put one end of it in his ears like the doctors in Wade's world, he plugged it into the side of the box. The screen came alive again with colorful charts and graphs. "Stand up, please."

Wade obeyed. Dr. Lyst held the coinlike end of the stethoscope between his fingers and began to move it a few inches from Wade's body in a scanning motion. He went from head to foot and side to side. Dr. Lyst watched the screen in the box.

"You had your tonsils removed," the doctor said.

"When I was five."

"You did something to your knee?"

"I cut it once and had stitches."

"Seven, to be precise. And you've been sick recently?"

"I had the flu."

"Flu? Hmm. I don't know what that is, and neither does my scanner."

"I feel better now." Wade was amazed. "This gadget is telling you all that?"

"That's what it was built to do," Dr. Lyst said. "Don't you have them in your world?"

"No, sir."

"Too bad." Dr. Lyst put down the stethoscope. "You seem to be in normal physical health as far as your skin, tissue, and bones are concerned. I'll make a note of the 'flu' you mentioned." He picked up the blood pressure gauge. "Hold out your arm, please."

Wade stretched out his arm.

Dr. Lyst rolled up Wade's sleeve, then wrapped the pressure cuff around his arm just above the elbow. Again, he plugged the other end into the side of the box. Wade felt as if someone had a tight grip on his arm.

"Is this reading my blood pressure?"

"It's reading your blood pressure and taking a blood sample."

"You mean, right now?"

"Yes."

"But shouldn't I feel a prick or something?"

"No. It was designed to take the blood without you realizing it." The box beeped at Dr. Lyst. He took the pressure cuff off Wade's arm. "All finished. The analyzer needs a little while to evaluate your blood, but all in all, I'd say you're no different from a normal, growing boy in our world."

"This is amazing."

Dr. Lyst put the box away. "Now let's talk about your world," he suggested. "Tell me everything."

Wade didn't know where to begin and shrugged helplessly.

Dr. Lyst smiled warmly. "Why don't you start with your family? Tell me about your mother and father, your brothers and sisters."

"I don't have any brothers or sisters," Wade explained. "It's just my mother and me until my dad comes home from the war."

"What does your dad do in the war?"

"He's a pilot, stationed in the South Pacific. But we don't know where he is right now."

"Why's that?"

"We haven't heard from him—nobody has—for a few weeks. All the other dads have contacted their families, but my dad hasn't. We don't know why. Mom keeps calling and asking, but nobody knows where he is right now."

"You're worried."

Wade nodded.

"How did your country . . ." Dr. Lyst's brow creased with sudden concentration. "What's it called?"

"The United States of America."

"Tell me how it became united, and then tell me why it went to war with the South Pacific."

Wade laughed. "It didn't go to war *with* the South Pacific. It went to war with Japan and battled the Japanese *in* the South Pacific. The South Pacific is an ocean. Here, I'll show you. Do you have some paper and a pencil? I'll draw it."

Wade drew a rough map of the world for Dr. Lyst and identified which countries were on whose side in the war. He explained about the Germans and the Japanese and the Italians, the Americans, the British, the French, and the Russians. He drew the United States and England to explain how the colonies became independent back in 1776 and had been dedicated to fighting for freedom ever since.

"So, the United States and its allies defeated Germany and Italy by sheer force and skill in battle, then resorted to dropping the atomic bombs to make Japan surrender?"

"Yes, sir."

Dr. Lyst drummed his fingers on the tabletop. "This is Tyran's goal, you know."

"What is?"

"To create weapons that are so superior to our enemies' that they'll have to unite with us or negotiate a peace. It's identical to what your leaders did." Dr. Lyst's eyes lit up. "Your arrival here is a . . . a miracle of sorts."

"I'm glad everyone thinks so," Wade said, feeling proud of his importance.

Dr. Lyst gazed earnestly at Wade. "You help us, Wade, and I'll do everything I can to get you home. I promise. Now, tell me about your technology."

Far into the night, Wade told Dr. Lyst everything he could. And when he finally felt certain he could trust Dr. Lyst, he pulled the drawings of the atomic bomb from his pocket. "Here," he said simply.

"What are these?"

"Drawings of the atomic bomb and"—he pointed to the other page with the list—"some of the materials they used."

Dr. Lyst peered at them for a moment. "Where did this information come from?" he asked. "How are you so privileged?"

"The father of a cousin of my best friend worked on the bomb. The cousin made these drawings from papers in his dad's briefcase for us to see."

"Why would he do that?"

Wade shrugged. "Because he knew we'd be interested."

"Fascinating! Crude, but fascinating."

Wade yawned and rubbed his eyes. Dr. Lyst noticed and said, "That's enough for tonight. You're tired. May I hold on to these?"

"Yes, sir. I was going to burn them anyway."

"Why?"

"Because the atomic bomb is a big secret in my world. I was afraid I'd get arrested or kidnapped by spies." Wade chuckled. It all seemed so silly now.

Dr. Lyst reached over to a button on the wall and pushed it. A servant seemed to appear from nowhere. "It's time to show this young man to his room," said the doctor.

The servant, a stiff-gaited old man, nodded. "Come along," he told Wade. He took Wade down another long hallway to a bedroom. It was luxurious, with a four-poster bed and velvet curtains, dark paneling on all four walls, paintings of rolling hills and countryside, an enormous fireplace with a marble mantelpiece, and two chairs and a table by a tall window. The servant pointed to a door next to the fireplace and said, "The bathroom is in there." He then pointed to a cord hanging next to the bed. "If you want anything, anything at all, simply pull that cord and someone will be here immediately to serve you."

"Thank you," Wade said.

A tabby cat suddenly leapt up onto the bed and meowed at Wade.

"That is Cromley," the servant said. "If he's a nuisance, I can put him out."

"He's all right," Wade said and scratched Cromley on top of his head. Cromley pressed himself against Wade and purred.

The servant retreated from the room, closing the door behind him. Wade wanted to have a look around, but he made the mistake of trying out the bed first. He lay down and absentmindedly stroked the cat. His last thought as he fell asleep was that life in this world might not be so bad after all.

Dr. Lyst stood in his laboratory and watched Wade on a screen, which had been hidden behind a curtain on the wall. Tyran walked into the room and stood next to the doctor.

"Well?" Tyran asked.

"I believe he's the genuine article," Dr. Lyst answered as he stroked his chin thoughtfully. "No one could come up with such an elaborately constructed fantasy world as he has. Certainly no one at his age. It all makes sense. He comes from some other place and time. I don't know how, but he has."

Tyran smiled. "Will you be able to take what he knows and turn it into something we can use?"

"I'll do my best," the doctor said.

Tyran patted him on the back. "Of course you will. But you know that time is working against us. If we're invaded . . ." he began, leaving the thought hanging.

"I'll work as fast as I can."

Wade was awakened by the sound of running water. He slowly sat up in bed. The servant who had brought him to the room the night before was in the bathroom. It sounded as if he was filling the bathtub. The servant emerged and looked pleased to see Wade awake.

"Good morning, sir," the man said.

"Good morning, sir," Wade repeated, stretching his arms.

"Your bath will be ready for you in a moment."

"Thank you. But you didn't have to go to any trouble. I could've run the bath myself."

"It's what I do, sir."

"Oh. What's your name, if I'm allowed to ask?"

"I'm called Thurston, sir."

"It's nice to meet you, Thurston." Wade scooted out of bed and shook Thurston's hand. "I'm Wade."

"Yes, sir. Did you sleep well?"

"Like a log."

"I assume that's a good thing?"

"Yes. Very good."

"I'm glad to hear it. Dr. Lyst is waiting for you in his laboratory after you've had your bath and breakfast. He seems quite eager to begin working with you today." Thurston began to make the bed. "I must say, I've never seen him like this."

"Like what?"

"Well, he's like a little child with a new toy."

"Am I his new toy?" Wade asked.

"I suppose you are, in a manner of speaking, sir." Thurston hesitated, clutching the bedspread. "If you don't mind my saying so, the entire castle is talking about you."

Wade self-consciously touched his hair. "Because of my hair, right?"

"I suppose for some. But most of them are talking about your knowledge. I'll speak honestly, sir: You have brought a tremendous amount of hope with you to this place."

"Me?"

"Yes, you. I dare say that you've become something of a celebrity."

Wade was impressed. "A celebrity," he repeated softly.

After his bath, Wade was given new clothes to wear. Unlike the tunic he'd worn at Arin's, he was given laced shoes; normal-looking gray trousers; a plain white shirt; and a V-neck sweater. Standing in front of the mirror, he thought of pictures he'd seen of students who go to colleges like Oxford or Cambridge in England. Thurston then took Wade to a large dining room where he was served eggs, toast, bacon, orange juice, and cereal. It seemed like ages since he'd eaten so much in the morning.

Dr. Lyst was pacing anxiously in his laboratory when Wade arrived. The doctor stopped in his tracks and smiled broadly. "Hello, young man," he said. "Did you sleep well?"

"Very well, thank you."

The doctor picked up a clipboard and assembled some sheets of paper on it. "We have a lot of work to do today," he said eagerly.

"We do?"

"I have to get everything I can out of that brain of yours."

"What if I don't know as much as you think I do?"

"But you do," Dr. Lyst said matter-of-factly. "It's all in there. I'm confident of it."

Wade grinned. If only the kids at school could see him now! They wouldn't dare laugh at him for the science-fiction comic books he was nuts about or the stolen moments at lunch and recess with the science journals that Mr. Curfew, his next-door neighbor, lent to him. The kids thought he was weird and often said so to his face, but now he was *important*. Oh, if only Steve Calloway could see him!

"Let's talk specifically about how explosives were developed in your world," Dr. Lyst said.

"All right," Wade replied. "But I'm a little rusty with my history."

"Do your best. Think hard. If I can establish any parallels between your technology and ours, I may be able to find the means to create here what you have created there. Now, tell me everything you can."

Wade took a deep breath. "Let's see . . . I think it all started with gunpowder."

"What's it made from?"

"Oh. Let me think. It's been such a long time since I read about that. Saltpeter and charcoal and sulfur."

"What is saltpeter?"

Wade had to think for a minute. Then it came to him: "Potassium nitrate. When you put all three together, it creates a black powder that—"

"Ah! Black powder."

"That's one of the names for it."

"It certainly was," Dr. Lyst said. "It's mentioned in the writings of our forefathers. But the exact formula has been lost for ages."

"Then what are you using now?" Wade asked.

"Solar bombs."

"You mean, you're using energy from the *sun* for your bombs?"

"Precisely. We created a catalyst that makes the solar cells explode. Not unlike the black powder, I suspect."

Wade was mystified. "That's what the planes are dropping at night?"

"Yes," Dr. Lyst said. "But we've gotten as much out of them as we ever hope to. They're a peacetime technology that's ill-suited for war. They don't have the power we need. Some explosions, fire, and a little bit of damage. That's all. It's more for show than for destruction."

Wade shook his head. "I just don't get it. This world seems so . . . so advanced with some things, but so backward with others."

Dr. Lyst folded his arms, his clipboard pressed against his chest. "You have to understand that war hasn't been a priority for us. For the most part, our nations have gotten along over the years. We had skirmishes and fights every now and then, but not major wars. Not until now. Now everyone has a bloodlust for power. Treaties are broken; trust is destroyed. Neighbor has turned against neighbor."

"Arin says it's because everyone lost their faith in the Unseen One."

The doctor grimaced. "That's just the sort of thing I would expect Arin to say," he responded with obvious distaste. "This has nothing to do with the Unseen One. It has to do with *us*—with the abuse of power. Tyran wants to change all that."

"By being the most powerful, right?"

"Power in the hands of a benevolent man like Tyran is a good thing."

Wade said carefully, "There's a saying in my world: Absolute power corrupts absolutely. Or something like that."

"That may be true in your world, but not with Tyran. I've known him most of my life. His vision for unity and peace is real. But he's no fool. The only way to impress these barbarians who call themselves our leaders is to carry a bigger stick than theirs. Now tell me: Your world started its explosives with black powder, but what was used after that?"

"Have you ever heard of dynamite and nitroglycerin?"

Their discussion went on from there. Wade told him all he knew about the discovery of nitroglycerin in 1846 by an Italian named Ascanio Sobrero. Dr. Lyst laughed when Wade mentioned that it had originally been used as a headache remedy. But it was too dangerous for Sobrero to use for blasting, so he gave up. In 1862, Alfred Nobel of Sweden began to experiment with it, accidentally killing his own brother in the process. But he persevered, and, in 1866, he successfully mixed liquid nitroglycerin with an absorbent substance called diatomite. As a result, dynamite was born. After that came TNT.

"TNT?" Dr. Lyst asked as he scribbled on his clipboard.

Wade rubbed his forehead. His head ached. "That stands for . . . for . . . tri-nitro-toluene. Or tri-nitro-toluol. One of those two. It comes from coal tar or gasoline, I think."

"Don't stop, keep talking," Dr. Lyst encouraged him, writing furiously.

"All the explosives and bombs we use are directly related to TNT," Wade continued. "There's dynamite and amatol, which is TNT and ammonium nitrate. There's ammonal, which has powdered aluminum, TNT, charcoal, and . . . and ammonium nitrate."

"Go on."

"I read that scientists just developed some new explosives in the war. Something called RDX, which is . . . is . . . hexamine and TNT. And something else called pentolite. That's some other mixture with TNT. I don't remember."

"Try."

"I can't. My head hurts."

"What do these explosives have to do with the atomic bomb?"

"Nothing."

"Nothing!"

"The atomic bomb is completely new. It's a whole different idea. But I wouldn't know how to explain it," Wade said.

"You explained it to the elders."

"Those were just the pieces. It's top secret. Most of us didn't even realize the bombs existed until we dropped them on Japan. We'd heard about tests in the desert and hush-hush goings-on in the government, but we never thought . . ." His voice faded. He rubbed his eyes wearily. "You have the drawings. That's as much as I know."

"That's enough for now," Dr. Lyst announced as he tossed his clipboard onto a lab table. He patted Wade on the back. "Well done. I'm sorry to push you so hard, but time is very important to us."

"But I didn't tell you anything."

"You told me a lot more than you think. I can now point my technicians in the right direction, which is something I couldn't do before. We don't have to start entirely from scratch. We have an idea of what we're looking for."

Wade stood up. His legs were stiff from sitting on the stool. "Do you really think you can create an atomic bomb?" he asked.

"I don't know. But you've given me the stepping-stones that your world walked on to reach that end. Anything we develop now is bound to be more powerful than the solar bombs."

"I hope so. My brain can't take very much of this."

"I'm sure it can. But you've done an amazing job this morning. I'm very proud of you." Dr. Lyst was standing at the window now. "Would you care for a walk to clear our minds for a while? It's a beautiful day."

The golden sun lingered high above them, a large dot in the middle of a clear sky. From the walk along the castle wall, Wade could see the entire city of Sarum. Skyscrapers, government buildings, hotels, and shops rose impressively from the ground in an array of formations and styles. The scene reminded Wade of the view he'd had of New York City from the Empire State Building, though not so high up. Once again, he was struck by the vividness of all the colors compared to his world.

"Quite a city, eh?" Dr. Lyst said.

"It sure is."

Telescopes were set up at strategic points so visitors could look at landmarks, interesting architecture, and historical sites. Wade put his eye up to one.

"Look that way," the doctor said, pointing. "I was born near the park. Do you see? There's a market area. Nadia's Market, we called it when I was a boy. Now they call it something else, a contrived name that's supposed to entice people to spend their money."

Wade focused the telescope until the stalls, displays, and tents became clear. He saw plenty of merchandise and food. But, apart from a few stragglers, it was surprisingly empty. "Where is everyone?" he asked.

"What do you mean?"

"I see the market and all the stalls, but there aren't any people around." Wade scanned the area. "Wait. There they are. They're crowded up at one end."

"I can guess," Dr. Lyst said.

Wade squinted to see more clearly. "They're gathered around someone. Listening to him. It's Arin!"

"That doesn't surprise me. He often preaches on market day."

Wade looked over at the doctor. "Preaches about what?"

"The end of the world, of course." Dr. Lyst wiggled a finger at Wade. "Would you like to see? I can show you."

Wade followed Dr. Lyst down a set of stairs and back into the laboratory. The doctor pushed a button on the wall, and a curtain

moved to one side to reveal a large television. "The market, please,"
he said to the screen. It suddenly came to life with a full-color picture of the crowd that Wade had seen through the telescope, only
the people were much closer and clearer. "Focus on the speaker,
please," Dr. Lyst said. The picture moved to the right and stopped
on Arin, who was gesturing at the crowd. "Sound, please," the doctor instructed.

Arin's voice suddenly boomed out. "Only in the shelter will there
be protection!" he cried. "Return to the Unseen One and be saved!"

Some in the crowd laughed.

"Why should we believe you?" someone shouted.

"I don't have to give you my credentials," Arin replied. "You
know me!" He moved and spoke with great energy, but he didn't
sound excited. "You know that I am truthful with you. More truthful than the leaders of this city, who wish to keep the truth from
you."

"Where's your golden-haired boy?" a woman asked. "Why don't
you parade him out for us?"

"He's gone," Arin said.

"Gone! You mean he's vanished into thin air?" a heckler called
out.

"I believe he was kidnapped."

The crowd laughed, and someone said, "Oh, that's handy!"

"Off, please," Dr. Lyst said to the television. The screen went
blank.

"He's probably worried about me," Wade said thoughtfully. "I
should let him know where I am."

Dr. Lyst smiled sympathetically. "I'll see that Thurston takes
care of the matter."

"You think Arin is crazy, don't you?"

"Not crazy. Simply deluded." The doctor rubbed his eyes wearily. "I think anyone who feels he has to rely on some supernatural force—like the Unseen One—is trying to escape from the realities of life."

Wade wasn't sure he agreed. Arin didn't seem crazy or deluded. But what did Wade know about things like that?

"It's a lot of superstitious hocus-pocus," Dr. Lyst said.

"But what if he's right?"

"If he's right, then we'll all die as he says."

Wade shuddered. "That doesn't sound very hopeful," he replied.

"As far as I'm concerned, we're going to die anyway if we don't unite under Tyran and defeat our enemies." The doctor gazed steadily at the boy. "We each have to make a choice, Wade. We have to decide whose side we're on. You can go the way of Arin or the way of Tyran. There is no middle ground."

"I don't have to make a choice, do I? Remember, I don't belong here. Sooner or later, I'm going home. Aren't I?" Wade felt a sharp sting of panic. He imagined what it would be like if he couldn't get back. Though he enjoyed being important to Dr. Lyst and Tyran, he couldn't forget his poor mother. She'd be worried sick about him.

Dr. Lyst smiled at Wade. "As soon as we get the job done for Tyran, I'll do everything I can to get you home."

"Do you really think you'll figure out how?"

"I'll do my best. I promise."

Thurston suddenly appeared at the door. "Dr. Lyst, Tyran would like to see you," he said.

"I thought he might," Dr. Lyst replied and immediately left.

Thurston entered the room and began to look under the counters, behind a curtain, and in the corners.

"Are you looking for something?" Wade asked.

"Cromley the cat, Mr. Wade," he said. "You haven't seen him, have you?"

"No, I haven't. Is he missing?"

Thurston opened a closet door and peeked in as he explained, "He hasn't been seen since last night, which is very unusual behavior for him." He suddenly sneezed, wiped his nose with a handkerchief, then resumed his search.

"Can I help you look? I'm pretty good at finding things. At least, my mother says I am." Wade began to hunt around the lab, without success.

"Then I'm sure you are," Thurston said.

After another minute's search of the lab, Wade left with Thurston to look elsewhere for the missing cat.

Dr. Lyst knocked on the large oak door of Tyran's study a few minutes later. He stepped in without waiting for a response, then paused. The beauty of the study always took his breath away. Windows stretched from floor to ceiling along the outside wall. Another wall was dominated by bookcases, the next wall contained paintings by some of Marus's greatest artists, and the fourth wall was fronted by more bookcases, filing cabinets, and an enormous desk behind which Tyran sat.

He was looking over some papers and spoke without looking up. "I have been watching the visual recordings of the boy on the television," he said. He poked his pen toward the large screen in the wall behind him.

"I had hoped you would," Dr. Lyst replied.

Tyran put down his pen and folded his hands under his chin. "It all sounds fanciful to me," he continued. "Is he telling you anything valuable?"

"I think his information is *very* valuable," Dr. Lyst said enthusiastically. "He's given us a whole new direction, a direction we wouldn't have thought of in our solar-based society. It's so simple . . . so primitive . . . it's little wonder we didn't think of it."

"But will it work?"

"Yes."

Tyran eyed him skeptically. "You sound awfully confident."

"Don't you see? All the elements for these bombs were right

under our noses, but we didn't realize it until now. All my technicians in Hailsham have been watching our interviews on closed-circuit television. I spoke to them briefly on my way here to see you. They're already starting to put the pieces together."

"Can we create these weapons he is describing? Can we manufacture an atomic bomb?"

"I think we can. But it will take a long time."

"We do not have a long time, my friend. I have just learned that the Adrians will probably join the Albanites to fight against us. We *must* have superior weaponry to scare them off."

"If it's a scare you want to give them . . ."

"Yes?"

Dr. Lyst spoke slowly, thinking aloud. "It'll take a long time to create an atomic bomb, but I think we can create some smaller yet very powerful bombs in a shorter time—they'll certainly be more powerful than the solar bombs we're throwing at each other now."

"How quickly can you produce these bombs?"

Dr. Lyst did an estimation in his head. "A month, maybe more."

"A month! We don't have a month! I must have something sooner, something *now*."

"You want the impossible."

"I *need* the impossible."

"My technicians are working around the clock."

Tyran paced with his hands clasped behind his back. "If I could stall everyone with a demonstration . . . just enough to impress them that we have the capability to inflict damage . . . even if we are not ready to mass-manufacture yet . . . then maybe those fool elders will listen to me."

"You want to bluff them?"

"Yes. Make them think we have a whole arsenal, even if we do not. Can you create just *one* bomb powerful enough to make them think twice about me?"

"Without testing it first—"

"Forget testing it! The demonstration will be the test!"

Dr. Lyst looked doubtful. "I can try."

"When?"

The doctor took a deep breath and closed his eyes. "Three days?"

"Make it two."

"Tyran!"

"Three days may be too late. Make it two days, my friend. I am meeting with the elders this afternoon, and I *must* have something with which to surprise them. Two days."

"Two days." Dr. Lyst sighed deeply. "I'll leave for Hailsham right away."

From his bedroom window, Wade watched Tyran climb into his black sedan and drive away. A moment later, Dr. Lyst left in his smaller car. Wade wondered where they were going and why Dr. Lyst had such a serious expression on his face.

Wade's attention was drawn from the window by a strange scratching sound behind the wall next to the bed. *Rats?* he wondered. But then a dark-wood panel sprang open, as if suddenly released from a latch.

Thurston stepped into the room. "Secret passageway," he said to Wade as he closed the panel behind him. "I thought Cromley had gotten in there, as he sometimes does."

Wade approached the panel and ran his finger along the almost-invisible seam. "Really? Where does it go?" he asked.

"To the various rooms, then down to an underground corridor that runs to a pump house at the edge of the gardens," Thurston replied. "I believe it was used by the servants in the old days to retrieve water."

"How does it open on this side?"

"I'll show you," Thurston said. He added cautiously, "But you mustn't go in there. It's off-limits to everyone except a few of the staff."

"Okay," Wade said.

Thurston reached up to the top-left corner of the panel, which was decorated with a small carving of a flower—just as each corner was—and pressed a petal. It released the catch, and the panel opened again.

"Cool," Wade said.

Thurston closed the panel again, then asked, "Any sign of him, sir?"

Wade turned to the room and resumed his search. "Not yet. But I haven't really looked in here yet."

He and Thurston called out, "Cromley? Are you in here?" and then looked around the room, behind the curtains, in the closets, in the bathroom, and under the furniture. In the darkest corner under the bed, Wade thought he saw something move. "I think I found him!" he called.

A few minutes later, Thurston had retrieved a lamp, and together he and Wade looked under the bed again.

"It's Cromley all right," Thurston said, then beckoned the cat.

The animal meowed weakly.

"He doesn't look very well," Wade observed.

Lying down on his back, Wade reached under the bed and, with a broad, sweeping motion, scooped up Cromley and brought him out.

Back on his feet, Wade asked, "What's wrong with him?"

Cromley looked emaciated and had a crusty, yellow substance around his nose. "I can't imagine," Thurston said. He left immediately to call a veterinarian.

∞

Tyran was ushered into the chamber of the elders and found the room virtually empty. Only Liven and Dedmon awaited him. The two men looked tired and impatient.

"Where are the rest of the elders?" Tyran asked.

"They're ill and couldn't join us today," replied Liven.

"Ill?" Tyran was skeptical.

"Yes, ill," Dedmon answered with a scowl. "You're familiar with the word, I think."

Tyran frowned. "I said I wanted to meet with *all* the elders."

"Well, you have the honor of meeting with Dedmon and myself," Liven said. "Are we not enough for you?"

"Frankly, no."

"That's too bad," Liven said and then shuffled a few of the many papers in front of him. "You'll have to make the best of it."

"This is insulting!" Tyran complained.

"Oh, please, Tyran!" Dedmon said. "We've listened to your rantings and ravings long enough." He groaned, then wiped his nose with his sleeve.

"Rantings and ravings?" Tyran asked indignantly.

Dedmon continued, "You're as bad as—what's his name?—the mad prophet."

"Arin?"

"He's the one. The two of you are cut from the same cloth."

Tyran's face turned scarlet, but he said with restraint, "You do not know what you are saying."

Liven snapped, "What's your business with us, Tyran? We have a lot to do."

"What I have to say must be said to *all* the elders."

"Well, that's clearly not possible," Dedmon said. "Speak your piece or get out."

"Dismissing me like a schoolboy, is that it?"

"Suit yourself."

Tyran fumed. "I will show you who is the master and who are the schoolboys! I have warned you."

"Yes, yes," said Dedmon with obvious boredom, "you've warned us again and again. The people will rise against us, we must unite under your rule or perish, and I'm sick of your noise. The people have *not* rallied behind you, and we have *not* perished without you. I'm so bored with indulging you."

Tyran's voice rose angrily. "See how bored you are in two days' time! You will regret speaking to me in this way!"

"I'm sure we will. But until then, if you please . . ." Liven gestured to the door.

"Remember this day, gentlemen, and make note of what has transpired here," Tyran threatened. Then he stormed out the door, pausing only long enough to hear the two men inside laughing at him.

F or the rest of the day, the castle seemed to bustle with activity, but none of it involved Wade. Dr. Lyst was gone for most of the afternoon, and when he returned in the evening, he locked himself in the lab to work. Even Thurston was unavailable to Wade, since he'd taken Cromley to a veterinarian.

With time on his hands, Wade wandered the castle like a small ghost. He tried reading but found the books in Tyran's collection too political for his taste. He walked up and down the halls, glancing at the various paintings and statues, but he soon tired of that. Then he peeked in the various unoccupied rooms, strolled along the castle wall, and felt generally bored. Without Dr. Lyst, he didn't know what to do with himself.

He thought about his mother and wondered if she were upset because he'd been gone so long. It was wrong of him not to try harder to get back to his world, he figured, though he didn't have the slightest idea how to do it. Dr. Lyst had promised he would attempt to figure it out, but could he? What if *he* didn't know how? Wade then thought of Arin, who'd suggested that the Unseen One might return Wade to America. *Did Dr. Lyst remember to have Thurston tell Arin I'm all right?* he wondered.

Arin . . . Dr. Lyst . . .

They were so different. Arin believed in the doom and judgment of the Unseen One—that the end of the world was near. Dr. Lyst believed in the hope and future of Tyran—that a new beginning was at hand. And somehow Wade was the missing piece to both their beliefs. How was that possible? Wade didn't know *what* he believed.

That night, he dreamed of Arin preaching in the streets and a giant mushroom cloud growing on the horizon behind the city. *The atomic bomb!* Wade tried to shout, but he had no voice. Thousands died from the explosion.

The next morning, Thurston came to Wade's room as usual and threw open the curtains. Wade flinched and covered his face, as if protecting himself from an explosion.

"Are you all right, sir?" Thurston asked.

Wade was breathless. "I had a bad dream," he said.

"I'm sorry," Thurston sympathized.

Wade sat up and asked, "How's Cromley?"

Thurston turned, clasping his hands anxiously in front of him before saying, "Bad news, I'm afraid. He died last night."

"Oh no!"

"I'm going to miss him terribly."

"Me, too," Wade said with a nod, then asked, "How did he die?"

"The veterinarian wasn't sure. He'd never seen anything like it." Thurston pulled the covers aside so Wade could get out of bed. "It's all very mysterious," he added.

Wade looked at him, perplexed.

"Not only about Cromley, but the others, I mean."

"What others?" Wade asked.

"Some of the staff have taken ill. We have only about half of our usual people in place."

"Does anybody know why?"

"No, sir," Thurston said. "Tyran called for a doctor."

Thurston went into the bathroom to start the water for Wade's bath. Wade got undressed and wrapped a robe around himself. He walked into the bathroom, where Thurston was testing the temperature of the water.

"Thurston . . ." Wade began hesitantly.

"Yes, sir?"

"Did Dr. Lyst ask you to deliver a message to Arin?"

"No, sir."

"Oh." Wade thought for a moment. "I'd like to go see him if you can arrange it."

"Arin?"

"Yes, please."

"I'm afraid that isn't possible," Thurston said.

"Why isn't it?"

"Tyran has given express orders not to allow anyone in or out of the castle right now."

"Why?" Wade asked in surprise.

"He and Dr. Lyst are in the middle of some very important work, and they fear that a breach of security could compromise them." Thurston stood away from the bathtub. "At least, that's what they've told me."

"In other words, he's locked us in," Wade said.

"Yes, I suppose you could put it that way."

Wade folded his arms and thought for a moment. He wanted Arin to know where he was and that he was safe. "Thurston," he said finally, "I have to get a message to Arin. I want him to know I'm all right."

"I'll see what I can do."

Wade was in the middle of his bath when it suddenly occurred to him what the "important work" was. *Dr. Lyst is making the bomb!* he thought excitedly. *He's figured out how to do it!*

Wade remembered how the atomic bomb was surrounded by top secrecy during its development. The Americans had been worried that the Germans might discover what they were up to, steal their secrets, and develop the bomb before them. Likewise, that must be why Tyran and Dr. Lyst had clamped down on security around the castle. They didn't want any of their enemies to create the bomb first. Wade felt excited and proud.

Later, during breakfast, Wade noticed how empty the castle seemed to be. Many of the staff and servants were missing, just as Thurston had said. Wade ate his toast and wondered about the illness that was going around. What kinds of germs and flus did they have in this world? Were they the same as in his?

His thinking drifted back to the atomic bomb and the effects it had on the Japanese at Hiroshima and Nagasaki. The newspapers had reported that many mysterious illnesses—some fatal—afflicted the survivors. Doctors were still trying to sort out the causes, but most agreed that the diseases were the aftereffects of the radiation from the bombs. They still had so much to learn, they said.

Radiation, Wade thought. *Does Dr. Lyst understand about the dangers of radiation?*

Wade jumped up from the table and raced to the laboratory. The doors were closed, as he expected. He knocked loudly. When no one answered, he knocked again. This time he didn't wait and opened one of the doors.

The laboratory looked empty. Then, through the doors leading to the walkway on the wall outside, he saw Dr. Lyst. The doctor was standing, looking out over the city.

"Dr. Lyst?" Wade called.

"Oh, hello, Wade," the doctor said pleasantly. He looked weary. In the distance, a ribbon of smoke rose from the city's horizon.

"What's that?" Wade asked.

"More riots."

"They're *rioting*?" Wade was concerned. "Why?"

"The war, a poor economy . . . it's always the same," the doctor replied. "What can they expect when they follow the fools who serve as our elders? But the moment is coming—is nearly here—when Tyran will prove himself."

Wade leaned against the wall and kept his eyes fixed on the city. "You've figured out how to build the bomb," he said as casually as he could.

Dr. Lyst sighed. "Not *the* bomb—not the atomic one—but we've come up with at least *a* bomb. A powerful one. My technicians and scientists are exhausting themselves to have it finished by tomorrow."

Wade turned to him, surprised. "Tomorrow?"

"Tomorrow," Dr. Lyst affirmed. "That's when Tyran will make his demonstration to the elders."

"That's why everyone's been so busy," Wade said.

"Yes."

From somewhere in the city, they heard a loud *crack*, like the sound of a whip snapping. It was followed by a muted scream.

"Can't the police stop it?" Wade asked.

Dr. Lyst shook his head. "They've been trying, but the people are panicked. A lot of them are sick."

"Sick from what?"

"No one is sure."

Wade waited a moment, then asked cautiously, "Did you know that a lot of people in the castle are sick, too?"

"I heard that something is going around." Dr. Lyst touched his nose. "I'm not sure I feel very well myself. But I don't have time to think about it."

"Dr. Lyst, have you been using plutonium or uranium in your research?"

Dr. Lyst turned his gaze fully to Wade. His expression was quizzical as he answered, "We don't have such things here, but we have our own equivalent. We call it viranium. Why do you ask?"

"Because in my world, the stuff that makes the atomic bomb work is radioactive," Wade explained. "If people are exposed to it, they get sick. Sometimes they die."

"Oh, I see now. You're afraid that I've brought some of those substances to the castle and that's what's making people sick?"

"Yes. Maybe the people in the city are getting sick from it, too. See, I've been thinking about it, and maybe if you weren't careful, it might get into the water somehow."

"Don't worry about it, Wade," the doctor said, his voice full of assurance. "We have the strictest precautions in place. I have everything under control."

"Then you're not keeping any of that viranium stuff here—anywhere near the city?"

Dr. Lyst smiled. "I said not to worry. We're scientists. We're careful."

Wade wasn't sure if he believed him, but he didn't get the chance to pursue the subject because just then, Tyran appeared in the doorway between the laboratory and the castle wall. "There you are," he said. "I have been looking for you."

"Well, here I am," Dr. Lyst said, his arms outstretched as if he were presenting himself for inspection.

"You have time to stand out here and look at the view?" Tyran teased.

"I *make* time, Tyran," the doctor replied, then lectured, "as should you. You're looking very tired."

"I *am* tired," Tyran said sharply. "Tired of those idiots who call themselves our elders. They will not return any of my messages now. It was bad enough that they laughed at me yesterday, but now they are ignoring me. I will not tolerate it any longer."

"Ah! You've decided how you want to handle the demonstration?"

"Yes, providing you have good news for me."

"Good news?" Dr. Lyst nodded. "I suppose I do. Our prototype should be ready to test by tomorrow morning."

"*Should* be?" Tyran challenged him. "*Will* be, you mean."

"It *will* be."

"Excellent." Tyran rubbed his hands together briskly. "I have determined the perfect site for the demonstration."

"Where?"

"The home of one of the elders."

"A *home*?"

"Liven's mansion on the outskirts of the city."

"Not someone's home, Tyran! You can't be serious."

"I am very serious, my friend. That will show them how powerful we are, and that we mean business."

Dr. Lyst lowered his head and said softly, "No, Tyran."

"No? You are defying me, doctor?"

Dr. Lyst locked eye contact with him. "I know you're upset with the elders," he reasoned, "but murdering one of them at home is not the way."

"Murdering?" Tyran said, then suddenly laughed. "You do not understand," he explained. "I'm not out to *kill* anyone. I merely want to blow up Liven's *house*, not Liven or his family."

"That's a relief," said Dr. Lyst.

Tyran continued, "My spies have worked out Liven's routine. His wife and children are gone every morning at 10:00. His servants use that time to shop for the evening meal. The house will be empty when we do our demonstration."

"You're certain?"

"I am certain." Tyran eyed the doctor for a moment. "You are not convinced."

"I'm not convinced that blowing up anyone's house is a good idea."

"What do you think bombs are for?" Tyran said with a humorless chuckle. "Do you think Wade's country hesitated to drop those atomic bombs on their enemies just because there were *homes* in the target cities?"

"We dropped them on industrial cities," Wade said defensively.

"All the same, you destroyed homes and families. It is what happens in war."

"We're not at war with our own city," Dr. Lyst said.

"We may as well be," Tyran snapped, then turned to Wade. "Thurston asked me for permission to send a message to Arin on your behalf."

"Yes, sir. I want Arin to know that I'm with you and I'm safe."

"I told Thurston no, he did not have permission to do what you asked," Tyran said. He pushed his hands into his jacket pockets. "These are volatile times, Wade. I cannot have one of my servants seen near Arin's compound. It would give the wrong impression. Besides, why should you care whether Arin knows you are all right?"

"Because he helped me when I first arrived," Wade replied.

"Your loyalty is commendable but misguided. He would have made a spectacle of you. He only helped you because it suited his own ends."

Wade thought that statement was unfair. Arin didn't seem self-ish. "And why are *you* helping me?" Wade retorted.

Tyran struck out, clipping Wade on the cheek. "Never question me in that tone again!" he ordered.

Tears sprang to Wade's eyes, more from the shock than from the blow itself. "Yes, sir," he said coldly and turned his back to Tyran to look out at the city again.

He heard Tyran march away.

Wade gently rubbed his cheek. Dr. Lyst also looked thoughtfully toward the city.

"He seems harder now, doesn't he?" Dr. Lyst said.

Wade nodded.

"He's under a lot of stress."

Wade didn't say anything.

"The demonstration will prove to the elders that it's time to listen to us. A lot is riding on its success."

Wade kept his gaze on the city.

"Things will be different after tomorrow."

Wade nodded, but he wasn't sure whether that was good or bad.

Now that he knew he wasn't allowed to leave the castle or get a message to Arin, Wade felt like a prisoner. "It's to keep you safe," Thurston said in the dining room, echoing the same thing Tyran had said that first night he'd arrived at the castle. Come to think of it, Arin had said the same thing about keeping Wade in the compound: It was to protect him.

Why, then, he wondered, *does being kept safe feel like being imprisoned?* He ventured to ask Thurston that question.

"Being safe and being imprisoned aren't so different," Thurston said reflectively as he picked up Wade's dinner plates. "In the hands of someone who loves you, being kept inside is safety. When you're ill, for example, your mother or father may keep you in your room so you'll get better. In the hands of someone who hates you, being kept inside is imprisonment. You're kept locked up so you'll stay out of the way or won't be able to speak or cause trouble, or to punish you."

"So who loves me?" Wade asked. "Tyran or Arin?"

Thurston smiled at him warily. "That's not for me to say," he replied.

Wade remembered how Tyran had struck him on the face earlier in the day. Was that the act of a man who loved him? Wade thought he knew the answer. It was easy to think now that all of Tyran's kind words and friendly gestures had been to get Wade to tell them about the atomic bomb. But what about Dr. Lyst? He had always acted like Wade's friend. Or was that a trick, too?

Wade felt foolish and thought again about Arin. Stay in the

compound, Arin had told him, so no harm will come to him and he wouldn't be used to cause harm. Wade had felt disappointed and trapped when Arin had said that. Now . . .

Now he had to wonder: *Is this what Arin meant? Have I been used to cause harm?*

"Will that be all, sir?" Thurston asked.

"Yes, thank you," Wade answered.

Thurston bowed slightly, and Wade noticed for the first time how pale he looked. "Are you feeling all right, Thurston?" he asked.

"Not very," he replied, then took a tray of dirty dishes to the kitchen.

That night, Wade dreamed that he had climbed to the top of the castle wall to see the city—just as he'd climbed the wall of Arin's compound. But the ladder fell and he was stuck on the wall. To his horror, he saw that the wall was rigged with explosives, and they were set to go off in two minutes. He didn't know what to do. Then a voice called to him from below. It was Arin, with outstretched arms, shouting, "Jump! I'll catch you! I'll protect you!" Wade was poised on the ledge, unable to make his decision, when the bombs went off.

Wade awakened to a dark room. Once he realized it was only a dream, he lay back and tried to calm his fast-beating heart. He rolled over to look at the small clock on the bedstand. It was after nine o'clock.

Nine o'clock at night? That didn't make sense. He had gone to bed at 10:00. Tumbling out from under the covers, he went over to the curtains and pushed them aside. A glorious morning greeted him.

"Where's Thurston?" he wondered out loud. Pulling on his robe, he went into the hallway. Everything seemed unnaturally quiet. He made his way to Dr. Lyst's laboratory and was relieved to find the doctor there. "Good morning," Wade said.

"Is it? I'm not so certain," the doctor replied, pacing around the room with great agitation. He looked pale and had dark circles under his eyes.

"I overslept," Wade explained. "Thurston didn't wake me up like he normally does. Do you know where he is?"

"What?"

"Where's Thurston?"

Dr. Lyst waved his hand impatiently. "I haven't the foggiest. Probably with the rest of the staff, finding vantage points from which to watch Tyran's demonstration."

"He's going through with it? You finished the bomb?"

"Please, Wade, don't bother me with questions now. I'm annoyed—*most* annoyed."

"What's the matter?"

"The matter?" The doctor looked at him as if he were stupid. "I was up all night at our laboratory in Hailsham, that's what's the matter. Half my scientists and technicians have come down with this blasted illness. And I had Tyran breathing down my neck the whole time."

"Did you finish your prototype of the bomb?" Wade asked.

"I wouldn't call it a prototype. A prototype means we'll make more like it, and we won't. No, sir, we won't make another one like it. It was a mess."

"You mean it won't work?"

Dr. Lyst suddenly blew his nose, then answered, "It'll work, all right. It'll blow that house to smithereens. But I wouldn't want to make another like it. We needed *time*, I kept telling Tyran. We have to test these things *carefully*. But he wouldn't listen. Oh no, he wouldn't. He'll have his demonstration, but I won't let him pressure me like that again. I want my bombs to be *right*. It's a wonder his men weren't blown up carrying the bomb to the house."

"*His* men?"

"Why do you keep asking so many questions!" Dr. Lyst shouted. "He wouldn't let me or my technicians set the bomb up. He had his *soldiers* do it—as if they know anything about my bombs. 'You'll be spotted,' he said. 'My soldiers will creep in quietly, set the bomb, and creep away. No one will know they were there. But you and your technicians would blunder in and give the whole thing away.' Can you imagine? He said we would *blunder* in! *Blunder!* Well, if it all goes wrong, he'll have no one to blame but himself."

Wade didn't know what to say.

Dr. Lyst looked at Wade as puzzlement moved across his face like a shadow. "Why are you still in your bathrobe?"

"Thurston didn't wake me up," Wade explained again.

"For heaven's sake, get dressed, Wade! This is a big day!"

Wade rushed back to his room and hastily washed himself, watered down his hair so it wouldn't stick up at odd angles, dressed, then returned to the lab.

Dr. Lyst was out on the castle wall with a telescope. He handed Wade a large pair of powerful binoculars. "We'll see everything from here," he said, then sighed. "I hope you're pleased with your creation."

"My creation?"

Dr. Lyst eyed him impatiently. "Must you always speak in question marks? Yes, it's your creation as much as it's mine."

Tyran made his demands clear in the elders' meeting. Liven and Dedmon, along with Acad, who was obviously ill, argued with him.

"You think we're going to hand the reins of power over to you simply because you *tell us* we should?" Dedmon asked. He sniffled, then blew his nose loudly.

Liven stood up to face Tyran. "We've been more than patient

with you, Tyran," he said. "Leave now or I'll have my guards throw you out."

Tyran smiled and said, "Your guards are currently being subdued by *my* guards."

"What?" Liven said. He marched over to the chamber door, threw it open, and found himself face-to-face with three of Tyran's men. They scowled at him and looked all the more menacing because of their sharp black uniforms and high jackboots. Liven turned to Tyran. "You can't do this!" he insisted. "It's treason!"

"It is only a temporary measure, to make sure we are not interrupted until my demonstration is finished," Tyran replied as if nothing were wrong.

"What demonstration?" Acad asked weakly from his chair.

Tyran looked at his watch. "The demonstration that will take place in about five minutes. But you gentlemen will have to come up to the roof with me."

"I'm not going anywhere," Acad said.

"Neither am I," Dedmon added.

"Shall I call my guards to help persuade you?" Tyran threatened.

The three elders looked to one another.

"We'll go," Liven said. "But this had better be the most remarkable thing we've ever seen."

"It will be," Tyran said. "It will be."

Tyran and the elders reached the roof in four minutes. Acad looked as if he might expire right then and there from the journey.

"Now what?" Liven asked.

"Look off to the east."

"What about it?"

"More specifically, look in the direction of the Cinemon

suburbs—that wondrously large and exclusive selection of houses there," Tyran said, pointing.

"You know that's where I live," Liven said with a frown.

"By no small coincidence, it is where you live!" Tyran said dramatically. "That single large house over on the Cinemon Ridge—off by itself—will be the site of our demonstration. Look through the telescopes I have provided, please." He gestured to the telescopes. "Go on. Everyone have a look."

"I see my house," Liven said, flatly unimpressed.

"In five seconds you will not."

"What do you mean?"

"Watch." Tyran counted down slowly. "Five . . . four . . . three . . ."

"Two . . . one," Dr. Lyst counted down. When he reached *one*, he tensed in anticipation of the explosion. It didn't come. "Something's wrong," he said a few seconds later. "Something's gone wrong!"

"This is ridiculous!" Liven said and pushed the telescope away.

Tyran was red-faced. "Wait! It will come," he assured them.

"I don't know what you're up to," Liven said with a scowl, "but your time is up."

"No!" Tyran said.

"Let's go back to our meeting, gentlemen," Liven suggested to Dedmon and Acad.

Tyran held up his hands to stop them. "No! It will happen."

Liven pointed a finger at Tyran. "And you'd better be glad that whatever you were doing failed. Because if you do anything to hurt my family or my house or *anything that is mine*, you won't live to regret it."

Tyran turned scarlet and suddenly grabbed Liven. "You will stay here and watch until I tell you it is time to go!" he demanded. "Now watch!"

Dr. Lyst was talking into something that resembled a walkie-talkie, trying to learn what had gone wrong with the bomb.

Wade continued to look at Liven's house through the binoculars. It was a large Romanesque building with pillars in the front. Tall windows lined the first and second floors.

"Well?" Dr. Lyst shouted into the communicator. "What happened?"

A garbled voice said something back to him that Wade didn't understand.

"Say that again?" Dr. Lyst commanded.

Wade scanned the house. It looked impressive in the midmorning light. The pillars cast shadows against the white stone. The sun glinted in the windows. Suddenly, Wade froze. Something had moved in one of the windows. He was sure of it. "Dr. Lyst!" he said, his mouth going dry.

He now saw a woman clearly in one of the upper windows. She had opened it and was shaking a large cloth—maybe it was a small rug—out the window.

"Dr. Lyst," Wade cried out, "there's someone in the house!"

"There can't be. It's supposed to be empty," the doctor said and pressed his eye against the telescope lens. "Oh no!" He lifted the communicator again and started to say, "Abort the detonation!"

Just then, the house exploded.

The brilliance of the flash made Wade wince. The sound rattled his rib cage, the windows of the castle, and the wall under his feet. Then, for a moment, a sickening silence hung over the city. No dogs barked, no birds sang, no horns sounded, and not a human being moved or breathed.

A moment later, from somewhere far below, Wade heard a baby begin to cry.

Liven slumped to the floor of the roof. His face had gone completely white. He stared into an emptiness only he could see. One second his house was there and Sheresh, his housemaid, was shaking out a small rug from his son's bedroom window—and the next second it was all gone. The house, the road leading up to it, the trees surrounding it, and even a large chunk of the Cinemon Ridge itself—all were obliterated. Only a scorched black smudge marked where his home had been.

"You're a madman," Acad whispered.

Tyran looked at them one by one and spat out, "You laughed at me! Well, now let me hear you laugh!"

Dedmon and Acad stared at him.

"My wife, my children," Liven said as if bringing himself out of his shock.

"They are safe," Tyran said. "Your wife is running her usual morning errands, and your children are at school."

"Sheresh was there."

"The house was empty."

"Sheresh the housemaid was there! I saw her! Right before the blast."

Tyran turned to one of his guards, who nodded quickly to confirm Liven's statement.

"If she was there," Tyran said, "she was not supposed to be."

"She's dead! You killed her!" Liven cried out. The rage contorted his face as he rushed to attack Tyran. Tyran quickly stepped out of his path. Liven stumbled and fell to the ground. He lay there, sobbing heavily.

Tyran turned to Acad and Dedmon. "You have seen the power I have," he said coldly. "My explosives will bring our enemies to their knees. Now, the question is, whose side do you want to be on? Mine or theirs?"

"What kind of deal are you offering us?" Acad asked.

"You make me the governor of this realm," Tyran said.

"You say 'governor,' but you mean 'dictator,' am I correct?" Dedmon asked.

"I am willing to allow the elders to serve as an advisory board in my new government. You will not have to lose your prestige or positions. But I expect your loyalty."

Acad wheezed for a moment, then asked, "And what if we don't agree?"

"Then perhaps *all* your homes will be destroyed as Liven's was." Tyran stared them down with cold eyes. "And next time, I may not care whether your families are still inside. Think about it."

Wade barely made it to the wall before heaving the contents of his stomach over the side. It was more than his mind could take: A woman going about her business as she probably had for years on end, casually shaking a rug out a window, was dead. Did she have a husband? Children? Friends? Other loved ones? None of it mattered now. The bomb had gone off, and she was dead. And for what? So Tyran could give a demonstration.

Wade began to shake uncontrollably as the tears fell down his cheeks.

Dr. Lyst angrily threw down the communicator. It shattered into small pieces on the hard stones of the walk. Then he kicked at the telescope until it fell over. "Does he realize what he's done!" he shouted.

"He killed her," Wade said.

"Yes, he did. He killed her," Dr. Lyst said. "And it won't bode well for our cause!"

Wade wasn't sure he'd heard Dr. Lyst correctly. "Our cause?" he asked.

"We want the people to follow Tyran because he's a man of power and of vision," Dr. Lyst said, "not because they're afraid of him."

"Didn't you see what just happened, Dr. Lyst?" Wade complained. "He *killed* an innocent woman!"

Dr. Lyst waved his hand dismissively. "Oh, that. Yes, yes, it's tragic. But worse, it could damage our plans."

Wade gaped at Dr. Lyst. "You don't care, do you?" he said, shocked by the revelation. "You don't care that she died."

"Oh, *please*, Wade," Dr. Lyst said. "I have more important things to care about than the life of a housemaid."

Suddenly, Wade remembered something Muiraq and Arin had said about the evil of this generation: The first thing to go when people turn their backs on the Unseen One is their humanity. "Men who commit heinous and immoral acts become heroes—giants in the land," Arin had said. "Lives become expendable to wicked ideals and causes. We celebrate inhumanity because we no longer understand what it is to be human."

Tyran returned to the castle within the hour. Wade followed Dr. Lyst to Tyran's office, where their leader was clearly delighted. "The elders have agreed to support me!" he announced happily. "Now I must seize the momentum and make a speech in the city square."

"Slow down," Dr. Lyst said. "I think we should have a chat."

"I do not have time," Tyran said.

Dr. Lyst persisted. "I'm afraid you're losing sight of your goals," he warned.

"What are you talking about? I am *achieving* my goals—as of this day!" He clapped Dr. Lyst on the shoulder. "And you made it possible with that wonderful bomb of yours. But you cannot waste time. We need more of them."

"Listen to me, Tyran—"

"My throat is getting raw," Tyran interrupted, deaf to Dr. Lyst's concern. "Does anyone have a lozenge?" He went to his desk to find one.

"Tyran!" Dr. Lyst snapped.

Tyran stopped where he was and looked at the doctor.

"I understood about blowing up the house," Dr. Lyst continued. "That was a solid demonstration of power. But . . ." He hesitated.

Impatiently, Wade picked up the thought. "But you killed an innocent woman this morning!" he said.

Tyran turned to Wade and said casually, "Yes . . . and?"

Wade didn't know what to say. He had hoped Tyran might feel some sense of remorse. "Aren't you sorry?" he finally asked.

Tyran's gaze went from Wade to Dr. Lyst. "Why is this boy bothering me with stupid questions?" he asked.

Dr. Lyst took another tack. "Whether you're sorry or not, the crowds may not be, shall we say, *appreciative* that you killed one of their own," he suggested. "She was a *worker*, Tyran. You're supposed to be representing the workers, not killing them."

"Why should I care what the crowds think? The destruction of that house—and her death—demonstrated that I mean business. They will strike fear into their hearts."

"Destruction? Death? Fear?" Dr. Lyst lashed out. "Is that what you're after now? I thought it was *vision* and *strength* and *freedom*."

"Sometimes the only way to persuade the people toward things like vision, strength, and freedom is to scare them."

"No. In the long run, fear only leads to more fear, and then to oppression."

"I am losing my patience, doctor. I have an important speech to make, and I do not need you to muddle my thinking. Now, I suggest you and the boy get dressed for our big moment."

"You want *us* to go with you?" Wade asked.

"Yes. You will be on the grandstand with me. I want the people to see the brains behind my bombs and"—he gestured to Wade—"the *inspiration* behind them. Now *hurry*."

"But—" Wade started to argue, but Dr. Lyst signaled him to be quiet. It was time to leave.

When they were out of Tyran's earshot, Dr. Lyst said, "There's no talking to him when he gets like that."

"What are we going to do?" Wade asked.

"I don't know. I'm afraid he's lost control."

"I don't want to go to his speech. I don't want anyone to think I'm with him."

Dr. Lyst glanced at Wade. "But you *are* with him," he observed.

"Not anymore," Wade said. "Not after he killed that woman."

"I'm afraid you have no choice."

Thurston was nowhere to be found, so Wade had to rummage around for clothes to wear. In a spirit of defiance, he decided to wear the clothes Arin had given him after he'd first arrived: light trousers and tunic with a robe. The outfit seemed just right for the warm, sunny day.

Wade considered trying to escape. He didn't like the idea of being on display at Tyran's speech. And the more he thought about it, the sicker he felt for his part in blowing up the house and killing the poor servant woman. *If I hadn't talked to them about the atomic bomb, it might not have happened,* he told himself. He looked over at the wall panel next to the bed, the one that led to the secret passageway. *Maybe I can escape through there.*

Before he could decide, however, a stern-looking guard came to the room and indicated that Wade should follow him. They walked down the main hall to the courtyard, where Tyran and Dr. Lyst were waiting. A flicker of surprise showed in Tyran's eyes when he recognized Wade's clothes. "Nice outfit," he said sarcastically. Then he motioned for everyone to get into the back of his black sedan, and they drove into Sarum.

Wade was startled to see the condition of the city. The windows in many shops and homes were shattered, more so as they drove to the center square.

"Did the rioters break them?" Wade asked.

"Maybe some, but most of the damage was caused by the explosion," Dr. Lyst explained. "It was a far more powerful bomb than even I suspected."

"Yes, it was," Tyran affirmed with a smile.

Wade also noticed that many of the shops were closed. "Is it a holiday?" he asked.

"It will be after today," Tyran said. "We will call it 'Independence Day.'"

Dr. Lyst ignored him and said, "A lot of the people are sick with this mysterious illness that's going around. The hospitals are packed with patients. The city health authorities are now calling it an epidemic."

"One more thing for me to blame on the elders," Tyran said.

"*You'll* find a cure for it?" Dr. Lyst asked skeptically.

"No," Tyran replied. "As my leading scientist, *you* will find a cure for it."

Wade was tempted to bring up the subject of the effects of radiation, but he thought Dr. Lyst might get angry with him. He decided to remind the doctor of it later, in private.

As they approached the town square, the crowds thickened. People milled around aimlessly, though some had picket signs protesting the morning's explosion.

Tyran instructed an aide in the front of the car, "Make a note of who the protesters are. We will deal with them later."

The aide nodded and lifted a communicator to his mouth. "Photograph and identify the protesters," he ordered someone on the other end.

The car made its way slowly through the hordes of people who were gathering for Tyran's speech. Many stopped to watch the black sedan drive past. Wade was struck by how pale and tired everyone looked. One man stumbled against the car, and Wade nearly cried out. The man had a sickly, yellow crust oozing from his nose. *Just like Cromley*, Wade thought.

Wade glanced at Dr. Lyst. The doctor shook his head as if to warn Wade not to say anything.

The car came to a halt, and guards gathered around the doors so Tyran, Dr. Lyst, and Wade could have safe passage to the large grandstand set up at the back of the square. Some of the people applauded as the three of them walked up the stairs. A few hecklers booed them, but they were instantly silenced by other members of the crowd.

Wade heard someone mention his blond hair. Then an old woman pointed at him and shrieked, "He's the one! He's the cause of our problems!"

"Ignore her," Dr. Lyst said as they sat down in chairs behind the podium.

Wade shifted uncomfortably in his seat. Hundreds and hundreds of people were crushed into the square, and they all seemed to be looking at him. He didn't like the attention. He wondered, also, if they would truly be angry about the death of the housemaid.

Tyran approached the podium and lightly tapped a sticklike object attached to the top. The tapping was amplified from speakers stationed all around the square. It was a thin microphone, Wade realized. It wasn't like the fat, oblong microphones used for radio and television speeches back in his world.

"Ladies and gentlemen, your attention, please," Tyran said, his voice booming throughout the square. The crowd quieted down. "This is the dawning of a new day for Sarum—and for the entire nation. Many of you witnessed that dawning in the power of the explosion that rocked our city this morning."

A hum of discussion worked its way through the crowd.

Tyran continued, "I confess to you that it was the house of Liven, our foremost elder, which was destroyed."

The hum of discussion grew louder.

"I confess to you that, sadly, his housekeeper was killed in the explosion."

The crowd grew louder still.

"I also confess to you that I, Tyran, was responsible for the explosion."

Now the crowd erupted in a cacophony of shouts and cries.

Here it comes, Wade thought as he braced himself. *They'll riot now.*

But the shouts and cries weren't in protest, he quickly realized. They were calling out things like "How?" and "Where did you get this power?" and "Tyran's a genius!"

Wade couldn't believe what he was hearing. They weren't angry or rebellious; they were *impressed.*

A handful of people off to one side yelled, "You murdered an innocent woman!" but they were shouted down by the majority of the crowd. Wade thought he saw some of Tyran's guards move in to arrest them.

Tyran turned to Dr. Lyst and Wade and winked at them. He went on, "We have developed this power through the genius of Dr. Lyst, whom many of you know, and through a young stranger who was sent to us by fate!" Tyran waved his hand toward Dr. Lyst and Wade.

The crowd began to applaud. The sound moved like a wave toward the stage. Then came the cheers and shouts. Tyran gestured for Wade and Dr. Lyst to stand up. The doctor obeyed. When Wade didn't move from his seat, the doctor reached over and pulled him to his feet. Wade blushed and wished the stage would collapse and swallow him right then. *They don't care,* he thought as the people cheered for a full five minutes. Wade thought of Arin again and all he'd said about the wickedness of this generation.

"The power you saw this morning was to prove the validity of my claims to leadership," Tyran said when the crowd had calmed down again and Wade and Dr. Lyst had retaken their seats. "You know well the work I have been trying to accomplish in this city on your behalf. You know well how I have fought for your rights and your prosperity. You know well how I have been thwarted time and again by the elders, who are more concerned about their own reputations and pockets than about the people of this city. Have they not allowed us to be attacked on all sides by our enemies? Have they not allowed a mysterious illness to run rampant throughout the city?"

At this the crowd began to shout and cheer again.

Tyran waved at them to quiet down. "Those days are over!" he continued. "They have seen the power that I warned them I have harnessed and have agreed to make me the *governor of Marus*."

The crowd howled and applauded.

"The days of privilege for the few are over. From this day forward, I will lead this nation into a new era, an era of prosperity and of victory over the many enemies who threaten us!"

The people seemed uncontrollable in their enthusiasm.

"Let them be warned!" Tyran cried out. "Let them all quiver in the face of our power! We, the people of Marus, are rising from the ashes to victory!"

The crowd responded with a deafening roar. Tyran basked in their approval for a moment, then waved them once more to silence.

"If you are with me—if you swear allegiance to my cause—then I swear allegiance to you," Tyran said. "Let us all bow and pledge ourselves to a united city, a united nation, and a united future together!"

Slowly, the crowd began to kneel. Tyran took the microphone from the stand and also knelt there on the stage. Dr. Lyst slid from his seat to his knees. Wade watched them with an ache in his heart. The doctor reached over and tugged at Wade's robe. Wade looked at him. He gestured for Wade to kneel. Wade shook his head. Dr. Lyst frowned at him and gestured more firmly. Wade whispered, "No. We don't kneel to leaders in our world."

"But you're in *this* world now," Dr. Lyst whispered back. "And I strongly urge you to kneel now."

Wade was suddenly aware that the audience had noticed his hesitation. Tyran looked at him from the corner of his eye, then hooked a thumb at one of his guards at the edge of the stage. The guard moved slowly toward the stairs. Wade had no doubt that he would be made to kneel whether he wanted to or not.

"You're only supposed to kneel to God," Wade said quickly, as if it would make a difference to anyone. It didn't. But Wade was now stubbornly determined to keep his seat. *Kneeling to Tyran would be like worshiping him,* Wade thought. *I won't do it.*

The crowd was silent. The only sound Wade heard was the guard's footsteps on the stairs leading to the stage. Wade glanced around, a panic growing in his gut. He would make a run for it if he had to.

The guard was only a few feet away when a voice cried out from the crowd, "Don't touch the boy!"

All eyes went to the source of the voice. A single man stood in the center of the kneeling crowd. It was Arin.

13

I s this what it's come to?" Arin shouted defiantly, his voice in no need of amplification. "Now you're kneeling to a man because he makes a few promises? Because he can destroy houses? Because he murders innocent people?"

"Go back to your compound, Arin!" someone yelled at him. "You have no place here."

Tyran stood up. "No," he beseeched the crowd, "I am glad the prophet is here."

Arin smiled. "Are you?" he challenged. "Will you try to bully me into kneeling just like you were going to bully the boy?"

"I am glad you are here," Tyran said, "because the dawn of our new age would not be complete without saying farewell to the old age. *You* are that old age."

"You will say good-bye to this age—and this world!" Arin said, pointing at Tyran. "Hear the words of the Unseen One: 'The stench of your wickedness has filled My nostrils, just as the stench of your dying bodies will fill the nostrils of the vultures who will feast on you!'"

"You preach doom, Arin, and the people of this city are tired of it," Tyran countered. "I promise that the next house to be destroyed will be your own. I will see to it personally."

"You will see to nothing, for your eyes will be filled with the disease of your sin."

"Witness for yourselves!" Tyran said to the crowd. "I bring you a promise of a new beginning, a new era, and Arin whines of doom and disease. Have we not all suffered enough from his words?"

The crowd began to rise. "Yes!" one man shouted. This affirmation was followed by more.

"Away with Arin!" someone else cried out. It soon became a chant that they shouted as one voice: "Away with Arin! Away with Arin!"

"As your new governor, I will make Arin my first case of judgment!" Tyran said. "I will show him how well our city tolerates his madness! Bring him to me!"

The crowd, now a mob, turned on Arin, reaching for him. Wade jumped to his feet, desperate to see what would happen next. At first he thought Arin might fight back—he raised his arms as if to swing out against them—but then he suddenly dropped down, as if falling to his knees. The crowd moved in to the center, but it soon became obvious that the people were confused. The men and women looked around helplessly. "Where is he?" many shouted.

Arin was gone.

Men dressed similarly to Arin were suddenly grabbed and beaten by mistake. This triggered more confusion and violence. In no time at all, the rally had turned into a riot. Tyran shouted for control, but no one listened.

The old woman who had yelled at Wade before now leaped to the stage. "Seize the boy!" she shrieked. "He is evil!"

Tyran's guards tried to grab her and the other people who also climbed onto the stage, but they were outnumbered. Dr. Lyst suddenly stepped between Wade and the oncoming swarm, pushing Wade backward. Wade stumbled to the rear edge of the stage. "Run!" Dr. Lyst shouted at him.

Wade saw a gap between the back of the stage and the wall of the building next to which it had been assembled. He wiggled down through the gap and found himself in the hollow underside of the grandstand. It was an empty catacomb of wooden cross-beams, completely enclosed from the crowds beyond. The mob's footsteps sounded like thunder above.

Wade half-ran, half-crawled in a hunched-over position away from the noise. He ducked and dodged the woodwork and finally reached the end of the grandstand. Squeezing through another gap, he found himself in the open again, but at the far rear corner of the stage. Most of the mob was still around to the front. He crouched low, hoping no one would see him. He heard a child scream. Startled, he turned to see that the child was screaming at *him*. He raced down an alley away from the square. Behind him, someone cried, "There he goes!"

The alley led to another alley, which in turn deposited him onto a main street. Wade slowed to a trot and tried to blend in, but the people soon noticed his blond hair and reacted with fear. Some tried to grab him once they realized he was being pursued by the crowd behind. He legged it down another alley, this one darker, with garbage littered along the walls and tattered clothes hanging from laundry lines above. He ducked into a doorway and started to tie the collar of his robe over his head to hide his hair. A pursuer reached the opening to the alley and said, "I think he went this way!"

Wade panicked and reached behind him. His fingers wrapped around a door latch, and he pushed on it. The door opened easily. Wade slipped in, closing the door behind him as quietly as he could. Breathlessly he waited. The mob rushed by with the sound of an angry lion, kicking garbage cans and tearing at the hanging clothes on the way.

Wade didn't know how he knew, but he suddenly sensed he wasn't alone. He turned to face the room he'd just entered. It was in deep shadows except for thin shafts of light that broke through old shutters. "Is someone there?" he asked.

A raspy whisper replied, "What are you doing in my house?"

"I'm sorry," Wade said. "Those people were chasing me, and—"

"Are you a thief?" asked the whisper.

"No."

"Come closer."

Wade squinted, hoping to see what he was supposed to get closer to. As his eyes adjusted, he made out a bed in the corner of the room. The whisperer was in it. Wade slowly made his way over.

"Take that cloth off your head," the whisper ordered.

Reluctantly, Wade obeyed.

The whisper chuckled, then broke into a harsh cough. "I thought so," it said eventually. "Don't you know me?"

Wade looked closer and was repulsed by what he saw. The gaunt face looked as if someone had draped a thin layer of skin on a skull. A mustache hung limply above the upper lip. Crusty, yellow patches gathered around the nose and the corners of the eyes. Yet Wade knew the face.

"You were one of the men who kidnapped me," Wade observed.

"Movan at your service," the whisper replied.

"What happened to you?"

The face turned away for a moment to cough, then said, "I got sick. Can't imagine what it is, but I'm having a hard time shaking it. I'm sure I will, though. Just a few days' rest, and I'll be back on my feet."

"You should see a doctor," Wade suggested.

"I already did. He told me to go to the hospital. I hate hospitals. They take you in the front door, then send you to the cemetery out the back. Not for me, thanks. I'll take my chances here in the comfort of my own bed." Movan wheezed for a moment. "So they're giving you a run for your money?"

"Sort of."

"You can lie low here for a while. I don't mind, if you don't mind making me some tea." The lips stretched across the teeth in a stark grin. The mustache drooped more.

Wade shuffled uncomfortably. "The crowd is gone. I should go."

"Tell you what: Stay here and I'll pretend to hold you hostage. Then we'll split the ransom money from the highest bidder. How about that?"

"No, thank you."

"Just a thought."

Wade moved slowly toward the door. "Good-bye, Movan," he said. "I hope you get better soon."

"I hope so, too. Maybe I'll see you around."

"Maybe." Wade carefully opened the door, checked the alley in both directions, then stepped out. He took a deep breath to try to recover from the sight of Movan. *He isn't going to live,* Wade thought. Wade was also sure that the radioactivity from Dr. Lyst's experiments with the bombs must have gotten into the water or the air or *something* that had reached the people. That's why so many were getting sick. Tyran's castle was probably saturated with the stuff, which is why Cromley died.

But why aren't I sick? he asked himself.

No answer was forthcoming, so Wade covered his head again and walked down the alley, making sure to go away from where the crowd had run. He approached the main avenue again and, staying close to the wall, inched around the corner.

Just then, a heavy hand fell on his shoulder.

14

"Don't move," Arin said quietly. He had a hood pulled over his head to shadow his features. "You move too quickly, you see. It arouses suspicion. But if you walk slowly and purposefully, people don't notice you."

"How did you escape the mob?" Wade asked.

"I am under the protection of the Unseen One. They couldn't harm me." He then said wryly, "Well, they couldn't harm me very much."

"What are we supposed to do now?"

"I would suggest we return to the compound," Arin said. "At least that's where *I'm* going. Will you come with me?"

Wade nodded, grateful for the offer.

"Come along then."

They strolled down the thoroughfare as if they didn't have a care in the world. And, as Arin had said, no one seemed to notice them.

"Now you see our world as it truly is," Arin said. "The innocent are sacrificed to the whims of wicked men. Even those who feign goodness are corrupt to the very center of their hearts. The people do not cry out with indignation or anger against evil. Now they join in, so long as it suits their own selfish ends."

"Is it really so hopeless?"

"I'm afraid it is, son. Oh, you'll find glimmers of what once was—a noble deed, a moment of self-sacrifice—but they are quickly snuffed out."

"I feel like an idiot!" Wade exclaimed. He still felt responsible for a lot of what had happened. "All I wanted to do was see the city," he said, then went on to explain how he'd climbed the wall and been lured down by Movan and Simpson, taken to the elders, and then delivered to Tyran. He concluded by saying, "Tyran tricked me."

Arin stopped and turned to face him. "Did you not climb onto the wall after I had said to stay within the compound?" he challenged.

"Yes, sir."

"Did I not warn you that everyone outside the compound was infected with evil?"

"Yes, sir."

"Then let's be clear about this: If you were tricked, you *allowed* yourself to be tricked. Correct?"

Wade hung his head and admitted, "I allowed myself to be tricked."

Arin gazed at him, but even under the shadow of his hood, Wade could see that his face wasn't stern. He looked sad and said softly, "It's the way of man—to be seduced to a place of power, a shelter of delusion. From there you can't see things as they really are. You see things only as you *want* to see them. But the Unseen One takes us to a place of humility, a shelter of grace. It's uncomfortable for us, mostly because we then see things as *He* sees them, which means we see them as they really are."

"You mean Tyran's castle versus your compound?"

"I mean your *heart*, Wade."

"I don't understand."

Arin nudged him to continue walking. "You will eventually."

As they approached the front gates of the compound, it was clear they couldn't get in that way. A mob of wild-eyed men and women was attacking it with rocks, bottles, and anything else the people could get their hands on.

"This way," Arin instructed. Wade followed him down a side alley and around to a pathway that led into one of the abandoned warehouses Wade had seen before. Arin produced a key for the tall, riveted door. He opened it, and they went inside. The warehouse was empty except for a few pallets and boxes. Arin pushed his hood back from his head. Wade took the cue and undid his makeshift hat.

They walked over to an elevator and got in, and Arin pressed the button to go down. Several floors below—Wade lost count of how many—the doors opened to a dimly lit corridor. Arin led the way, and after a few minutes they came to a long metal staircase that reached up into blackness. Wade stayed close behind Arin, clinging to the handrail, as they went up and still farther up. Lights seemed to turn on and off as they passed, always just enough to show them the way in front.

Finally they reached another door, which Arin opened with a second key. They stepped through into the sunlight and beauty of Arin's compound. Wade looked back and saw that the door was part of what appeared to be a small toolshed.

"A secret tunnel," Wade observed. "I heard that Tyran's castle has one of these."

Arin replied with a slight smile, "All the best places have them."

Back in the house, where the noises of the mob became merely a background irritation, Wade was reunited with the rest of Arin's family. Muiraq doted on him and gently chastised him for disappearing the way he had. Arin announced that there would be no discussion on that subject since they all had work to do.

"The end is coming now," he said simply.

"*Now?*" Wade asked, shocked.

"Within the next few days, yes."

"How do you know?"

Arin waved his hand toward a set of newspapers scattered on the table. They were filled with headlines like "Epidemic Takes Over City!" "Health Authorities in Crisis!" and "Death Watch Begins: Illness Is Fatal for Some."

Wade read the headlines and thought again of his theory about the radiation. "I think I know what's causing this," he said. "Tyran has been working on bombs with the same kinds of ingredients we use in my world for the atomic bomb. They're radioactive. Somehow he's storing it in a place that's reaching the people. That's why they're sick."

"An explanation isn't necessary," Arin said. "The judgment of the Unseen One has come."

"But it doesn't have to! Not now!" Wade exclaimed. "Don't you see? If we can find out where Tyran is storing the radioactive stuff, we can get rid of it and save everyone. He may have some of it at the castle. But I think most of it is . . ." Wade looked around. "Do you have a map?"

"It's no use, Wade," Muiraq said, trying to calm the boy. "It's time."

"Maybe it isn't. Maybe you're wrong," Wade insisted. Riv handed him a map of Marus. Wade found Sarum, then found Hailsham. "Here. I heard Dr. Lyst say he has a laboratory in Hailsham where they developed the bomb they used on Liven's house. It's not very far away." Wade's eye scanned the area between Hailsham and Sarum. He found what he was looking for: a river that flowed between the two of them. "In which direction does this river flow?"

Riv looked at the map. "From Hailsham to Sarum," he answered.

Wade tapped the map with his finger and explained, "That's probably it! I'll bet the water has something radioactive in it, and that's what's making the people sick."

"Bet? This is a wager to you?" Arin said sternly. "You don't understand, Wade. The judgment of the Unseen One is here. You can't stop it no matter what you think is its source."

"But we *can*," Wade insisted. "We can tell the people not to drink the water! We can go to Hailsham and find out where the radioactivity is coming from! There are lots of things we can do! We don't have to give up!" He was shouting now.

Arin and his family watched Wade quietly. Then Arin said in a gentle tone, "You feel responsible, and you want to do something to stop this."

Wade choked back tears. "Yes," he answered simply.

"And if I tell you it's impossible, that there's nothing you can do, you won't believe me, will you?"

Wade shrugged. "I don't know what to believe."

Arin glanced at his wife, then sighed and announced to Wade, "I have brought you here for nothing. You weren't ready to come."

Muiraq put her hand on Arin's arm. "You're not letting him go back out there?" she asked.

"I can't stop him. The Unseen One wouldn't have me keep him here against his will."

Wade stammered, "I wasn't thinking *I* should go out again. Can't we call somebody? Tell the authorities?"

"We could, but who would listen to us? Anyone connected to this compound is without a voice in the city."

"And I doubt that Tyran would listen—or allow anyone to interfere with his bomb making," Oshan added.

"Dr. Lyst would listen," Wade said. "He's in charge of the bombs. He would understand."

"Dr. Lyst is in Tyran's pocket," Pool said.

"No," Wade responded. "He doesn't agree with everything Tyran's doing. We could persuade him to take action."

"*You*—not us," Arin said.

"I have to try."

"I promise you, son," said Arin gravely, "you will not alter these events by a single fraction."

Wade was resolved now. "Maybe you're right," he admitted, "but I'd feel awful for the rest of my life if I didn't try."

"Then try. And when your heart is ready, try to come back to us. This is the only place where you'll be safe."

Arin let Wade use a communicator, not unlike a telephone. He told an operator who sounded like a robot to connect him to Tyran's castle. The request caused some confusion since there was no listing for a "Tyran's castle," but eventually things got sorted out and Wade heard a rapid series of tones. He found himself talking to some kind of automatic switchboard, which put him through a series of questions, requests for passwords, and identification after he'd asked for Dr. Lyst. Finally he said angrily, "If you tell him it's Wade Mullens, he'll want to talk to me!"

The line seemed to go dead. Wade was just about to hang up when suddenly Dr. Lyst's voice crackled to life.

"Wade? Wade!" Dr. Lyst said.

"Hello, Dr. Lyst," Wade replied.

"Are you safe?" Dr. Lyst asked. "I've been worried about you."

"I'm safe. Where are you? In the laboratory?"

"No, I'm in my car, searching the streets for you." He paused to cough violently, then continued, "Tell me where you are, and I'll come get you."

"Wait a minute," Wade said, then cupped his hand over the communicator. He told Arin, "He wants to know where I am."

"Tell him to meet you in front of the Dome," Arin instructed.

"The Dome?"

"He'll know where it is."

"I'll meet you in front of the Dome," Wade said into the communicator.

"Right," the doctor said. "Oh, and cover your head. There are people out here who'd like to see you dead." He hung up.

Arin led Wade back the way they'd come, through the corridor to the warehouse and back into the alley. He then guided him through the city streets until they came to a large courtyard with a building shaped like a dome in the center.

"It's a museum," Arin explained. "It was once filled with great works of art dedicated to the Unseen One. Now it's filled with the chronicles of man's folly."

"Thank you for bringing me," Wade said.

"My heart's desire is for your safety."

"I know. I'm grateful."

"Are you certain you want to go through with this? I don't trust Tyran or his Dr. Lyst."

"I don't trust Tyran either, but I think Dr. Lyst will watch out for me."

"I hope you're right." Arin glanced around and said sorrowfully, "From this moment on, the people of Sarum will not see or hear from me. My duty is fulfilled. My family and I will finish what's left to do in the shelter and go in until the Unseen One tells us it's safe to come out."

"Even if we can stop the illness?"

Arin looked as if he felt sorry for Wade. "You won't stop it any more than you can stop the turning of the tide or the rising of the two moons," he said gravely. "Look to the Unseen One, Wade, and return to us if you can."

"I will."

Wade looked over at the large front steps leading up to the Dome's entrance. He recognized Dr. Lyst's car waiting at the bottom.

"There he is," Wade said. But when he turned back, Arin had disappeared.

How does he do that? Wade wondered. He walked over to Dr. Lyst's car. The door opened just as he reached it. But it wasn't Dr. Lyst inside; it was one of Tyran's guards. Wade backed away and into another guard, who quickly grabbed his arms.

"Into the car, young man!" the guard ordered. "Tyran and the doctor have been waiting for you."

Tyran blew his nose and then pondered Wade, who was slumped in a large chair in front of Tyran's desk. Wade wondered where Dr. Lyst was.

"You were at Arin's compound," Tyran said with a hint of accusation in his tone.

"Yes, I was. How did you know that?" Wade asked.

"Dr. Lyst's communicator identified it when you called. What did Arin want with you?"

"He took me to the compound to keep me safe from the crowds."

Tyran smiled. "We will have to thank him for that one day in the future."

"He says there won't be a future. He says the end is coming now, through the mysterious illness."

"That is predictable." Tyran leaned forward against his desk. "But I do not understand. You were safe with him. Why did you make contact with Dr. Lyst?"

"Because I think I know what the illness is that's going around."

"Oh? Please enlighten me."

"First I have to go to Hailsham."

"Hailsham? Why?"

"I think the illness is a reaction to the radioactivity from your bomb experiments."

Tyran thought about it a moment, then encouraged Wade, "Go on."

"Dr. Lyst told me about the viranium he's using. If it's like our uranium or plutonium, it's radioactive. That's what's making everyone sick."

"Fascinating."

Wade sat up in his seat. "Dr. Lyst has some of the viranium here at the castle, doesn't he?"

"Yes, we have a small amount in a storage area. He has needed it for tests in his laboratory. He assured me that there was no health risk involved."

"He was wrong."

"How do you know?"

"Because Cromley died."

"Cromley—the *cat*?" Tyran laughed unbelievingly. "You will have to come up with a better example than that, my boy."

"The staff have been sick, too."

"That does not mean the viranium is causing it."

"Then let me go to Hailsham to see if the viranium has somehow gotten into the water supply. Maybe it's contaminating the river that comes to this city."

Tyran placed a hand on his chin thoughtfully. "Our laboratory *is* positioned on the river, now that you mention it," he admitted.

"Then please let me and Dr. Lyst go to check it out."

"I am not sure we can do that."

"Why not?" Wade asked, then added as an enticement, "You'll be made a hero if you can stop the illness."

Tyran looked at him skeptically. "Is that what is important to you now, making me look like a hero?"

"No," Wade replied honestly. "Stopping the sickness is what's important to me."

"Why? You do not belong here. You do not even appear to be sick. Why should you care?"

"Because . . ." Wade hesitated. He didn't want to confess the truth to Tyran, but he felt as if he had no choice. "Because I think some of this is my fault, and I want to try and make it right."

Tyran said soothingly, "You are not to blame for anything, Wade. Just the opposite. You have helped me to usher in a new age."

"I know," Wade said in a way that couldn't be mistaken. He blamed himself for Tyran's success.

"You do not like me anymore, do you?" Tyran asked.

"No."

"Why not?"

"I think you're going crazy with your power."

Tyran looked impressed. "That is interesting," he said. "Dr. Lyst made the same comment."

"He did?"

"Right after the riots. He told me to my face that he thought I was losing my grasp on reality."

"He's right."

"On the contrary, he is terribly wrong. And he is suffering for it even now."

"Suffering!"

"I do not take kindly to traitors, Wade." Tyran pushed a button on his desk. "But the two of you are too valuable for me to dispense with. So here is what I am going to do: I am going to put you in my own personal prison in the tower. That will give you a chance to think things over. It is not too late to prove your allegiance."

Guards suddenly appeared on both sides of Wade's chair. He stood up, and they led him to the door.

"Wade," Tyran said before they left the room, "your refusal to kneel was deeply humiliating to me. Even though I suspect you have more information that would be of use to me, a part of me regrets that you were not killed in the riots. Your martyrdom would have brought more sympathy to my cause. Now we will have to come up with other plans for you."

The guards took Wade away.

The tower was exactly that: a tower on one side of the castle, with a long, narrow staircase leading to the top. At various landings were doors leading to small cells, each containing a straw mattress on a wooden frame, an old blanket, a wooden table, and a bucket to use as a toilet. Each cell also had a narrow slit in the wall that had once been used by archers to fight off enemies. It was called an arrow loop, Wade remembered reading in a history book. When they got to his cell at the top of the tower, Wade looked out and took in the entire city of Sarum. But the view was small consolation for his loss of freedom.

The door slammed behind him, and the key grated in the lock.

What am I going to do now? he wondered. *And what's happened to Dr. Lyst?*

He hoped the doctor would find out where he was and come rescue him. But what if he wasn't able? What if Tyran had tortured or killed him? Sinking into despair, Wade lay down on the mattress. Within seconds, he felt fleas biting at him. He leaped up, slapping his skin. When he thought he had killed them all, he grabbed the blanket, beat it against the wall, then sat on it away from the bed. There he remained as the sun faded and night claimed the sky.

He couldn't sleep. The cell was cool and damp and made his bones ache. He paced around the room to keep from getting stiff. Somewhere outside, he thought he heard women crying. Occasionally something exploded and he wondered if the city were being attacked by planes again. Peeking through the arrow loop, he saw bright reds, greens, golds, and silvers erupting in the sky. Fireworks?

He jumped when he heard a key in the door.

"Stand back from the door!" a man shouted.

Wade watched from his place by the arrow loop as the door opened and a guard entered. He was an older man with white hair and a face drawn into a permanent frown. He wore a shabby version of Tyran's guards' uniforms—the smart black had faded to a dull gray, and the shiny jackboots were scuffed and worn. The guard sniffled and, without saying a word, dropped a tray of food onto the small table. He then turned to leave again.

"Excuse me," Wade said.

"What do you want?" the guard snarled.

"My bed is full of fleas."

"So what?"

"Don't you have something I can use to kill them?"

"What's wrong with your hands?"

"I mean, a powder or something like that."

The guard shrugged. "I'll ask."

"Oh, and—"

"What?" the guard asked impatiently. He suddenly and violently sneezed into his hands and wiped them on his trousers. "Well?"

"I was wondering about the fireworks. Is a celebration going on?"

"Tyran has negotiated treaties with the Albanites and the Palatians. They won't be attacking anymore. The Adrians, Monrovians, and Gotthardites are expected to agree to a peace as well. Any more questions, your highness?"

"When can I leave here?"

"When Tyran says." The guard went to the door.

"Will you please tell Dr. Lyst that I'm up here? He may want to talk to me."

"Dr. Lyst is in no condition to talk to you."

"Why not?" Wade asked.

"He's sick. I think he caught what a lot of the rest of us have."

"Oh, no . . ."

"But I'll tell him if I see him, which won't be likely."

"Thank you."

"Good night."

"You'll be back in the morning?"

"Maybe."

The guard left, slamming the door and locking it again.

Wade looked down at the tray of food. It contained a bowl of a murky brown broth, a piece of bread, and a cup of water. He sat down, slowly dipped the bread into the broth, and began to cry.

Wade had curled up under the blanket next to the wall, but he hardly slept. The guard returned the next morning with another bowl of brown broth, bread, and water. Wade asked him about the flea powder, but the guard merely grunted. "I don't feel very good," he complained. "I haven't had time to ask."

The guard certainly didn't look good. His face was pallid. His eyes were bloodshot, and his nose was red and raw from wiping it. He coughed with a deep-chested raspiness.

"Is the sickness still spreading in the city?" Wade asked.

"Yes. Everyone seems to have it."

"Have the doctors found a cure?"

"Doctors!" he snorted. "They're useless. People are dying left, right, and center, and the doctors can't do a thing about it."

Wade was shocked. "People are *dying*?"

The guard's expression told Wade that he didn't want to talk about this anymore. "I'll be back at lunchtime," he said with a tone of finality. He left again.

Wade listened for the click of the lock. He then went to the door and looked it over carefully. It was made of solid wood, with the hinges on the hall side. The lock was basic: The key turned the bolt into the frame. Wade peeked into the lock itself and could see the dark hallway beyond. The guard obviously took the key with him.

Wade sat down to his breakfast. The brown broth turned his stomach, so he pushed it away. He absentmindedly chewed on the bread. What was he going to do? How long would Tyran keep him locked up? Was this a quick punishment for his rebellion, like being sent to his room, or a long-term sentence?

The morning dragged on slowly. Wade took to pacing from one end of the room to the other, which wasn't far at all. His mind raced with all the events that had brought him to this point. He thought of Arin and his family, of the compound that Arin had said was the birthplace of this world, and of the Unseen One. Arin was so certain about his faith in this person no one could see; he was convinced of the reality of the message he'd spent most of his life proclaiming. "Repent!" Arin had said again and again to those who wouldn't listen. And now he stood alone—just he and his family—sure that the end was imminent. *What if it is?* Wade mused. *What if the end comes and I'm still trapped here? Will I die here?*

Wade kicked at the table leg. This was all his fault. He was so quick to ignore Arin and so ready to believe in Tyran and Dr. Lyst. Why? Little wonder, really. Tyran and Dr. Lyst made him feel important; they appreciated him for all the things he got teased about at school; they made him think he was part of a glorious new day in this strange world. Arin, on the other hand, told him he was a sign of the end of the world. Wade didn't like to think about being part of the end of something; he wanted to be part of its beginning.

But Arin might have been right. Whether the world ended because of radiation sickness or because Tyran blew it up with an atomic bomb, it was still the end. And Wade had played his part in it. His efforts to undo the damage were worthless as long as he was trapped in the tower. Who else could do it? Tyran didn't care as long as he had his position of power. Dr. Lyst wasn't around.

Oh, if only I could get out of here! he thought. *I could still save the day.*

He frowned to himself. Save the day? How could he save anything when there was no one there to save *him*?

The guard returned at lunchtime with yet another tray of brown broth, bread, and water. He didn't speak to Wade at all, nor did he answer any of Wade's questions. He simply coughed and sneezed. His cheeks were flushed, and his eyes looked feverish. He left again.

Wade's mood shifted from anger to despair. He took to kicking at the door and screaming out of the arrow loop for someone to let him go. No one responded.

A siren sounded off and on throughout the afternoon, then went silent.

As night fell, Wade saw fires down in the city. When the guard eventually came late with the dinner tray, Wade asked about them.

"Funeral pyres," the man mumbled. "They're burning the dead."

He set the tray down on the table, and Wade saw that it held only a piece of bread and some water.

"The cook is out sick," the guard coughed. His speech was slurred, and his movements were slow and weak, as if he might collapse at any moment. Wade secretly wished he would. He also wondered if the guard could catch him if he ran for the door.

The guard grumbled to himself, then staggered toward the door before Wade could make up his mind. After going out, he closed and locked it.

In a furious burst of energy, Wade threw himself against the door and screamed, "Let me out of here!" His tantrum lasted a full

15 minutes, after which he felt drained and depressed. He cried himself to sleep.

That night he dreamed about Movan, lying in that dark room in the alleyway, his nose and eyes covered with yellow muck. He reached out for Wade and asked him in a raspy death rattle to take him to Arin's compound. "I've realized the error of my ways," Movan said. "Take me to Arin, where I'll be safe again."

Wade picked Movan up—in the dream he was no larger than a small boy—and carried him to the gates of Arin's compound. The gates were torn from their hinges. Arin's house was ransacked. The once-beautiful compound was desolate and scorched, as if an atomic blast had blown it away.

Still carrying Movan, Wade rushed to the shelter. The door was sealed shut. Wade put Movan down and pounded on the door for Arin to let them in. No one answered. Exhausted, Wade turned to Movan to apologize for his failure. Movan was now nothing more than a skeleton with a mustache above its upper teeth. It leered at him. Wade tried to step away, but the skeleton had hold of his ankle and wouldn't let go. Wade kicked at it, screaming again and again, "Get off! Get off!" He finally gave the skeleton the hardest kick he could manage, and it shattered into hundreds of pieces.

Wade went back to the shelter door and banged at it with his fists. "Please let me in!" he cried. "I'm sorry! I was wrong! I repent! I repent!"

When Wade woke up, he was standing at his cell door. His hands and arms were bruised. He'd been pounding at it in his sleep.

He slumped to the floor and wept until he ran out of tears. He thought of the Unseen One. "If You're the same as the God in my world," he heard himself praying, "then wake me up from this nightmare. Take me back to my coal cellar. I'm sorry for what I've done. Please . . . save me!" He sobbed again, "Save me."

The guard didn't come the next morning. Wade tried to convince himself that the guard had simply forgotten about him. It was a mistake. He had no reason to worry.

When the guard didn't come for lunch, Wade grew anxious. Surely they had replacement guards. If his regular guard was sick, they'd send someone else.

Wade watched the city from the arrow loop. Except for the occasional car or man or woman rushing down the street, it seemed unnaturally quiet. A few times he thought he heard what sounded like rioting or looting, but the buildings blocked his view. Smoke from various fires rose continuously until a dull brown haze hung over the city like an old ghost.

He paced from the door to the arrow loop and back again. His stomach ached from hunger. He prayed again to the Unseen One for help, but he also started to give up believing it would come.

The city was dying, he knew. The end had arrived, just as Arin had always said. And Wade was doomed to watch it all from the window of a tower, where he, too, would die.

It was another dream, Wade thought. Dr. Lyst, gaunt and dying, had him by the shoulders and was shaking him.

"Get up," the doctor rasped at him, then coughed.

Wade winced as spittle hit his cheek.

It wasn't a dream. Dr. Lyst was leaning over him, a gray morning light on the walls behind him.

"Doctor?" Wade said, sitting up.

The doctor braced himself against the table. "I thought you were dead," he wheezed.

"I thought I was dreaming," Wade replied.

The doctor went into a coughing fit. It sounded as if every ounce of liquid in his lungs was coming up. When he finished, he said, "Tyran is dead."

Wade was speechless.

"He came down with the sickness. It seemed to attack him more quickly than some of us. I don't know how it is I'm still alive. But last night, right before he died, he muttered something about you being locked up here. I was too weak to find the keys. But I felt a little stronger this morning and . . . came . . . up . . ." He coughed again, then collapsed on the floor next to the table.

"Thank you," Wade said. "Thank you, thank you. I didn't know how I was going to get out."

"Help me back down the stairs," the doctor instructed. "I don't want to die up here either."

The journey was slow and difficult, but they eventually made it down the tower stairs. Dr. Lyst fell into the first chair they found in the hallway at the bottom.

"The old fox tricked me," Dr. Lyst explained. "As soon as I agreed to meet you at the Dome, he cornered me. I think he had a listening device on my communicator. Anyway, we argued, I told him what I really thought, and he put me under guard in my laboratory."

"He sent his guards to capture me."

"I'm sorry. I should have known better. Arin would've taken care of you."

"I came back to see you," Wade said. "I figured out why everyone was getting sick, and I thought we could stop it."

Dr. Lyst smiled weakly. "You were born to be a scientist," he said fondly. "Always thinking. Always speculating. I used my time under lock and key to investigate this illness. I was my own patient, you see. My notes are in the lab. You should read them." He went into another coughing fit. Then, recovering a little, he continued, "It's too late now. I'm dying. We're all dying."

Wade knelt next to the doctor. "Maybe not. By finding the source of the radiation leak—the viranium—we could seal it up."

The doctor looked at Wade with bloodshot eyes and slowly shook his head. "No," he said, then coughed again. "Take me back to the cot in my lab. I don't want to die in this hallway."

"You're not going to die."

The doctor grunted, then stretched out a hand for Wade's help. Again, slowly, they made their way to the lab. The halls were empty. The castle was silent. Wade suspected they were the only two living people inside.

Wade helped the doctor lie down on a cot near the lab table. The man didn't speak but breathed heavily and coughed occasionally. Wade thought he'd fallen asleep.

Unsure of what to do next, Wade went over to the desk and found a leather-bound book, the doctor's journal. The notes were scrawled in an almost illegible way. He scanned the pages and stopped at an entry from a couple of days before where the doctor had tersely described the symptoms of the illness.

"The timetable seems to vary from person to person," the doctor had written. "But the symptoms are nearly the same. In the first 48–72 hours, coldlike symptoms: runny nose, congestion, sore throat. All symptoms intensify over the next 24 hours or so, including a high fever. Gradual breakdown of the immune system."

A few pages held notations that Wade couldn't figure out. Then he found an entry that said, "Investigated viranium poisoning as possibility. All containers sealed. No leakage. No exposure. I have one more theory—"

"Wade," the doctor called from the cot.

Wade went over to him. "Yes, doctor?"

"Go to Arin."

"Now?"

"Yes."

"But what about you?"

"I'm dying."

"Come to Arin with me."

"No. I won't survive the journey. I'm very nearly dead now."

"You won't die."

Dr. Lyst chuckled. "It can't be helped. There's no cure."

"I don't understand," Wade said, his eyes brimming with tears. "You said in your journal that it wasn't the viranium. It wasn't poison from radioactivity."

"It wasn't."

"Then what is it? Where did this sickness come from?"

"Dear boy," the doctor said, then coughed. "It came from you."

A terrible burning worked its way through every ounce of Wade's body. "What?" he whispered.

"You are the host of this illness," Dr. Lyst said. "You brought this plague to us."

"No. No!" Wade cried.

Dr. Lyst closed his eyes. "Do you remember how I did a physical on you that first day you came here? I did blood tests then, remember?"

"I remember."

"You said you had just recovered from a flu, and I didn't know what that was. Well, after exhausting every other theory about this sickness, I studied your tests. Then I studied the samples of my own blood. There it was. Your flu is the thing that's killing us."

"But it was only a small flu," Wade protested. "It wasn't anything serious."

"It wasn't serious in your world. But in this world, which hasn't seen anything like it, it's fatal. Our immune systems don't work against it because it's completely new to us."

Wade put his head down, feeling overwhelmed by the truth.

Dr. Lyst stroked his hair gently. "There, there," he comforted. "It's not your fault. How could you know?"

"But . . . I caused this," Wade said into his lap. "Everyone is dying because of me."

Dr. Lyst wheezed for a moment, then said, "Or maybe Arin was right. It is the judgment of the Unseen One on all of us. You were simply His final sign, as Arin said. You were the means through which the Unseen One judged us."

Wade looked up at Dr. Lyst's face.

The doctor attempted to smile. "Terribly unscientific to say so, I know. But I'm dying now, and it doesn't matter anymore. Now, be a good boy and hand me that controller on the table."

The controller was a small device with a dozen electronic buttons on it. "What is it?" Wade asked as he placed it in the doctor's hand.

"My final gesture," he replied. "I've always had a backup plan in case things didn't go the way I thought they should. I'm going to blow this place to smithereens."

Wade gasped out, "You can't!"

Dr. Lyst worked his lips into a smile again. "Yes, I can. Do you think I want anyone in the future to learn my terrible secrets? Let *them* figure it out if they're so determined to blow each other up."

"But Doctor—"

"Go quickly to Arin, Wade. I'll make sure you're safely away before I push the button."

"But I don't want to leave you here!"

"Now is not the time to be sentimental. You always hoped to go back to your world anyway. You would have said good-bye to me then. Say good-bye now and be done with it."

Wade fought back the tears. "Good-bye."

"Hurry. And don't dillydally."

Wade ran out of the room without looking back.

W ade had the presence of mind to grab some fruit from a
bowl on his way out of the castle. He ate it as he ran through
the courtyard, across the bridge, then down the winding drive. He
didn't know how long Dr. Lyst would give him before pushing the
button, but he didn't want to take any chances.

At the bottom of the drive, Wade encountered a figure lying
prone in the street. He went up to it to see if he could help. As he
got closer, he saw it was a woman. The dead, staring eyes told him
there wasn't a thing he could do.

Hers was the first of many bodies he saw as he raced blindly
through the streets, hoping he was going toward Arin's compound.
Not only were the people dying, but the animals had collapsed as
well. Birds fell from the trees and struggled against their illness
with flapping wings. Bloated horses lay dead along the streets. Dogs
whimpered, then expired. Dead cats dotted the sidewalks.

Wade passed one shop where feverish looters tried to drag out
merchandise. What was the point? he wondered. Or was it that the
old habits refused to yield to the dying souls?

"It's the boy!" a man shouted.

Wade suddenly realized he'd forgotten to cover his head.

"He's the cause of all this!" a woman yelled. A small band of
men and women headed for him. They stumbled weakly, like pup-
pets held up by only half their strings.

"Stop!" another man shouted.

Wade dashed away and down an alley. He easily outran them.

Fires poured out of some of the shops and buildings. The streets were covered with broken glass, debris, and the occasional corpse. Wade tried not to look. The sight was too horrifying, particularly when he remembered he was the cause. *This is all my fault,* he said to himself again and again.

An old man stumbled in front of him, lurching and reeling, grabbed for him, then collapsed onto the road. He gasped once, then twice, then breathed out long and hard until he breathed no more. Wade fell against a nearby wall and shoved his fist into his mouth to keep from screaming or throwing up—he didn't know which was more likely.

Regaining a little composure after a few moments, Wade pressed on. A few blocks down the road, a younger man in a black uniform— one of Tyran's guards—recognized Wade. He blew a whistle and was soon joined by three more guards. They took up the chase after Wade.

These four weren't so easily outrun. Wade ducked down various streets and alleys, but they cut him off. They knew their way around the city much better than he did. Finally he jumped through a doorway into a large building. It looked like a hotel. The guards followed him.

He ran up one flight of stairs, down a hall, then up another flight. Up and up he went with the guards always behind, always pushing him on. Spotting an open window at the end of the next hallway, he went to the ledge and saw a fire escape that would take him back down to the street. He climbed out onto it and began his descent.

When he had gotten halfway down, one of the guards spied him from a window he was passing, opened it quickly, and grabbed for him. Wade sidestepped the guard's hand, but in the process he stumbled and fell off the side of the railing. Clawing wildly at the air, he caught hold of a rung on the fire escape ladder. It came unhitched from its spring and shot out horizontally, carrying Wade with it. When it reached its full length, it stopped suddenly, then coasted down toward the ground. As soon as it seemed safe, Wade leaped off, regained his footing, then sprinted away without looking back.

As he rounded a corner, he was nabbed by the first guard who'd seen him. "I've got you now!" the man announced with a leer.

At that instant, an enormous explosion rocked the city. Dr. Lyst had pushed the button, Wade knew, and there would be little left of Tyran's castle. The force of the blast caused windows to shatter around them. The guard, wanting to protect himself from the debris, let go of Wade, who immediately dived under a nearby car. He heard something strike the guard, and the guard yelled in pain. Wade looked out from beneath the vehicle. The guard, now on his knees, blood pouring from the side of his head, shouted at Wade and then sputtered as he tried to blow his whistle. Wade turned away, crawled out from under the other side of the car, and took off at high speed, turning into the next alley he found.

This alley led to another main street. He had no idea where he was. He hesitated. Should he go left or right? The rush to get away from the guards had turned him all around.

Help me, he prayed, then ran to the right. After 50 yards or so, the street deposited him onto a large courtyard—and the Dome. He was relieved to see something he recognized. Up at the top of the stairs, looters were carrying works of art out of the museum. One said something about the "blond-haired boy," but Wade didn't stick around to hear any more. He thought he remembered how Arin had brought him to the Dome a few days before and headed in that direction.

Several minutes later, Wade approached the gates of Arin's compound. They were torn off their hinges, just as Wade had dreamed in the tower. His heart sank. He hurried into the compound and over to the house. Also as in the dream, it was ransacked. Half of it was a charred ruin, with its black timbers thrusting this way and that. But, contrary to Wade's dream, the forest was still there.

Wade took the path that he knew led to the shelter.

Once in the thick of the forest, he slowed down and tried to catch his breath. He also wanted to be careful. Whoever had ransacked the house might still be nearby. He looked around and noticed that the trees looked grayer somehow, as if even they were ready to give up on life. The flowers had dropped their petals and withdrawn their scents. The whole garden now smelled of soot, smoke, and ash like the rest of the city. Arin's paradise looked like an old, decaying park.

Reaching the shelter, he went around to the door. It was scratched, scuffed, and dented as if people had tried to break it down. Wade wondered where the attackers were now. Had they given up and gone away?

What would Arin and his family think if Wade pounded on the door now? Would they dismiss him as just another crazed native?

He knocked on the door. His small fist made tiny taps against the large steel structure. He knocked again, harder. Then harder still. Finally as hard as he could. Nothing stirred on the other side. He began banging more heartily, pretending he was playing some sort of game. When no one responded, he attacked the door out of fear that they might never open it to him.

He started to shout, but he quickly realized his voice would probably draw a mob or Tyran's guards, if any of them were left.

His pounding on the door got him nowhere, so at last he sat

down and waited. Still nothing happened. The shelter showed no signs of life. He was locked out and completely alone.

He tried to decide what to do next. Should he leave? Perhaps. But where would he go? Soon he would be the only living boy in the city. If Arin were right, he might be the only living boy in the entire world. How long were Arin and his family planning to stay inside the shelter? Days? Years?

Then, like a seed of terror, a thought grew in his mind. What if Arin and the others *couldn't* let him in? What if they were afraid that they'd catch whatever sickness Wade was carrying? *They should be afraid*, Wade realized. *Why would they be immune to it?*

No, they *didn't dare* let Wade in.

He struggled with this thought and fell into a deep despondency. He could no longer imagine what to do or where to go. He wished he had stayed in the tower—that Dr. Lyst had never opened the door—and then he would have died without experiencing this hopelessness, this final consequence of the sickness he'd brought to this world.

I am totally and completely alone, he thought. *Even the Unseen One has probably deserted me and gone into the shelter. I deserve to die out here.*

With nothing else to do, he lay down in the dirt and curled up into a small ball.

The nightmares came not long after he'd fallen asleep. Out of the darkness, the dead came to accuse him of killing them. Their faces were twisted into grotesque masks. Their accusing, skeletal fingers were draped with decaying skin. But Wade didn't run from them. He stood his ground and listened to their harsh, raspy voices that called him a murderer.

"You're right," he replied to them. "And now I'm suffering for what I've done. I'm alone in a dead world. Alone."

He heard the sound of a crypt opening, with rusty hinges and the smell of moss. Hands reached out for him, beckoning him into the casket. He closed his eyes. The hands wrapped around his arms and shoulders and pulled at him. He felt his body being swept away . . . caught like a dead fish on a wave . . . pulling him . . . pulling him . . .

And then he saw a bright light and heard the voice of Arin whispering for him to wake up.

Wade's heart jumped at the sound of the voice, but he didn't open his eyes. He feared that he would look up and see nothing more than the closed shelter door. He feared the hope that the voice kindled inside him. He couldn't bear to have it dashed.

"Are you playing a game with us, boy?" Arin whispered.

Wade slowly opened his eyes. Arin's face came fully into view. Wade reached up and touched his cheek, wanting to make sure he wasn't dreaming. The skin was real. Arin was real. Wade looked around and saw the faces of Muiraq, Oshan, Etham, Pool, Nacob, Riv, and Hesham gazing back at him with worried expressions. He was inside the shelter with them.

Arin smiled at him with relief. "We were worried about you, boy," he said.

Wade threw himself into Arin's arms and cried as he'd never cried before.

"We thought we heard someone knocking, but we didn't want to open the door until we were sure it wasn't a trick," Arin explained to Wade. They were all sitting around a large metal table in what they called the "dining room" of the shelter. In the distance, Wade heard the lowing of cattle, the occasional bleating of sheep, and the chirping of many kinds of birds.

"We waited until night fell and then opened the door," Muiraq continued. "There you were, all curled up, sleeping so deeply. We pulled you in as quickly as we could and then closed the door again."

"The door is sealed tight from now on," Arin said. "You are the last to join us, and only because the Unseen One made it clear to me that you were allowed."

Wade hung his head low. "I don't deserve to be here," he said solemnly. "Why did the Unseen One tell you to let me in?"

"Because of your heart," Arin replied.

"What about it?"

"Did you not pray to the Unseen One and ask for His forgiveness? Didn't you ask Him to help you?"

Wade remembered his time in the tower. "Yes, I did."

"It was more than anyone else in this world did," Arin said gravely. "So He opened the door to you."

"But how did *you* know that?" Wade asked, mystified once again.

Arin shrugged.

"What will happen to the world now?"

"For 40 days and nights, it will go through a terrible upheaval. All living things will die—not only people, but the animals and plants as well. The world will drown in the illness you brought."

"The illness *I* brought," Wade said softly.

"Everything that humanity has trusted in until now will be obliterated: its technology, its knowledge, its lies. After 40 days, my family and I will rise up from the shelter to begin anew. The Unseen One will start pure again what had been corrupted."

Wade looked puzzled, then asked, "But why aren't you sick? Why didn't you catch the disease I brought? You should be afraid now."

"I told you when you arrived that the Unseen One would pro-tect us. And He has, us and all the animals and other living things here. Whatever illness you brought simply hasn't affected us."

Muiraq stood up. "This is enough talk for now," she announced. "There are chores to do, and then we must eat our dinner. Go on now!" She shooed them all away as if they were birds on a fence.

Later, when Wade was standing near one of the large aquari-ums, watching the saltwater fish gliding around carelessly, Arin approached him.

"You have something on your mind," Arin said.

Wade almost asked him how he knew, but he decided it was a mystery he would never understand. So he said directly, "I feel ter-rible about what happened. I'm responsible for this catastrophe."

"In what way?" Arin asked.

"I came here and introduced terrible bombs, and worse, I spread a sickness that"—it seemed incredible, but he said it anyway—"that killed everyone. If I hadn't come, then . . ." He paused and gently bit his lower lip. He was tired of crying and didn't want to start again.

"There now, stay strong," Arin said warmly. "Let's try to untangle this mess you're in."

"How?"

"Well, the first thing you should remember is that you didn't come here on your own. I believe the Unseen One brought you here for a purpose."

Wade thought about it for a moment. It was true that he hadn't asked—or done anything—to come to this world. One minute he was in his coal cellar, and the next minute he was here. "That's right," he agreed. "But my purpose was to bring sickness and death."

"Sickness and death, yes. Just as at another time you could have come and brought life and light to our world. But you didn't. The Unseen One brought you here to convey His justice to an evil world that demanded it." Arin picked up a broom and leaned on the handle as though it were a staff. "Sooner or later the Unseen One's promises are always fulfilled, you see. You happened to be the way He fulfilled this promise."

"It's still a terrible promise to fulfill."

"I agree," he said. "And I don't suppose you have to like it any more than I liked preaching a message of doom for so many years. Do you think I enjoyed that? I was cut off from my relatives, ostracized by my neighbors, ridiculed in my community. When they weren't laughing at me, they were cursing me. But that's the nature of things in this world. The truth will always set us apart. Sometimes that truth soothes and heals, and sometimes it cuts to the marrow. As a result, our service to the Unseen One will always put us at odds with unbelievers. But we have to take our part and do what He wants us to do."

"But if I hadn't come . . ."

Arin looked at Wade like a disapproving teacher. "That's a useless question, now, isn't it? Granted, you did some foolish things once you got here. But those things played themselves out as they should have. You allowed wicked men to deceive you, and they ultimately paid the price for it."

Wade considered that notion. "What price did *I* pay for what I did?" he asked.

"What price do you *think* you should have paid?"

"I don't know."

"Should you have paid more?" Arin stroked his chin in consideration. "Well, now, I believe you've suffered as much as you needed to suffer to realize your foolishness. You saw where you went wrong, and you asked the Unseen One to forgive you."

"Yes."

"Then what else is there to be said? What else is there to be paid?"

Wade struggled to understand what Arin was saying.

Arin put his arm around Wade's shoulders, and they began to walk. "I know how you feel, Wade," Arin said softly. "Deep in your heart, you feel guilty because you're in this shelter and you don't think you deserve to be. Am I on the right track?"

Wade nodded.

"You think that maybe if you suffered *more*, you might feel less guilty. Is that the idea?"

Wade didn't reply, but he knew it was so.

"Then listen to me and listen closely," Arin went on. "There's no amount of suffering you can do to deserve the love of the Unseen One. He saved you because of your *repentant heart*—because you realized there was nothing more you could do. You had to give up and ask for His help. That's as much as any of us can do. The truth

of the matter is that none of us deserve to be saved. We should all
be outside, dying with the rest."

"But you're all so good and wise and—"

"Don't be ridiculous!" Arin corrected him. "We're men and
women, flesh and blood, as prone to disobedience as anyone. The
only thing we did was to listen to the Unseen One when no one else
would."

Wade didn't know what to say.

Arin smiled. "You think about it for a while. Maybe it'll make
sense one day. Meanwhile . . ." Arin handed Wade a feed pouch. "I
want you to go over and see that the horses get their dinner. You
can start with Bethel. The feed is in that long box against the wall."

Wade looked at Arin curiously. It seemed like a strange turn to
their conversation.

"Go on," Arin said. "Just put the pouch over her mouth and the
strap over the top of her head. But be careful. She *does* bite." In the
dim light, Wade thought Arin looked a little sad, but he couldn't
imagine why.

Wade went over to the feed box and filled the pouch with oats.
He then went to Bethel's stall, hesitating at the door.

Arin was still watching him. "Go on," he said again.

Wade shrugged and stepped into the stall. It was dark. "Bethel?"
he called out. He spotted her toward the rear. He approached her
slowly so as not to scare her, then put the feed pouch up to her
mouth. She began to eat. He then reached up to put the strap over
the top of her head. "There you go," he said and turned back to the
door.

Something crunched under his feet.

"What is that?" he asked and lifted his foot to look. He lost his
balance and fell over on his side. Embarrassed, he laughed to himself and said, "You're such a clumsy oaf."

"What did you say?" a woman asked.

Wade replied, "I said I'm such a clumsy oaf." And then he real-ized that the woman was his mother and he wasn't in the stable with Bethel at all. He was lying in his bed—his *own* bed—in his own home in his own world.

Wade looked at his mother, his face wide open with surprise. "Mom?" he said.

Her eyes were moist. She'd been crying. "Hello, son," she replied.

"What happened?" he croaked and started to sit up. He felt too weak, though, and decided to stay where he was.

"You've had a terrible relapse," she answered. "A high fever. I was worried sick. I knew I shouldn't have let you out of bed. You never should have been down in the coal cellar."

"How long?" His throat was dry; he was dying of thirst.

"Since this morning," she replied. "I got the telegram and went down to tell you about it, but you were unconscious in the coal cellar. The doctor said you must have fainted from trying to fill the bucket." She began to cry again. "I shouldn't have let you do that."

Wade patted his mother's hand. "It's okay, Mom. I feel a little weak, but I'm all right. I had the strangest dream, though."

"You rest while I get you some soup. Then you can tell me all about it." She dabbed her eyes with a tissue, then walked to the door.

Wade suddenly realized something she'd said. "Mom—"

"Yes, son?"

"What telegram? Is there news about Dad?"

She reached into her pocket and pulled out the folded yellow sheet of paper. "There's news," she said and started to cry all over again.

Wade held his breath.

She composed herself and continued, "Your father is alive and well, Wade! He had to parachute out of his plane and wound up breaking his leg in the jungle, miles and miles from anywhere. Some island natives have been sheltering him until they could find help. Isn't that wonderful?"

Relief washed over him. "Yeah, it's great."

She came back over to the bed and hugged her son tight, then made a fuss for crying so much and went out to make him some soup.

"Sheltered," he said softly to himself and stretched long and hard. "What a dream!"

Only after he'd finished his soup did he remember the top secret atomic bomb plans. He searched his robe and under his pajamas, then noticed that he was wearing a different pair. His mother had changed his clothes.

"You had coal dust all over your other pair of pajamas," she said when he asked her about it. "And they were soaking wet from your fever."

"What did you do with the papers I had?" he asked hesitantly.

"What papers?"

"I had some papers tucked under my pajama top, with drawings and a lot of writing."

"You didn't have any papers," she said.

"How about down in the coal cellar?" he persisted.

She looked at him impatiently. "You didn't have any papers, I'm telling you. I would have seen them. Were they school papers?"

"No."

"Then you must have left them somewhere else, because they're not around here."

Suddenly he remembered the exact moment when he had handed them over to Dr. Lyst.

And he wondered.

PASSAGES™
MARUS MANUSCRIPT 3

THE CHRONICLES OF INTERCESSION
ANNISON'S RISK

Manuscript date: September 18, 1927

PASSAGES™
ANNISON'S RISK

LIZAH

KRAWLE

ADRIA

Desert

The Wilderness

RAUNDAL

DORR

M
RULED

MONROVIA

Fiel
Grea

LEAPFORD

GOTTHARD

Great Canyon

RELLEN

Forests of Gotthard

MUIRK

← Mining Camp

PALATIA

Palatian King's Cottage

Age of
Apostacy

Arin

Timeline = 2000 years

Glennall

II

IV

FANGETALL

ALBANY

EASTCLIFF

The Downs

Ibany Road

SARUM

US

ALATIA

hailsham

University of
Hailsham

Arinshill

Legend

~~~~~ River

--- --- Road

+++++ Railroad

GLENDALE

of the Rocks

URNCHANCE

Mines

Caves of Laurel

Fendar	Period of the Judges		Darien		Draven			BOOK 3 ANNISON
VI			I		V			III

"Ready or not, here I come!" a child's voice called out from somewhere behind the shed.

Madina Nicholaivitch giggled and scrambled to find a hiding place. She'd already hidden once behind the well and once in the garage, and now she had to think of somewhere little Johnny Ziegler wouldn't think to find her.

Johnny shouted, excitement in his voice, "I'm coming, Maddy!"

Everyone called her Maddy now except her grandparents, who still spoke in Russian and called her Dreamy Madina in that tongue. It didn't matter to them that they'd been living in America for 10 years now. "We will not forsake our traditions, no matter where we live," Grandma had said.

On the other hand, Maddy's father, Boris, now refused to speak any Russian. He said he was protesting the Russian Revolution of 1917 that drove them, persecuted and destitute, from their home in St. Petersburg. "We're in America now," he stated again and again in his clipped English. "We must speak as Americans."

"The revolution will not last," Maddy's grandpa proclaimed several times a year, especially in October, on the anniversary of the revolution.

"It is now 1927, is it not?" Maddy's father argued. "They have killed the czar, they have destroyed everything we once held dear, and they are closing our churches. I turn my back on Russia as Russia turned its back on us. We are Americans now."

So Madina became Maddy and spoke American because she was only two when they came to America. She never really learned Russian anyway, except for odd phrases from her grandparents. Refugees that they were, they'd started off in New York and drifted west to Chicago as opportunities from various friends and relatives presented themselves. Boris had been an accomplished tailor back in St. Petersburg, so his skill was in demand wherever they went. Then they'd heard from a cousin who owned a tailor shop in a small mid-Western town and wanted Boris to join him in the business. They called the firm Nichols Tailor & Clothes, Nichols being the English corruption of their original Russian name, and made clothes for nearly everyone, including the mayor.

Maddy was unaffected by all the changes and upheaval in their lives. She seemed contented and happy regardless of where they were. The world could have been falling apart around her, and she would have carried on in her pleasant, dreamlike way, lost in fantasies like *Alice in Wonderland, Peter Pan,* and the many other stories she read at the local library.

She often pretended to be a girl with magical powers in a fairy-tale world. Or she played out a dream she'd been having night after night for the past two weeks. In the dream, she was a lady-in-waiting to a princess with raven black hair and the most beautiful face Maddy had ever seen.

"You must come and help me," the princess said to her every night in the dream.

"I will," Maddy replied. And then she would wake up.

She had told her mother about the dream. But her mother smiled indulgently and dismissed it as she had most of Maddy's fanciful ideas.

Apart from pretending to be in fairy tales, Maddy enjoyed playing games like hide-and-seek with the smaller neighborhood children. Her mother often said that she would be a teacher when she grew up because she loved books and children so much.

Maddy circled their old farm-style house that had been built with several other similar houses on the edge of town. It had gray shingles, off-white shutters, and a long porch along the front. She ducked under the clothesline that stretched from the porch post to a nearby pole. The shirts and underclothes brushed comfortingly against her face, warmed by the sun. She then spied a small break in the trelliswork that encased the underside of the porch. That would be her hiding place, she decided—under the porch.

She pressed a hand down on her thick curly, brown hair to keep it from getting caught on any of the trellis splinters and went only as far under as she dared, to the edge of the shadows. The dirt under her hands and bare legs was cold. She tried not to get any of it on her dark blue peasant dress, which her father had made especially for her. She could smell the damp earth and old wood from the porch. In another part of the garden, she heard her little brother squeal with delight as their mother played with him in the late-summer warmth.

"I'm going to find you," little Johnny, the boy from next door, called out.

Maddy held her breath as she saw his legs appear through the diamond shapes of the trellis. He hesitated, but the position of his feet told her that he had his back to the porch. Maybe he wouldn't see the gap she'd crawled through. He moved farther along, getting closer to the gap, so she moved farther back into the shadows and darkness. The hair on her neck bristled. She'd always worried that a wild animal might have gone under the porch to live, just as their dog Babushka had when she'd given birth to seven puppies last year. But Maddy's desire to keep Johnny from finding her was greater than her fear, so she went farther in.

The porch, like a large mouth, seemed to swallow her in darkness. The trelliswork, the sunlight, and even Johnny's legs, now moving to and fro along the porch, faded away as if she'd slowly closed her eyes. But she knew she hadn't. She held her hand up in front of her face and wiggled her fingers. She could see still them.

Then, from somewhere behind her, a light grew, like the rising of a sun. But it wasn't yellow like dawn sunlight; it was white and bright, like the sun at noon. She turned to see, wondering where the light had come from. She knew well that there couldn't be a light farther under the porch, that she would soon reach a dead end at the cement wall of the basement.

As she looked at the light, she began to hear noises as well. At first they were indistinct, but then she recognized them as the sounds of people talking and moving. Maddy wondered if friends from town had come to visit. But the voices were too numerous for a small group of friends. This sounded more like a big crowd. And mixed with the voices were the distinct sounds of horses whinnying and the clip-clop of their hooves and the grating of wagon wheels on a stony street.

Crawling crablike and being careful not to bump her head on the underside of the porch, Maddy moved in the direction of the light and sounds. The noises grew louder, and, once she squinted a little, she could see human and horse legs moving back and forth, plus the distinct outline of wagon wheels.

It's a busy street, she thought, but then she reminded herself, *There's no busy street near our house.* The sight inflamed her imagination, and she ventured still closer and closer to the scene. *It's like crawling out of a small cave,* she thought. Then her mind raced to the many stories she'd read about children who had stepped through a hole or mirror or doorway and wound up in a magical land. Her heart beat excitedly as she thought—*hoped*—that maybe it was about to happen to her. Perhaps she would get to see something wondrous; perhaps she was going to enter a fairy tale.

At the edge of the darkness, she glanced up and realized she was no longer under the porch. The coarse planks of plywood and the two wheels directly in front of her and two wheels directly behind her made her think she must be under a wagon. More startling was that the porch, the trellis, Johnny, and even her house had disappeared.

A man shouted, "Yah!" and snapped leather reins, and the wagon moved away from her. She stayed still, afraid she might get caught under the wheels, but they didn't touch her. In a moment she was crouched in an open space, sunlight pouring down onto her. People were crowded around, and she stood up with embarrassment on her face, certain they were wondering who she was and where she'd come from.

A man grabbed her arm and pulled her quickly into the crowd. "You'd better get out of the road, little lady," he warned. "Do you want to get run over by the procession?"

Besides that, no one seemed to notice her. But she noticed them. Her eyes were dazzled by the bright colors of the hundreds—maybe even thousands—of people lined up on both sides of the avenue. Trees sprung out from among them like green fountains. Tall buildings stood behind them with enormous columns and grand archways. Maddy blinked again. The colors seemed too bright somehow, much richer than the colors she was used to seeing. Then she smiled to herself: They looked just like the colors in so many of the illustrated stories she'd read.

She noticed that some of the people clutched flags and banners, while others held odd-looking rectangular-shaped hats to their chests, and a few carried children up on their shoulders. What struck Maddy most were the peculiar garments everyone wore. The

women were in long, frilly dresses, not unlike Maddy's own peasant dress but far more intricate in their design, billowing out at the
waist like tents. The men had on long coats and trousers that only
went to just below their knees. The rest of their legs were covered
with white stockings. On their feet they wore leather shoes with
large square buckles. The men had ponytails, she noticed, and hats
that came to three-pointed corners.

The scene reminded her of the last Fourth of July, when she had
stood along Main Street with the rest of the townspeople for the big
parade, followed by fireworks and picnic food in the park. Some of
the people in that parade had dressed the same as the people she
saw now. It was the style of clothes worn when America won its
independence.

Unlike the parade back home, however, this parade didn't seem
very happy. Most of the people stood with stern expressions on
their faces. A few looked grieved. Several women wiped tears from
their eyes. Maddy suspected she had formed the wrong impression
of what she was seeing. Maybe it wasn't a parade; maybe it was a
funeral procession.

"Did someone die?" Maddy asked the man who'd pulled her
from the street.

He gazed at her thoughtfully and replied, "Our nation, little
lady. Our nation."

A regiment of soldiers now marched down the avenue. The men
were dressed in the same outfits as those in the crowd, but all were
a solid blue color, and they had helmets on their heads and spears
or swords in their hands. They broke their ranks and spread out to
the edge of the crowd.

"The king is coming, and we want you to be excited about it,"
one of them said gruffly.

"He's not *our* king!" someone shouted from the thick of the crowd.

The soldier held up his sword menacingly. "You can be excited or arrested," he threatened. "The choice is yours."

The soldiers moved off to stir up other parts of the crowd. Across the avenue, a fight broke out, and Maddy watched in horror as three soldiers began to beat and kick a man they'd knocked down. They dragged him away while the rest of the soldiers stood with their swords and spears at the ready.

What kind of parade is this, she wondered, *where the people are forced to enjoy it or be beaten?* As if to answer her question, Maddy remembered the stories her father told of the Russian revolutionaries who demanded that people parade and salute even when they didn't want to.

Halfhearted cheers worked their way through the crowd as a parade of horses approached and passed, soldiers sitting erect on their backs, swords held high in a formal salute. Then a large band of musicians with woodwinds and brass instruments came by, playing a lively song of celebration. Next came several black open-topped carriages, each with people dressed in colorful outfits of gold and silver that twinkled in the sunlight. The men wore white shirts with lacy collars. The women wore hats with brightly colored feathers sticking out of the backs. They waved and smiled at the crowd.

Maddy noticed one man in particular who seemed almost as unhappy as some of the people in the crowd. He had a pockmarked face, unfriendly eyes, a narrow nose, and thinning, wiry hair. Unlike the rest of the parade, he didn't wear a colorful jacket but one of solid black—as if he, too, were mourning something. Occasionally he lifted his hand in a wave, but Maddy was struck by the look of boredom on his face. It seemed to require considerable effort for him to be pleasant to the crowd.

At the end of this particular procession came the largest carriage of all. The carriage was gold on the outside; its seats were made of a plush, red material. A man sat alone on the rear seat—propped up somehow to raise him higher than he normally would have been— and waved happily at the crowds. He was a pleasant-looking middle-aged man with ruddy cheeks, big eyes, and wild, curly hair.

"I was wondering if he'd wear that stupid wig," someone muttered nearby.

"It's no worse than that coat," someone else commented.

The man's coat displayed the colors of the rainbow and had large buttons on the front. Maddy smiled. It made him look a little like a clown.

"I can't bear it," a woman cried as large tears streamed down her face. Even with the tears, she waved a small flag back and forth.

"What's wrong?" Maddy asked the woman. "Why are you crying?"

The woman dabbed at her face with a handkerchief. "Because it's the end of us all," she replied with a sniffle.

"Aye," an elderly man behind her agreed. "When the barbarians parade down the streets of Sarum, it's the end of Marus."

Suddenly a group of soldiers who had been following the golden carriage with muskets slung over their shoulders spread out to the crowds, thrusting flags and banners into their hands. "Take these and follow us to the palace," they commanded.

"Only after I've had my brain replaced with a beetroot," the elderly man said defiantly.

A soldier hit him in the stomach with the butt of his musket. The man doubled over in pain. "You'll follow no matter what kind of brain you have!" the soldier growled.

"Leave us alone!" a woman shouted. "Why don't you go back to Palatia where you belong?"

"And deprive our king of his spoils?" another soldier called back. "That wouldn't do."

The man who'd been hit recovered his breath, grumbled something Maddy didn't understand, then stepped out onto the avenue to follow the soldiers. Maddy was swept along with him and the rest of the crowd around her. Before she knew it, the man's flag—a small, rectangular cloth of red with a single star in the middle— was in her hand. He smiled at her. "You'll enjoy waving it more than I will," he suggested with a pained expression on his face. Eventually, she lost him in the crowd.

Worried that she might get in trouble, Maddy held the flag up and swung it as she walked. It didn't occur to her that she had no idea where she was or if she could find her way back to her porch. If this was a dream she was having or, better still, a magical place she'd found like Alice in Wonderland, she was curious to see what would happen next. "Dreamy Madina" was like that. But she wasn't too pleased about the nasty soldiers or the unhappiness of the people.

Maddy followed the crowd up the avenue until it joined yet another broad street. They seemed to walk for miles. Because she was surrounded on all sides by the crowd, she couldn't see much of the city. Only occasionally did a large building poke skyward beyond someone's head or shoulder. She wished she could stop to look longer at the great pillars and round towers or to read the names on the statues of men in brave and noble postures. Otherwise, she caught only glimpses of shops and homes made of brick and stone.

Just as Maddy's legs started to ache from the long walk, the crowd slowed to a halt. Then, after a moment, it slowly moved forward again, now through a large gate made of wrought iron and gold posts. She found herself in a parklike area with level grounds and manicured grass. A single driveway curved around in a half-moon shape and stopped at the double front doors of a palace. At least Maddy assumed it was a palace, for she'd never seen such a majestic building in her life.

The front door stood at the center of two wings, made of yellow stone, that spread out to the left and the right. There were three stories, each with rows of tall windows that reflected the day like jewels. Maddy's eye was drawn to a gold rotunda over the center section, where the front doors were. On top of the rotunda was a statue of something that looked to her like an angel.

The crowd was instructed by the soldiers to sit down on the grass. The man in the golden carriage stood up to address the throng. His voice was deep and booming but still hard to hear since he was some distance away.

"I, King Willem, declare a national holiday for my subjects, the people of Marus," he declared.

"We're not your subjects!" a man shouted from somewhere deep in the crowd. Soldiers instantly moved in to find the culprit.

The king ignored him. "Let this be a time of celebration!" he continued. "A time of feasts and banquets unlike anything seen in your lifetime!"

"As if I ever expected to see a *Palatian* king on the throne in my lifetime," an old man with a craggy face growled softly off to Maddy's right.

"Let the musicians make music, let sweet drinks flow, and let the food fill our bellies!" the king called out. "From this day forward, Palatia *and* Marus are intertwined, united by fate and by victory."

"It's *our* fate thanks to *his* victory," the same man muttered sarcastically.

The king continued, "And now I beseech every man, woman, and child to join me in celebrating my marriage to one of your own, the pure and gracious Annison!"

With this, a woman stepped out through one of the palace's front doors. Maddy gasped. The woman had raven black hair and a slender face, with a smile that seemed to light up everything around her. It was the most beautiful face Maddy had ever seen.

"It's the princess from my dream," she said out loud to a woman next to her.

The woman grunted and turned away.

Maddy craned her neck to see better. Annison wore a beautiful red-velvet dress that highlighted the redness of her lips and the blush of her cheeks. She looked shy and slightly embarrassed to be standing in front of so many people. Lifting her hand, she gave an awkward wave.

Though it was a slight gesture, the crowd came alive now, with all the people leaping to their feet to cheer her. They cheered in a way they hadn't cheered for the king at any point in his procession—wildly and exuberantly. He didn't seem to mind, though. He stretched out his hand to her, his face filled with pride.

"I can't believe she's marrying him." A woman nearby sneered in the midst of the shouts and cheers. "She's a Marutian. She should be ashamed."

"She's an orphan girl," another woman said with a shrug. "Who knows what her lineage is? For all we know, she's a Palatian herself."

"She may be our only hope," an old man observed thoughtfully. The two women looked at him uncomfortably and shut up.

Maddy didn't understand what any of it meant. All she knew was that the princess of her dream was real in this strange world, and now she'd lost sight of her because of the crowd.

"You must come and help me," the princess had said in the dream.

And Maddy had promised she would. With that thought in mind, she pressed herself forward through the crowd. She was determined to get to the front door of the palace—and Annison.

The king, who had resumed his speech while Maddy worked her way to the front of the audience, had just finished when she reached the edge of the lawn and the gravel driveway. The wheels of the golden carriage were within her reach. The king stepped down from the carriage, allowed Annison to put her arm through his, and walked with her into the palace. The large doors closed. Maddy was overcome with disappointment.

The soldiers began urging the crowd to disperse. Maddy stood alone where she was, her eyes fixed on the front doors, unsure of what to do next. She wanted—*needed*—to get to Annison. The feeling stabbed at her heart. She didn't know why it was so important, yet the longing, the yearning, demanded that she make good on her promise to help Annison. But how could she get inside the palace?

The answer came from a stern-looking, matronly woman who suddenly appeared at her side. "You, child," she said.

Maddy looked up. "Me?" she asked.

"Didn't I see you with the choir?"

"Choir?"

"Stop answering my questions with questions. Are you with the choir or aren't you? If you are, you should be inside with the rest."

Maddy decided not to risk the wrath of this woman by asking what she was talking about. Besides, if joining the choir meant she might get to see Annison again, she was glad to join the choir. "How do I get in?" she inquired.

The woman grunted as if she had known all along that Maddy wasn't where she was supposed to be. "That way," she said and, taking Maddy's arm, led her to the double front doors.

A servant opened one of the doors before they reached it. He lifted a quizzical eyebrow.

"She's with the choir," the matronly woman explained.

He nodded and took Maddy's other arm, gently pulling her away from the matronly woman and into the front hall. It was an ornate foyer filled with paintings, statues, and a wide marble staircase. The walls were trimmed with gold-leaf borders. A set of chandeliers hung like large diamonds on each side. Up above, Maddy saw that the inside of the rotunda contained frescoes of angels all around.

"I do wish you children would stay together," the servant said impatiently. He took Maddy down a grand hallway lined with more paintings and small alcoves with statues. Eventually they reached another double doorway. "They're preparing to rehearse here in the Great Hall," he said and nudged her inside.

Maddy's jaw dropped at the sight of the room. It truly was a great hall, with high walls of carved wood, cornices, ornately framed portraits, and mirrors. The tall windows she'd seen outside were ablaze with the daylight, which flooded the room. Dozens and dozens of tables were set up and being laid by more servants than Maddy could count. At one end of the hall was a small stage where a group of girls and boys stood, dressed in smart gray outfits.

Maddy navigated her way past the tables and servants and approached the group cautiously. "Are you the choir?" she asked a girl with reddish hair who shifted uneasily from foot to foot.

."Yes," she replied. "We're going to sing for the king and his bride-to-be at the banquet tonight. My name is Sarah. Who are you?"

"My name is Maddy."

"You're not part of our choir," Sarah observed, then looked her over. "You're not in uniform."

"I know that."

"Then what are you doing here?"

"A woman outside told me to come in."

"To join us? Can you sing?"

"A little."

"I can sing, too." Sarah smiled. "I have a solo."

Maddy looked around, hoping to catch sight of Annison again. "Do you know where the princess—I mean, Annison—is?"

"She's probably in her chambers now," Sarah replied. "I think she's beautiful, don't you?"

"Yes, I do," Maddy said dreamily, then asked, "Do you know who she is?"

"She's Annison. You just said so."

"But *who* is she?"

The girl didn't seem to understand the question and shrugged.

Maddy decided to try a different approach. "I'm a stranger here—"

"Where are you from?"

"I come from the mid-West."

"Is that in Marus or Palatia?"

"It's in America."

Sarah looked puzzled, then shook her head. "I don't know where that is. But my father said that people were coming from all over the world for the wedding."

Maddy pressed on. "What I'm trying to say is that I'm a stranger, and I don't know anything about this place or your king or—"

"Oh." Sarah lowered her head a little and said softly, "Well, for one thing, he's not really our king."

"He isn't?"

"No. He's not from Marus. He's from Palatia."

"So?"

Sarah looked at Maddy impatiently. "They beat us in a war and killed our old king—King Jarrod—and now Willem says *he's* our king, even though a lot of people here don't like him. My father says he's trying to turn Marus into Palatia."

"Then why don't the people throw him out?"

"We're not strong enough."

Maddy understood now. It was a little like Russia, where one side beat the other and took over everything. Something still didn't make sense, however. "But Annison is from Marus, isn't she?" she asked.

"Uh-huh."

"Then why is she marrying the king?"

"Because he's the king and he said she has to," Sarah answered simply.

"Oh." Maddy suddenly felt sad that Annison was being forced to marry the king. That kind of story never had a happy ending in the fairy tales she'd read.

Sarah seemed to sense that more needed to be said and explained, "You see, the king was looking for someone to be his wife, and he made a command that all the prettiest girls in Sarum had to come to a big party he had here at the palace. Annison came, and she was the most beautiful girl he had ever seen, and so he asked her to marry him."

"Like Cinderella," Maddy said.

Sarah looked blankly at Maddy. "What?"

"Cinderella." Maddy was so relieved that she didn't notice Sarah's confused expression. "If this is like Cinderella, it might turn out all right."

"I don't know what you're talking about."

Maddy was still lost in her thoughts about the fairy tale. She asked, "Is Annison the daughter of a man who marries a terrible woman and has wicked stepsisters who make her work hard but won't let her come to the royal ball?"

Sarah pondered the question for a moment, her mind trying to sort out what Maddy had just asked. "Nobody really knows anything about Annison," she finally said, hoping it fit in somehow. "I heard she was an orphan who was raised in secret here in Sarum. My mother says she's probably the descendant of one of our ancient kings and would have been queen anyway even if King Willem hadn't conquered us. The king says she must be of royal lineage or she wouldn't be so beautiful. My father says it's just a move by the king to make the people of Marus like him better."

Maddy thought about it for a moment and concluded excitedly that maybe she was there to help Annison escape from the king, and then she could marry her true love, who was probably a handsome country lad who was really the son of a nobleman.

A thin, storklike woman walked in. Her hair was pulled back in a tight bun, and her dress hung on her skeletal frame like tissues wrapped around a coatrack. She clapped her hands. "Attention, children, attention!" she called.

All the children suddenly formed into two rows. Maddy tried to stay behind Sarah in the back.

"Is everyone here?" the woman asked.

"Yes, Mrs. Leichter," the children said in unison.

At the far end of the hall, a tall man entered. Maddy immediately remembered him from the parade. He was the one with a pockmarked complexion who looked bored and miserable. He made his way toward them. His hands were clasped behind his back, and he eyed them with the look of a vulture considering its next meal.

"Quickly," Mrs. Leichter said when she saw the man coming. "It's the king's personal assistant. Let's impress him with our singing by doing 'Fair Maiden.'"

The children stood up straight and waited for their cue to begin. Mrs. Leichter raised her arms and brought them down quickly. The children began to sing a lively tune about a fair maiden who was lost and lonely but met a handsome prince on a deserted road and won him over with her purity. Maddy stayed in the back, pretending to mouth the words. The tune was so catchy, though, that by the fifth verse she knew the words of the chorus and found herself singing along:

"Fair maiden, fair maiden," the prince said so sure,
"In all of my life there is no one so pure.
I'll take you as bride, I'll make you my queen
And rule o'er the land, and rule o'er the sea."

What Maddy didn't realize was that after the fifth verse, only the first half of the chorus was sung, with the rest of it hummed in harmony. So when the other children began to hum, she continued to sing loudly.

She realized her error right away but kept singing in hopes that it might not sound like a mistake. The other children began to giggle, however, and soon the song was completely undone.

Mrs. Leichter turned to the pockmarked man. "I'm so sorry, Lord Hector," she said in humiliation.

Hector grunted. "I hope it'll be improved before your performance tonight." He sneered and strode away.

Mrs. Leichter screwed up her eyes angrily and looked at Maddy. "Who are you, and what are you doing in my choir?" she demanded.

"I'm Maddy."

"But you don't belong in my choir."

"No, ma'am."

"Then I must ask you to step aside."

"But she can sing," Sarah said in her defense.

"I just heard her singing abilities," Mrs. Leichter said. "And while her voice is lovely, she obviously doesn't know the songs we're going to sing for the king and our future queen."

Maddy looked away sheepishly.

Mrs. Leichter flicked her hand at Maddy as if she were shooing a fly away. "Go on, my dear. If you wish to join our choir, have your parents come to the Academy and fill out the appropriate forms."

Maddy stepped away from the choir.

"Good-bye," Sarah said sadly.

"Good-bye." Maddy turned away, worried that Mrs. Leichter or one of the servants would now step forward and escort her from the palace. Any hope she had of meeting Annison seemed to vanish.

Mrs. Leichter turned her attention back to her choir and called out, "Attention, children. We will sing 'Fair Maiden' again, but correctly this time." She began to wave her hands, and the children started to sing as Maddy made her way across the Great Hall to the doors.

As she entered the long hallway again, it occurred to her that she had no idea of where to go. Worse, she realized she was being reckless. Why was she so desperate to see Annison? Why did the desire burn in her heart as it did? She'd had a dream, that was all. She had no reason to be there, no sensible excuse for wanting to meet Annison. It was all nonsense, Dreamy Madina lost in a fairy tale once again. What if her parents were worried about her at that very moment? What if they had the neighbors looking for her? She should leave the palace right away and find her way back home.

She intended to go. She really did. But at the very moment when she turned in the direction of the front doors, a man stepped into the hallway from a side room. He was short and had white hair, a full, friendly mouth, and deep laugh lines around his eyes. He wore a dark blue coat with gold buttons and epaulets on his shoulders. Maddy thought he looked like a merry policeman.

"Hello, young lady," he greeted Maddy pleasantly. "Are you lost?"

"No, sir," Maddy replied.

He came closer. "Where are you going?"

"I wanted to go to Annison's chambers," she said honestly, but before she could finish her statement, the man interrupted her.

"Our future queen's chambers? You have business there?"

"I wanted to meet her," Maddy said.

The man seemed distracted, as if he hadn't heard her properly. After a moment he suggested, "If you're going to her chambers, you might be of service to me."

"Me?" she asked.

He scrutinized her briefly. "Only if I can trust you. Can I trust you?"

Maddy nodded vigorously.

He wiggled a finger at her. "Come with me," he instructed.

Maddy followed the man down the main hallway, down a smaller hallway to a quick left turn, and then down one more hallway to a door. It led into a small room with a writing desk and long shelves with papers piled up from end to end. The man bent down behind the desk and arose with a large vase of flowers. Red and pink carnations, Maddy thought, and yet they were somehow different from carnations she'd seen at home. Again, the colors seemed brighter, more intense.

"I would be grateful if you'd take these to her chambers," the man said with a gentle smile. "Deliver them to Annison personally.

There's a card for her inside. But when you give them to her whisper—and I mean *whisper*—that these are from Simet. Do you understand?"

"I'll give these flowers to her personally and then *whisper* that they're from Simet," Maddy repeated.

"Good girl," the man said.

"Are you Simet?" Maddy asked.

The man nodded solemnly. "Yes, I am."

"Then why don't you give them to her yourself?"

"For one thing, men are not allowed in those chambers. For another thing, I don't want anyone else to know these flowers are from me. It's a great secret that I trust you to keep. Do you know how to get to Annison's chambers?"

"No, I don't."

Simet chuckled. "I've been working in this palace my entire life, and I still get lost. Let me show you." Dabbing a quill pen into a pot of ink, he drew directions from his office to Annison's chambers. Maddy was glad. She never would have found them otherwise. "If anyone stops you," Simet added as he tucked a slip of paper into the pocket on her dress, "just present this slip of paper and say you have been approved by a lieutenant in the palace guards. That's me."

Maddy took the flowers—they were heavier than she expected—and began her trek through the corridors to Annison's chambers.

B y the time Maddy reached Annison's rooms, her arms hurt from carrying the vase of flowers. In spite of Simet's map, she still got lost once or twice—going down a hall that reached a dead end, walking into rooms filled with people preparing for the evening banquet, and even wandering into the main kitchen. No one seemed to notice her at all, and only one man in a uniform asked to see the slip of paper Simet had given her.

A large, muscular, bald-headed man stood guard at Annison's door. He eyed Maddy with a cool indifference, looked at the slip of paper, then opened the door for her to go in. Maddy's heart quickened a little at the thought of finally seeing Annison, though a part of her still felt like a silly little girl for wanting something so much when there was no apparent reason for wanting it. *It was only a dream*, she thought. *Maybe this is nothing but a dream, too.*

Maddy stood alone in a large room with marble pillars reaching from the floor to a high ceiling. It was simply furnished with a few couches and chairs with large cushions, one or two tables, and velvet curtains that hung around huge glass doors. The doors led to a balcony that overlooked a mazelike garden. From where Maddy stood in the middle of the room, she could see that the garden was an explosion of greens, reds, yellows, and purples.

Off this main room were several closed doors. Maddy wasn't sure what to do or where to go with the flowers, so she waited a moment, hoping someone would come.

"Well?" a woman's low voice asked.

Maddy was startled. The woman was sitting on one of the couches but was so big and lumpy that Maddy had thought she was a collection of cushions.

"I assume the flowers are not for me," the woman said with a chuckle as she shifted her position and rose from the couch. She had dark hair, which she tucked under a weblike hat, and a full, round face. Her eyes were friendly in spite of the sagging bags under them. She had a pug nose and thick lips that made her jowls shake as she spoke. "For Tabby?"

Maddy was so surprised by the appearance of this woman that she didn't know what to say.

"Not for Tabby?" the woman asked, feigning disappointment. "Then I suppose they're for Annison. Give them to me." The woman reached for the vase.

Maddy pulled it away from her. "I was told to give these to Annison personally," she insisted.

"Don't be silly," the woman argued. "I am Tabitha, Annison's nurse. I will see that she gets them."

Maddy refused to hand the flowers over. "I have to give them to Annison myself." Clutching the flowers awkwardly, Maddy pulled Simet's note from her pocket and gave it to Tabby.

Tabby read the note and grunted. "This doesn't mean a thing. This only gives you permission to be here, not to tell *me* who may receive the flowers." She reached for the flowers again.

Maddy stepped back defiantly.

Tabby growled, "Oh, you wicked child!"

"A wicked child?" asked a gentle voice from one of the doorways. "Surely not." To Maddy's delight, it was Annison.

"I say she is," Tabby complained. "She will not give me these flowers for you."

"I was told to give them to you personally," Maddy explained.

"Then you are right not to give them to anyone but me," Annison said with a smile. Again, she looked radiant.

Tabby harrumphed.

"But *you*, my dear nurse, are right to be on guard for me," Annison added. "You would have been negligent to allow a strange girl to wander our chambers."

Tabby looked slightly appeased, gave Maddy a final disapproving look, then turned on her heel and left the room.

Annison held out her arms. "Now you may deliver the flowers personally."

Maddy gave her the vase and then, just as Annison was closest to Maddy's face, whispered, "They're from Simet."

Annison's smile widened, but tears filled her eyes. "Oh, I should have known." She placed the flowers on a small pedestal near the glass doors and lingered there, her back to Maddy. The shaking of her shoulders made Maddy realize she was crying.

Maddy went to her and implored, "Please don't cry."

Annison straightened up to compose herself. "I'm not sad," she explained as she wiped her nose with a handkerchief. "I'm happy."

"You don't look very happy."

Annison looked at Maddy and began to cry again. She sat down on one of the couches, burying her face in her handkerchief.

"Oh, dear," Maddy whispered, her heart aching as if the tears were her own. She sat down next to Annison. "I'm here to help you."

Annison looked up at Maddy. "Help me?"

"I had a dream about you, and you asked me to help you, and I promised I would," Maddy explained.

"You dreamt about *me*?"

Maddy nodded.

Annison looked quickly around to make sure no one was near or listening. She leaned close to Maddy and said softly, "Tell me about your dream."

Maddy told her everything: about living in America, about the dream, about hiding under the porch, and about arriving in time for the king's parade.

As Maddy spoke, Annison's eyes grew wide, and her red lips parted in an expression of awe. "This is wondrous," she concluded.

"I think so, too," Maddy said with a smile. "I'm like Alice in the looking glass. It's magic."

Annison frowned. "I don't know your friend Alice, but no, this isn't magic. At least, not the magic of stories or pagans. This is something more."

Maddy confessed that she didn't understand.

Annison now spoke in a whisper: "It is the Unseen One."

"The what?"

"The Unseen One." Annison suddenly stood up and paced the floor, wringing her hands as she did. "But what does it mean? Why were you sent to me?"

"I came to help you," Maddy reaffirmed.

Annison wasn't listening. She paced and spoke softly, mostly to herself. "I know the stories of old, the writings in the ancient manuscripts that tell of voices, protectors, and messengers who came from other places—strange places—to help us." She suddenly sat next to Maddy again and gazed steadily into her eyes. "But your eyes—they aren't different colors."

Maddy blinked. "Different colors?"

"Oftentimes the ones who came had eyes of two different colors. But yours are both green. What am I to make of it?"

Maddy felt again as she had when she stood in the crowd: confused and unsure. "I think," she suddenly announced, "that I'm here to help you find your true love."

Annison looked at her, surprised. "What do you mean?"

"Your true love," Maddy replied. "Just like in the stories. You don't love the king, so I'm going to help get you back to your true love."

"You don't know what you're saying," Annison said sharply. "I have no true love."

Maddy was hurt by Annison's tone. "You don't?"

"Has the Unseen One sent you to test me? Or is this a message I must heed?" She paced again. "Is it something cryptic, like a riddle? What do you mean by 'true love'?"

"I mean someone that you *really* love."

"I love no one the way you mean," Annison said simply. "I'm marrying the king."

"But you don't love him," Maddy insisted, though she now doubted herself. "Do you?"

"Love has nothing to do with it," she stated. "I'm doing my duty, for my country." She wrung her hands again. "Oh, I wish I could speak with Simet. He'd know."

"Why can't you?"

"I'm not allowed to see or speak with any men without the king's permission until after the wedding. And to ask to speak with Simet would raise many difficult questions." Annison's face suddenly lit up with an idea. "But *you* can talk to Simet. You can go back to him and tell him what you've told me. Will you do that?"

Maddy shrugged. "If you want me to."

"Then take this." Annison took a ring off her finger. "It's my own. If anyone stops you, show this ring. I am the king's betrothed. No one will harm you as long as you have this ring. It proves that you serve me."

The ring fit on Maddy's thumb. She held it up proudly.

"Beware of one man in particular," Annison then warned. "Lord Hector."

"I've seen him. He doesn't look like a very happy man."

"He isn't. He hates Marus and wants everyone in it to be as miserable as he is." Annison guided Maddy to the door. "Pay close attention to whatever Simet tells you."

"I will." Then Maddy smiled. "You see? I'm going to help you already."

Annison smiled and patted her on the head. "So you are. And I have no doubt that you will help me more than you know. Now go."

Maddy left through the door she'd come in, past the large bald man, and walked confidently down the hall. Then down another. Then around another. Finally she realized she had wandered into sections of the palace not found on Simet's map. She had no idea where she was going. She stopped a young housemaid and asked for directions. The housemaid rattled out a stream of confusing instructions. Maddy pretended she understood and wandered off again.

Every now and then, she peered out the windows to see if the scene might guide her. It never did. Every view looked different. After another 10 minutes, she stopped at a pair of glass doors that led to a balcony. Outside, three men leaned on the stone handrail, their backs to Maddy. They spoke softly to one another.

"We must strike quickly," one of the men said.

The second man agreed: "If we act even as early as tonight, we may cause enough of a stir to bring the rebellion we need."

"Kill the king right before his wedding? It's a treacherous idea," the third man observed with a chuckle. His shoulders, covered by a black coat, shook gently.

"Our people will think the Marutians assassinated him to save the dignity of their beloved Annison," the first man added. "It will give our soldiers a cause to rally around—"

"*Someone* to rally around, you mean," the second man interjected.

"Yes. And who might that someone be?" the third man asked knowingly.

"Who else? It must be *you*, my lord," the second man replied. "With the king disposed of, you can legally declare yourself the lord protector. Then, with the allegiance of the army, you can march back to Palatia, arrest the king's brother and heir as a member of the conspiracy, and secure your place on the throne there."

The first man shook his head. "But what about the Marutians?" he objected. "Will they not also rally their forces while Palatia is in turmoil? We risk losing this country after so recently claiming it."

"If a pampered fool like Willem can conquer Marus, I can conquer it again in my sleep." The third man sneered. "Marus is the least of my worries. It's a despicable little country with donkeys for citizens."

"I happen to like it," the first man protested. "And I would be glad to rule it as a reward for my allegiance."

The third man chuckled again. "You haggle even now? You're shrewd, my friend. Yes, if I become lord protector of the kingdom, you may have Marus."

"Good. Maybe I will take Annison as a bride of my own. She's pretty enough."

"If I were you, I would kill her as a member of the conspiracy," the third man advised. "It would show the Marutians that you aren't to be trifled with."

"And what of me, my lord?" the second man asked. "Will you give me Albany as you promised?"

"Albany has always been yours," the third man replied.

"Then let us shake on it," the first man said. "The king's chalice will be poisoned at the banquet tonight by a man in my employ, and you will become lord protector, and we will become the regents of Marus and Albany."

"So be it," the third man agreed.

The first man turned to shake hands with the others. He was a handsome young man with dark hair and a thin goatee. He saw Maddy out of the corner of his eye and spun on her quickly. "Who's this?" he snapped.

The second man, who was older and had sharp features and graying hair, also turned. "What do you want?" he growled.

The third man didn't turn but froze as he was, with his back to Maddy.

"I'm lost," Maddy said nervously.

The young man grabbed her arm roughly. "What did you hear just now?" he demanded.

"Nothing," she stammered. "I only came to ask for your help."

The young man glared at her. "I don't believe you. What did you hear?"

"Nothing," she said more fearfully. He was hurting her arm.

"Ease off, Stephen," the older man said. "She's only a child."

"A child with big ears," Stephen said, lessening his grip on her arm. "Does she have the mouth to match?"

"I'm lost!" Maddy pleaded. "I only want to find the front of the palace."

The older man laughed and told her, "You're well out of your way if you're trying to find the *front* of the palace. Let me tell you how to get there."

"Terrence—" the young man began.

The older man held up his hand to silence him. "How much could she have heard? And who would believe a young girl anyway?" He knelt down closer to Maddy and produced a jewel-handled knife from his belt. "Besides, she wouldn't want her tongue cut out, would she?"

Maddy shook her head. "No, sir."

"Then you will keep your tongue still and go about your business, correct?"

Maddy nodded quickly. "Yes, sir."

The older man kept his eyes fixed on her. "Go down this hallway to the right until it dead-ends, then turn left. Follow that hallway until *it* dead-ends, and then turn right. One right, one left, one right. That will take you to the grand hallway along the front."

"Thank you," Maddy said as she inched away from them.

The older man held up the knife again before tucking it away. "Remember what I said."

"Yes, sir." Maddy didn't waste another second but rushed off down the hall. When she was certain she was out of their reach, she stopped and leaned against the wall. The stone was cool against her hot back. Her face felt flushed, and she thought she might cry. Then she realized, *I've just overheard a plot to kill the king—this very night at the banquet!*

What was she to do? If she told anyone and the man called Terrence found out, he would cut out her tongue. But if she didn't tell anyone, the king would be killed—and Annison, too.

At that moment, she wished she could melt into the wall and somehow go through the other side to her home. This wasn't the fairy tale she wanted to have. This was more like a nightmare.

And she didn't know how to get out of it.

"Why are you so pale?" Simet asked when Maddy finally reached him. Even after finding the front doors to the palace, she had needed help from another two servants to get to Simet's office. His brow furrowed with concern. "Is Annison well?"

"She's well, but she wanted me to come back and talk to you," Maddy said. Her mouth clicked from dryness. Simet poured her a cup of water and insisted she drink before continuing. Maddy did, gulping the water down. Then she took a deep breath. "I have to tell you about my dream."

Simet sat on the edge of his desk. "Your dream?"

Maddy looked deeply into his kind eyes and knew she could trust him with anything she had to say. And, like Annison, she believed he would have the answers to help them. So she told him everything she'd told Annison.

Simet listened with a thoughtful expression. He moved only once, and that was to close the door to his office when he feared someone might overhear Maddy's remarkable story.

When Maddy had run out of things to say, he nodded at her. "Yes, this is the work of the Unseen One," he observed.

"I don't know who the Unseen One is," Maddy confessed.

"I'm not surprised to hear it," Simet said sadly. "Only a few of us now acknowledge the Unseen One. Our kings turned their backs on Him and stopped proclaiming Him, so it's little wonder that we've been conquered. And now King Willem is here with his Palatian religion, a religion of man and man's powers, with no room for faith in greater, eternal things. He has already closed our houses of worship. And if Lord Hector had his way, all believers in the Unseen One would be locked up or executed because they deny his religion. Men who do not love the Unseen One often loathe Him and want to wipe any belief in Him from the face of the planet."

"But *who* is the Unseen One?"

Simet scratched his chin as if trying to think of a simple way to explain a complicated idea. Finally he responded, "The Unseen One is the Creator of us all. He is the King of all worlds. He is God over all gods."

"God," Maddy repeated, latching onto a word she understood. "I know about God. I learned about Him in church. And He's all the things you just said."

"Then you know about the Unseen One," Simet said hopefully.

Maddy pondered the idea for a moment. "But I don't remember ever hearing that He took people from one place to another, like He took me from my world to this magic one."

Simet chuckled. "You think this world is magic? The people of this world wouldn't think so. On the contrary, the people of this world would probably consider *your* world magic."

Maddy hadn't thought of it that way. But she stuck by her question. "Still, it seems strange that He brought me from my world to this one."

"It's not for me to guess the ways of the Unseen One. He does as He pleases. And I'm certain the same is true for how He works in your world. No matter how much He has revealed of Himself in our sacred writings, He remains a mystery greater than our finite minds can solve. You're here—that's evidence enough for me that He is at work for some purpose."

"What purpose?" Maddy asked. "What am I doing here?"

"You're not a messenger or a voice or a protector," Simet observed as he looked into her eyes. "But in your dream, you promised you would help Annison. So the Unseen One must have sent you to be her helper."

"I'll help her find her true love," Maddy declared.

Simet looked puzzled. "Whatever do you mean?"

Maddy explained how so many of her favorite stories involved a princess who was in love with a handsome young man but was being forced to marry a mean king. In the end, the handsome young man, who vanquished the mean king, rescued the princess.

"Ah, I see now," Simet said. "But my child, this is not a children's fairy tale. You're not in a story of wishful thinking or fanciful dreams. You're now in a place where the happy endings of childhood give way to the reality of faith."

Maddy looked crestfallen. This was not what she wanted to hear.

Simet patted her arm in comfort. "Dear girl, you wouldn't want to spend your life drinking baby's milk, would you?"

Maddy gazed at him quizzically. "No."

"Well, that's what your fairy tales are," Simet explained. "They're the milk of an innocent faith. But you must never stop at the milk. There comes a time when you must have the nourishment of other things, grown-up things like meat and vegetables. Otherwise you'll never grow as you should. Do you understand?"

Maddy shook her head. "I'm not sure."

"Allow me to try another example." Simet clasped his hands together and looked as if he were in deep thought. Then he continued, "Children's stories and fairy tales often help to light the spark of faith. They help us to see that there are realms much bigger than our own world. They teach us to believe in things we can't understand while they point to other greater things. But we must eventually fan that spark of faith—allow it to grow into a mature flame that will burn in our hearts throughout our lives."

Maddy didn't reply. It was a lot for her to think about.

"You've been brought to us as a helper," Simet went on. "But not to help as a child helps in a fairy tale, with dreamy fantasies of romance, handsome princes, and true love. You're here to help in the raw reality of faith—with sweat and muscle and pain."

Maddy thought again of the dream and of her promise to Annison. Was it possible that the Unseen One had sent her to uncover the plot to kill the king? Even if it meant losing her own tongue? "Sweat and muscle and pain," Maddy repeated softly.

With an unexpected resolve that filled her heart, Maddy knew she could not sit by and allow anything to happen to Annison, no matter what happened to her in the meantime. "There's something else I have to tell you," Maddy said, and then she told Simet about the three men and their plot to poison the king.

Simet's face went white, and he clutched the edge of his desk as if to steady himself. "What did you say the names of the men were?"

"I didn't see who the third man was," she replied. "But the other two were called Stephen and Terrence. The one called Terrence said he would cut my tongue out if I blabbed."

Simet nodded. "There's only one Terrence who would dare do such a thing. But don't fear. He won't have the chance to hurt you. I will see to that."

"Then you'll warn the king?"

Simet hesitated. "No. I think it would be best if *Annison* warned the king. What better way to show her loyalty and ensure his favor toward her?"

"I don't understand," Maddy admitted, phrasing her question carefully. "If she's from Marus, why is it so important for her to be so chummy with the king?" She thought about it again and quickly added another question. "Why is it Annison's duty to marry someone she doesn't love?"

Simet sighed deeply. "For years we have believed the Unseen

One has chosen Annison for a very special place in the destiny of our nation. We were never sure how or what role she would play—not until the day King Willem saw her and decided to marry her. Then we knew. She would marry the king in order to influence him."

"Influence him how?"

"We don't know yet. But it burns in our hearts that her role as the queen may make the difference between life and death for many people."

"You keep saying *we*. What *we?*"

"A small gathering of true believers in the Unseen One, including Annison and myself."

Suddenly Maddy thought she understood and gasped, "You're her father!"

Simet smiled. "No, I'm not her father, though she would call me by that name if I allowed it. Her parents were killed when she was a small child, and their wish, written in their will, was that I would raise her in the faith."

"But why is it such a big secret?"

"To protect her. And to protect me. And to protect our gathering of believers. The less anyone knows about us or our connections to one another, the safer we are."

"You're like a secret club?"

"Something like that. But our secret is a dangerous one. Under the kings of Marus, we were frowned upon for keeping our faith in the Unseen One. Under King Willem—or I should say, under *Lord Hector*—we could lose our lives."

"But that means the king is marrying a believer in the Unseen One, and he doesn't even know it."

Simet smiled again. "Exactly."

A knock came at the door, and then it was pushed open without an invitation. Lord Hector himself peered in. He looked at Simet first and said, "Simet, I want to discuss the security for this evening's banquet." Then he saw Maddy, and a flash of surprise lit up his eyes for a second and then disappeared. "Forgive my intrusion," he added quickly.

"Not at all, my lord," Simet replied.

"Then come to the Great Hall. I wish a word with you and the other guards."

"Yes, my lord."

Lord Hector glanced at Maddy again and then turned to leave. In the moment he did so, Maddy noticed the back of his black coat and the shape of his shoulders, and she knew. "It was him," she whispered after the door was closed and she heard his retreating footsteps.

"What's that?" Simet asked.

"He was the third man on the balcony."

"Lord *Hector*? In a plot to poison the king?"

"Yes."

"Are you sure, Maddy? You must be completely sure."

"Yes. He wants to do it so he can take over Palatia."

Simet looked like a man who had suddenly found the last two pieces to a jigsaw puzzle. "I've often wondered about him. I've watched how he speaks to the king, the look in his eyes. He's a man who covets power. So I should not be surprised."

"Shall I go back to Annison now?"

"Yes, hurry and tell her what you know."

Maddy stood up and went to the door. Just as her hand touched the knob, Simet added earnestly, "Maddy, you've been sent to help us, and help us you have. But I don't think your part in this drama is finished. You must keep your eyes and ears open. Assume nothing about what you see and hear. Report *everything* to Annison or to me. Do you understand?"

Maddy nodded, suddenly feeling very important.

The royal banquet to celebrate the forthcoming marriage of King Willem and Annison was a lavish affair. Hundreds of dignitaries and noblemen from Palatia, along with the well-to-do of Marus, crowded into the Great Hall. The men wore frilly lace collars and matching coats and trousers of deep blue, light green, or gold that seemed to sparkle. The women wore velvet or silk dresses, each with elaborate designs of flowers, birds, or stripes, some with colorful shawls draped over their shoulders. Many of the women *and* men wore wigs that rose up from their heads in piles like cotton candy or bird's nests. Those women who didn't wear wigs had their hair done in large curls. The men favored long hair, carefully combed and kept in place by what looked to Maddy like oil or wax.

The guests took their places at the many tables, now set with white linen, plates of china, and solid silver cutlery. Blazing torches shone from wall sconces in between colorful tapestries that had been hung for the occasion. Candles were lit at every setting, giving the entire hall a yellow tint. The chandeliers, also alight with candles, looked like clusters of stars, ready to explode over them all.

Enormous trays of food were brought out by the palace servants—seven courses in all—and served to the many guests. The room was an intoxicating mix of smells. Considering the number of guests, Maddy was impressed by the speed with which the servants did their work. They began as the sun set and continued serving well past 11:00.

The king and Annison sat side by side at the head table. For tonight, the king didn't wear a wig but combed his ginger-colored hair forward in a style that reminded Maddy of a picture of Julius Caesar she'd once seen at school. Annison was dressed discreetly in a simple pink gown with fringes of lace and bowed ribbons attached to them. To the royal couple's left and right were Lord Hector, who still looked bored, and several other men and women Maddy didn't know. Stephen and Terrence were at the head table, too, and kept looking at each other anxiously. As a member of Annison's court, Maddy was given a seat at a table in the corner nearest the head table. She sat next to Tabby, who ate with great enthusiasm.

Maddy was too nervous to eat. Ever since reporting her news to Annison, she had been on a knife's-edge of suspense, wondering how the evening would play out.

Near midnight, flasks of a sweet red drink were poured into the guests' chalices. It was time for the royal toast, and now Maddy found herself sitting on the edge of her seat. She had told Annison of the plot to poison the king, but she had no idea what Annison had done with the information or how she had passed the word to the king. She watched Stephen and Terrence, who watched the king's every move. Lord Hector maintained his usual bored expression.

The king stood up, raising high his chalice—a large goblet with green and red jewels encircling the cup. "Ladies and gentlemen," he said in his booming voice, "I am grateful for your attendance tonight. To honor the occasion, I promised my betrothed that I would not make a lengthy speech."

A titter of laughter worked its way through the crowd.

"It is enough for me to say thank you to all, to wish prosperity on the united kingdoms of Palatia and Marus, and to invite you back in a week's time for the wedding."

The crowd responded with scattered applause.

"Now for the royal toast," he announced.

There was a rustling throughout the room as all the guests stood by their chairs and raised their chalices.

"To my betrothed, the future queen," he stated happily.

"To the future queen!" the crowd responded.

Maddy watched the king, her eyes growing wider and wider. The chalice moved toward his lips. Annison remained seated and still, her face betraying nothing but her usual shyness at being the center of attention. Had Annison not told him about the poison? Was the plot to kill him going to succeed?

"My king!" Lord Hector suddenly shouted from his place.

The king hesitated, the chalice only an inch from his lips. "Lord Hector?" he asked, lowering the cup.

"Do not drink from that chalice," Lord Hector warned.

The king looked puzzled. "This is most unusual, Hector. It's the royal toast. Why shouldn't I?" he inquired.

"Because, on this very day, I have uncovered a plot to assassinate Your Majesty—by poison in that very chalice."

The crowd, shocked, stood where they were, many not sure how to react. Several of the noblemen instinctively drew their swords. Maddy's jaw dropped. What kind of game was Hector playing? Why would he stop the plot that he had helped to mastermind?

Stephen and Terrence watched Hector with bewilderment on their faces. Maddy noticed that Terrence's hand subtly moved to his belt, his hand resting on the handle of his knife.

The king remained composed. "And who would dare to attempt such an assassination?"

"Two trusted men in your very midst," Lord Hector announced, then pointed dramatically. "Stephen and Terrence!"

Suddenly the palace guards burst through the doors, including Simet, and rushed to the head table. Stephen held up his hands in surrender, but Terrence pulled out his knife and lunged at the king.

Lord Hector was quicker, though, and leapt between the two men. He also had a knife in his hand—Maddy had no idea where it had come from—which he thrust into Terrence's chest. They both fell to the ground, disappearing behind the ornate tablecloth. Seconds later, Lord Hector reappeared and dusted himself off as if he had merely tripped over something.

The crowd erupted in shouts and applause.

There was a commotion at the back of the hall as two guards grabbed one of the servants. Maddy assumed it was the one the conspirators had hired to poison the drink.

Simet and the other guards had grabbed Stephen, who offered no resistance. He now leered at Lord Hector. "I should have known," he growled over and over as they dragged him out of the hall.

"Well done, Lord Hector!" the king said happily once the offenders had been removed. His eyes danced and his cheeks were apple red from the excitement. He raised his chalice again. "I salute you!"

And then, to everyone's horror, he gulped down his drink.

"Your Majesty!" Hector cried out.

The king slammed the chalice down on the table and laughed. "You are quick, Lord Hector, but my beloved Annison is quicker. She was already privy to the traitors' plot to poison me, and I made sure to change chalices. Little did they realize that had we drunk our toast, both Stephen and Terrence would have fallen dead from their own poison, which I had placed in their cups!"

Lord Hector bowed in homage to Annison. "Our new queen is a remarkable woman," he said smoothly. "I wonder, if I may ask, how she knew of the plot?"

"We women have our ways," Annison replied pleasantly.

Lord Hector forced himself to smile. "I have no doubt that you do."

For an instant, Annison's eyes caught Maddy's, and she winked at her.

∞

The attending maidens in Annison's chambers were abuzz with what had happened at the banquet. They speculated about how Annison had learned of the plot and if there were any others involved who weren't caught, and then they told and retold the dramatic moment when the king nearly drank the chalice—and then did, to everyone's surprise.

"What a joke!" one said.

"How brave of the king," another observed.

Only after Tabby threatened them with hard chores the next day if they didn't go to bed *that minute* did the chattering stop.

Maddy was given a small bedroom annexing Annison's main bedroom and a wardrobe of day and night clothes. She had no idea how Annison managed it, but the clothes were all the right size. Maddy slipped into a nightgown and snuggled into the soft down mattress, but she was too excited to sleep. Her mind counted unanswered questions like sheep. She thought she heard a sound from Annison's room and decided to sneak a peek to see if Annison had gone to bed. She hadn't; the bed was empty. A gentle breeze blew the pale curtains back and forth. The glass doors leading to the balcony were open, and Maddy could see Annison's silhouette pacing outside. Maddy crossed the room and stopped at the doorway.

Annison had her eyes closed and seemed to be talking to herself. Maddy realized she was praying. "Thank You" was all Maddy heard her say. And then Annison opened her eyes and gazed peacefully at Maddy.

"You should be asleep," Annison chided gently, gathering her robe close around her as if warding off a chill. But the night was warm, crickets chirped somewhere below, and pale moonlight filled the clear sky.

"Oh, look!" Maddy gasped, her eyes fixed on the light overhead. There in the sky was a bright moon—and right next to it, a little smaller and more orange, was *another* moon. "You have two moons!"

Annison glanced up at them. "Yes, we do. How many do you have in your world?" she asked.

"Just one," Maddy replied. The sight mesmerized her. *Imagine having two moons in your world,* she thought in amazement. She stood looking at the double orbs for a few moments.

Annison watched her, a tiny smile betraying her affection for Maddy. "You remind me of someone," Annison observed.

"Who?"

"Me."

Maddy turned to her, an unformed question on her lips.

"I once looked at the world with the wonder you have. I believed in fairy tales and happy endings."

"You don't now?"

"In my heart, I still do," she said warmly. "But I've also learned a great deal about the world, and sometimes the happy endings don't come the way we think they should. But they come eventually— beyond this world—thanks to the Unseen One."

"Simet told me I'm not here to help you find your true love. He said I need to help you the way the Unseen One wants me to help you. He said I need to grow up."

"We all have to grow up, it's true. But that doesn't mean we must lose our sense of wonder and awe. The mystery of faith is too great for that. Even now I look around me—at the beauty of those two moons, at the secrets of the stars, even at the extraordinary way you have come to me—and I realize there's so much I don't understand. But I know what I must do."

"You'll marry King Willem."

"Yes, I will."

Saying his name reminded Maddy of the drama at the banquet and her many questions about it. "I can't figure out what happened," she stated. "Lord Hector was one of the men who plotted to kill the king, but then he turned on Stephen and Terrence at the last minute."

"Lord Hector is a shrewd and cunning man. I suspect he knew somehow that their plans had been found out. He must have decided to turn it to his advantage."

Maddy remembered how Lord Hector had come into Simet's office when Maddy was there. It was possible that he'd seen her on the balcony or recognized her voice and assumed she would tell Simet what she'd heard in spite of Terrence's threat. "But you told the king that Lord Hector was one of the men, didn't you?" she asked.

"No, I didn't."

"Why not?"

"It's one thing to accuse underlings like Stephen and Terrence of treason," she replied. "It's another thing to accuse the king's most-trusted adviser. I would have needed more proof than your word to persuade the king to take action against Lord Hector. As it is, this will warn him to be careful."

Maddy felt uneasy at the thought. If Lord Hector knew that Maddy had told Simet and Annison about his plans, wouldn't he want revenge against her? Maddy gave it some thought but decided not to say anything to Annison. She was there to help her, not add to her worry.

"I think it's time for bed," Annison suddenly announced. "We have a lot to do tomorrow."

"What am I going to do?" Maddy asked.

Annison smiled at her. "You'll help me to prepare for the wedding, and perhaps you'll be my eyes and ears in other parts of the palace. We'll see."

6

Preparing for the wedding was an enormous task, far more complicated than Maddy would have ever thought. There were flowers to be ordered, dresses to be made, food to be chosen for the reception afterward, seating arrangements to be secured for the wedding itself and the reception, an order of service for the ceremony to be decided upon, a schedule to be devised for the royal "ride" from the palace to the royal chapel (where the wedding would take place), a procession through Sarum to be planned, and on and on.

For most of the day after the banquet, Maddy sat next to Annison, scribbling her dictation of things that needed to be seen to in the days leading up to the wedding. Then, shortly after lunchtime, Tabby entered the main room of the chambers and whispered something to Annison. Annison nodded quickly and signaled Maddy to follow her into one of the side rooms. After they entered, Annison closed the door.

The room appeared to be some kind of study, with squares of dark paneling covering three of the walls. A fireplace took up most of the fourth. In the center were a writing desk and small tables holding a selection of books and decorative items like china vases and busts. The floor was covered with a large colorful rug.

"Is something wrong?" Maddy asked.

"I have an errand for you to run," Annison replied. She went to the fireplace and tugged at a small piece of marble that hung like an icicle from the side. Suddenly a panel on the wall behind them opened a couple of inches.

"A secret door?" Maddy asked, amazed.

Annison pressed a hand against Maddy's back to urge her forward. "Simet has worked in this palace most of his life," she explained. "He knows every inch of it, including the secret passageways. He told me about this the day I moved in."

"Where does it go?"

"It leads to many different rooms. But—" Annison pulled a piece of paper from her sleeve and handed it to Maddy. "Follow this map and these directions. They'll take you to the king's reception room."

"You want me to spy on the king?"

"Lord Hector is about to have an audience with King Willem to discuss what happened at the banquet last night. I need to know what he says."

Maddy took a step into the passageway but stopped. "It's dark," she complained.

Annison reached up and grabbed something on the inside wall. It was a torch that, from the smell, must have been doused in oil. Using flint from the fireplace, she lit the torch. Its flame was small but adequate. She gave the torch to Maddy. "Don't get lost this time," Annison teased her.

Maddy giggled and stepped into the passageway. The torch surrounded her with moving shadows.

Annison gestured to a small lever on the wall. "This will open the panel to let you back in," she informed her.

"Okay," Maddy said.

Annison closed the panel door.

Maddy moved forward slowly until she was sure of her footing and of the passage's width. It was surprisingly wide. Following the

instructions, she crossed several side passages, then turned right
and passed more doorways with levers. She wondered where they
all led to and imagined the trouble she'd cause if she suddenly
appeared in one of the rooms. Counting the doorways carefully,
she turned left after the eighth door and walked for a long time
before she found the passage Annison had marked on the map. She
turned left again and followed it until it reached a dead end. There
she found a hook in the wall to hold the torch.

The map indicated that she wouldn't find a lever on the wall but
a small knob, which she was to slide carefully to one side. She did.
It opened a small rectangular peephole. She found herself looking
at a large room with a throne sitting on a small stage. Large velvet
curtains surrounded it. Empty chairs stretched out from the foot of
the stairs in two rows. King Willem suddenly appeared through a
door behind the stage and walked casually to the throne, where he
sat down and inspected his fingernails, then adjusted the sleeves
on his coat.

A moment later, a large double door opened and Lord Hector
strode in. He was dressed in the same mournful-looking black coat
and trousers. He stood at the foot of the stage and bowed stiffly.

"Your Majesty," he intoned.

"My dear Lord Hector," the king greeted, waving him forward.
"Good day to you, and thank you once again for your chivalry on
my behalf."

Lord Hector dipped his head and cleared his throat as if embarrassed. "Yes, of course, my liege," he began. "Now—to business?"

"If you must."

Lord Hector clasped his hands behind his back and announced,
"I have interrogated Stephen and his treasonous servant in the
dungeon."

"In your usual meticulous manner, I have no doubt."

"Yes, sire. Sadly, neither was made of strong stuff, and they expired in the process."

"How sad," the king said without meaning it. "Oh, well, I didn't really want to execute them in the week of my wedding anyway."

Maddy put a hand over her mouth. The easygoing way that the two men spoke about death appalled her.

"Did you learn anything valuable?" the king asked.

"The conspiracy to overthrow you is far-reaching."

The king raised an eyebrow. "Is it?"

"I was able to learn that Stephen, Terrence, and the servant they employed to poison your chalice are all part of that terrible cult I've warned you about."

"Cult?"

"The believers of the Old Faith."

"Oh, that nonsense about the Unseen One and all that."

"Exactly."

Maddy couldn't believe what she was hearing. Did Lord Hector really think he could get away with such a lie?

"I thought you outlawed that when we arrived." The king crossed his legs and leaned back comfortably into his throne.

"I did, sire," Lord Hector replied without any variation in the drone of his voice. "But their members still meet secretly, as evidenced by the cunning plan they nearly succeeded with last night."

"It's curious, though."

"Sire?"

"I had always understood that the believers in the Old Faith were nonviolent," the king said. "All they've ever wanted is to be able to worship that strange God of theirs as they saw fit. Why would they want to kill me?"

Lord Hector answered as if teaching a child. "You are a Palatian, sire. The members of the Old Faith are Marutians. In matters of national honor and identity, even the most peaceful cults will resort to violence if they feel they have no other choice."

"Then why don't we let them worship the way they want and be done with them? They have no complaint against me if I grant them that."

Lord Hector shook his head slowly. "Because it won't end there, sire. Their faith is bound up in the destiny of this nation. If you allow them to worship freely, it will be no time at all before their faith will spill over to the people at large. And once that has happened, there will be a trickle, then a river, and finally a flood of patriotism. With that patriotism will come patriotic acts—against you, to free themselves from your rule. History has shown it to be true time and again."

"Oh, dear!"

"I have outlawed the Old Faith to hold back the tide of their zeal," Lord Hector explained. "And, frankly, I find it offensive. For them to superstitiously believe in ancient gods when it's clear that *we* are the keepers of our fate, the champions of our destiny, is ignorance at its worst. I cannot tolerate it."

"As usual, you speak eloquently and poetically," the king said appreciatively. "What do you propose?"

"I propose that outlawing the Old Faith isn't enough. We must use our forces to come down on them like a hammer. We must drive them from their hiding places and arrest them."

The king sighed wearily. "If you insist. But be discreet about it. I don't want a lot of fuss distracting from my wedding day."

"Of course, sire." Lord Hector bowed and walked away.

Maddy waited a moment to see what the king would do next. He sat, yawned, and inspected his fingernails again. Then the door opened and a page stepped in.

"The mayor of Sarum to see you, sire," he announced.

The king waved a hand at the page. "See him in," he commanded, barely stifling his boredom.

Maddy closed the peephole and stepped back into the passageway. She felt numbed by what she'd just heard. Lord Hector was actually placing the blame for the assassination attempt on the believers in the Unseen One! It made her blood boil to think about it.

She had to hurry back and tell Annison. Retrieving the torch, she rushed down the passageway in the direction from which she had come. She followed the map carefully while moving as fast as she could. Then, as she passed one particular side passage, she thought she heard footsteps. They were terribly close to her, but she didn't see a light.

I hope there's nobody else in here, she worried.

She pressed on, quickening her step.

A harsh sound, like a loud, throaty cough, made her stop in her tracks. It was unmistakably human. Someone was in the passageway with her.

She looked around quickly, her torch throwing very little light into the shadows. Should she call out? *No,* she thought. *Keep moving. Don't stop for anything. And try not to be afraid.*

But the fear seized her anyway, and she misread the map once or twice, winding up down the wrong passageway or stuck at a dead end. Still, she was certain that someone was nearby. She thought she heard heavy breathing off to the left. And there was the clear sound of a heel scuffing against the stone floor somewhere off to her right. Was she being followed, or was her imagination playing tricks on her?

Finally she arrived at the last passage that would take her back to Annison's chambers. She sprinted the length of it, gasping with relief when she got to the lever. But just as she reached for it, a pale white hand shot out of the darkness and grabbed her wrist.

She started to scream, but another hand clamped down over her mouth. Wide-eyed, she looked up into the face of Lord Hector.

"I've often wondered if there were rats in these passageways," he hissed softly. "Now I see that there are."

Maddy tried to tell him to let go, but he kept his hand firm.

"I haven't been able to figure you out, little girl," he growled. "Are you a spy for someone? Or do you just have the uncanny luck of being in the right places at the wrong time? Which is it?"

He didn't remove his hand for her to answer.

"One moment you're singing in a children's choir, and the next you're an unwanted guest on a balcony. One moment I see you talking to Simet—and I can guess the subject—and then, like magic, you're a member of Annison's court. It mystifies me. And I'm not a man who mystifies easily. Are you working for Simet or for Annison—or is there some connection between the two of them I don't know about? *Who are you,* little girl?"

He still didn't take his hand away.

He leaned his face so close that she could smell cabbage on his breath. "I have many questions about you. And I want you to know that, one way or the other, I *will* find the answers. It's only because I'm not sure about you that I'm going to let you go." He finally released his grip on her. "But if you're the rat I think you are, *you will be exterminated.* Consider it a warning." He paused to correct himself. "No. Consider it a threat."

With that said, he stepped back into the shadows and seemed to disappear.

Maddy waited to hear his retreating footsteps. Her heart raced, her breath came in short gasps, and those were the only sounds she heard. When she was certain he was gone, she pulled the lever and stumbled into the study.

Maddy told Annison about Lord Hector's plans to arrest the believers in the Old Faith. She also described what had happened with him in the passageway.

Annison was concerned but reassuring. "Lord Hector is clever enough to be careful with you," she said soothingly. "He won't do anything to you as long as he can't figure out who you're working for and why. For all he knows, you may be working for the king himself."

"But he threatened me," Maddy reminded her.

"To *scare* you," Annison replied. "All it means is that we must be careful. We must trust no one. We may be surrounded by his spies."

Annison then sent Maddy to tell all the news to Simet.

On the way to Simet's office, Maddy was on edge, sure that everyone she encountered worked as a spy for Lord Hector. By the time she reached Simet, she was in a cold sweat.

"We don't want to turn you into a nervous wreck," Simet said sympathetically. "I think we must establish a secret routine, a set time in a secret place where I'll meet you and we can swap messages. Otherwise you may well be followed if you keep coming to me more than once a day."

"Where and when?" Maddy asked.

Simet thought about it, then suggested, "There's a door leading to the old bell tower on the east side of the palace. It's dark, with a private courtyard that no one uses anymore. Better still, there are no windows or doors nearby from which anyone can spy on us."

"I don't know where it is."

Simet smiled. "As usual, I'll draw you a map. But you must memorize the directions and then destroy the map. The less we have in writing, the better." Simet quickly drew the map and handed it to Maddy. "Let's meet every evening at six. In case of an emergency, leave one of Annison's smaller scarves tied to my office doorknob. Then I'll know to meet you right away."

"But what about Lord Hector's plans?" Maddy asked.

"I'll inform the other believers in the Old Faith of his devious plans."

Everyone was so busy over the next few days with the wedding details that they hardly noticed when Lord Hector sent out a proclamation to the palace staff. It said:

"As an oath of allegiance to the king and his queen, all members of the royal staff must sign a declaration of loyalty, renouncing any duty, obligation, or fealty to any other faiths, powers, or provinces. Signed, Lord Hector, Chancellor to King Willem IV of Palatia, Marus, and Albany."

"It's a test," Annison observed when Maddy brought the proclamation to her attention. "Lord Hector wants to see if he can trick any of the true believers into the open. Fortunately, with the chaos surrounding the wedding, I don't believe he'll be able to force everyone to sign the proclamation. As it is, I will insist that my court be exempt. Lord Hector has no authority over me. Only the king can force us to obey."

"Will you sign if the king makes you?"

"No," Annison replied. "And let us hope the king does not try."

The situation was far more difficult for Simet, however, as Maddy discovered when she spoke to him at the bell tower that night.

"He's a cunning devil," Simet observed. He was more agitated than Maddy had ever seen him. "The audacity of the man, to insist on allegiance when he himself wants to kill the king!"

"But what will you do?" Maddy asked, growing worried for this man who had fast become a good friend.

"As a true believer, I cannot—*will not*—sign such a proclamation."

"Then how will you get out of it?"

Simet tapped a finger along the side of his chin for a moment, then responded, "I can't. I can only hope to stall him until he becomes so busy with other things that he forgets who signed and who didn't."

"I don't think Lord Hector is the kind of man who'd forget," Maddy said forlornly.

"Me, either," Simet agreed with a frown. Then, as if to wave away the worry that hung like a cobweb over them, he continued, "One night soon after the wedding, I want to take you to one of our meetings."

"Of the true believers?"

"Yes. I want them to meet you, to see with their own eyes a helper from the Unseen One."

Maddy suddenly felt shy. "I won't have to make a speech or anything, will I?"

"No, of course not."

"Good."

"I'll let you know when," Simet said, then urged, "You must go back. Tell Annison that she's in my thoughts and prayers as we approach the wedding day. The Unseen One will bless her for her faithfulness to her duty."

As Maddy left the courtyard, she thought she saw someone or

something move in a dark shadow near the palace wall. She watched for a moment, her heart racing. A few seconds later, a cat meowed and strolled into the open. Maddy breathed a sigh of relief and strolled on, trying to appear casual.

Simet emerged a moment later, his thoughts consumed by Lord Hector's proclamation. He was oblivious to anything unusual about the small courtyard. Had he been paying closer attention, he would have seen the same cat move back into the shadows—and rub itself against a man's leg.

The wedding day of King Willem and Annison finally arrived. It nearly made Maddy's adventure seem like a fairy tale again. The sun shone bright, and the sky was a rich blue. Annison, dressed in a long, white silk gown with headdress and veil, looked like a true princess. She was taken to the chapel in a large gold-trimmed coach, which drove first around the major roads of the city so the people could cheer her. They did, with an enthusiasm Maddy hoped was heartfelt and not forced by soldiers in the crowd. The king went directly from his palace chambers to the chapel.

Maddy, Tabby, and the other members of Annison's court were also dressed in white dresses of lace and silk, and they were transported to the chapel in a special black-and-silver open-topped wagon.

The chapel, normally a cold and austere place, came alive with the colors of the many flowers brought in for the occasion. Maddy thought the smell was heavenly. She noticed that Lord Hector, still dressed in black, clenched a handkerchief to his nose as if the smell were offensive to him.

Simet was there as well, dressed in his best uniform of dark blue, with gold buttons and epaulets. He clutched a blue tricornered hat to his chest and occasionally pulled a lace handkerchief from his sleeve to dab his forehead as if he were hot. But Maddy noticed that it was a ploy. He was secretly signaling Annison, who also tucked and untucked a handkerchief from her own sleeve. Maddy imagined that they were expressing their love for each other. Or maybe Simet was reminding Annison to be brave while she did her duty. Whatever it was, Annison seemed to straighten up, a look of resolve in her eyes. Maddy then saw tears in Simet's eyes.

The king was dressed in a brilliant gold coat and trousers, with silk stockings and gold shoes. He wore another wig, this one blond, but it looked more like a hat than anything hairlike.

The wedding ceremony itself was a disappointment to Maddy. Once the bridegroom and bride came together at the altar, the words of the service became legalistic. Maddy thought it sounded more like the two of them were signing a contract than getting married.

"This is so unromantic," Maddy whispered to Tabby at one point. "It looks like a fairy tale, but it sounds like a business meeting."

Tabby rolled her eyes in an annoyed fashion and whispered back, "Palatians aren't known for romance. This is how they conduct their weddings. I think they're long and tedious. It would be even longer if they hadn't cut out any semblance of the old religious service. Good riddance to it, I say."

Annison had told Maddy that, though Tabby was loyal to Annison, she wasn't a believer in the Old Faith. She considered it a lot of superstitious nonsense. So they had to be careful what they said around her. Maddy often wondered why Tabby, a Marutian, had gone against the traditions of her ancestors and given up on the Unseen One, but she never dared to ask.

Two long hours went by with exchanges of vows, of documents, of rings, of scepters, of crowns, and of other symbolic things Maddy lost track of. After the formal ceremony finished, everyone returned to the palace grounds for another banquet, this time under several pavilions on the grounds.

Everything about the banquet was as wonderful as the banquet they'd had the week before, except no one tried to poison the king this time. Many speeches were made by visiting dignitaries, and the king himself—half drunk, Maddy thought—gave an hour-long speech that declared his love for Annison, his hopes for the kingdom, and his optimism about the future.

The sun set, the two moons rose, and the king and queen left by the king's golden carriage to tour the city once more and wave to those who came out to greet them. Then they went off to somewhere in Palatia—a secret place belonging to the king—for their monthlong honeymoon.

With Annison gone, Annison's court now had to move all her belongings to rooms next to the king's own chambers. Maddy asked Tabby why they still had separate rooms now that they were married. Tabby rolled her eyes and quickly explained that it was Palatian custom for the queen to have her own rooms apart from the king's, and then he could summon her when he wanted her. Maddy still didn't understand and persisted in questioning the arrangement until Tabby impatiently told her to mind her own business and go back to work. Maddy shrugged and obeyed.

The queen's court was busy from morning until night, packing Annison's things and filling trunks with her clothes, jewelry, and personal mementos.

On the third evening, a grandfather clock in the corner struck six, and Maddy suddenly remembered that she hadn't been to the bell tower since before the wedding. She had assumed there was no reason for her to meet Simet while Annison was away since there were no messages to send. But suddenly she doubted her assumption and thought she should slip away to make certain all was well with Simet.

It had rained most of the day, but now the sun came out just in time to set. Pools of water lay around the courtyard like large footprints. Simet was waiting for her just inside the belltower door. "You came after all," he said without reproach.

Maddy felt ashamed. "I'm sorry," she apologized. "I assumed we wouldn't meet while Annison was on her honeymoon. I should have asked you first."

"Don't worry," he offered with a smile. His face was half shadowed by the dusk, but she saw his eyes darting quickly around the courtyard.

"Is something wrong?"

"We're going to meet the true believers."

"*Tonight?*" she asked. "Right now?"

"Now," he answered and gently took her arm. "Come with me."

Simet guided her across the courtyard to an outer wall that ran along the palace grounds. The grass was squishy and wet. In a few minutes, they reached a small wooden door. He pulled a key from a loop on his belt and unlocked it. They stepped through into a wooded area. Simet stopped and made sure to lock the door again behind them.

"This way," he said, and she followed him through the woods until they reached an alley shrouded by old buildings of timber and stone. They crept along until the alley reached a larger street. People, horses, and wagons made their way in opposite directions on the two sides of the street. Simet seemed determined to lose them both in the congestion. Once or twice Maddy worried that she would get separated from him, but he always reached out to take her hand or her arm so she wouldn't get lost.

The entire way, Maddy wondered what to expect from the group of true believers. Would there be magic or miracles? Would something marvelous happen because she was with them? Maybe the Unseen One would somehow appear to them.

They ducked down another alley and wound up in a small court of townhouses. The Tudor-style beams, crooked doorways, and angled windows peered at them. Large boxes filled with flowers stretched along the windows and at the base of each house. Simet directed Maddy to a door on the far right, where he tapped on it in a rhythm that reminded Maddy of Morse code. A spy hole opened briefly, then closed again, and the latch lifted on the inside of the door. It was opened by a small silver-haired woman with a skeletal face. She smiled when she saw Maddy.

"Oh, dear girl, come in," she greeted and gestured with a bony finger. "Come in, Simet." She looked cautiously out the door again and then closed it quickly. They stood in a dark hallway for a moment until she moved around them. "In here," she instructed and led them to a room at the far end of the hall. It was a modest sitting room with a sofa and divan, one or two end tables, a carpet with pink and blue flowers in it, and thick blue curtains over the windows. The woman stooped and suddenly pulled the carpet back. "They're waiting," she said.

"Aren't you joining us, Annigua?" Simet asked her.

She shook her head vigorously. It seemed so fragile that Maddy thought it might fall off. "It's my turn to keep watch."

Simet knelt and grabbed hold of a small ring inset into a floorboard Maddy hadn't noticed. He gave the ring a tug and a trapdoor lifted up. The old woman took it from him and held it while he stepped onto unseen stairs. Maddy carefully followed him.

At the bottom of the stairs was a large room, cool like a cellar but decorated in comfortable-looking chairs. Oil lamps were lit and hung from the beams crossing the ceiling. Banners on the walls contained symbols Maddy had never seen before. A small group of men and women was gathered in the center. The people were on their knees and looked as if they'd been praying. One man rose to greet them. He was stocky, with a round, pudgy face, salt-and-pepper beard, and mostly gray hair pulled back in a ponytail.

"Simet," the man said pleasantly, then turned his gaze to Maddy. "And you are Maddy."

"Yes, sir."

"I am Petrad."

"He's the elder of our group," Simet added quickly.

The rest of the group now stood. Petrad introduced each man and woman to Maddy, but they were a blur of names and faces. Once the formalities were over, they drew the chairs into a circle and sat down. Maddy was aware of everyone staring at her, but she tried to ignore it, choosing instead to look at her hands folded in her lap.

"What's the latest news from the palace?" Petrad asked Simet.

"Hector is putting more pressure on some of us to sign his oath of allegiance. He has cornered me twice about it."

"What did you say to him?"

"I told him that the oath was buried in a stack of papers in my office, and I would get to it when I could. I suggested it wasn't a priority over my many other duties for the king."

"Did he accept that?"

"He gave me that cold look that only he gives so well. I don't know how much longer I can put him off. In any event, I don't trust him. I believe this oath is a first step to bigger things. He wants us annihilated."

"So he does. He's already sending his soldiers to the homes of suspected members." Petrad pursed his lips as if his statement brought back a painful memory. All he said, though, was "We will continue to pray for you and the others."

"Thank you," Simet said.

Suddenly they all lowered their heads, and Petrad prayed to the

Unseen One to give Simet strength and guidance in his role at the palace. Maddy watched out of the corner of her eyes, wondering if something bizarre or exciting would happen. Then they lifted their heads again.

"And what about you, Maddy?" Petrad asked. Maddy looked at him. "Do you have any messages for us from the Unseen One?"

The question scared her. "No, I don't think so."

Petrad smiled. "I just thought I'd ask. Meanwhile, is there anything we can do for you?"

Maddy shrugged. "For me? I don't think so."

"Tell me: How is your faith?" he asked.

"My faith?" She was feeling more confused.

"Yes. Tell us the condition of your soul."

"Oh, don't be ridiculous, Petrad!" a woman with a scarf on her head said sharply. "She's a young girl. 'Condition of your soul,' indeed. You can't expect her to know what you're talking about."

"Then *you* ask her, Bridga," Petrad insisted.

The woman called Bridga smiled at Maddy. "You came to Annison as a helper from another world, which is a wondrous thing to us," she explained. "But Simet tells us you are unsure of your faith."

"I am?" she asked. She couldn't figure out what they were getting at.

"He suggested that you think you may be in a dream or a fairy tale," said the woman.

Maddy looked at Simet helplessly. He gave her an embarrassed wink and spread his hands in resignation.

"I see what you mean," Maddy began. She tried to form an answer. "I think . . . I understand now that this isn't a fairy tale. What I mean to say is that I wasn't very happy that Annison had to marry the king when she didn't love him. But she did it anyway. Out of duty to the Unseen One. I guess that's how it happens sometimes. Real life isn't always a fairy tale, but sometimes . . ." Maddy paused, unsure of her words or how to finish her thought. Finally she said, "What I mean is, when I grow up, I hope to be as brave and courageous as Annison is."

The group seemed to approve. Petrad clapped his hands together. "Well said! Bravo!"

Bridga looked at Maddy earnestly, but she had a faraway look in her eyes. "The time will come soon when you *will* have to be as brave and courageous as Annison," she suggested. "Perhaps more so. But you must give up your ideas of magic tricks."

Maddy's mouth went dry. "What do you mean?"

"You're still thinking as a child," she said. "Even now you want magic tricks from the Unseen One. You hope to be amazed and astonished, like a member of an audience watching a magic play. But the Unseen One does not stand on the center of this stage. He watches from the wings while *you* play your part. Do not wait for magic and miracles, dear child. Play your part and play it well. That's what you're here to do."

The group was silent now. Maddy felt the heat of their watchful eyes. She didn't know how the woman called Bridga had known to say what she said, but she was right. Maddy was still thinking like a child.

Just then a small bell on the far wall rang. The men and women leapt to their feet, leaving Maddy to sit, unsure of what was happening.

"We have guests," Simet said softly, coming close to Maddy.

"Guests?" Maddy asked.

Simet put a finger to his lips. "We must be quiet and wait."

Above them, heavy footsteps beat against the floor as a large group of men—"Soldiers," Petrad whispered—entered the house. There were shouts. Something hit the floor and crashed. They could hear the old woman, her voice squawking like a bird's, rebuke the men for barging in on her. Then the heavy footsteps came closer. They were right overhead, the voices now clearer. Someone said that an illegal meeting was taking place in her house. Did they see a meeting? she asked. Did they see anyone else there? The old woman demanded that they leave.

The men thumped and crashed around. Everyone watched the stairs to the secret hatchway, waiting to see if the soldiers would find it—and them. The tension was like a low hum in Maddy's ears.

"We should leave," one of the men suggested. "Quickly. Through the tunnel."

The rest agreed, and they moved to the far corner of the cellar. Petrad pulled a small chest away from the wall, revealing a square hole behind it. The women began going through, while the men looked at them and back at the stairwell anxiously.

Maddy hesitated where she was. "What about Annigua?" she asked.

"Yes," Simet said, also lingering, his eyes fixed on the stairs. "I don't like this."

Petrad returned and put his hands on their shoulders. "She'll be all right," he assured them.

But even before the words were out of his mouth, they heard the distinct sound of a slap, and Annigua cried out with pain. One of the soldiers shouted questions at her, demanding to know where the meeting was.

"They're roughing her up," Maddy stated, alarmed.

Simet rushed to the bottom of the stairs. Petrad followed, grabbing his arm. "Don't, Simet," he warned. "If you go up now, you'll be arrested, and then they'll have the evidence to convict her, you, and any of the rest of us they can catch. They'll also know about this secret room."

"I can't let them hurt her," he answered sternly.

"They won't do her much harm. You live in the palace, so you don't know what it's like for the rest of us. They'll knock her around, mess up her home, and then leave. But if you go up to help her . . ."

Simet clenched his fists as he tried to decide. Then, angrily, he spun on his heels and went to the tunnel. The rest had already gone.

"We're going to leave her?" Maddy asked.

"We have to," Simet said sadly. Maddy thought she saw tears in his eyes, and then he ducked into the tunnel.

"Come along, child," Petrad said and nudged her along.

Maddy bit her lip. The last thing she heard as she entered the dark passage and Petrad pulled the chest back against the wall behind them was the sound of glass breaking and Annigua crying out a loud, "No!"

The tunnel led under several houses and emerged in a stairwell, flooded from the day's rain, at the bottom of a large, industrial-looking building. The people went their separate ways without acknowledging one another. Simet and Maddy traveled in silence. Neither could escape the feeling that they'd abandoned poor Annigua.

To get back to the palace, they had to circle around to the street leading to Annigua's front door. As they walked, Maddy noticed a man in a long coat walking toward them. He looked at them, his eyes reflecting recognition, and then turned his face away ever so slightly. Maddy thought it was a curious action, but then she felt a twinge of recognition as well. She had seen the man somewhere before: the high forehead and heavyset eyes, the square jaw—at the palace, she was certain.

She intended to mention it to Simet, but they were now passing the small street leading to Annigua's house. Glancing in that direction, they could see the door standing open, a dim light coming from inside, the silhouette of someone moving about in the hall.

"It's no use," Simet groaned.

Maddy hated feeling so helpless. It seemed wrong to leave Annigua to the mercy of those terrible soldiers. Suddenly, without thinking, she turned and marched toward the door.

"What are you doing?" Simet asked, trailing her.

"Petrad didn't say we couldn't visit a friend, did he?"

Simet understood and nodded. Then, moving so quickly that Maddy almost didn't see him do it, he snatched up a handful of flowers from one of the boxes along the street. "Flowers for our friend," he explained.

They reached Annigua's door, a commotion of crashes and bangs still coming from inside. Simet pounded on the door and shouted out, "Hello? Are you at home, Annigua?"

A soldier appeared in the hallway. "What do you want?" He sneered at them.

"We have come to visit our friend." Simet held up the flowers as if to prove the statement. "Is there a problem here?"

"Your friend is busy," the soldier growled. "Come back tomorrow."

"But I'm very busy tomorrow. I must see her tonight."

The soldier approached them, eyeing them from head to foot as if to decide whether he could hurt them easily. "I said to go away!" He grabbed the edge of the door, intending to slam it in their faces, but Simet shoved his foot in the doorway. The soldier looked at him indignantly. "Do you want to be arrested?" he demanded.

"And do you want to explain to the king why you've arrested one of his palace guards?" Simet challenged.

The soldier was clearly surprised and took a second look at Simet. "What's that you say?" he asked.

Simet stepped into the door. "I am Simet, a palace guard for the king." He gestured to Maddy. "This is my protégée. Now, we've come to see our friend. And unless you can show me a warrant authorizing your insolence, we *will* see our friend."

Simet pushed the soldier aside and marched down the hallway. Maddy smiled at the guard, who stood with a numb expression on his face, and followed Simet.

The damage was worse than it had sounded. It looked as if they had literally turned the room upside down and shaken it until everything had either fallen or emptied. Three other soldiers stopped their destruction to look dumbfounded at Simet and Maddy.

Annigua sat like a crumpled doll in a chair off to the side. Her hand barely covered a red welt on her right cheek. Maddy's heart lurched at the sight. *It will be a deep black and blue in no time at all,* Maddy thought.

"Annigua?" Simet said.

Annigua looked up, her face alight with the surprise of seeing him. Her eyes quickly went to the rug and the trapdoor as if he'd come up through it and she had somehow missed the moment.

"We brought you flowers," Maddy said brightly. Simet gave them to her. She took them uneasily, as if she still couldn't figure out what had happened.

"We were passing by and thought we'd stop in to visit you," Simet explained. "But I see you have visitors. What goes on?"

"They're ruining my house!" the old woman sobbed, tears filling her eyes. "They're accusing me of things! What's our nation coming to when barbarians can invade an old woman's home like this?"

"That's a question I would like answered, too," Simet said, scowling at the soldiers.

The soldier who had met them at the door entered the room. He seemed to have gotten over his shock. "Look, you two, we're here on the business of Lord Hector," he declared. "And if you don't leave right this minute, I *will* arrest you for obstructing justice."

"Then you'll have to arrest us," Simet challenged. "And let the consequences fall heavily upon your shoulders."

The soldier looked at Simet for a moment. Then he shrugged and barked at his companions, "Take them to Lord Hector."

W ell, well," Lord Hector said disapprovingly a short while later. He stood next to a large bookcase in his office, as if posing for a portrait. He lightly fingered one of the books. "What am I to make of this?"

"Make whatever you like of it," Simet replied. His eyes were cold, his jaw set as he dropped himself into a chair across from Lord Hector's desk. Maddy had never seen him look so angry. She sat down in another chair nearby.

"I can't help but wonder why you two were visiting a known criminal," he said in a voice of satin. "Come to think of it, I can't help but wonder why you two were together at all. Are you friends?"

"We have mutual friends," Simet answered. "Annigua is one of them. And she is *not* a criminal."

"So *you* say." Lord Hector clasped his hands behind his back and sauntered to his desk with a forced casualness. "I happen to know she is a fanatic of the Old Faith, an illegal cult. I also happen to know that she conducts secret meetings in her house. Quite a coincidence that you were there tonight."

"No one has yet said that visiting a friend whenever I like is a crime."

Lord Hector smiled. "You should choose your friends more wisely."

"Are you now determining who can and cannot be friends in Marus?"

"In the interests of the king, I may well determine *a lot* of things, including that." Lord Hector sneered. "You know that believing in the Old Faith is contrary to the king's wishes, and I am determined to eliminate that faith. Even tonight, my soldiers are paying surprise visits on suspected members."

"Visits—or attacks?" Simet asked.

"That depends on whether they resist."

"Annigua didn't resist," Maddy suddenly said, "and your soldiers still beat her up."

"Oh?" Lord Hector countered. "Were you there when it happened? How do you know whether she resisted? Is that what she told you, or are you going by some other source of information?"

Maddy pressed her lips together and lowered her head. She was afraid that if she said any more, she might reveal that she *had* been there.

Then a question came to Maddy's mind. Did Lord Hector already know that? Was it possible that she and Simet had been followed to Annigua's house? Maddy remembered the man she'd seen in the street. Was he one of Lord Hector's spies? If so, Lord Hector knew full well that they were there. He might even have sent his soldiers in to catch them in the act. If that were the case, he was merely toying with them now. *Can he do anything to us without proof?* she wondered.

"I'll allow that you happened to be in the wrong place at the wrong time," Lord Hector offered, as if pardoning them. "But there are other matters on my mind. Your oath of allegiance, Simet—I want it on my desk in the morning."

"You will not have it," Simet replied.

Lord Hector's face went red. "What?" he sputtered. "Do you openly defy me?"

Simet stood up. "I appeal to the king."

"You can't."

"As a member of his royal guards, I have the right to appeal anything you or any of his other officials decree. So I appeal."

"Why will you not sign an oath of allegiance unless you're not loyal to the king? Or perhaps you really are one of those fanatics of the Old Faith?"

"I am a Marutian and bound by no Palatian oath of allegiance. I will appeal to the king on that basis. Even *he* respects the differences between our two nations, united or not."

"He is king over all, which means you are bound by his laws!" Lord Hector nearly shouted.

"Then I will wait to hear him declare that for himself," Simet said calmly. "Until that time, I will remain under our Marutian law, which says that no Marutian in a royal position can sign an oath of allegiance to any other government."

Lord Hector grunted. "You quibble over technicalities."

"If necessary. But you can do nothing to me until he returns from his honeymoon to settle the matter."

Lord Hector narrowed his weasel-like eyes until they were mere slits. "We'll see about that," he threatened. He walked over to a window and pulled the curtain aside. "By the way, tonight I issued a new decree. We'll call it *Lord Hector's Decree*."

"How original."

"It says that to follow or subscribe to the Old Faith is now punishable by death." He let the significance of his announcement settle into Simet's and Maddy's minds. "And in anticipation of the great number of superstitious fools my soldiers will catch, you see"—he nodded toward the window—"I have begun the construction of a new gallows." Lord Hector smiled devilishly. "It's been specially designed for them. They will be allowed to *kneel* before they're hung."

"No!" Simet said in an appalled whisper.

Lord Hector turned to him. "As a member of the palace guard, you may have the right to appeal to the king, but the rest of your countrymen do not. They are average citizens who must enjoy the justice of *my* courts. Now get out! I have work to do."

Simet glared at Lord Hector, then turned to leave. Maddy stood up, but Hector suddenly added, "No, I want the girl to stay for a moment."

Maddy looked at Simet, worry in her eyes. He nodded at her as if to say, "Be brave." He walked out and closed the door behind him.

Lord Hector sat down in the chair behind his desk and gazed at Maddy. "You, dear girl, are a puzzle to me. My people can find out nearly anything I want to know about anyone, but you don't seem to have a history. You might have fallen from one of the two moons for all I know."

Maddy didn't respond.

"Because you seem to be a favorite with our new queen, I want to give you the benefit of the doubt. I want to believe you're merely young and impressionable and have slipped under the misguided influence of Simet."

He waited a moment to see if she would now speak. She didn't.

"Do you understand what's happening in this kingdom? It isn't a conflict between Palatia and Marus. It's not a battle over geography or heritage. It's a battle over *ideas*. The *new* ideas of Palatia are those of a world made better by the supremacy of mankind. We reject the *old* ideas of those fools who still believe in unseen gods, who have faith in things outside our control."

Maddy watched him silently.

He rested his elbows on his desk and folded his hands in front of him. "You seem to be a perceptive girl. Surely you must see where—and with whom—the future lies. Join the winning side.

Use those sharp eyes and ears of yours for those who will benefit you the most. Put them to use for your king and beloved queen. Work with me and help me to root out the believers in the Old Faith. It will put you in good standing with our monarchs." He paused again. "Well?"

Maddy wanted to say a resounding *no* right away, but she thought better of offending him. Simet could appeal to the king, but could she? Would her ties to Annison be enough to protect her?

"An answer, if you please," Lord Hector persisted.

Maddy cleared her throat nervously and spoke as diplomatically as she could. "I would like to speak to Queen Annison about it, to seek her advice," she declared.

Lord Hector's expression, which had been alive from his anticipation of her answer, now fell back to its normal boredom. "If you insist," he said coldly.

"I wouldn't dare do anything without her permission," Maddy explained and stood up.

Lord Hector leaned back in his chair. "In the meantime, you had better be careful, child. Anything can happen to you in a large palace like this. People can disappear and not be missed for days."

Maddy didn't reply but left the room as quickly as she could.

Maddy was awakened the next morning by Tabby's loud voice. She sounded agitated as she spoke with one of the other servant girls.

"Riots!" she said. "It's as if the people have lost their minds! They're in the streets, fighting the king's soldiers, tearing the city apart!"

Maddy got out of bed, wrapped her robe around her, and went into the main chamber. Tabby stood in the center of the room, gesturing wildly as she spoke.

"It's all because of Lord Hector's decree. He's going to *execute* anyone associated with the Old Faith. Mind you, I couldn't care less about superstitions like that, but I hate to see Marutians slaughtered for such an absurd reason. I wonder if the king knows? I wonder if anyone has told Annison? It's an outrage, that's what it is. An outrage!"

"The believers in the Old Faith are rioting?" the servant girl asked in a shrill voice.

"Maybe some of them, I don't know. But the decree has brought *all* Marutians into the streets. Don't you see? They're rioting because the decree violates their civil liberties. They say this is the first step to complete domination."

The servant girl clutched her apron and strangled it nervously. "What will happen to us? Do you think the mobs will win against the soldiers?"

"Anything is possible."

Maddy leaned against the doorway, trying to take it all in. Was this the rebellion that might overthrow King Willem's forces in Marus? Was it possible that Annison hadn't needed to marry the king after all?

Maddy spent the day going about her duties—more packing for the queen—but kept her ears open for news about the riots. Occasionally, through the open glass doors, she could hear a distant roar of people, then muskets being fired, but the palace seemed like a remote island otherwise. At midday, she heard a rumor that Lord Hector had several regiments positioned around the palace to make certain it was safe.

Deep in her memory, she recalled the stories from her grandparents about how the Russian revolutionaries stormed the cities, vandalizing homes and palaces, driving those who resisted into the streets. Some members of her family had crowded into a church for sanctuary, only to have the church burned down around them. Several had died.

Now she was on the other side. She *wanted* the Marutians to win. She wanted the mobs to force the Palatians out of the country so they could believe and worship freely again. But could they do it? How could a disorganized mob fight against a powerful army?

Maddy also wondered about Simet. Would he take to the streets to help the mob, or would he stay to protect the palace? Where was his allegiance at a time like this?

As midday turned into afternoon and afternoon turned into evening, Maddy decided to go to the bell tower at six to see if Simet was there. She crept cautiously along the halls, even going the wrong way several times to make sure she wasn't being followed. Though it was a period of crisis, she didn't doubt that Lord Hector might have someone keeping an eye on her. But it seemed as if all the men were out of the palace, and the few maids and servant girls she saw didn't seem to pay her any attention.

The old wooden door to the bell tower was already ajar when Maddy reached it. Normally it was closed and locked unless Simet was already there, in which case he would open the door as she approached. They then met either in the doorway or, if they were worried about being seen, just inside the tower, at the base of the stone steps that curled up to the top.

Maddy peeked her head through the open door. "Simet?" she whispered.

No one answered.

She thought about turning around and going back to Annison's chambers, but it occurred to her that she'd never been to the top of the tower. Her meetings with Simet had always been so rushed that she hadn't asked him to let her see what it was like. Glancing around quickly, she closed the door. A pale light spread down like a fan from somewhere above. She went to the stone steps and began her ascent.

She had no idea how high the tower went, and she lost count of the steps somewhere around 100. They continued to circle upward, and she was now determined to make it to the top. She hoped Simet was up there somewhere.

Then she wondered what she would do if Simet *wasn't* up above. Perhaps no one was there and the door had been left ajar by accident. Or, worse, what if Lord Hector were there? How would she explain her presence in the tower? But her aching legs told her it was too much of a waste to go back now. So she persevered.

Eventually she reached another wooden door, similar to the one at the bottom. It, too, was slightly ajar. As quietly as possible, she pushed it open and stepped out onto the belfry. It was enclosed on four sides by walls nearly as tall as Maddy and pillars that reached up to the bell encasement. She looked up, expecting to see a large bell, but it had been removed. Pigeons' nests now littered the wooden slats where a bell had once hung.

A man stood at the opposite end of the belfry, gazing out at Sarum. Without seeing the face, Maddy knew who it was.

"Simet?" she said softly.

He didn't turn but responded, "Do you see?"

Maddy could. The view was breathtaking. Tall, monumental buildings rose up amidst smaller roofs. Towers reached upward like large pencils. The streets and avenues, obviously based on old horse paths rather than planned roads, crisscrossed like a spider's web. In the distance was a large bridge that stretched over a river. It was a magnificent sight.

There was more to see than just a view of a beautiful city, however. Billows of smoke rose up like black cotton over whole sections. Every now and then she thought she heard the pop of a gun, and then she realized it was a cannon. Buildings in some sections of the city lay in ruins.

"It's more than I can bear," Simet groaned. Only then did Maddy realize he was weeping. "The Palatian army has broken up the mob. Most of the fighting has stopped. Lord Hector has won."

"What will happen now?"

"Lord Hector will come down like an iron fist on the dissenters. He will execute those who actively fought against him and then resume his persecution of the Old Faith."

Maddy felt heartsick at the news. Things could only get worse now.

"Oh, who will come and save us?" Simet implored. Maddy realized he was praying out loud. "Who will be our deliverer? Send us an intercessor. Otherwise, the night will fall and we will never see the day again." He bowed his head and wept uncontrollably over the city.

Maddy put her arm around his waist, and he pulled her close. Tears formed in her eyes, and she found herself praying along with him. "Help us," she whispered. "Send us a deliverer."

Simet was right. Lord Hector fell on Marus like an iron fist. The jails and dungeons were filled with many of the rioters, and his soldiers raided the homes of anyone suspected of being involved with the Old Faith.

Just as disturbing was the effectiveness of a special group of secret police Lord Hector had created. They worked diligently to spread propaganda that the members of the Old Faith had started the riots that nearly destroyed the city. They claimed that Lord Hector had uncovered a plot in which the members of the Old Faith planned to kill Queen Annison when she returned from her honeymoon. Then the secret police not only spied on the people of Sarum, but they also encouraged the people to spy on one another. Soon neighbor turned against neighbor, reporting suspicious activities or offhand statements that sounded treasonous. Petrad was betrayed by a neighbor and arrested.

Maddy heard all this through Simet as they continued to meet every other day. She worried about Simet. As time passed, he began to look worn out. He seemed to be aging right before her eyes.

"Lord Hector is winning," he said to her in their latest conversation, his voice old and tired. "In only three weeks, he has brought us to the edge of destruction. I don't know how many of us will be left by the time Annison returns."

"But Lord Hector hasn't executed anyone," Maddy reminded him. "He's waiting for the king to come back. You said so yourself.

He wants to hand them over like trophies just to show what a good job he's doing."

"But how many will be left by the time the king gets here?" Simet asked. "He tortures them daily. I have no doubt the weak among them will succumb to disease, if not starvation, around the time the king returns. Lord Hector will kill them off before they can be formally executed."

After a moment of silence, Simet confessed, "I went back to Annigua's house the other night. It's been boarded up. I learned from a neighbor that she was arrested and locked in the dungeon. After only a week, she died."

Together Maddy and Simet prayed. Then Simet said quietly, "I've come to realize that Annison may be our only hope. She must persuade the king somehow to reverse what Lord Hector has done."

Meanwhile, Lord Hector was unrelenting. On the eve of King Willem and Queen Annison's return, he called the entire palace staff, including Annison's court, to the Great Hall. He stood before them dressed in his usual black coat, with the usual leer on his face. Many of his soldiers and secret police stood behind him on the stage. One of them was the man with the high forehead that Maddy had seen in the street outside Annigua's house that night of the meeting. Maddy knew then that he'd been following either her or Simet. The thought sent a chill up and down her spine. How often had she been watched or followed without her realizing it?

"I have an announcement," Lord Hector declared. "Tomorrow, when the king and queen return, I will inform them that I want to celebrate their new reign in Sarum with a cleansing of the king- dom. We're going to scrub out the old ideas, the old ways, and the old faith once and for all. We will have a final *purge* of those who resist the new ideas, the new ways, and the new faith in the suprem- acy of our king!"

Some of the Palatians in the crowd cheered. The rest listened in stunned silence. Maddy felt her heart drop to her feet.

Lord Hector continued, "I want the entire city—no, the entire *nation*—to join in as we dig up the last of the weeds in our beautiful garden. What better way to present the kingdom to His Majesty!"

The Palatians applauded, many of them nudging the rest of the crowd to join in. Soon the room was a roar of applause. Maddy kept her hands at her side. Giving her a sharp elbow in the side, Tabby whispered, "Even if you don't agree, applaud. People are looking."

Maddy didn't care and stubbornly kept her fists clenched. She thought only about that phrase "a final purge." She imagined the frenzied soldiers riding through the streets, trampling or bayoneting their suspects; the mobs of sympathizers setting fire to the homes and buildings that were suspected havens of the Old Faith; and innocent people being dragged out and beaten, probably killed, by anyone with a desire to do so.

She looked around the room for Simet but couldn't see him anywhere. What was his reaction to the news? Maddy then saw him standing near the doors. He was stone-faced, his expression empty, betraying nothing. She wanted to go to him, to find out what he thought they should do. But she knew that Lord Hector or one of his men would be watching.

Their eyes caught each other. Maddy wanted to see some sense of hope in his expression. But he simply shook his head and walked out.

The despair in his expression filled her with dread.

King Willem and Queen Annison arrived at the palace early the next afternoon. Protocol demanded that the staff line up in the front hall to present themselves to the returning couple. They applauded as the king and queen stepped through the front doors.

King Willem took a dramatic bow. He looked happy and rested. He had begun to grow a beard and mustache while he was away, which made him look more mature. And he had gotten rid of his wild wigs and now let his own hair be seen. He looked like a proper king, Maddy thought.

Queen Annison looked as beautiful as ever. Her raven hair was longer and pulled back in an unfamiliar style. "She's been to one of those awful Palatian hairdressers," Tabby whispered to Maddy. "We'll put that right in no time."

Apart from that, nothing about Annison's appearance made Maddy think anything had changed. She had the same gentle smile, and her eyes reflected an inner resolve, a strength, that comforted Maddy.

"Do you think she knows what's been happening here?" Maddy asked Tabby.

Tabby shook her head. "Probably not," she replied. "The king wouldn't think it's a woman's place to know or care about the affairs of government. In fact, I wouldn't be a bit surprised if Lord Hector kept even the king in the dark about what he's been doing. But the king will find out soon enough."

Maddy stood by, barely maintaining her patience, while Tabby gave Annison a tour of her new chambers.

"They're larger than the others," Annison said, pleased. She went out to the balcony. "And I believe I like the view of these gardens better than our other view."

Maddy realized that even if Annison hated the new chambers, she was too kind to have said so.

"Tabby, please be sure to thank everyone for their hard work in moving all my things so efficiently," Annison instructed.

"Of course, my queen."

Annison giggled. "Don't be silly," she chided gently. "When we're in these chambers, I am, and always will be, Annison. You may save the formalities of calling me *queen* for the formal places."

Tabby bowed slightly. "Yes, Your Highness."

Annison laughed and waved her away. "Leave me with Maddy for a few moments."

Tabby frowned. "I think you'd be wise to allow me to inform you about—"

"No, Tabby. I want to speak with Maddy first, and then you can tell me all the latest news and gossip."

"As you wish," Tabby said unhappily and retreated from the room.

Annison sat on the edge of her bed and patted a spot next to her. "Come, Maddy. Sit down and tell me everything. Is Simet well? When can we exchange messages again?"

Maddy didn't sit down but stayed where she was near the window. She opened her mouth to speak but suddenly felt a ball of tears rise in her throat. She swallowed hard to make it go away.

A shadow crossed Annison's face. "Maddy, what's wrong?"

"You were gone such a long time" was all that Maddy could say.

"We were at the king's cottage in the southern mountains of Palatia," Annison explained. "The king received regular reports from one of his servants, but he never shared them with me. Has something happened? Is Simet all right?"

Maddy went to the bed and sat down next to the queen. She couldn't look Annison in the eyes and lowered her head.

Annison touched her face, lifting her chin with a gentle hand. "Tell me what's wrong, Maddy."

Then, like a dam bursting, the words came—as did the tears— and Maddy told Annison everything that had happened after she left for her honeymoon.

Annison's face went pale as Maddy spoke, but she struggled to keep her composure. Agitated, she then stood up and paced, wringing her hands, her eyes darting back and forth as her mind tried to work through the terrible news.

"Where is Simet now?" she asked once Maddy had finished.

"I don't know. But one of the last things he said to me was that you are the only hope. You must persuade the king to undo what Lord Hector is doing."

"Me?" Annison paused again to think. Then she returned to the bed, sat down, and took one of Maddy's hands in hers. Her voice shook as she spoke. "Listen to me, Maddy. Now is not the time for tears. We'll weep together later. Right now we must do something to avert this horrible plan."

"Do what?" Maddy asked helplessly.

"I need more information . . ." Annison's sentence trailed off as an idea came to her. "The passageway."

"Passageway?"

"Yes. If you go to the king's reception room now, you may hear what Lord Hector is reporting to him."

"There's a passageway from these chambers?"

"Yes." Annison was on her feet again. She went around the bed to the side nearest the wall. In the corner, she felt along the edge of one of the panels, then pressed her hand down. The edge gave way, and the panel sprung open.

"But I don't know the way," Maddy complained.

Annison held up her hand and went to a small end table. She picked up a piece of paper and a pen and quickly scribbled the directions. "This will take you to the same main passageway where you were before. You'll remember it." Annison thrust the paper into Maddy's hand and guided her to the entrance. She reached up into the passageway and retrieved a torch. After lighting it, she gave it to Maddy and sent her on her way.

Annison had moved so decisively that Maddy didn't have time

to think about what had happened in the passageway with Lord Hector. But the memory returned as she crept through the dark shadows. In a few minutes, she reached the peephole she had used to watch Hector and the king before. She slid the cover back and peeked through. The king, dressed in lime green, was sitting on his throne, looking bored as usual. And Lord Hector, in his black coat, stood in front of him, his hands clasped behind his back. He was talking about the finances of the region and how much money was in the king's treasury. This went on for a few minutes.

Finally the king said, "I've heard enough about money and economics, Hector. I want to hear what you've been doing to this city while I was gone."

Lord Hector smiled. "Of course, Your Majesty," he replied. "I was saving the best for last."

The king frowned. "I was greatly troubled by the reports of riots."

"No more than I was when they happened, sire," Hector said innocently. "But I've learned that they were incited by members of your nemesis, the Old Faith, and I've been working with particular diligence to capture them."

The king rested his chin on his hand. "Tell me everything."

With great embellishment, Lord Hector told the king how he had sent his soldiers to suspected meeting houses to break up illegal worship services. He claimed that many of the members actively resisted the soldiers, even resorting to violence, whereupon his men had to use greater force. "A few of the culprits died before we could bring them to justice," he said, as if saddened by their deaths. "One or two of our soldiers were scratched and bruised."

Maddy was astounded by the unflinching way Hector lied. She wanted to scream at him from where she was but resisted the temptation.

"As a result," Lord Hector continued, "I issued a decree forbidding the Old Faith in your kingdom and stepped up our efforts to rid the land of the vermin. They retaliated by causing riots among the gentler and good citizens of Sarum."

The king scratched his chin. "It still puzzles me. I was certain the believers in the Old Faith were against violence."

"As I've told you, Your Majesty, they seem peaceful enough until threatened. And then they come roaring forth like lions."

"So where is all this leading to?" the king asked impatiently. "I have a game of golf to play this afternoon."

"I'm pleased to say that I have diminished the threat to you by the members of the Old Faith. I believe we have captured most of the ringleaders and destroyed their meeting places."

"Then the crisis is over," the king said as if concluding the discussion.

"Not quite," Lord Hector replied. "I'm calling on all law-abiding and peaceful people in the nation to engage in one final purge to rid the kingdom of this infestation—as a celebration of your return from your honeymoon."

"Meaning what?"

"Meaning that this coming Saturday, all good Palatians and Marutians who are loyal to Your Majesty will drive the Old Faith out once and for all. Then I will empty the dungeons and jails of the traitors and execute them, according to Your Majesty's pleasure."

"Yes, I noticed the new scaffolds you were building," the king said in a doubtful tone. "Are you sure the Marutians are behind this idea of yours? I wouldn't want them to get upset and revolt or anything like that."

"The Marutians are as tired of the Old Faith as we are, Your Majesty. They welcome our efforts to get rid of it. Like us, they wish to turn their faces toward the bright sun of your new and enlightened ideas."

The king rubbed his hands together as if to end the meeting. "Good. Well done. Let me know how it all turns out."

That's that, Maddy thought with a sense of defeat. *The king has approved the purge.*

Lord Hector cleared his throat before the king could get to his feet. "There is one other matter, sire."

"What?" the king asked, annoyed.

"One of your palace guards . . ."

"A guard? What about him?"

"Well, I have tried repeatedly and in a reasonable manner to get him to sign the oath of allegiance to Your Majesty. And now," Lord Hector said with a chuckle, "he insists on appealing to you rather than signing the oath."

"Appeal to me?"

"Apparently it's his right as a palace guard to appeal directly to the king," Lord Hector replied, then added offhandedly, "It's one of those Marutian laws I want to change as soon as we can."

"I see. Well, what about it?"

"I have evidence—not cold, hard evidence, mind you, but evidence nonetheless—that this particular guard won't sign because he is a fanatic of the Old Faith."

"Why are you telling me about this?" The king now stood up. "Why haven't you locked him up and interrogated him?"

"As I said, he appealed to you, and I can't touch him without your permission."

"Then consider his appeal heard and denied. I can't be bothered with this nonsense." Without saying anything else, the king stepped down from the throne and left the room.

"Of course, Your Majesty," Lord Hector said to the empty room.

Maddy wasted no time rushing back to Annison's chambers. After emerging in the bedroom, she burst in on Annison in a side room that served as a reception room. Annison was listening intently to Tabby.

Tabby glowered at Maddy, displeased by the rudeness of the interruption.

"I'm sorry, Your Highness," Maddy said breathlessly, "but I have news."

"Leave us, Tabby," Annison commanded.

"But Your Highness—"

Annison gave Tabby an uncharacteristically stern look. Tabby stood up, bowed, and left the room, nearly slamming the door behind her.

Maddy reported what she'd seen and heard in the king's reception room. Annison's eyes went wide, and she reached out to take Maddy's hand. "You have to run and warn Simet," she urged. "Tell him to escape and hide until it's safe again. Go, dear girl, *go!*"

Maddy left in a flash and hurried down the many hallways of the palace. She had no fear of becoming lost now; she was getting to know her way around pretty well. She got to Simet's small office just as he was coming out.

"Simet!" she said with a gasp.

He was surprised to see her. "Hello, child," he greeted. "Your timing is perfect. I am about to seek an audience with the king to discuss my appeal—and to tell him all the terrible things his chancellor has been doing."

"Lord Hector . . . has beaten you to it," Maddy said in heaving tones. "The king has given him permission for the purge . . . *and* to arrest you. Annison wants you to escape. You have to hurry!"

Simet looked bewildered, as if Maddy had suddenly walked up and hit him in the face with a rock. "This can't be," he said in a half whisper, then cried out, "Where is justice? Where is the Unseen One?"

"He's only in your imagination," Lord Hector said as he approached from the end of the hall. "It's where He's always been. But thank you for confirming what I always suspected, that you're one of the fanatics of the Old Faith."

"Run, Simet!" Maddy implored. "Run!"

But it was too late. Lord Hector's guards swarmed around them like bees and grabbed Simet by both arms.

One of them, the man with the high forehead, punched Simet in the mouth. "That's for making my job so difficult," he spat.

Simet shook his head as if shaking off the blow, but a trickle of blood slipped from his lip.

Maddy gave the man a hard kick in his shin.

He winced and then suddenly laughed at her. "You're a feisty one," he observed. "I've enjoyed watching you."

Lord Hector stepped in between Maddy and the man. "Take Simet to my *special* interrogation room in the dungeon," he commanded.

Simet said nothing as the guards took him away.

Lord Hector grabbed Maddy roughly by the arm. "I warned you to choose your side carefully," he said coldly.

Maddy looked at him defiantly. "I am on the *queen's* side," she challenged. "Are you going to arrest me, too?"

Lord Hector grunted and let go of her. "You'd be advised to stay very close to the queen, then. And stay clear of anything to do with Simet. He's as good as dead."

10

"What are we to do?" Annison asked over and over as she paced from one end of her bedroom to another.

Maddy watched her go back and forth. "Can't you talk to the king like Simet said?" she asked. "You're his wife, after all."

Annison shook her head. "It isn't that easy. According to Palatian law, the queen can only be summoned by the king. She can never approach him on her own initiative."

"What happens if you break their law?"

"He could divorce me or, worse, have me arrested and put to death."

"That sounds like a stupid law."

Annison agreed and then worried aloud, "He warned me when we returned that he would be very busy this week. I don't think he planned to see me again until next week sometime—*after* Hector's purge. And after Simet has been murdered."

"What if you bumped into him by accident?" Maddy suggested. "What if you just happened to be somewhere that *he* happened to be?"

Annison considered the idea for a moment, then commented, "I don't know of any Palatian laws against that."

"Then you could talk to the king and make him understand."

"But that's another question," Annison said thoughtfully. Tired of pacing, she sat down in a chair. "What can I say to make him understand? He doesn't believe women should be involved in affairs of state to begin with. Worse, if I appeal to him on behalf of the Old Faith, he'll wonder why I'm doing it. That would leave me with only one choice: to tell him the truth."

"The truth?" Maddy asked. "The *whole* truth?"

"Yes. I'll have to confess that I myself am a believer and that Simet has been like a father to me."

"What do you think he'll do if you say all that?"

"I don't know." Annison contemplated the consequences. "He might very well feel betrayed and allow Lord Hector to kill me along with all the others."

"Then maybe you shouldn't do it. Maybe there's another way."

"What other way, Maddy? You've been sent here by the Unseen One to be my helper. Now *help* me. Tell me of another way to save my people, and I'll do it. Otherwise, don't distract me from what I know, and you know, I must do."

Properly chastised, Maddy fell silent. Her mind went back to when she'd first arrived in Marus with her fairy-tale hopes and storybook dreams and hadn't understood Annison's commitment to duty. Then it was the duty of marrying a man she didn't love. Now Maddy realized that marrying the king was only a small thing to do. Her real duty for the Unseen One meant that she might have to give her life to save the people she loved.

Annison gazed at Maddy as if she knew her thoughts. "You see now, don't you?" she quizzed. "What good is our faith in anything if we're not willing to sacrifice ourselves to it completely—even die for it?"

Maddy nodded and made up her mind. If Annison were going to sacrifice, she would sacrifice, too.

Annison looked at the clock on the mantel. "If the king is golfing this afternoon, he'll return to his chambers around five o'clock. That gives me a few hours to prepare. Come help me get dressed."

Maddy looked at her questioningly.

"If I'm going to bump into the king, I want to look presentable," she explained with a smile.

As she dressed, Annison discussed her options with Maddy. Annison decided that her panic about Simet and Hector's purge mustn't rule her thinking. If she had to appeal to the king, she needed to do so in a subtle and intelligent manner.

"I must learn from Lord Hector," she told Maddy. "I must have a plan even more clever than his own. Then I must speak to the king as Lord Hector does."

"You mean lie?" Maddy asked.

"Of course not!" Annison replied. "But there are more ways to appeal to the king than simply throwing oneself at his feet or confronting him with our cause. We must get him in the right frame of mind to consider other notions before we make our case."

Maddy was impressed with Annison's calm and collected manner. Maddy, on the other hand, was a bundle of nerves. All the subtlety and cleverness in the world wouldn't make a difference if the king rejected Annison and her faith.

Annison went to her desk and pulled out a small red book. She sat down and began to write in it. After a moment, she seemed self-conscious about Maddy's standing nearby and dismissed her. Maddy waited in the other room, wondering what Annison was up to.

It was close to 4:30 when Annison came out of her room. "Tabby has learned from one of the king's servants that he'll return from his golf game through one of the entrances in the east garden," she told Maddy. "I'll make it a point to be strolling in that garden when he arrives."

"I'll go with you," Maddy said.

"No, you won't," Annison stated firmly. "This is dangerous. If it all goes wrong, you must leave the palace immediately. One way or another, you must find your way home."

Maddy was distressed. "Home? How am I supposed to go home? I don't know how I got here in the first place!"

"Then we'll hope and pray that the Unseen One will send you back if our plans are undone."

"But I want to go with you," Maddy pouted.

"No. You wait here." Annison clutched the small red book against her chest. She then adjusted her shawl, gathered up her dress, and strolled casually out of the room. For a fraction of a second, it was easy to think she was merely a woman going for a walk in a garden—and not to her possible doom.

Maddy lasted all of five minutes in the room alone. Then her eye caught an umbrella leaning against the wall, and she decided Annison would need it to shield her from the sun or protect her from the rain, if it happened to fall. It seemed like a good excuse either way, so she grabbed it and headed for the east garden.

It was a beautiful summer's day, and the sun poured golden rays down to highlight the lush greens, blues, purples, yellows, and reds of the garden. Maddy looked around for Annison but couldn't see her. Suddenly a hand was on her arm.

"What are you doing here?" Annison asked as Maddy turned to face her.

Maddy smiled up at her and said feebly, "I brought you this umbrella."

Annison wagged a finger at her. "You've disobeyed me," she stated. "Now go back to my chambers."

Maddy opened her mouth to argue, but the sound of an approaching coach stopped her. It was the king's coach, coming up a gravel path that traveled along one side of the garden. The driver drew the horses to a halt only feet away from where Annison and Maddy stood. The door swung open and the king stepped out.

"Hello, my dear," he said pleasantly as soon as he saw the queen. "What a nice surprise!"

Annison bowed to him and nudged Maddy to do the same. "Thank you, my king," Annison replied. "I've been enjoying the garden."

"May I walk with you for a moment?" the king asked, blushing a little like a schoolboy.

"I would be honored."

The king took the queen's arm in his, and they strolled toward the large fountain that stood at the center of the garden. Maddy followed at a discreet distance, but she could hear what they were saying.

The king initially dominated the conversation with talk about his golf game. Then, when it was clear they had exhausted that topic, Annison said, "My lord, I know you're terribly busy now that we've returned. But I would like to ask a favor . . ."

"A favor, my queen? Name it and it's yours, even up to half my kingdom," he said playfully.

"I would be grateful if you and Lord Hector would come to lunch in my chambers tomorrow."

"We would be delighted!" the king replied, then added sourly, "But do I have to bring Hector? He's been getting on my nerves lately."

"As your queen, I think it would be wise for me to be in good standing with your chancellor. Don't you think?"

"You are diplomatic as well as beautiful!" the king exclaimed. He kissed her hand. "I am to meet Hector in a few moments and will present your invitation."

"Thank you, sire. It will be a modest meal, but I treasure any time we have together."

The king blushed again, then stroked his growing beard with the back of his hand. "You are a joy to me, Annison. I will see you at lunchtime tomorrow."

"Until then," Annison said, and she handed him the book she was carrying. It was covered in red velvet and had a small gold clasp along the front. It was the one Maddy had seen her writing in earlier. "This is a small gift from me in the meantime. It's a story I wrote for you. But you mustn't read it until later."

"I'm intrigued," the king said and took the book gratefully. He kissed Annison's hand again. "Thank you." With only a passing glance toward Maddy, he walked to the back door of the palace, whistling a jaunty tune.

Once the king was out of earshot, Annison took Maddy aside. "You must be quick now," she instructed. "I want you to go back down the passage to hear what's said between the king and Lord Hector. Hurry now!"

Maddy found most of the conversation between the king and Lord Hector boring. They discussed more financial details, legislation about Palatians living in Marutian homes, the positioning of troops, and a series of meetings the king was to have with local business-men. The king hardly seemed interested.

Then, when the meeting was drawing to a close, the king said, "My Lord Hector, I hope you don't have any plans for lunch tomorrow."

"I don't, sire," Lord Hector replied. "Why do you ask?"

"The queen has invited us to lunch in her chambers."

"Us? The two of us?"

"Yes. She asked for you specifically."

"Well, I'm honored, Your Majesty. I wouldn't miss it."

"And so you shouldn't."

The king left the reception room by way of a back door, and Maddy nearly closed the peephole to return to Annison. But Lord Hector did a curious thing. He suddenly marched up to the throne and sat down on it, slinging his leg over one of the chair arms.

"Well, well," he said aloud.

The man with the high forehead came forward from the door. Maddy wasn't sure if he'd been there the whole time and she just hadn't noticed him, or if he'd only just entered. "You look rather pleased with yourself," he observed.

"Why shouldn't I be, Reginald?" Lord Hector responded. "Things are looking up."

"Are you talking about the purge or the king's golf score?"

"I'm talking about being invited to the queen's chambers for lunch tomorrow. What do you make of it?"

Reginald shrugged. "I'm not sure I make anything of it."

"But why invite *me* when she could have the king all to herself?"

"A very good question. I suppose you think you have an answer?"

"I do. I believe it's a gesture on her part to win my friendship. I think she's a very shrewd woman, and she knows where the real power in this kingdom rests. With me. She also knows that now is a very good time to win my favor."

"You read a lot into a simple invitation."

"In the business of politics, one has to. Nothing is as it seems. No one is kind unless they will gain from it. No one is nasty unless there's an advantage. That's how the game is played."

"But she's only the queen," Reginald said. "She has no real power."

"It's true," Lord Hector conceded. "But she's a beautiful woman. And I believe she has the king's heart." Hector sat up, abruptly changing the subject. "Tell me how Simet is holding up. Has he given you any worthwhile information? It would be gratifying to me if he would blab the names of all the other leaders of the Old Faith."

"No, sir. He defies us at every turn. He has surprising stamina for an old man."

"You won't kill him."

"Of course not. I leave that pleasure to you on Saturday."

Hector chuckled low and wickedly. "He will be the first to die on my new gallows." Hector then stood up, his tone turning light. "I wonder what I should wear to the queen's chambers tomorrow?"

"Your black coat, I assume."

"Yes," Hector said thoughtfully. "It's my favorite."

Maddy finally went back to Annison's chambers. Annison was in the midst of finalizing the menu for the next day's lunch with the king. Tabby took copious notes, offering suggestions on one or two items, and then hustled off to inform the royal chef.

"What did you learn?" Annison asked Maddy once they were alone.

"Lord Hector thinks you've invited him to lunch because you want to be his friend," Maddy replied. "And they're trying to get Simet to give them the names of the leaders of the Old Faith."

"They're torturing him," said Annison softly.

Maddy nodded somberly. "But he hasn't told them anything."

"And he won't. He'll die first."

"They won't let him die," Maddy said. "Lord Hector wants Simet to be the first one hung on the gallows this Saturday."

Annison clutched her hands to her breast. "If the Unseen One would permit it, I would poison that evil man's food tomorrow. But that's not His way. It's not what I believe I should do."

"What *are* you going to do?" Maddy asked. "Inviting them to lunch . . . the book you gave to the king . . . I don't understand what you're up to."

"I told you I'm going to appeal to the king in Lord Hector's way. If it works, I may beat him at his own game. If it doesn't, I may be the second person hung on the gallows this Saturday."

That evening, Tabby, breathless and red-faced, ran into Annison's chambers just as the clock struck eight. "A servant has just come from the king!" she exclaimed.

Annison, who was trying to decide what to wear for the next day's lunch, looked up anxiously. "A servant from the king?" she asked.

"He wants you to come to his Reception Hall immediately. He wants an audience with you."

Annison swallowed hard. "What on earth could he want with me now?"

"The servant didn't say. But you must hurry."

Annison raced to a standing mirror to be sure her dress and hair looked all right. "Do I look presentable?" she asked anxiously.

"There's no time!" Tabby cried impatiently.

"May I come with you?" Maddy asked.

"The king wants her *alone*," Tabby emphasized.

Annison leaned to Maddy's ear. "Watch from the passageway," she whispered.

Annison and Tabby hurried out. Maddy waited for a minute and then, when she was sure it was clear, went to the hidden door in the bedroom, lit the torch, and rushed down the passageway to the peephole.

Maddy got to the peephole before Annison reached the Reception Hall. The king was seated on his throne, flipping through the small red-velvet book Annison had given him earlier. His expression was one of deep concentration. He looked puzzled and worried, an unusual combination for him. Then a servant entered and announced that Queen Annison had arrived. The king stood up, tucked the book in his belt, and said, "Please send her in."

Queen Annison entered, and, glancing quickly in the direction of the peephole, she bowed. The king went to her and took both her hands in his. "Thank you for coming on such short notice," he greeted.

"The pleasure is mine, sire," she replied.

He kissed her hands and then led her to two of the chairs at the base of the podium on which the throne sat. She sat down in one, and he sat in the other.

"How may I serve Your Majesty?" she asked.

"I want to talk to you about this story you've written." He pulled the book from his belt and held it up.

"What of it, sire?"

"I found it both moving and frustrating at the same time."

"I'm glad my writing could touch your emotions."

"You knew very well that it would. I may not be a particularly brilliant man, but I'm not a fool. You wrote this story for a purpose."

"What purpose might that be, sire?"

"Don't be coy, Annison. I had hoped that you respected me more than that."

"I'm sorry if I sound coy."

"Let's talk about this story." The king fiddled with the pages of the book as he spoke. "You tell about a man who works in a palace and has raised an orphan girl like his own daughter. He works hard and serves his king well, but his greatest reward is to see his foster daughter rise to great heights of power and popularity. But this man never reveals that he's the girl's foster father and carries on in his meager duties. Then one day he learns of a plot to kill the king. He secretly informs the queen, who then tells the king, who then thwarts the plot. But because the king didn't know of this man's loyalty, he believes the slander of those in his court who falsely accuse the man for their own gain—they themselves were in on the plot to kill the king but cleverly disguised the fact. The king has the man locked up, tortured, and then, finally, hung on the gallows."

"That is the story I told, yes."

"The ending leaves me furious, my queen. My sense of injustice at this man's fate makes my blood boil."

"As you are a just king, I thought it might."

"Confound it, Annison, is this story true? Am I the king?"

"Please, Your Majesty," Annison said carefully. "May we continue to speak of the story as only a story, to see what we may learn from it?"

The king snorted unhappily. "You Marutians love your stories, don't you? It's as if you don't know how to speak directly."

"I don't wish to offend you."

"No, no," he said. "We'll do it your way. Let us speak of this man hypothetically."

"Since the story outraged you with its injustice, do you think, then, that the king should free the man?"

"Of course he should." The king suddenly stood up and paced, his hands clasped behind his back. Maddy wondered if it was a habit picked up from Lord Hector by the king or the other way around. "More than freeing him, the king should honor the man! No generosity should be withheld."

Annison breathed a sigh of relief. "I am happy to hear you say so, my lord."

"Now tell me, Annison. Is this story of yours true or not?"

"It is true, Your Majesty."

The king groaned. "And who is the man?"

"His name is Simet. He's the one who told me of the plot to poison you, which he'd heard from a reliable source."

"I think I know him. He's one of the palace guards."

"He was, Your Majesty. But even now he is in the dungeons, being tortured."

"I will soon remedy that. And his foster daughter? Have I met her as well?"

Annison opened her mouth to answer, but at that moment a knock came at the door.

"What is it?" the king bellowed.

Lord Hector entered, clutching a handful of papers. "Your Majesty, I have these papers for you to—" He stopped when he saw the queen sitting with the king. "I'm so sorry, sire. I didn't realize you were busy."

He bowed as if to retreat, but the king called him forward. "You are just the man I want to see," the king declared.

"Sire?"

"Yes," the king replied. "There's a grave injustice I want to correct. Will you help me?"

"With pleasure, sire."

Annison suddenly interrupted. "Perhaps Your Majesty should speak *hypothetically* to Lord Hector, to gain his wisdom on the subject," she suggested.

"An excellent idea, my queen," he said, boylike, as if he were about to play a game of charades. "Lord Hector, what would you think if I said there was a man who saved a king's life but was not properly rewarded for it?"

Lord Hector looked from the king to the queen and back again before responding, "Then I would assume Your Majesty would want to reward him in some way."

"With great honors, yes?"

"If Your Majesty pleases." Lord Hector's face lit up, and then he asked, "Do I know this man?"

"I'll say only that he has served me with great diligence in the past month, and I'm afraid I haven't given him his due."

"In the past month?" Lord Hector suddenly blushed.

"Yes," the king went on. "Now, I wonder what *you* would do to honor such a man."

"Well . . ." Lord Hector began, again blushing, "I would suggest a banquet, inviting all of his family and friends and the notables of the city, and then I would present him with a medal or medallion of some sort, proclaiming his value to Your Majesty. And"—he paused to clear his throat—"if you felt that this particular servant was worthy, you might give him a house and lands in the countryside. But that is for Your Majesty to decide."

Something about Lord Hector's expression and the way he spoke gave Maddy the impression that he thought he himself was the man about whom the king was talking.

"I'm so glad to hear you say it!" the king exclaimed. "We will do all that for the man—and more."

Lord Hector smiled. "Your Majesty is too kind."

The king frowned. "If I were kind, this man would not be in the dungeon in the first place."

Lord Hector looked puzzled. "In the dungeon?"

"Yes. And it's my intention to find out who put him there in such an unjust manner."

"It . . ." Lord Hector suddenly seemed to have trouble speaking. His mouth moved, but the words were slow to come. "It goes without saying. But, sire, who is the man?"

"His name is Simet."

Lord Hector's face contorted as the blood rushed from his face. His expression went from shock to confusion to fear. "Simet?"

"Yes. I assume you know him."

"I do, Your Majesty." Lord Hector struggled to maintain his composure. Maddy was sure his mind was working quickly to turn this to his advantage somehow. "But—oh, dear—this is most awkward."

"Why?"

"*You* authorized his arrest."

Clever man, Maddy thought. *He has turned the tables on the king.*

"Did I?" the king asked, unsure.

"Earlier today. He's the palace guard of whom I told you. He refused to sign the oath of allegiance."

The king looked thoughtful. "Odd, then, that a man who refused to sign your oath is also a man who may have saved my life."

"True, Your Majesty. *If* he did as you said," Hector offered.

"You have your sources of information about this man, and so do I," the king retorted. "For the time being, I will believe *my* sources."

"As you wish, sire. But there's more to it than that. I have reason to believe he's a fanatic of the Old Faith."

"Yes, so you said earlier today."

"Which is one more reason he was put in the dungeon, as *you* authorized."

The king pondered this statement for a moment. "So I authorized his arrest based on *your* claims against him?"

"Yes, sire."

The king looked down at the red-velvet book thoughtfully, then gazed at the queen with a knowing expression. She simply returned his gaze with a look of expectation.

"I think I understand now."

Lord Hector seemed sure he had won his case. "So to release him from the dungeon might be folly on your part—"

"Folly?" the king bellowed, suddenly turning on Hector. "You speak to your king of his folly?"

"No, Your Majesty. Of course not," Lord Hector said evasively. "I didn't mean *your* folly. I meant—"

"I know what you meant," the king growled. "Regardless, you will release the man. And not only will you release him, but I also want you to begin preparations for the honors you mentioned."

"The honors?" Lord Hector gulped loudly.

"I want him to have a banquet and a medal and a house and lands."

Hector closed his eyes as if enduring great pain. "If you insist, Your Majesty."

"I insist. We will discuss the matter further tomorrow."

"Perhaps we could discuss it at our luncheon together?" Annison suggested.

"That would be perfect," the king agreed. "A woman's touch for such an occasion would be welcome. You are dismissed, Lord Hector."

"Yes, yes," Hector stammered, still dumbfounded by this turn of events. "Thank you, sire."

When Lord Hector reached the door, the king suddenly called out, "Hector, have you been *interrogating* Simet in your usual fashion?"

"*I* haven't as yet. But he has been asked a question or two, I'm sure."

"Then you had better make sure the palace doctor attends to him. I want him in perfect condition for his banquet."

"Yes, sire." Lord Hector bowed and backed out of the hall.

Once the door was closed, the king turned to Annison again. "Satisfied?" he asked.

"Thank you, sire."

"Well, I'm not," he stated. "You haven't told me everything. I believe there's more to this story than you've said. And I am now suspicious of its outcome."

"There is more," Annison replied. "But it can wait until our luncheon tomorrow."

"Perhaps I won't wait. I have my own ways of finding things out."

Annison smiled at him noncommittally.

The king looked at her warily. "Why do I have the feeling you're toying with me?"

Annison looked offended at the idea. "Your Majesty is far too astute to be *toyed* with."

"Nonsense! People have been toying with me my entire life. From the nursery to the grave, a king is but a toy to be tossed to and fro between his lords and ministers."

"But by his wife?" Annison asked.

"I hope," he said earnestly, "that my wife does not."

He kissed her hands again, and Annison left. Then, alone, he returned to his throne and sat down wearily. His fingers lightly brushed the velvet on Annison's book. He held it to his chest for a moment. Maddy suddenly realized that the king was truly in love with his queen.

He abruptly stood up and went to the door. A servant appeared in the doorway. The king whispered something Maddy couldn't hear. The servant nodded and rushed off, and the king returned to his throne with a wan smile on his face.

Simet was taken to a wing of the palace Maddy had never seen before. The royal doctor kept an infirmary there, made up of small rooms with comfortable beds. Simet lay in his bed, his face puffed and bruised, but he didn't look as bad as Maddy had feared.

"What has happened?" Simet asked, his voice weak. "Why was I released?"

"Annison spoke to the king," she answered.

His eyes grew wide. "She spoke to him? About what? What did she tell him? Is she in danger?"

"No," Maddy assured him. "She is well, and you are free."

"But what about Lord Hector? His purge is coming in only a few days."

"Annison is doing the best she can to stop it."

"But how?"

"By the inspiration of the Unseen One," Maddy replied, repeating what Annison had told her to say.

"I don't understand," Simet said, sweat forming on his brow. "You have to tell me everything."

"She'll tell you nothing more," a voice said from behind Maddy. It was the doctor. He stood looking like an unmade bed, his white hair sticking out in all directions. Had he been roused from bed to attend Simet? Probably. "This girl is going to leave you now so you can rest. I also want to tend to the results of your *interrogation*." He said the word disdainfully, as if he'd seen too many of the victims of Lord Hector's torturers.

"No, wait," Simet requested.

The doctor intervened and forced Maddy out. She waved quickly from the door and said comfortingly, "Don't worry."

But Maddy herself was still worried. It was one thing to tell a clever story and get Simet released from the dungeon, but it was another to save hundreds if not thousands of believers from Hector's purge. Maddy didn't fully understand Annison's thinking or how she still hoped to influence the king, but she hoped and prayed that Annison would succeed somehow.

As Maddy rounded the corner to the hall leading back to Annison's chambers, Lord Hector stepped forward.

Maddy cried out.

"Calm down!" Lord Hector snapped. "You'll come to no harm."

Maddy continued to walk toward the chamber doors.

"You are the linchpin to all this somehow," he observed, walking alongside her. "But how? Are you influencing the queen? What is your connection to Simet?"

"I'm sorry, but I must return to the queen," Maddy said, picking up her pace.

"What's the connection between the queen and Simet? Why did she intercede for him? *How* did she intercede for him?"

Maddy didn't answer. The chamber doors were in sight now.

Lord Hector suddenly grabbed Maddy's arm just as she reached the doors.

"Ouch!" she cried out, though it didn't hurt much.

"What is the queen up to?" Hector demanded. "Is she for me or against me?"

"Does it matter?" Maddy asked as she grasped the door handle. "She's only a simpleminded woman. What can she do to you?"

Maddy pushed the door open. The large bald-headed guard was just inside and approached them menacingly. He relaxed when he saw Maddy but looked suspiciously at Lord Hector's hand on her arm.

Lord Hector let go. "Tell your queen that she should be careful," he warned. "I've been playing this game—and the king—for years."

"Maybe the rules are changing," Maddy retorted and closed the door on him.

Safe inside the chambers, she found herself grabbing a cup of water. She felt sick to her stomach from the sheer anxiety of everything that had happened. Once she felt calm again, she went into Annison's bedroom to tell her that Simet was all right.

Maddy's dreams that night were fitful. She saw hundreds of people being led to the gallows, their bodies swinging lifeless at the ends of hundreds of ropes. Lord Hector had succeeded with his purge. He had played the "game" better than Annison.

Then she sat at a table with the king and Lord Hector. They were eating lunch. But Annison's chair was vacant.

"Where is she?" Maddy kept asking.

Finally Lord Hector smiled and replied, "She was a fanatic of the Old Faith. You will find her hanging outside."

"No!" Maddy cried.

"What do *you* believe?" the king questioned her. "Are you a fanatic, too, or are you willing to embrace our *new* ideas?"

"What new ideas?" Maddy asked.

"Whatever ideas I approve of," the king responded. He dabbed a napkin against his lips and tossed it carelessly on the table.

"What do you believe?" Lord Hector pressed. "Tell us now so we may decide whether you live or die."

Maddy felt a burning in her eyes. "I believe in the Unseen One," she replied, her voice quavering.

"I'll kill you for that," Lord Hector said with a smile as he tugged on a long rope hanging from the ceiling. A curtain suddenly parted on the far side of the room. Behind it was a small scaffold. A noose hung from the top. "Custom-built for a girl your size," he noted.

"Are you *sure* you believe in the Unseen One?" the king asked with a yawn.

Maddy looked at the scaffold and then back at the king. "Yes," she said as firmly as she could muster. "Yes, I do."

And then she awoke in a cold sweat.

"Whatever happens at lunch tomorrow," she found herself praying to the Unseen One, "let me be brave."

The morning was filled with preparations for the lunch. A large table was placed in the center of the queen's chambers for Annison, the king, and Lord Hector. Smaller tables were brought in to hold the various dishes of fowl, vegetables, fruits, and several types of bread.

Annison checked and double-checked to make sure everything was as perfect as it could be. Tabby huffed and puffed as she double-checked Annison's double-checking. Maddy ran several errands from the chambers to the kitchen and had to endure the complaints of the royal chef as he upbraided her for interrupting him so much.

Finally the the king and Lord Hector arrived. Annison's entire court stood at strategic places around the table—some to serve, some to make sure the cups were always filled with drinks, others to clear away any unused dishes, and the remainder to do whatever was asked of them. Maddy was assigned to be Annison's special attendant, to stay near Annison in case she needed anything. Maddy was pleased to obey. She had feared she would be sent from the room and not allowed to watch what happened.

"What are you going to do?" Maddy whispered to Annison in the final seconds of silence before the knock came at the door.

"I don't know," Annison answered honestly.

"You mean you don't really have a plan?" Maddy asked, surprised.

"I have planted some seeds, which I hope we will see grow," she replied. "Unless, of course, the birds have plucked them from the ground before they've had a chance."

Maddy wasn't sure of what she meant, but there was no time to question further. A loud rapping sounded on the door. Tabby opened it, and the king and Lord Hector strode in together.

"Oh, my!" the king exclaimed as he looked at the table spread out before him. "I thought we were having a modest lunch. This looks more like a banquet."

"I am undeserving of such a feast," Lord Hector said. His voice was smooth as silk.

They sat down with Annison, and her staff began to serve them. They chitchatted about the wonderful weather they'd been having and the flowers in the garden, and the queen advised Lord Hector about some of the shops for men in Sarum where he could buy the best-made clothes. He seemed grateful for the advice.

Finally the meal was finished, and the servants brought them coffee, tea, and small chocolates. Both the king and Lord Hector made a fuss about how wonderful the food was and how gracious a hostess Annison had been.

"I do not know Your Highness very well," Lord Hector admitted to her. "But I'm so pleased to find you as charming and delightful as I'd heard you were."

"Thank you," Annison replied.

"You have outdone yourself, my queen," the king said contentedly. "Ask me for anything, anything at all, and it's yours!"

Annison smiled. "I want only what you want, my king— truth and justice in our kingdom."

The king leaned back in his chair and nodded. "Truth and justice, yes. Two things we must have. Shall we begin with truth?" The king then pulled Annison's red-velvet book from his coat pocket and set it down on the table. "Do you read much, Hector?"

Lord Hector looked at it distrustfully. "Occasionally. Books of trade, mostly."

"You should read stories," the king suggested. "Stories can be far more interesting than books of trade. They can also nudge you toward great truths that might otherwise escape you." He patted the book. "This story, for example. Simple as it is, it has caused me to reconsider many things."

"What kinds of things, sire?" Lord Hector inquired.

"That man, for one, the guard who was in the dungeon . . ."

"Simet," Annison reminded him.

"Yes, him."

"I released him as you commanded, sire," Lord Hector said quickly.

"I know you did. And I've been informed that he's recovering nicely from your interrogations."

"I did not interrogate him," Lord Hector corrected him.

"No, you didn't. True. Your man Reginald actually did the interrogation."

Lord Hector raised an eyebrow. He clearly didn't expect the king to know about Reginald—or anything to do with what went on in the dungeon. "Reginald?"

"You know him, of course. Suspicious-looking fellow with a rather high forehead."

"Yes, I know him."

"So you should. He does a lot of your dirty work, I understand."

Lord Hector didn't reply but waited to see what the king would say next.

"The same sort of dirty work he did for his previous employer."

"I'm at a loss," Lord Hector said. "I don't know who his previous employer was."

"But you must," the king insisted. "His previous employer was that traitor Lord Terrence."

Lord Hector feigned surprise. "Was he?"

"Yes, he was." The king suddenly patted his pockets as if he'd forgotten something. He then dug into an inside pocket and produced a piece of paper. "Late last night, I got him to tell me all about it."

Lord Hector paused for a moment, then signaled to one of the servants for more water. "You spoke to Reginald yourself?" he asked.

"At length," the king replied. "You see, I read this story—written by my dear wife—and it caused me to think about the men who had tried to poison me. Of course, I hadn't investigated the case myself. I left it to *you*, my trusted chancellor, to do that. Sadly, everyone who might have been forthcoming with information died from your interrogations."

"I reported that to you at the time," Lord Hector reminded him.

"One of the men was a servant," the king went on. "You accused him of being in the employ of one of the two lords and claimed he had been the one who actually poisoned my cup. But I've learned from Reginald that the accused servant was innocent. It was Reginald who poisoned my cup."

Lord Hector's jaw dropped. "No, my king! Tell me it isn't so!"

"I'm afraid it is. Reginald confessed it all."

"I am stricken!" Hector declared, putting a hand to his mouth. "I had no idea I was employing a *traitor*. Until this moment, I didn't know he was Terrence's man."

"It surprises me what you know and do not know, Lord Hector."

"What do you mean, sire?"

"You said conclusively that Lords Stephen and Terrence were both fanatical members of the Old Faith. I have learned otherwise. In fact, the two of them, along with Reginald, actively *hated* the Old Faith. So how did you draw your conclusions?"

"From my interrogations, sire. But under such duress, they may have lied to me about their cause."

"Perhaps they did." The king drummed his fingers on the book. "Or perhaps you put the lie into their dead mouths."

"Sire!" Hector cried indignantly and stood up.

"Sit down, Hector."

"But Your Majesty—"

Maddy wasn't sure how it happened, but the king suddenly had a knife in his hand. "I said, sit down."

Lord Hector obeyed.

"We were speaking of truth, and now I want it." The king kept the knife steadily pointed at Lord Hector. "You and Lord Stephen and Lord Terrence conspired together to do two things, kill me and—"

"No!"

"And rid the land of those who subscribe to the Old Faith. You failed at the first, but you've worked very hard at the second."

"You accuse me unfairly!"

"And you continue to lie to me." He turned to Annison and asked, "How did you know I was going to be poisoned at the banquet?"

"Simet told me."

"And how did Simet know?"

Annison hesitated. Maddy knew she was trying to protect her, to keep her out of what might happen.

Maddy stepped forward. "I told him, Your Majesty," she admitted.

"You?"

"I'd be wary of anything this girl has to say, sire," Lord Hector interjected.

"Quiet!" the king commanded. To Maddy he said, "How did *you* know?"

"I overheard Lord Stephen, Lord Terrence, and Lord Hector plotting to poison you the day of the banquet," Maddy reported.

"You're certain it was the three of them?"

"Yes, sire."

'Don't believe her, Your Majesty!" Hector pleaded, his voice rising. "She is easily influenced and may be confused by what she saw and heard."

The king ignored him and asked Maddy once more, "Are you *certain* Lord Hector was one of the men?"

"I am positive, sire."

Then, catlike, Lord Hector leapt to his feet and raced for the doors. They opened, but the way was blocked by several guards. He stopped, took a few steps in another direction, and then moved in another, but every exit was covered by the king's men. They grabbed him and dragged him back to the table.

The king stood up and slapped him across the face. "I trusted you, Hector, and you have fed me nothing but lies," the king stated.

"What else could I give you?" Lord Hector spat at him, his eyes narrowing with hatred. "The truth is too hard for you to swallow. It gets in the way of your golf games and wigs and stupid parades. The truth in your hands is like giving a diamond to a fool—you would play marbles with it!"

The king observed him silently for a moment, then confessed, "Yes, you're right, Hector, but I'm willing to change. No, I *will* change. But what am I to do with you? Can *you* change?"

Lord Hector, seeing hope for a reprieve, nodded quickly. "Yes, Your Majesty, I can change. Show mercy to me. Please! You will then see such an amendment of life that even my closest family will not recognize me. Mercy!"

The king turned to Annison. "What does my queen say?" he asked.

"It's not for me to decide," Annison answered. "I can only hope you show him the same mercy that he has shown the believers in the Old Faith over the past month."

The king understood and signaled the guards to take Lord Hector away.

"No!" he cried as he was dragged out, kicking and screaming. "No! Please! Have mercy! Noooooo!"

Everyone was shaken by Hector's exit except the king. He sat down again and calmly picked up Hector's uneaten piece of chocolate. Popping it into his mouth, he told Annison, "And now I want the truth from you."

"Sire?"

"Who is Simet?"

"A member of the palace guard," she replied, then added, "and the man who raised me as his daughter."

The king nodded as if he'd already figured it out. "He is also a leader in the Old Faith, a faith that I myself have outlawed."

"Yes, Your Majesty."

The king kept his eyes fixed on Annison. "Then I may assume that you are also a believer in the Old Faith?"

Annison gazed back at the king. "Yes, Your Majesty."

"So, by the law of Hector's decree and the purge he ordered for this coming Saturday, Simet should be executed."

"Lord Hector planned for him to be the first," Annison stated.

"And, by law, you should also be executed."

"Yes, sire." Her gaze never wavered, her eyes staying firm on the king. "In the end, I would not deny my faith—or my foster father."

The king averted his gaze, looking down at the table thoughtfully. He touched the red-velvet book again. "I would have preferred that you told me the truth in the beginning."

"I was afraid to," Annison confessed. "The man I knew a month ago seemed so fickle and uncaring that I was certain he would have sent me away. And then what would have happened to my people?"

"And now?"

"Now I see a man to be respected. A man I believe loves me. A man I have grown to love."

The king seemed startled by her remark. "Is that true?"

"It is, sire. I would now trust you with my life—and the lives of those I hold most dear."

He sighed. "So be it." He stood up again and seemed taller somehow, rising to a majestic height. "In light of Hector's treason, I will repeal his decree. Further, because Simet, as a believer in the Old Faith, showed his loyalty to me by being instrumental in saving my life, I will repeal any and all laws that oppress or persecute those who believe in the Old Faith. The gallows that Hector constructed will be used on him alone for his treachery."

Annison fell to her knees and, grabbing the king's hand, kissed it. "My king!" she declared.

"Rise, my queen. What I do, I do because I want to be a just king." He then looked down at her tenderly. "And because I want to be a good husband."

Before Annison could respond, he withdrew his hand and marched from the room.

Annison rose to her feet and stood until he was gone, and then she slumped into her chair again. Her face in her hands, she began to cry.

Maddy went to her and wrapped her arms around her neck. She, too, cried.

From the corner, Tabby grabbed a handful of chocolates and said, "I'm going to find another job. This one is too stressful!" And she popped the chocolates into her mouth.

The banquet for Simet was held in the Great Hall on the following Saturday. It was a magnificent feast and included all those
of the Old Faith whom Lord Hector had thrown into the dungeon.
Together they, along with the king and queen, lamented those who
had died at Lord Hector's hands. Then the king made a passionate
speech asking for their forgiveness and promising a new day of
religious freedom for the people of Marus.

Simet, whose bruises were now faded, was touched by the occasion. He was teary-eyed when the king pinned the medal to his
chest. "I don't know when I became such a baby," Simet sniffled.

The king laughed and then announced that Simet was now *Lord*
Simet, with a manor house and lands to the east of Sarum, and
would replace Lord Hector as his adviser.

Annison had the last word, though, when she stood up and, in
defiance of all known ceremony and protocol, offered a toast to her
father, Simet.

Everyone, the king included, rose to his feet and saluted Simet.
Afterward, the guests all applauded the queen, for everyone knew
by then that she had truly saved their lives.

Alone, in a courtyard on the other side of the palace, Lord Hector was executed for his crimes against the king and against Marus.
The executioner and a lone witness confirmed his punishment and
signed the death certificate. He was buried in an unmarked grave.

O n your next birthday, you'll be old enough to be made a royal lady-in-waiting," Annison told Maddy several days after Simet's banquet. They were in the east garden, walking among the many rows of flowers. The smells were intoxicating.

Maddy smiled. "I don't know what a lady-in-waiting does, but it sounds very chivalrous," she said happily. "Just like something from the days of King Arthur."

"King who?" Annison asked.

Maddy giggled. "I'll tell you about him sometime," she replied.

On the edge of her giggle, though, she had a strange feeling, a sweet sadness. She knew somehow that she would never tell the story to Annison. It was time for her to go home. But she had no idea how or when it would happen.

"You're happy here, aren't you?" Annison asked.

"Yes, I am," she answered. But her tone betrayed her home-sickness.

"You miss your family."

Maddy nodded.

"There's a meeting of the Old Faith tonight. I suggest we put it to the leaders to pray that the Unseen One will take you home."

"Can they do that?"

Annison tilted her head a little. "They can *try*."

The king was on a patch of green grass several yards away. He stood over a small white ball with a golf club in his hands.

He was practicing his golf swing and had been doing so for the past hour. So far he had succeeded in hitting only one ball in the direction he'd intended.

Now he swung his club backward and then forward, hitting the ball hard. He looked ahead expectantly, hoping to see it fly farther out onto the manicured lawn. Instead, however, it spun off to the side and landed under his royal coach, which had been parked there by the driver.

"Oh, blast!" the king said.

Annison laughed.

He looked at her with a pained expression and informed her with mock sternness, "It isn't funny."

Annison put a hand over her lips to hide the smile, but it lit up her face too much. "I'm sorry," she giggled.

The king then laughed, too. "Maybe I'll take up bowling," he said. He patted his pockets and then added, "I'm out of balls anyway."

"I'll get you one," Maddy shouted and ran to the coach to retrieve the ball he'd just lost. She looked around the wheels for it but couldn't see where it was. Then, stooping down, she saw it sitting under the center of the carriage. Crawling carefully so as not to get her dress dirty, she went to the ball and grabbed it.

"You shouldn't be under there!" she thought Annison called out. But it didn't sound like Annison.

"What?" she asked as she turned to look back. Her mother was peering in at her through the gap in the trellis. Maddy gasped, jerked up, and nearly hit her head on the underside of the porch.

"Come out of there!" her mother ordered. "You'll get your dress all dirty."

Maddy crawled out from under the porch.

Her mother *tsked* at her and brushed at her dress. "Why do we make you new dresses when you insist on getting them dirty?" she asked. "Why?"

Johnny Ziegler suddenly rushed up to her. "There you are! I found you!" he screeched happily, touching her as if to ensure that it was her turn to find him.

Maddy blinked. "You won't believe what just happened to me," she told her mother.

Her mother sighed as the baby cried from the other side of the lawn. "You're right," she said as she walked away. "I probably won't."

"What's that?" Johnny pointed at her hand.

"What's what?" Maddy asked. She felt a little fuzzy-headed.

Johnny pointed again.

Maddy lifted her hand. She was clutching something she'd found under the porch.

It was a golf ball.

PASSAGES™

ABOUT THE AUTHOR

Paul McCusker is a writer and director for *Adventures in Odyssey* and the award-winning Focus on the Family Radio Theatre.® He also has written over 50 novels and dramas. Paul likes peanut-butter-and-banana sandwiches and wears his belt backward.

ABOUT THE ILLUSTRATOR

Mike Harrigan is the art director for *Focus on the Family Clubhouse*® and *Clubhouse Jr.*® magazines for kids. He loves the art of visual storytelling and, when he's given the chance, will doodle on just about anything.